VASILY MAHANENKO

THE SECRET
OF THE
DARK FOREST

*Books are the lives
we don't have
time to live,

Vasily Mahanenko*

THE WAY OF THE SHAMAN
BOOK 3

MAGIC DOME BOOKS

The Secret of the Dark Forest
The Way of the Shaman, Book # 3
Second Edition
Publ;ished by Magic Dome Books, 2017
Copyright © V. Mahanenko 2016
Cover Art © V. Manyukhin 2016
Translator © Natalia Nikitin 2016
All Rights Reserved
ISBN: 978-80-88231-16-5

ALL BOOKS BY VASILY MAHANENKO:

***The Way of the Shaman* LitRPG series
by Vasily Mahanenko:**
Survival Quest
The Kartoss Gambit
The Secret of the Dark Forest
The Phantom Castle
The Karmadont Chess Set
Shaman's Revenge
Clans War

***Dark Paladin* LitRPG series by Vasily Mahanenko:**
The Beginning
The Quest
Restart

***Galactogon* LitRPG series by Vasily Mahanenko:**
Start the Game!
In Search of the Uldans
A Check for a Billion

***Invasion* LitRPG Series by Vasily Mahanenko:**
A Second Chance
An Equation with One Unknown

***World of the Changed* LitRPG Series by Vasily Mahanenko:**
No Mistakes
Pearl of the South

***The Bard from Barliona* LitRPG series
by Eugenia Dmitrieva and Vasily Mahanenko:**
The Renegades
A Song of Shadow

TABLE OF CONTENTS:

Chapter One. The Emperor....................................1

Chapter Two. Seathistles.....................................43

Chapter Three. Anhurs...86

Chapter Four. Departure for the Free Lands........134

Chapter Five. The Guardian of the Dark Forest....178

Chapter Six. The First Battle of the Dark Forest...226

Chapter Seven. The Black and White...................272

Chapter Eight. The Patriarch.............................312

Chapter Nine. The Lieutenant.............................359

Chapter Ten. Unauthorized Actions.....................411

Chapter Eleven. The Traitor Shaman...................455

Chapter Twelve. The Birth of the Dragon..............500

Chapter Thirteen.The Judgement of the Goddess 538

CHAPTER ONE.

THE EMPEROR

"MAHAN, IS THERE MORE INTERESTING STUFF on the way or can we start getting some answers out of you?"

Anastaria's simple question sounded like a crack of thunder in the surrounding world, snapping everyone out of it. The world exploded: after seeing a dragon with their own eyes, hearing the announcement that they could play on the side of Kartoss and, in general, after a long and hard battle the players tried to get everything off their chests all at once. The area was shaken by various exclamations, like: "Whoa! A Dragon!," "They said they didn't exist, but this small-fry knows them!," "Who the heck is that?" There was such a din that I couldn't hear myself think, let alone try to answer Anastaria.

Because of the noise, few heard the quiet clap of the opening of the portal: a little way off a new

Herald had appeared in Barliona. The Emperor ascended the throne and his envoys appeared the very same moment. With Advisors it was more complicated, since they had to come with a background, but I had a feeling that this matter would be resolved in the course of the day – it's not as if the developers would have launched all of this without the necessary preparations. As I glanced around the raging crowd of players, the herald came up to Tisha, who was gazing into the distance, eyes wide. The girl was still in a state of shock and unable to come to terms with seeing two of her closest relatives became heads of Empires.

"Princess," the herald bowed, "Please follow me. The Emperor is waiting for you and your young man," the envoy bowed to Slate, "at the Palace."

"Me? Us?" The Intellect Imitator inside Tisha did a stellar job in playing a girl who was still in a state of shock and struggling to understand what was going on. Her vacant gaze, wandering over the players, her grip on Slate's hand, as if it was the only thing keeping the Headman's daughter in this world ... such an exquisite piece of programming really should have been seen in a theatre instead of wasting away at the edge of the world.

"That is correct, Princess," the Herald once again bowed his head.

"But I can't come alone. My brothers, they are still in Beatwick, tied up and ..."

"Unfortunately," the Herald's cheerful expression faded and his tone became more subdued, "we cannot take them with us. They are being sent Kartoss, where they will continue to serve the Dark Lord. Please, Princess, the Emperor is expecting you."

"What will happen to Beth? And to Mahan? Will they come with me?" Tisha had to make sure. I can't say much about Beth, but the fact that the Princess has remembered me is a good sign. As soon as I get away from this madhouse, there may be a chance of getting a nice bonus from this member of the Imperial family. I wouldn't say no to some extra gold!

Instead of responding, the Herald pointed to Elizabeth, who clung to her newly-regained husband and children. While Mariana hid her face in her Father's embrace, Clouter tried to slip out of his mother's strong grip and get a better look at everything. Totally irrepressible, that boy! Another portal appeared next to Beth, out of which stepped a different Herald.

"High Priestess, you are expected in Anhurs. I'm sorry, but the matter cannot wait."

"Yes, of course. My husband and children ..."

"They shall come with you. Please come this way," the Herald pointed to the portal.

"Mahan," Beth turned to me, "when you come to Anhurs, please make sure to come and visit me."

"Thank you, High Priestess. I will definitely drop by," I bowed my head, noting Anastaria's narrowing eyes. Aha! She had no idea that the High Priestess of Eluna in Malabar had been replaced.

"Beth." smiled the Priestess, "Just call me Beth. I await you in Anhurs." With these words the woman disappeared into the portal, pulling Mariana and Clouter after her. Theodore, Beth's husband, glanced at the portal and at the Herald and then came over to me.

"I usually pay my own debts, regardless of any position that my wife may hold," he said in a low bass and handed me a scroll. "Two years of imprisonment have inspired me to write this work. Read it; perhaps you may find it useful."

Item acquired: "A Treatise on Imprisonment and Ways of Staying Yourself."
Number of pages: 240.
Upon reading and providing correct answers (70%) to the questionnaire on this treatise: +20 Intellect, +3 Agility, +3 Stamina, +3 Strength.
Duration: Unlimited.

Theodore shook my hand and entered the portal. Only at that moment did I realize that we were surrounded by a strange silence. It felt like déjà vu. Had Renox dropped in on us again? I looked around and saw that the players had split into two groups. The first, the larger one made up of about 90% of the players that escaped from Beatwick, withdrew a little way off and started to summon their pets for returning to the more populous regions. These players tried not to make too much noise and disturb the second group. The latter consisted of the leaders of all the clans, their deputies and shadow leaders, such as Evolett; they were now observing the conversations of the NPCs with some interest. Anastaria, who stood next to me, was even making a video of the whole thing, a movie camera icon flashing above her head.

"Princess," the first Herald once again reminded us of his presence. "It's time. The High Priestess is already in Anhurs and as for Mahan, the Emperor will speak to him in person, right after you. He will be taken to the palace a little later."

"All right," Tisha brightened up and turned towards the blacksmith. "Let's go, darling. Father won't dare to keep us apart."

When the couple disappeared into the portal, other portals began to open, one after another. Heralds stepped out of each one, walked up to the rescued Beatwick villagers and took them to the 'mainland'. I don't know how it was for other players, but for each rescued villager I received a 10-point Reputation increase with the Malabar Emperor. One hundred and thirty-five Beatwick residents tuned into 1350 Reputation points. After a few minutes, only players remained by the destroyed Kartoss castle.

"I see that you found yourself in possession of an interesting scroll." Just as I thought, Evolett was the first to speak. Anastaria may be a strong-willed girl, but she wouldn't barge in with her 'uncle' present, assuming he really was her uncle. The chain of command had to be respected! Ehkiller wasn't present among the fighters, so Evolett clearly intended to take the situation in hand. "I have a rough idea of what that is, so I won't ask you to show me its properties. Read through it carefully before you try answering the questions. It may not be clear from the description, but you'll have only two attempts to complete the questionnaire. And now we have to move on to less pleasant things. You probably realize that you've put all the high-level players at a very big disadvantage today. Just think: some upstart, excuse my bluntness, took it upon himself to do what even Anastaria could not – direct an inter-clan raid. And we're talking about an upstart who is completely unknown, without any kith or kin or any real levels. Can you imagine the storm this will kick up on the forums? The clans' ratings will take a big tumble and you'll be the only one to blame. This is the tricky situation I would like to discuss with you."

"Stop handling this moron with kid gloves! Stick him on the blacklist and rub him out every chance you get!" interrupted Plinto.

"Plinto, I will settle this matter myself," Evolett's voice was frosty, putting the sham clan leader back in his place.

"Quit shutting me down all the time! 'Don't do that', 'don't say this': I've really had it with you! This jackass has decided that he's better than our clan! Sitting on his high horse and showing off how the clans mean nothing to him! Those cursed chess pieces are his handiwork!"

"Plinto!" Evolett didn't shout, but his voice was sharp enough to send one for respawn. "I've been putting up with your shenanigans for what seems like ages, but enough is enough! You will stop bringing our clan into disrepute as of now!"

"You and your clan and your decisions can go to hell!" Plinto fired back. "You can take it all and stick it where the sun don't shine! You've got me really shaking in my boots. And as for you, you little shit," he said, turning to me, "we'll catch up in person later. You'll regret making that pawn for a long, long time! Our meetings will be frequent and will all end the same way. Like this!" Suddenly Plinto dashed towards me, unleashing throwing knives that left a trail of green poison behind them. I only had enough time for a brief chuckle. 350+ level mobs were unable to bring me down, but this one unbalanced individual was apparently going to finish the job.

"Chill it, handsome," came Anastaria's voice and a dome surrounded me. A bubble! "Phoenix, attack!"

Phoenix's entire raid group reacted immediately. Plinto didn't even have time to get near me before he was slowed, had Petrification cast on him and was sent for respawn a few seconds later. In other words, he was disposed of quickly and professionally. Something else was bugging me now. Earlier, the system, on behalf of the Emperor, informed the players of the ban on PvP fighting. Had the Emperor's previous order been revoked? Strange, I had no memory of any announcements of that sort ...

"Legion!" There came a shout. "Phoenix has broken the truce! Waste them!"

"Phoenix, circle formation!" Anastaria's reaction was instantaneous. "Vlad, Paul! Make a portal, and bring all our fighters here!"

"SILENCE!" I never thought that Evolett was capable of shouting so loudly. The two groups that were about to dive into battle froze, looking at each other in surprise. The other clans got out of the way and were also murmuring in indignation. Hardly surprising, since they had just been deprived of one heck of a spectacle! "The Dark Legion clan has no claims against the Phoenix clan and thanks them for subduing Plinto," said Evolett, quickly diffusing the situation. "There will be no battle now. I will personally throw anyone that attacks any Phoenix player out of the clan. Even if they do it in self-defense! Is that clear?" Evolett confirmed my hunch that the PvP mode was still forbidden. Its shutdown wasn't system-wide, but localized, so both Plinto and a number of Phoenix members were about to be docked some Reputation points.

Silence descended on the ruins of the castle. The Legion players stared at their leader in incomprehension and the players of other clans started to whisper amongst themselves, wondering who the heck this was and why was he suddenly commanding the Dark Legion clan.

"Dammit!" came a grumble from Anastaria, as she read the message that appeared in front her. "Our reputation with the Emperor has gone down!"

"Has everyone calmed down? Then let's get back to business." Evolett looked over the bewildered players, and turned to me, "As I already said, damage has been done to the reputation of all the clans, so I'll make an official statement. I call upon a Herald, and request your assistance!"

A Herald immediately appeared next to Evolett: "You called me, Evolett. If your summons lacked a good reason, you shall be punished."

"According to the decision of the clan assembly, I am now the leader of the Dark Legion clan. I ask you to bear witness to this fact," Evolett said, handing the Herald a sheet of paper. "Plinto is being excluded from the clan. We are no longer responsible for his actions."

"Accepted." The air was filled with the ringing voice of the Herald. "Henceforth, Evolett is the head of the Dark Legion clan. Is this all?"

"No. On behalf of the Dark Legion clan, I declare Shaman Mahan *persona non grata*. He is now officially added to the blacklist and all clan members will be informed of the fact. Starting tomorrow, any clan member that has had a chance to attack him, but failed to do so, will be automatically excluded. Herald, I ask you to verify that this directive is being adhered to."

"Do you agree to the conditions for adding Mahan, who has positive reputation with the Malabar Empire, the Malabar Emperor, Goddess Eluna, Priestesses of Goddess Eluna, Pryke Mine Guards and the Krong Province to the blacklist?" the Herald's voice now had an icy edge to it, "his reputation with other factions will not be taken into account." Anastaria, Undigit and other clan leaders were looking from me to Evolett and back again in surprise. In Evolett's case it was on account of his words, but I didn't get the meaning of the surprised looks shot in my direction. Nor did I get why the Herald listed all the Malabar factions that I had encountered when playing as a Shaman and why he had left others out, such as the Shaman Council and the Dark Lord of Kartoss.

"Yes! This is the decision of the clan assembly." Evolett handed the Herald another paper. The new clan leader didn't simply look pleased, but rather had turned into one big smile – as had the other Number Twos standing nearby. "Now we just have to write a name here – and that name is Mahan. The Dark Legion clan is putting him on the official blacklist."

"So be it!" The Herald took the paper from Evolett, after which a gong sounded some way off. "Is that all?"

"Yes, thank you, Herald." Judging by Evolett's expression, what had just taken place was something that he'd waited a very long time for. I seriously didn't get it, but clearly something unusual had just gone down: some of the players were still wearing expressions that read 'No way did this just happen!'.

"Thank you." I decided to clear the atmosphere, which was beginning to grow a little too charged. "Not everyone has the privilege of being put on the official blacklist of the second clan in the Empire."

I'm not sure if it was something I said, but the surrounding world exploded for the second time in the past hour. Many of the players were speaking to each other or shouting things, while others stood there with glassy eyes – probably typing up forum messages, after hopping back into reality. A minute later the buzz had somewhat died down and Evolett smiled once again.

"It seems that you are not too familiar with what being put on the official blacklist actually means, so allow me to enlighten you. Each clan has two blacklists: a general one and an official one. The general one contains players who've been making trouble for the clan, for example, Anastaria, Hellfire, and so on. When a player from our clan runs across a player from the general list, they get a message that there is an enemy nearby and they should take heed. It's quite easy to end up on the main list, since any player with the relevant level of authorization can add you. But then there is the second list, the official one, where for each player the clan pays a tax to the Empire and sacrifices its reputation. For example, you will be costing us five thousand Gold a day, as well as daily Reputation reduction with all the factions listed by the Herald. The Reputation of each clan member that signed under the list will fall. On the first day it will fall by 1 point, on the second by 2, the third – by 4, the fourth by 8 and so on. All this irrespective of whether the player on the blacklist is inside the game or has logged out. The timer is ticking in any case. Thus, in just three weeks' time any Reputation, whatever its initial level, will tumble down to Hatred. This will be true for all those who signed under it. Putting a player on the official list requires at least five hundred signatures and the paper that I just handed the Herald contains just over four thousand.

"Now we come to the main point of putting someone on this blacklist. As soon as someone from the clan runs across the player on this official list, they must do all they can to send that player for respawn. They would not be penalized with a PK mark and would be able to do this even inside a town. Members of other clans or unaffiliated players will receive a message that the Dark Legion clan will pay them 5000 Gold for killing you. The Heralds are responsible for ensuring that clan members comply with the compulsory attack policy. They will also count the number of times you're killed by other players. Even the safe zones are ineffective against the official list. This blacklist is very popular with those who wish to punish some particular person. It is expensive, of course, but sometimes it's worth it. There are around forty thousand players in my clan, with an average level of 137. You have a day to run and hide. In the following two weeks our people will be looking for you very thoroughly. As soon as the Reputation of each person that signed under the list gets reduced to Hatred, you will be removed from the blacklist automatically, if I do not do so earlier. But that's never going to happen." Evolett looked like the cat that got the cream; "That's all from me."

"Evolett, what are you up to?" came Anastaria's subdued whisper. So that's that. She was no longer interested in Mahan-the-Dragon; she had to get to the bottom of whatever plot the leader of Number Twos had concocted.

"You'll find out soon enough, my dear." Evolett

gave another radiant smile. "Mahan, you're really quite a find! You've gained positive Reputation with so few Malabar factions – and all of them exactly the ones I was after!"

"Mahan, the Emperor wishes to speak with you." With all this talk I hadn't even noticed that a Herald had appeared next to me.

"Yes, of course," I mumbled, but before I could step into the portal, I was stopped by a gentle touch from Mirida. Everyone seemed to have completely forgotten about her.

"Wait – " Mirida bit her lip, as if trying to come to a hard but necessary decision. She finally breathed out, leant over to me and quickly blurted out, "I want to tell you why I came to Beatwick. It doesn't matter what you'll think of me, but you ought to know the truth. My name is Marina. Yes, that very same," she said when she saw my reaction. "I'm marking a spot on the map, let's meet up when there's a chance. Please come. There is a lot I must tell you." A message flashed before my eyes; a location somewhere near Anhurs had been marked on my map. "If you don't turn up, I'll understand, but give me a chance to explain, please!" Marina let go of my hand and stepped aside. It was just as well that I was already pumped full of emotions by this point, so I took the news that I was looking at the cause of my eight-year prison sentence calmly enough.

"A day, Mahan, you have a day," repeated Evolett, "then the hunt will begin!" It came out rather overplayed and over the top, like a villain in an old film giving his final speech. I don't know why, but it made me smile. Bearing in mind that all of this was being recorded on video and would be uploaded for public viewing, I knew the Dark Legion clan would be looking forward to some dark times. A bit of a tautology there. Putting a low-level player on an official blacklist just for successfully directing an inter-clan raid looked stupid and cast the clan in an extremely unfavorable light. But Evolett didn't look like a stupid man and he had probably thought this through in advance.

"Please wait here." As soon as I stepped out of the portal, the Herald gave me a few minutes to look around and enjoy the view of the Palace after its 'rearrangement' by Geranika. Even in this sorry state, the Malabar Emperor's residence was magnificent: the stones, the dust, the pockmarked walls and broken statues scattered around the territory – all this destruction only underlined the excellence of the spectacle. You got the feeling that it took several teams of designers to achieve the proper 'ruined palace' look.

"I even somewhat regret that I didn't see all this splendor in its better days," came the words of the former Beatwick Headman, the ex-Master of the Empire of Kartoss and the current Emperor of Malabar as he walked up to me. "You have to give it to the previous Emperor , he had taste. Come, it's time to reward our hero."

I don't know what it was: the destroyed palace or the moon being in Aquarius, but as I walked behind the Emperor, I totally failed to experience any excitement over the anticipated bonuses. I had a feeling that my inner zoo was immediately disheartened and succumbed to apathy. The Hoarding Hamster was an especially sorry sight: under normal circumstances he should have been flying after the Emperor, trying to get his paws on all possible bonuses and stuffing them in his pockets. Far from it! He was sitting and gazing sadly at the downcast Greed Toad, barely holding back his tears. I opened my quest log and scanned through its contents to stave off the infectious melancholy:

'Night Terror of the Village.' Rare. Completed. Reward: +400 Reputation with the Krong Province, +500 Experience, +80 Silver Coins, a Rare Item from Headman's Stores.

'Search for the Dark Coordinator.' Unique. Completed. Reward: +4000 Reputation with the Malabar Empire, +4000 Experience, +10,000 Gold Coins, a Scaling Item from the Emperor's stores.

'The Last Hope. Step 3.' Rare. (Time until the wolves respawn: 2 months, 21 days.)

'The Eye of the Dark Widow.' The Quest will become available at level 100. Legendary.

'The Way of the Shaman: Step 3: Completion of the trial to become a Great Shaman'. Class-based.

'Restoration of Justice.' Class-based. Unique.

I was about to remove the Wolf Quest, but

something within me objected. You don't just ditch quest chains. It's not like I have to feed it or as if there's a limit on the number of quests. At the same time, it would be very interesting to see what crazy things the developers cooked up with this quest chain. Pulling out those arrows was something else! Just remembering it made me shudder. In all likelihood it comes with a pleasant reward at the end, even if it's a low-level one. The happy squeak of the Hamster, who caught a whiff of a bonus, was barely audible. My brain gears seemed totally out of whack!

'Restoration of Justice' is a good quest, but to complete it, I would have to hike all the way to Serrest Province, where my Reputation is at Hatred, thanks to its Governor. I wondered if my Reputation with the Governor could be higher than with that of the Province itself. Would they kick me out straight away or would I actually have a chance to speak to Prontho? I guess I'll find out when I get there.

It will still be a while until I'm able to do the 'Eye of the Dark Widow' quest. Two quests are completed, so it looks like I have nothing left aside from the 'Path of the Shaman' and 'Restoration of Justice'. According to the timer, the trial for becoming the Great Shaman was still 2 months away. Even that made me a bit sad. In Beatwick I started to feel like a protagonist in global game events, but as soon as it was all over, I immediately turned back into a standard ordinary player, of which there's a multitude in Barliona. Once again, I became one of the many.

Other than access to the palaces, there are no

benefits aside from the positive regard of the Emperor and the Dark Lord. With my level of Reputation I could only walk around the Palace, watch it being restored and regain its former brilliance, and watch covetously as Anastaria and Hellfire receive unique and rewarding quests. There was little doubt that the entire Phoenix leadership had gained Esteem with the Emperor.

The Emperor took me to a small room lit by a couple of torches. Aside from a hint of daylight from a narrow window, the place was submerged in gloom. A small wooden table on curved legs was the only object that interrupted the surrounding emptiness. I would never have thought that such rooms could exist in the palace ...

"From what I've come to know of you, you have no special need of elaborate rewards." The Emperor smiled and picked up a scroll from the table: "You are being given this item for completing the 'Night Terror of the Village' assignment. I no longer hold the position of the Headman, but I can't fail to reward the man who found my Sklic. You did a good job." With these words Naahti handed me the scroll.

Reward for the 'Night Terror of the Village' Quest: +400 Reputation with the Krong Province, +500 Experience, +80 Silver Coins, Jewelcraft Recipe 'Malachite Jewelry Box with Lapis Inlays.'

I quickly learned the recipe, opened the recipe book and looked at its description:

Malachite Jewelry Box with Lapis Inlays.

Description: A neat and sturdy box for jewelry. Can carry 10 items. Crafting stat bonus: the box can carry an additional (Crafting) number of items. Item class: Rare. Minimum level: 50.

Crafting requirements: minimum Jewelcraft level 40.

Ingredients: 2 pieces of Malachite, 2 pieces of Lapis Lazuli, 4 Bronze Wires.

Instruments: Jeweler's tools.

Well ... that'll do, I guess. On the one hand, it's a new recipe, on the other ... a bit of a disappointment. I was hoping for more. The expression on my face made the Emperor laugh:

"You definitely need to work on controlling your emotions better. You look like someone just offered you something disagreeable. Bear in mind that the assignment to find the Sklic could have been removed altogether as soon as the battle started in Beatwick, but I decided to leave it in place. Now let's move on to a reward that should be more to your liking: the search for the former me.

Reward for 'The Search for the Dark Coordinator' Quest. +4000 Reputation with the Malabar Empire, +4000 Experience, +10,000 Gold Coins, a Scaling Item from the Emperor's stores (the choice of the item is up to you).

I noticed that exactly 10,000 Gold coins fell into my purse. It turned out that this amount was already free of the usual Imperial tax. I quickly tried to calculate what it should have been in the first place, but couldn't come up with a round number, only fractions. Never mind.

"There are five items on the table that would suit you," continued the Emperor. "You can choose one of them. You wouldn't be able to buy these items from Thricinians even if your reputation with them was Exulted. You will be able to see the properties of the items only after you make your choice, so choose carefully."

No looking at their properties? How the heck am I supposed to make a choice like this? Five items were lying on the table in a neat row: a Shaman's Hat with horns, like the one Almis had; a feathered Cloak, almost identical to the one I was wearing; Boots; Pants; and Bracers. Disbelieving the Emperor, I checked the properties of each item, but they really were hidden. How to make a choice? My spirits sunk even further. How long can I keep playing these guessing games? Bah! They can go to hell with their rewards!!

"I respectfully decline your gift," I said, firmly returning the Emperor's gaze. "I refuse to make an uninformed decision. It's better to refuse everything than forever regret picking the worst out of the lot. I would like to thank the Emperor for this opportunity, but no – I will not choose."

"Your choice has been made," the Emperor

replied calmly and immediately the table with all the items disappeared. "The Heralds will see you out."

My Hoarding Hamster lifted his head, looked me in the eye and then let it drop again. He had no fight left in him.

"Mahan! You're here!" As soon as we left the room, Tisha suddenly appeared next to us. "Father, have you thought of a reward for him?"

"He refused it," the Emperor replied just as calmly. "Mahan thinks that the Emperor is unworthy of granting him a reward."

"Mahan," Tisha froze next to me, astonished, "is this true?"

I don't think I like the direction that this conversation is taking – the Intellect Imitator is doing a great job of making me look like an obnoxious and ungrateful bastard who rudely refused a gift. In your dreams! I happen to be capable of standing up for myself! I took out five cursed rings and, after hiding their properties, handed them to Tisha.

"Choose one and put it on, without looking."

"But, they can't be 'read'!" said the girl in surprise.

"Exactly. Just choose one and put it on."

Tisha took one of the rings, which reduced Strength by 5%, put it on her finger and exclaimed:

"It's a Cursed Ring! Mahan! What is the meaning of this?"

As soon as the ring was put on, its properties became accessible to the wearer. Tisha angrily pulled off the ring and threw it towards me.

"Why did you do that? I trusted you! You ..."

"Hold on, Tisha," the Emperor interrupted her and turned to address me: "Open the properties of the other rings and hand them over to me."

There didn't seem anything wrong with Naahti's request, so I picked up the ring Tisha threw down and dropped it together with the rest into the Emperor's hand.

"Did you make them?" The Emperor took a careful look at each ring.

"Yes. I made them from the materials gathered in Beatwick, but after the Inverters did their job only items like these came out, no matter what I did."

"What do you plan to do with them?"

"I'll take them to Elizabeth. She can bless them, they're quite useless otherwise."

"Do you still have any of the amulets that you made in Beatwick?" The former Headman kept up his confounding line of questioning. Something began to stir in me that I thought was gone forever – genuine interest. What can the Emperor want with my rings and Amulet? Strange.

"Yes, here it is." I took out the Novice's Amulet out of the bag and handed it to Naahti. I thought that as soon as he took the Amulet, he would immediately turn into a Vagren, but Emperors were immune to such things by the looks of it. Naahti gave me back four rings, leaving only one for himself. He took it in one hand and the Amulet in the other and then did something I thought completely impossible. He combined them together. A bright sun shone through his hands and when the glow faded both the ring and the Amulet disappeared, as if they never existed. A pleased smile appeared on the Emperor's face.

"Dad?" Tisha was looking wide-eyed at her father, "You just ..."

"Destroyed something that belonged to another?" The Emperor raised an eyebrow. "I know. Mahan's losses will be reimbursed. A hundred Gold for the ring and a thousand for the Amulet." As soon as he uttered those words I received a message that 770 Gold had fallen into my purse. "But that's not the important part. Firstly, Mahan showed me that I was wrong to offer him a blind choice and, secondly, I have an assignment for him."

"A blind choice?" asked Tisha.

"Yes. I offered him a choice of five items with concealed properties. He refused to choose. Now I understand why. It seems that he hasn't forgotten who I was before becoming Emperor, so his suspicions are not groundless." I was lucky that the Emperor was so clever. He came up with the reason, explained it and, most importantly, believed in what he was saying. I was slowly coming back to normal and was hit by the horrible realization how my refusal must have looked. Here was a prideful Shaman, turning his nose up at the gifts of the Emperor. I was lucky not to get docked Reputation points for this.

"You've shown me that I was wrong," continued the Emperor, "so we should once again return to the reward. This time you will have no choice: I will decide what your reward should be. But this can wait. I can't stop thinking of the chess pieces standing in the main hall. They could've only been created by a Cursed Artificer. Did you hold such a title?"

I nodded, not understanding where the Emperor was going with all of this. And why did he say 'did' rather than 'do'?

"The Amulet of the Novice of Eluna could be made by any sentient that has a positive reputation with the priestesses. But you were a Cursed Artificer, therefore, in order to create such a thing, you had to become a Blessed Artificer. Is that the case?"

I nodded once again, beginning to lose track with all these Artificers. There were altogether too many of them.

"Dad, I really don't understand what this is all about," said Tisha, who was still standing next to us. Truth be told, she was voicing my thoughts too – I had no idea what it was that the Emperor wanted.

"Come," the Emperor waved his hand and a portal opened nearby, "I must show you something."

You have gained access to the Emperor's Throne Room. Current level of Palace access: 46%. Next interior: The Emperor's Office.

I waved away the message – for which many players would have easily given two years of play – and stepped into the portal. What was it that Naahti needed?

The answer was very unusual: a dagger was stuck right in the center of the throne. I could tell that this was a Cursed Object without even looking at its properties. The waves of darkness emanating from the dagger were being contained by statuettes of Eluna placed around the throne.

"A present for the future Emperor from Geranika," explained Naahti. "No-one can touch the dagger – neither the Emperor nor the Dark Lord. It can only be destroyed by combining it with a holy object, as I have just done, but there are very few of these throughout the Empire and all of these are located in temples. Neither the throne nor those objects can be moved, otherwise they will lose their properties. The new High Priestess has shielded the effect of the dagger on the Palace, but I cannot take my throne. An Emperor cannot exist for long without his throne. In four months' time I will disappear."

"No!" came a cry from Tisha.

"Calm down, my dear. Not all is lost. In a week I will gather all the heroes of the Empire and ask for their help. According to these scrolls," – some scrolls appeared in the Emperor's hands – "a lost Relic of Light is located somewhere in the depths of the Free Lands. With its help it will be possible to destroy this dagger. The heroes will have to meet very strict requirements, including a minimal level of 200. Their Reputation with the Emperor will not be a factor – I am prepared to meet any exiles half way and give them a second chance. Although I'll weigh up all the pros and cons first..."

"So where do I fit into all of this?" It looked like the scenario for the opening up of Kartoss as a player faction was set to continue a week later and involve high-level players.

"You are a Blessed Artificer. One can't depend entirely on the search for the Relic being successful ; for example, it may not be found within the given time. It is my duty as the Emperor to protect my Empire from any risk and you've given me a very interesting idea. Aside from the heroes of the Empire, I will give an assignment to each of the craftsmen. Instead of joining the search effort they will have to create a holy artifact capable of destroying the dagger. Perhaps someone will succeed. You will be given this assignment right now, even though you don't meet the necessary parameters. As Beatwick had shown, sometimes it's worth taking a risk and trusting a low-level free citizen."

Quest available: "Creation of a Holy Artifact."

Description: The Malabar Empire is facing a calamity: A cursed dagger has been plunged deep into the heart of the throne. If it is not destroyed within four months, the Emperor will perish. Create a holy item that could destroy the dagger.

Reward: +500 Reputation with the Emperor, +15 Levels, +50,000 Gold Coins, a Scaling Item from the Emperor's stores.

Penalty for failing the quest: None.

Quest type: Scenario.

Requirements: at least 100 levels in the main Profession (the quest cannot be completed if

the level of the main profession is less than 100).

Level restrictions: None.

Time limit for completing the quest: 127 days from the moment it has been given out.

"I will do everything in my power to destroy the dagger," were the only words I could force out of myself after reading through the quest description. +15 levels ... for this Anastaria and Hellfire would drop everything and start crafting like mad. It's hard to get your character to level 100, but it is possible. Reaching level 200 would require a special effort. After level 300, however, each level gained is a real cause for celebration. And with this you would get +15 all in one go.

"I had no doubt that you would take up the challenge," said the Emperor solemnly. "Now, let us once again return to the question of your reward. I think this would suit you better than the rest," with these words Naahti handed me the boots. "Wear them with pride!"

I bowed as I accepted the Emperor's gift and finally had a look at the properties of my reward. What kind of an item was it impossible to get from the Thricinians?

Item acquired: "Shaman's Boots of Brisk Running".

Durability: unbreakable.

Description: Shamans spend most of their lives on the road. Comfortable shoes are a

guarantee of a happy, and living, Shaman.

+40 to maximum level of Energy, Spirit summoning time is reduced by 50%, +(Player Level*10) Intellect, +(Player Level*5) Stamina, +(Player Level*3) Agility, +(Player Level*7) defense from all damage types.

Item class: Scaling, Integrated.

Level restrictions: None.

Finally the Hamster shook off his apathy. He was jumping happily around the boots, blowing specks of dust off them and looking at the Emperor with love-filled eyes, solemnly promising to craft the holy artifact the very next day: anything to get another bonus like this.

"And one last thing, you may try to create the relic in Anhurs, with the aid of the High Priestess, but I advise you to travel to the Free Lands. There are many untapped resources there, some of which are probably of the hallowed kind. The choice remains up to you, I can only advise. And now please excuse me, I have to leave you."

The Emperor gave me a brief nod, opened a portal and a moment later I was alone with Tisha. I quickly put on the boots, in case anyone changed their mind, and sadly noted that the bonus from Rick's set disappeared. I had to choose – either to put on this new wonder or keep the bonuses from all the eight items in the set. The boots were a clear winner: Rick's gear would have to be changed soon in any case. I've outgrown it.

"Where are you off to now?" it looked like Tisha would be sticking with the stunned princess role for some time. The change of Emperor took place almost painlessly and the developers had already come up with a mass quest for the players, but Tisha was still walking around in a state of shock. Could there be a quest tied to all this?

"I'm going to pay Beth a visit now. She asked me to drop by as soon as I came to Anhurs. Then I will go to the registrar and finally register my clan. And then ... we'll see. Princess, can I be of any help to you?"

"'Princess': ... that sounds so ... strange. Well ... no ... I ..."

Judging by the fact that Tisha was struggling to make up her mind about something, I must have been on the threshold of being given a new quest. I looked at my Attractiveness to her. 39 points. Strange, with the ordinary girl Tisha in Beatwick it was as high as 83 or thereabouts, but here, with her a Princess it was just 39. Of course: these were two different Imitators despite there being only one NPC! They reduced it by too much. It looks like I'll need at least 40 points to be given the quest. Damn, I have no way of increasing my score either. I remembered the Dress that I gave to Reptilis and my inner Greed Toad came out of hibernation. Not only did that lizard fail to pay me the rest of what he owed me (although maybe he did do it – I've not been to the Bank yet), I handed him an item that would have been really useful right now. All I would have had to do was make a gift of it to Tisha and the Princess would have been putty in my hands! Any quest, any help – within reason, of course. I was so stupid!

"Tisha," I said, risking calling the girl by her name. In Beatwick there was no problem with calling NPCs by their first names, but this was the palace and she was now the Princess, so it could land me in real trouble. "How about this: right now I'll go and settle my affairs, then come back to the palace in the evening and we'll have a chat. I have access, even to the Throne Room, so we can meet on this very spot. We can have a proper talk then."

"All right," smiled the girl, as if a great weight had been lifted from her shoulders. "Until evening, then."

I barely had time to notice that I was alone: Tisha was gone in a flash. Great! So how will I make my way out of here? It's not like I know the plan of the palace!

"The Emperor asked me to accompany you." Like a genie from a bottle a Herald popped up next to me. "Where would you like to go?"

"I need to get to the High Priestess of Eluna," I said, quickly recomposing myself. "Please transport me there, or, if you can't take me there directly, to the place where I can ask for an audience with her."

"Please come this way." The Herald opened a portal, saying, "The High Priestess is ready to receive you."

* * *

Beth's office had quite a Spartan look. There was a simple table, snowed under with various papers, a wooden chair and, pale modest curtains that completely covered the walls. If this were reality the curtains would have been sure to conceal a number of guards, ready to strike down anyone that threatened their mistress. In Barliona, however, I was quite sure that the curtains concealed shelves full of books and scrolls not meant for the eyes of ordinary mortals. Although ... ordinary mortals wouldn't have dreamt of being admitted to the office of the High Priestess, so the matter with the scrolls was worth further thought.

"Mahan!" Beth was clearly happy to see me. "It's so good that you managed to get here quickly. I have started to sort out the mess left behind by the previous High Priestess, which is mind-bogglingly terrible. There was no semblance of a system or proper record-keeping. I already demoted her to the rank of a Novice – it's better for her to bring light and warmth to ordinary people than to do paperwork. That was never her strength. I'm sorry, but I have very little time, so I'll get straight to the point. What are your plans in the next three or four months?"

"I must create a Holy Item for the Emperor in order to free the Throne," I answered honestly. There was little sense in doing anything else. My Attractiveness with the High Priestess was at 91 and I was Friendly with the Priestesses of Eluna, so I could speak the truth, whatever it may be.

"So you already know? The Emperor has shared this secret with you?" Beth froze for a moment. "Then again, I shouldn't be surprised, after everything that you've done ..."

After pausing briefly Beth started to dig around amongst the files on her table. For a few moments, all I could hear was the rustle of paper and the subdued mutterings of the Priestess: "Where is it? You could lose a herd of elephants in here. It's not an office, it's just one big mess! ... Finally!"

"I can't give you back the ring," Beth continued, giving me a scroll. "It vanished the moment I was back in Anhurs. But I owe you a great deal, so I'm offering you the rank of a Priest of Eluna. You would skip the Novice stage and immediately become a Great Priest. This matter has already been discussed with the Emperor and he promised to help. Here's the draft of your agreement regarding the change of your class, you only have to sign it."

To the player located in a prisoner capsule: In view of your arrival into the main Gameworld and possession of a positive Reputation with the leading NPCs of Malabar, court decision No. 45-RS344328 grants you the permission to change your character class.

Proposed class – Great Priest.

Chosen deity: Eluna the Light-bearer.

Do you agree to change your class? Yes/No.

"This offer is insufficient to express my gratitude, but I have to start somewhere," added Beth, awaiting my reply.

Suddenly, a veil seemed to obscure my sight and a ringing sound filled my head. It was as if my blood pressure had shot up as a result of what I just heard. I even thought it a good idea to simply close my eyes and try to imagine that everything that just happened was a mistake and that when I opened them again it would all disappear. But no! The system really was offering me to change my character class from the unpopular Shaman to one of the most universal and esteemed classes. The ability to revive players during combat alone was worth a lot! And I would get all of this right now, on the spot!

"I can't … " I spoke with some effort, trying not to look Beth in the eye. Experience had taught me that those who consider Shamans a weak class understand nothing in this game. And those who know the truth are keeping shtum about it.

"You refuse?" Elizabeth lifted her eyebrows in surprise.

"Beth, please understand. Do you think I would have managed to do everything that I have if I wasn't a Shaman? It's more than just a class – it's a certain way of thinking, acting and feeling. You can't describe Shamans in words; you can only feel them. I may make a good Priest, but I would have to destroy an excelled Shaman."

"These are all just words! You think my gift unworthy of you?" Overcome with emotion Beth jumped up from the chair. Why are women so difficult ... ? Will I really have to lose Reputation with the High Priestess if I wanted to remain a Shaman?

"Beth, I never said anything of the sort. I can't become a Priest, I'm a Shaman!"

"You're a coward, not a Shaman! You are being offered a big responsibility and you're trying to wriggle out of it!"

So that's how it is? Then it's time to bring out the heavy artillery.

"Beth, if Clouter ... I mean Avtondil and Mariana were kidnapped by Kartoss minions and you were given an ultimatum: either become a Warrior or your children will die. What would you choose?"

"What?! How dare you compare such things?" shouted the Priestess. My level of Attractiveness in the NPC's properties began to plummet. Currently it amounted to just 63 points and if the conversation kept going in the same direction, I could forget about remaining in the High Priestess's favor. With all the ensuing consequences ...

"Yes, I do dare!" I had also raised my voice in response to Beth's shouting. "Do you think you're the only one in this position? You think that because I'm a Shaman I have no responsibilities? Tell me, what would you do?"

"You are forgetting yourself, Elemental Shaman," Beth cut me off sharply, emphasizing the last word. By now Attractiveness had reached 47.

"Fine, I will reply for you," I continued. "What did you say in Beatwick? 'Let the children go, we'll stay behind and try to slow them down.' You're prepared to face death for the sake of your children, so why do you think that I ..."

"YES! I would give up everything just so they could live!" Attractiveness was at 34. "But what do you, a male free citizen, know about children?! How can you compare parts of me that have gained their own being with your Shamanism?!"

We had arrived at the moment of truth, the point towards which I had been driving all this time. I was ready to get to the heart of my argument with Beth. Let's see, oh High one, what you'll say to this, I thought. I wasn't even looking at the change of class message. The constantly flashing 'Yes / No' buttons distracted me only for the first few seconds. Now, as our conversation had descended into shouting, they had grown dim and almost evaporated. I don't need this: I'm a Shaman!

"Draco, come to me, we need to sort something out."

"Coming."

"Hello, brother. Did you call me?" Draco appeared right next to me.

"Do you remember him?" I asked Elizabeth, who stared at the Dragon, eyes wide. "He was playing with your son. If I become a Priest, he will disappear. Forever. Tell me, does he really deserve to be destroyed? Is the rank of the Great Priest worth the knowledge – for the remainder of my life – that I was responsible for destroying a Dragon? I'm prepared to fall out with you completely and forever be barred from Eluna's temple, as long as my brother remains alive!" Damn, I failed to restrain myself and broke into screaming towards the end. It came out altogether too emotional in the end.

"I forgot," said the Priestess, stunned, and I was pleased to see that my Attractiveness returned to its initial 91 points ... even overshooting to reach 93! I even gained Reputation now! "Forgive me ... I ..." The Priestess's eyes filled with tears. "Forgive me ..."

"Beth, I am very grateful to you for your offer, but you can see for yourself that it was never going to be possible for me."

"But I wished it for all the best reasons ... I thought being a Priest was such a high honor. Do you see this pile?" Beth nodded in the direction of the pile of papers. "These are all requests from free citizen Priests to re-take the rank initiation test. Currently there are over a million of these Priests of Eluna in Malabar and that number is growing every day. I don't know how many Priests other gods have, but they are also quite numerous. So, I thought ..."

"And you thought you would make me a Great One straight away, right? When I know nothing about what it means to be a real Priest? After all, there's a reason that people spend so long in the rank of a Novice. You have to learn how to communicate with the goddess and how to master your power. And here a former Shaman would become a Great Priest ... everyone in Anhurs would laugh if I tried to say a prayer."

"That's not that important. You would have learned quickly, so I wouldn't have accepted such a reason for your refusal, but a Dragon ..." Beth came up to him and looked at me. "Can I touch him? I really wanted to do that when my son was playing with him, but I was too afraid."

"What about you, Draco? You don't mind?"

"Of course not. I like it when people pet me," Draco put out his head towards the priestess, expecting to be stroked.

"Now I can see that for you he is a person and not just a totem," the High Priestess said solemnly, in fact not reaching out to touch the Dragon after all. "You are a worthy Shaman and long may you remain this way."

The choice of the character class has been made.

Changes have been recorded.

Current class: Elemental Shaman.

"Now, let's get down to business." Beth quickly changed the topic. "I asked you about time for a reason: Mahan, the Priestesses of Eluna need your help!"

Quest available: "Restoration of a Holy Relic. Step 1: The History of the Missionaries of Eluna."

Description: Listen to the High Priestess

and learn the story of the Missionaries of Eluna.

Requirements: Reputation with Goddess Eluna = greater than 0; Reputation with the Priestesses of Goddess Eluna = Friendly or higher.

Quest chain class: Rare.

Reward for completing Step 1 = +1500 Experience, +100 Reputation with the Priestesses of Eluna.

Reward for the quest chain: Variable.

Penalty for failing / refusing the quest: Neutral status with Goddess Eluna.

"I will do everything I can to help the Priestesses." I didn't hesitate for a moment in accepting the quest. Something interesting was afoot and I wanted in.

"Ten years ago ..." Beth began the tale after settling in a seat behind her table, before abruptly interrupting herself: "Let your Dragon go, there's no reason for him to keep doing laps in my office." She continued, "Now then: ten years ago, as soon as I was removed from the position of the High Priestess and sent into exile, a missionary expedition was sent to the Free Lands. It was comprised of forty Novices, ten junior and five ordinary Priests and the mission was headed by the Great Priest Midial. Other than the priests, two hundred warriors and fifty mages joined the expedition. All of them were at level 200. The official purpose of the mission was to expand Eluna's zone of influence in the Free Lands, but this was a cover. Midial's main aim was to find the Tear of Eluna

– the lost amulet of the High Priestesses. According to our archives it was last seen in that region. As you can probably guess, the missionary party disappeared. Neither Midial nor anyone else from the group ever came back and all their communication amulets ceased to function. What happened to them is anyone's guess. What is more important is that the Great Priest took with him the Stone of Light, and it hasn't been seen since."

"The Stone of Light?" I interrupted Beth, seeking a bit more detail on this point "What's that?"

"A concentration of Divine Light. With its help Priestesses can either drive back darkness or completely restore their strength. With just one use the Stone can restore the power of two Great or twenty ordinary Priests. Afterwards it needs to be recharged. The recharging happens in a temple: if the Stone is placed on an altar just two hours later it's ready for use again. These Stones can have different appearances; some look like ordinary rocks and others are statuettes. All the Stones of Light located in Anhurs are currently standing around the Emperor's throne, shielding the palace from Geranika's Cursed Dagger. The recipe for making the Stones has been lost, so each specimen is precious. This is the complete story. On behalf of the Priestesses of Eluna, I ask that you travel to the Free Lands and return with the Stone of Light!"

Quest: "Restoration of a Holy Relic, Step 1: The History of the Missionaries of Eluna" has been

completed.

Reward: +1500 Experience, +100 Reputation with the Priestesses of Eluna.

Quest available: "Restoration of a Holy Relic. Step 2: Search for the Stone of Light".

Description: Go to the Free Lands, find the lost Stone of Light that was once in the Possession of the Great Priest Midial and find out what happened to the missionaries.

Requirements: Reputation with Goddess Eluna = greater than 0; Reputation with the Priestesses of Goddess Eluna = Friendly or above; combined group level = 600.

Quest chain class: Rare.

Reward for completing Step 2: +35 000 Experience, +500 Reputation with the Priestesses of Eluna, +100 Reputation with Goddess Eluna.

Reward for the quest chain: Hidden.

Penalty for failing/refusing the quest: none.

"One more thing," added Beth at the end "you can't travel to the Free Lands alone. You will need helpers. I will mark your map with the place where the missionary expedition was headed, but if the level of your group is insufficient, this mark will disappear. Please, don't go by yourself – it's very dangerous!"

"I won't go alone," I assured Beth, turning over all my acquaintances in my mind. The combined level of 600 is quite a lot. On the one hand, that's just Anastaria and Hellfire together, but I had no intention of handing this quest over to them. I had to get back in touch with my old connections, find Eric and co. and quickly level up.

"How much time do I have to find it?" If the quest could be postponed by a month, I might have a chance to level up at break-neck speed and gain a dozen levels, irrespective of Evolett's emphatic threats. That would be great.

"The sooner the better, but you do have two months. Gather your team and return to me – you will all be sent by teleportation to the borders of the Free Lands. A month later I will send other teams. I'm sorry, but this matter is just too important. If we don't hear news from you, I will have to appeal for help from the heroes of the Empire. The Stone must be returned."

Changes to the quest "Restoration of the Holy Relic. Step 2: Searching for the Stone of Light."
Time given for completion: 2 months.

"I hope you will return with the Stone," said Beth, finally. "And now you must excuse me, I am catastrophically behind in getting my affairs in order. Oh! What's wrong with me? I still haven't thanked you for the rescue! The Great Priest rank wasn't even the main reward. It's this," said Beth taking out a small box from under her table. Eluna's High Priestess is really quite something – so changeable that you end up feeling you're dealing with a child: ...she switches to a new topic every ten minutes, any longer than that and her brain just gets too tired. It made me wonder if this Imitator got a concussion in Beatwick.

"It may not be the Emperor's ring, but you may still find it useful. Wear it honorably." Beth opened the lid of the box and took out a ring. She looked at it closely for a couple of seconds, as if searching for a flaw, and then handed it to me.

Item acquired: "Holy Ring of Eluna".
Description: +20% Experience gain.
Requirements: Reputation with the Priestesses of Goddess Eluna: friendly or higher.
Item class: Unusual, Blessed.

Minimal description, but the effect was simply amazing! So, Blessed Items can be rather useful! That's it: Blessed Items!

"Beth, I also have a certain matter to discuss with you! I've made so many cursed things in Beatwick it's crazy! I still have some of that dubious ore left as well. Can you bless all of these things? I can't sell them and it seems a pity to just throw all of it away."

"Of course, put them all on the table. It's time to give my Priestesses some proper work – they could use a break from all the heavy-duty flirting with the guards. You can come and collect all of this tomorrow."

"Great! Then I'm off to gather my team. The Stone will be found!"

I put on the new ring and headed for the Bank

of Barliona. A flashing pictogram in the form of a letter had been trying to catch my attention for the best part of the last ten minutes. This could mean only one thing – I had a message in the mail. Of all possible limitations, I only had Tax and the Presence of Pain remaining, so little comforts like notifications and internal clan chats were now accessible. But who could be so keen to get hold of me?

CHAPTER TWO

SEATHISTLES

"HOW CAN I HELP YOU?" the bank of Barliona gremlin asked in a squeaky voice as his dark eyes looked up at me.

"I'd like to get a personal mailbox that would permit me to send mail from anywhere. I was finally getting around to buying the most important item in Barliona: the Basic Portable Mailbox. Many players head to the Bank and buy this useful device on the very first day they roll up a character. Now there would be no need to run to the Bank every time I had to send a message or read a letter: I'd have it all right there in my pocket. Of course, the basic version doesn't have all the nice features with settings, content-sorting and use of the mail Intellect Imitator, but I saw little sense in buying the enhanced version to get all these things: it's not like I was expecting mountains of mail.

"The annual cost of the Basic Portable Mailbox service is two hundred gold. Do you wish to make the purchase?"

"But it used to cost five hundred!" I exclaimed involuntarily, greatly surprised by the unexpected decrease in the cost of the service. Lowering prices in any way, let alone halving them, seemed out of line with the Corporation's usual way of doing things.

"This is the policy of the Bank of Barliona towards persons that have achieved Respect with the Emperor," the gremlin said somewhat pompously, tearing himself away from his papers. "Should you reach Exalted, this service would be provided free of charge. Do you wish to acquire the Mailbox?"

Well, I'll be ... ! When I played as a Hunter I hadn't managed to increase my Reputation with the Emperor by a single point and had no idea about a nice perk like that. The saving of three hundred a year may not be huge, but was still nice.

"Yes, I do. Please deduct the sum from my account." I confirmed the message that popped up about the deducted amount and again turned to the gremlin.

"Your Portable Mailbox." I was handed a small folder, showily tied together with a red ribbon.

Item acquired: Basic Portable Mailbox.

Description: You shall now be able to send and receive mail in any location in Barliona.

Annual service cost of Mailbox: 200 gold. Does not take up inventory bag space.

I thanked the gremlin and entered my Personal Room. The flashing icon indicating new mail didn't go anywhere and was telling me that I had five letters waiting for me now. I sat down on the uncomfortable chair, noting that I should look into expanding my personal space here to reduce general discomfort, and opened the first letter:

"Only today! New erotic show with a copy of the Great Anastaria! 21+. Ticket price: 2300 gold, video recording prohibited. Show venue: The Anhurs Dating House!'

Well I'll be ... spam! Real, genuine spam! It really has been a while! The filters that I had turned on when I was in Beatwick blocked all mail except that sent directly by other players, so in the past six months I hadn't seen any bulk messages. After adding the sender to the blacklist to prevent similar messages getting through, I continued to read the rest:

"Clan 'Pwnage Meisters' invites you into its ranks. We have a friendly and fun team and all you need to do is bring your 'First Kill'. Repair covered by the clan (we have our own repair experts)."

"Clan 'XXX' invites you ..." and twenty more letters with similar offers. I went through them one by one, wondering why I was never notified of their

arrival and then noticed their date. Most of the letters had arrived well before the events in Beatwick, when I was still under my parole limitations. Five had arrived just in the two hours that had elapsed since my virtual freedom. And here was I thinking that I had received something important ... got my hopes up, and all that. I continued looking through the letters with dampened enthusiasm, gradually forming a 'blacklist' of my own: just in the last few minutes four more spam letters had arrived. Then I finally came across something unusual: a letter from Evolett.

The envelope had a pictogram of a box next to it, indicating an attachment. I pressed the pictogram and saw the list of things that had been sent to me: fifty-seven scrolls – all Jewelcraft recipes – judging by the description. Riiight ... What's in the message then?

"Hello Mahan,

First of all, I would like to apologize for the performance that I had to put on today, but everything had to look genuine to the Heralds: Imitators – no way around it'. I believe that the enormous boon that you managed to hand my clan merits an explanation on my part. So here it is.

The idea of letting people play on the side of Kartoss has been floating around the Corporation for some time. They did their best to keep a lid on it but you can't get away from the human factor in the workforce, so if you know your way around the net not only can you find the description of all the new races and classes, but also make an approximate prediction of the update's release date. About six months ago it became clear that all the preparations have been completed and that the Corporation was ready to launch the scenario. By some unfathomable miracle you have ended up being part of it, so I can only hope that your luck will hold out. As soon as the Heralds told us that members of the clan have been banned from appearing in the Krong Province, it became clear that the scenario had commenced.

Constantly coming second can get very tedious, so the decision to transfer the clan to Kartoss was taken at the clan assembly. We conducted a clan-wide survey and established our base: four thousand players who were prepared to move to Kartoss. The rest of the rabble was removed from the clan, just as Plinto was. Unfortunately people like him are uncontrollable. Please keep that in mind when creating your own clan. So all we had to do was wait for the start of the transfer and become the First Clan of the Dark Empire.

That is when I had a very interesting idea. According to the rumors that reached me, the worse your Reputation with the Emperor and the Empire, the easier it would be to transfer your clan, even going as far as gaining Respect with Kartoss and the Dark Lord. At the clan assembly we decided to put a player with a positive Reputation with both required factions on our official blacklist so we could end up deep in the minus. It's not possible to just add people to this list on a whim – you need approval of a Herald and a dramatic performance. Everything had to be official and clear, including the over-the-top rhetoric, otherwise it wouldn't have worked. So I played my part in the theatrics. We've spent some time looking for a 'victim', even considering adding Ehkiller at first, but he had positive Reputation with too many useful factions with which we also would have preferred to remain on good terms – Thricinians, for example. And then you turned up. The Emperor expressed his gratitude to you and this could only mean that your Reputation with him is higher than Friendly. Then I took a chance, and, as you can see, hit the mark. Aside from the Malabar factions you don't have any Reputation leveled above Friendly.

Just moments after the Herald took you away I was contacted by the representatives of the Corporation expressing their thanks for finding a 'loophole' that allowed a very favorable migration to Kartoss. This move has already been blocked, so it can't be used a second time, but our clan was left as it was. We acted within the framework of the Game and didn't break any rules, so there won't be any penalties imposed on Dark Legion. Thus, when in three weeks' time we migrate to the other Empire, we will ALREADY have Respect with Kartoss and the Dark Lord.

I realize that the next three weeks will be very tough for you and would like to offer you at least some compensation for the moral damages suffered on my account. I know that you are a very skilled and exceptional Jeweler (the Cursed Chess Pieces are proof of this), so I'm sending you Jewelcraft recipes that cannot be bought from the trainers. All of them are drops from Dungeon bosses and all are of Rare (and some even Epic) quality, so I believe they should be sufficient to compensate you for any distress you might experience. I don't want to send you money, as that's unimaginative and will mean that I've bought you.

Yours sincerely, the Head of the Dark Legion Clan, Evolett.

P.S. I hope my idea will not affect the clan's Reputation with the Dark Lord. As far as I know, you are in good standing with him as well. It would be a great pity to make that mistake.

P.P.S. Try to vanish from places frequented by players for the next three weeks. Take a trip to the Free Lands, go on a walkabout or focus on leveling up. Neither I nor the Dark Legion clan have any desire to be constantly sending you for respawn.

P.P.P.S. (Hmm, rather a lot of postscripts here.) The only thing I will really miss is the Cursed Chess Pieces. They will disappear the moment we move to Kartoss – this has already been verified. I hope that the recipes that I sent will aid you in creating something as beautiful and magnificent."

All this hit me like a bolt out of the blue. There was so much information and all of it so interesting: it was quite overwhelming. Plinto was removed from the clan because he was uncontrollable. I now have a ton of recipes that were not normally available for sale! The Dark Legion is preparing to migrate to the dark side. Stop! Shouldn't I have a letter about that as well?

Only two unread letters remained. I looked at the senders: Barliona Administration and Reptilis. Reptilis' letter came with an attachment – that green lizard probably sent me the rest of the money he owed me, so that can wait.

"Dear player!

We would like to inform you that from today you have the opportunity to transfer your character to the side of the Kartoss Empire. If you decide to take this step, utter the phrase: 'I call upon a Magister, I request your assistance', and you will be teleported to the Nameless City (the capital of Kartoss) and offered the choice of a new race and class (you can find the description of all races and classes in the game manual). Number of times you can refuse to change your Empire: not more than 2. After the second refusal the transfer of the character will become impossible.

Duration: a month from the moment you read this letter.

To the owners of the clans: you can transfer your clan to the side of Kartoss only if you have the written agreement of each clan member.

Yours sincerely,

Barliona Administration"

Hmm ... a transfer to Kartoss. ... Maybe I should just throw in the towel now and become a 'dark one'? I opened the manual and immersed myself in reading.

Trolls, thaurun, undead, ogres, dark bloods,

ashen elves ... well, I'll be! Over twenty previously inaccessible new races. For players who love everything new – this was paradise! New quests, new lands, new skills, new ... new everything! I thought about moving to Kartoss for a few seconds, but then smiled and shooed that thought away. I'm quite happy in Malabar, as it happens.

"Hi, Mahan!

This is Reptilis, the one you sold the Dress to. Here is the remainder of the money and huge thanks for the Dress. I'm lost for words in expressing my gratitude. Once again, please accept my apologies for trying to lead you like a sheep to the slaughter. I had no idea that things would turn out this way. If you ever need help – just say the word. I'll do all that's in my power straight away.

Tillis"

So it looks like Anastaria did like my Dress after all. The Greed Toad heaved a deep sigh one last time and with sadness saw the 24500 gold drop into my purse. The time had come for me to reap the results of my work. I opened the folder and started to write letters.

"Hello Marina,

Listen, you know that I've been put on the Dark Legion blacklist, so I'll be in hiding for the next three weeks. Consequently, it won't be possible to meet up with you in the near future. Let's do the following: as soon as I know that I'm no longer under threat, I'll contact you.

Daniel"

This player is not currently in the Game. Your letter will be delivered later.

First of all I postponed the meeting with Mirida to an unspecified point in the future. I had already decided that we should meet, so it made sense to warn her that I was about to vanish for an uncertain amount of time. Something was telling me that I had to speak with her, but to be honest I had to admit that I was afraid of this meeting. In the first few months, I would've given a lot to look Marina in the eyes but now, after I had actually seen those eyes, even just those of her avatar, I had no negative feelings towards her: I realized that I felt neither anger nor rage. Emotions had ebbed away, leaving only the harsh reality behind. Still, it felt so strange to sign with my real name! I had become so unused to it in the last half a year that I had begun to forget it. I had to try to use it more often, or after my release in seven years' time I would still be insisting that my name is Mahan.

Right after the letter to Marina, I wrote letters to my former acquaintances, with whom I've played for almost a year and a half, and asked to meet with them. I urgently had to gather my own team, preferably made up of people that I had known before.

Elenium was a junior Priest of Eluna. Since we

were going on a quest handed to us by Priestesses, he was bound to get some special bonus out of it. Just a few months before I ended up in prison, Sergei, as he was called in real life, had become a father, so he disappeared from Barliona for a while. I hoped that his little son was doing well and that Elenium was still playing.

Duki was a Rogue. In real life he was Johannes, from some Berlin suburb. He was an interesting guy, with whom you could talk about almost anything, ramble through an adventure together and generally have a great time. That's as long as he keeps his feet on the brakes. If Duki really lets rip, you'd better hang on! I've hardly ever seen such a nitpicky brainiac.

Sushiho was a Necromancer. Real name, Paolo: a genuine citizen of Rome. He was a two-meter-tall teacher of eastern martial arts, but chose a little gnome as his game character. He wanted to cast himself against type and he managed it very well: we met up outside the Game a couple of times and we always treated this giant as a shorty.

All of us spent a great deal of time together and even wanted to form our own clan, but never got around to it. Now there was finally an opportunity to make those old dreams a reality. On several occasions, after getting out of the mine, I almost wrote to them, but each time something stopped me. Although this was no 'something'. I know exactly what it was: I didn't want to hang my problems on others. Even if I wrote to them that everything was fine, I would have had to tell them about everything that had happened. What was the sense of burdening them with such boring and unnecessary information as my imprisonment?

After these guys, the list of my good acquaintances had run out. Now only Eric, Clutzer and Leite remained. I had known these three for only two weeks, but in that time they had shown themselves to be real men so I immediately wrote a letter to each of them, proposing that we should meet up tomorrow morning at the Jolly Gnoom tavern. The blacklist kicked into action only at the end of tomorrow, so I had a little bit of time on my hands. I think that's it. Although ... no!

There was one more outstanding debt that simply had to be settled. I opened the map of Kartoss that I got from the leader of the Dark Goblin mining incursion. It contained 20% of the old Kartoss territories. I wondered whether the map remained current or became seriously outdated after the game update. A good question to which I would have loved to know the answer. But this wasn't that important right now. When he sent me that small mountain of Jewelcraft recipes, Evolett handed me a truly massive gift. I had to give him a corresponding reply. I highlighted several areas of the map close to the capital, made a copy of these and sent it to the leader of the Dark Legion clan under the heading 'A favor returned'. I may have only shared half of my 20% with him, but I thought this was sufficient not to feel indebted for the rest of my life. The Greed Toad prevented me from sending the entire map, having risen up in arms in defense of its interests.

Now I really was done. I've sent out all the warnings, meeting requests and thanks. I could now proceed to pat myself on the back. Although, on reflection, there was one more thing I needed to take care of: Anastaria. The thought of my Scaling Items was bothering me – what if they get forgotten? Despite there being an agreement in place, unbreakable as it was, I'd still rather play it safe and refresh the memory of the party involved.

"Speaking!" Anastaria's divine voice filled my personal Bank room.

"Anastaria, this is Mahan! Have you already been transported?"

"No, we had to port ourselves. To what do I owe the honor? I'm beginning to fear calls from you," judging by the girl's cheerful voice, she was laughing, "You either chuck me into some backwater shrubbery or turn up demanding to steer a raid. What did you find this time?"

"No, I'm calling you about a totally mercantile matter right now. When can I get the Thricinian items that Phoenix promised me? You see, Evolett just declared open season on me, so it would be good to get them now and not in three weeks' time."

"Not right now – I'm not in Anhurs. Let's meet in two or three hours. It will be just gone midnight and there will be fewer people around – you could barely squeeze through the crowds stomping through the city right now. Let's meet on the central square, the Thricinian place is located nearby. That work for you?"

"All right, I'll see you in a couple of hours. I am already on the square, just dial me as soon as you're here and I'll come right away. I'll have a look around the shops in the meantime."

"Good, catch you later then," Anastaria disconnected, but I was wary of her good mood. She was suddenly very calm and approachable. ... Something wasn't right here. I would have to be very careful during our meeting and keep my tongue in check.

I was about to leave, but then saw that I had just received another letter. Strange – everyone seems to be writing to me these days. I opened the folder and looked at the author. It was Evolett.

Mahan, we urgently need to meet. In 10 minutes in the Golden Horseshoe tavern, it's on the central square in Anhurs. I've reserved a table. Evolett.'

* * *

"I'm looking for a decent clan for transfer to Kartoss!"

"Those headed for Kartoss – join us! It would be easier in a clan!"

"Selling 20 Black Fox pelts! 10 gold each!"

The last message stuck out of the general flow of messages like a sore thumb: Anhurs had descended into the chaos of people preparing to move to the Nameless City and I cringed as if beset by toothache. How could I forget that aside from the advantages of being a free citizen, there were also the downsides, such as general city chat? Although Farstead also came with various messages from players, they didn't form such an endless din that was now stressing out my ears. Until you fix the general chat settings, filtering out the unwanted channels, you end up hearing and reading everything on offer from players across Anhurs. Obvious trolling and flooding were forbidden, with the Imitators keeping a close eye on this, but even just the shouts searching for groups and seeking sale or exchange of goods combined into an endless clamor. When I was walking to the Bank I didn't take any notice of this, but now the players were really letting rip: Kartoss beckoned for many.

I quickly went to the settings and added a filter, which sorted types of messages into groups, then breathed a sigh of relief and headed to the tavern. On the outside, with its grey walls, dingy doors and dirty windows, the Golden Horseshoe didn't stand out in any way, but that didn't stop it being the most expensive tavern in the capital, and therefore the whole of Malabar. This was the place where Barliona's elite would head to celebrate the successful completion of a mission or a raid. Phoenix is thought to have started this tradition by holding a great party there after it won its first prize for completing a Dungeon. Only players who specialized in Cooking could be chefs in the Golden Horseshoe and they were paid a handsome salary for their work. Each year this elite tavern held contests for the best chef in Malabar, offering a job to the winner, and the competition for this position could be stiffer than for gaining the 'Best Clan' title. Just the names of the dishes here were quite taxing on the brain as you struggled to imagine something like: 'Grilled flying Kamarton with slices of Devilsaur served under rwondian rosemary sauce', 'Sautéed Crocolisk in Foxrabbit skin'. ... The dishes' names certainly created an impression.

I opened a squeaky door, noting that at least in this regard the developers didn't have to overdo it, and found myself in a fairytale.

Firstly, I immediately found myself in a tuxedo. The system determined that I had a right to enter the building and dressed me in what suited the status of the establishment. The tux was an ordinary illusion, not affecting the stats of my gear in any way, but it still felt very strange. You had to know how to wear a tuxedo – otherwise it would end up looking like it was stuck on a mannequin. A couple of steps later I realized that it was a skill I completely lacked. Secondly, the inner décor of the establishment presented a stark contrast to its external look. There was gold, crystal, sparkle and, for some reason, red satin – that pretty much summed up the dazzling sight that met me. Everything was so rich and expensive that I couldn't help feeling totally out of place here. With my paltry 60-and-a-bit thousand gold, I had no business being here. It would've only bought me the entrance fee and a couple of appetizers. Drinks were out of the question.

"Please, you're expected," one of the waiters distracted me from close examination of a statue depicting a battle of an Orc and a Dinosaur. I was being addressed by a player – that was the way things were done in the Golden Horseshoe.

"Well, hello once again, you walking surprise," Evolett greeted me cheerfully from a sumptuous armchair. An identical tuxedo to the one I was wearing looked so natural on him that I felt embarrassed by my own stiffness. A snow-white napkin – as if any spills or crumbs were even possible in Barliona – was lying on his knees. The table occupied by the leader of Dark Legion was laid out for two people and the selection of silverware provided was pushing the boundaries of reason: five spoons and six forks. What was this? Did someone want to humiliate me and show up my lack of proper table etiquette? In your dreams! Clouter, I should find you and definitely make you another dog figurine, or even two. Even though I didn't really have much practice in applying my posh table manners, the lad had drilled them into me so well that I was quite sure of myself. So, my good sir, two can play this game. Especially if I keep in mind that I've been given a chance to enjoy top-notch exotic food, at someone else's expense, no less. I had no intention of paying. So where's the menu and what does their drinks assortment look like?

"Hmm." Evolett grinned when I used the salad

fork in the right place and sent off the waiter to get another one for the fish. "You continue to surprise me. I'll be honest with you, I expected you to stare at the cutlery in complete bewilderment and make silly mistakes, but it looks like I could learn a thing or two from you instead. Where did you learn all this?"

"Everyone has their secrets," I said meaningfully, finishing the contents of my glass. It had to be said that the food at the Golden Horseshoe completely justified coming here: I was currently sporting all kinds of buffs: +20% Experience for 4 hours, increase of all stats by 10% and the ambrosial drink with a faint greenish glow increased my Energy to 200 points. It would only last 3 hours, but the taste that I was experiencing was out of this world.

Speaking of the taste, despite the fact that the majority of the players in Barliona didn't experience any sensations, the sensory filters were turned off in the taverns. Giving a player, who might be on a strict diet in real life, a chance to enjoy a very delicious cake without a worry about the millions of calories ... This was a very effective marketing move on behalf of the corporation. There weren't all that many places where the sensory filters were turned off: Taverns, Dating Houses, Arenas and, as it turned out, certain quests, such as 'Saving Grey Death'. The rest of the time players didn't have to think about feeling anything inside the game.

"Since we've already begun the conversation, allow me to tell you why I sent you this urgent invitation," Evolett took a break from his food, "the answer is simple: the map. I received your present, looked at it and saw that I absolutely had to have the full version."

"The full version?" I decided to feign utter surprise, playing at being totally clueless about what he meant. At the same time I was trying to figure out how the leader of the Dark Legion clan could have found out about the map. The goblin prisoner? Unlikely. Perhaps the Herald let it slip? Quite possible, but then ...

"Yes, the full one" smiled Evolett, as if listening in on my internal monologue. "It looks like you're still a beginner Cartographer if you don't know that each copy created contains the description of which part of the original has been provided. You've sent me 50% of the map and I found it quite fascinating. So much so, in fact, that I am prepared to discuss the matter of acquiring the second half."

I took a break from the food, opened the map and prepared a copy of a small part of it. I looked at the properties of the copy and cursed through my teeth – it was true, not only did it bear the record of the author, but also the source from which the copy was made. Moreover, everything was editable and if I had wanted to conceal the information all I had to do was delete it. If I had only known ...

"I see you're not taking the old man at his word." I was once again greeted by Evolett's smile: he was clearly enjoying all of this. He leant back into his armchair and was in such good spirits that I immediately wanted to do something bad and unpleasant to him to wipe that smirk off his face, even for a minute. I could just take this fork and ... hmm ... What's happening to me? I somehow never noticed such bloodthirsty tendencies in myself before. Something wasn't right! After looking through all my buffs and debuffs I found the reason: Berserker, lasting 10 minutes. Bugger it! Looks like one of the dishes that I ordered caused this effect. As soon as the buffs started to land on me in droves I stopped keeping track of them, clearly a mistake. I copied Evolett's pose and tried to control the upsurge of adrenaline. The capsule did its job well – right now I felt like I could turn the whole world upside-down, run a marathon, tear Hellfire apart with my bare hands or punch Geranika's face in. Yup! The main thing now was not to lose it and not to allow myself to express any emotions. In my case attacking another player would mean returning to the mines, and was to be avoided at all costs. Unlike buffs, which could be cancelled at will, there was no such easy option for debuffs. I lost all interest in Evolett, in the food and the surrounding world and turned into a statue. I'm a lump of rock, which sees and feels nothing. I'm a windmill, through which the wind blows without toppling it. I'm ...

"Mahan, please drink this." I came to myself as a waiter shook me by the shoulder and handed me a glass containing a liquid of some kind. There was still seven minutes of the Berserker left, so it took some effort to suppress my desire to punch the waiter in the face and instead focus on what he was saying.

"Please drink this. It will remove the debuff."

With some difficulty and shaking hands I poured the liquid down my throat. It burned, but my head cleared straight away; the overwhelming impulse to act left me and I could look around with normal eyes. Hmm. Where did all these people come from? There were two waiters, standing in a line, a plump dwarf, wringing a chef's hat in his hands, an elven lady in a luxurious dress and a Herald. That was all, aside from Evolett who was warily examining my face.

"Mahan, how are you feeling?" The tension was broken by the Herald's question. The crowd had exploded: the waiters were shouting threats at the chef, the lady at the waiters, Evolett at the lady and only the dwarf stood silent and downcast, his eyes on the ground.

"What exactly happened here?" I asked the Herald in return "Why did I end up with the Berserker debuff?"

"A chain of coincidences," came the chef's whisper through the surrounding din. "Who would have thought that mixing elysks and karpatosses, while washing them down with swanna and snacking on shurpilus, could result in a Berserker? This is pure Alchemy and I'm no expert in that. No-one before you has ever ordered such an original collection of dishes, so totally unsuitable to each other ..."

Yeah, that's me all right! Fear the Shaman who has landed a freebie.

"Mahan, could I have a moment of your time?" said the Herald in an official tone. Everyone around me immediately fell silent. No-one wanted to interrupt a Herald. "Please sign Form 12.4a to submit an official complaint about a premeditated attempt to make you cause damage to bystanders and send you back to the mines." At this news the lady in the dress gave a subdued shriek and went pale. I didn't even know that a player's avatar could lose color, something to remember. "This complaint will be examined in the course of an hour. The minimal punishment for this offence stipulated by the law on Prisoners of the Malabar Empire in Barliona (and consequently the real world) amounts to a year-long confinement in the mines. The punishment will be applied to the executive manager of the Golden Horseshoe tavern ..." At this the elven lady turned a shade whiter, which previously seemed impossible "... and to the chef who cooked these dishes. The form has already been filled out; all you have to do is add your signature."

A text with 'Signature' button appeared before my eyes. The dwarf didn't lift his head and everyone else froze expecting my decision.

"Why am I not on this list?" I asked the Herald after reading the statement. "I was the one that chose the dishes – no-one was exactly force-feeding me here. This means that I'm as much to blame as these two." I nodded towards the chef and the manager.

"According to the rules of sensory establishments," volunteered Evolett, "the checking of the dishes and their combinations is the responsibility of said establishment. Even a crazy combination like the one you ordered should've been checked for compatibility and any eventual negative results. Those who fail to follow procedure will be punished. From what I can remember, this is the ninth time this sort of thing has happened, am I right?" He looked questioningly at the pale-faced elven manager. The latter was only capable of giving a weak nod and swallowing. "The Golden Horseshoe values its clients too much to permit itself such errors."

I read over the statement once again, looked at the dwarf, the elf, Evolett and the Herald, found the small 'Refuse' button and, with a swift move of my virtual hand, pressed it without hesitation.

"Please explain your choice," asked the Herald, his words devoid of any emotion. Even the usual ringing in his voice seemed subdued.

"I've done time at the mines and I know what it's like. You have to be a complete bastard to wish ill towards someone who has tried to achieve perfection with his creation. I don't need this."

"Your choice had been made." There was a clap of the portal and the Herald sped away to his other errands.

"You're fired," the manager, who had now come to herself, hissed to the chef "I want you out of my sight and out of the tavern this very second!"

"Will you let us eat and to talk in peace already?" Evolett got their attention by leaning over the table and banging a knife on a glass. "Please sort your problems out after my meeting."

After throwing me a meaningful gaze the

manager departed. The waiters blurred into the scenery and the chef simply vanished. He was probably automatically removed from the building.

"It was a mistake to let it go," chided Evolett as soon as everyone was gone, "she will still be fired – the owner will not stand for such a disgrace. This tavern's reputation has taken a serious blow in any case. When it comes to it, don't agree to anything less than three free meals a day for a year. You can send the request within the next seven days – they will agree to all of your demands. I'm sorry that I've become the unwitting cause of this situation. Nothing would've happened had I not invited you here. But let's not lose any more time. The map: I really need the full version. The change in Kartoss locations has meant an automatic update of all the maps so old maps have not become obsolete. I won't ask how you got it; I'll just say that I need it. What would you ask for it?"

"This is a very abrupt jump," now it was my turn to smile "from fighting the Berserker debuff to selling the map – please let me catch my breath a little. I never thought that the map could interest you quite that much, so I haven't thought of what I could ask in return. What can you offer?"

"It's not very nice to try to shift responsibility onto others. How am I supposed to know what it is exactly you might need? Are you suggesting that I should decide instead of you?"

"You've missed the mark in trying to appeal to my pride. Unlike me, you know very well just how much this map is worth, so we are on very unequal footing here. After all, you've most likely already decided what you're prepared to pay for the second half, so there's no point beating about the bush. Make your offer and I will agree or decline."

"Are you feeling so completely unperturbed when talking to one of the most influential players in the Game?" Evolett had adopted a familiar, informal manner and was addressing me more directly now. "One gets the feeling that speaking to players of my level is something you do every day. Emperor, Heralds ... almost all the players that I know start to worry, stutter or confuse their words when speaking with someone of my standing. You, on the other hand ..."

"Have I understood you correctly that you have no intention of making an offer?" I interrupted the leader of the future best clan of Kartoss.

"One million gold," Evolett finally decided. "That's excluding the compulsory 30% that, as I know, you get deducted from every payment."

A million gold for a copy of the map? This isn't just a good deal – it's the deal of the century!

"But I have one condition," Evolett brought me down to earth "we sign an agreement that no-one else except you is to use this map. After this it couldn't be sold, gifted or exchanged. I don't wish to see another clan in Kartoss in possession of this information. This is my offer."

"I agree." I didn't even have to think about this deal. A million gold for a bunch of virtual numbers is a very good investment.

Skill increase:

+2 to Trade. Total: 9

Achievement earned!

Moneybags level: 1 (9 transactions worth over a million until the next level)

Achievement reward: the amount of money dropped by mobs has increased by 10%. This ability affects any players under your command.

You can look at the list of achievements in the character settings.

"I didn't think there existed a man capable of surprising me twice" a pleased Evolett stretched in his armchair after putting away the full copy of the Kartoss map I gave him. "After Beatwick and the opening up of Kartoss everyone forgot that Dragons have returned into the game and you are directly connected to this development. You even know one of them. And then the map. You are simply a mine of surprises. I have a proposal for you: if you're able to surprise me a third time I'll give you a present. This has no time limit – you can take forever, if you like. I'm just curious if you'd manage it a third time."

"'Forever' is just too long. I prefer to act in the moment." With that I opened my sack, took out the Eye of the Dark Widow, uncovered its properties and put it on the table before Evolett. I'd been intending to start showing off the Eye for some time, since I had to start gathering the team to complete this quest, so now was as good a time as any.

The Dark Legion's leader's hands jerked in a

grasping movement towards the Eye and his face turned into one big question: HOW? But he quickly controlled himself and regained his impassive demeanor.

"In just two days you will receive the promised present." After a pause Evolett asked, 'How much?"

"It's not for sale. I'd like to try this myself."

"Then I propose an alliance. As soon as I cross over to Kartoss, only competent players will remain in the clan. We can help you do the quest. Naturally, all the loot will be yours and I'm prepared to pay for my clan to be included. Think about it, no need to decide now. Making an alliance with the first clan on Kartoss would bring many benefits.”

"I'll definitely think it over," I promised Evolett and returned to my food.

At the tavern's exit I was met by a respectable-looking goblin, the owner of the place, by the look of it. After a brief bout of bargaining I was granted the opportunity to come to the tavern three times a day for two years. I could also bring up to three people with me. Keeping in mind the buffs one could gain in the tavern, I considered this a good investment for my future clan.

Speaking of the clan. With all these meetings, I completely forgot that I had been planning to drop by the Registrar. While there still time, it was a mistake I had to quickly remedy.

* * *

The mark in the shape of azure Seathistle looked simply magnificent on my cloak and the see-through flower before my name indicated that I belonged to a clan. The Seathistles clan has made its début in Barliona.

At first I wanted to pick a serious and intimidating name, like 'Wings of Terror', 'Night Legion' or 'Dragon', but then some common sense clawed its way back: why? Who was it that I was trying to impress? And for whose benefit was I thinking up excuses? Myself? It's just that the alternatives were even worse.

The registrar, an old plump man with an impressive moustache and similarly impressive potbelly, stood by the desk, patiently penning something down. Registering a clan was abominably simple: you pay five thousand gold, pick a name for the clan from the list of available names and you've got your clan. The system automatically generated the emblem, which could be edited later – should you ever get around to it – then the clan emblem was slotted next to the player names and that was pretty much it.

After paying the required fee, I opened the list of names. Just like player names, clan names had to be unique within each continent. The list of recommended names numbered over ten thousand and I had no idea which filter to use to narrow down my search.

"Dragon." I tried my luck and saw a message that this name was unavailable. The recommended names of 'Red-nosed Dragon' and 'Gold digger Dragon Killers' and so on sounded like the products of someone with a small imagination and a big hangover. After going through a couple more possibilities that sounded interesting, I finally gave up. Will I really have to name it 'I don't care, I've been playing in Barliona for many years now'? I think not. After playing around with name filters and setting them to look for single-word clan names, I looked at the list of the names that came up: 'Phartizans', 'Floodland', 'Seathistles', 'Croutonistas' ... Hmm ... 'Seathistles' ... Why not?

Name of newly-created clan: Seathistles. Please confirm.

There were two buttons: 'Yes' and 'No'. I could see, of course, that the name sounded stupid and off-the-wall, but I liked it.

Clan Seathistles has been created.
Clan leader: Mahan
Current clan level: 1
Next level gained: 20 million clan points

That was that. The registrar handed me a paper confirming my right of clan ownership and returned to his desk. I would have to go and read up in the manual what these clan points were and how to go about getting them.

Due to the presence of players that have earned the 'First Kill' achievement in the Mushu Dungeon, clan Seathistles receives:

+2 Resource Points for all gathering professions

+2% chance of creating a copy of an object for all crafting professions at no extra resource cost

These properties combine with the properties of other Dungeon First Kills.

I'll take two of those! How could I forget about this? The First Kill! Now I saw why Phoenix tried so hard to get at least one person with this achievement to join its ranks. At higher profession levels, especially with gathering (of Diamonds, for example) getting +2 to the gathered resource ... Mm ... I think I want another First Kill!

After accepting the flower generated by the system as the clan symbol, I went around the Profession Trainers.

First I dropped by the Mining and the Cartography trainers, where I increased the Hardiness and Scroll Scribe specializations to 10%. The next 5% would come at level 150 of the profession, so it was still some way off. I didn't even bother visiting the Cooking and Repair trainers – with my level in these professions there wasn't much for me to do there. Now only Jewelcraft remained.

"Welcome, how can I help you at such a late hour?" A colorful gnome greeted me elaborately.

Sporting a red velvet dressing gown, tied with a patterned belt, the Jeweler constantly fiddled with his beard as if he had no other purpose for his hands.

"I've come to be trained," was my simple reply. I had a brief chance to look through the scrolls sent by Evolett and not one of them was for someone with a profession level lower than a 100. I was still too much of a beginner for them with my 42 levels.

"Please touch the book," said the trainer, clearly losing interest. It was a strange that only Jewelers required you to touch the skill book; other trainers that I had known managed without it. Not wishing to disappoint the gnome I put my hands on the book, where some incomprehensible symbols immediately appeared and came together to form a text.

The gnome quickly glanced at the emerging lines, turned around, took a step away and then froze. Extremely slowly he turned his head again toward the book, took another slow step back and stared intently at the text. An eternity seemed to go by (no more than a minute in actual fact) before the trainer recovered from the shock. What a strange Intellect Imitator this NPC has – it seems altogether too involved in playing out the role.

"The Cursed Artificer that has turned into the Blessed Artificer; the author of the Cursed Chess Pieces and the Orc Warriors from the Karmadont Chess Set; the creator of exact copies of the Dwarf Warriors from the Karmadont Chess set," the trainer breathed out loudly, tore his gaze away from the book and looked at me. "It's been a while since I've had such an interesting student," he paused and then said, chuckling, "with just 42 levels in the profession. Did you level up in your skill only by creating Rare and Unique items?"

"No, I ..."

"It doesn't matter," the Jeweler interrupted me "you've come to learn and I will teach you. What would you like to know?"

"I need all the recipes for my level and want to offer you this one." I opened my Jewelcraft recipe book, created a scroll with the Stone Rose recipe and handed it to the gnome. "I would also like to learn how to sift Ore so I can get precious stones from it. I think that's it."

The gnome gave me a businesslike glance, chuckled, took out a piece of granite from under the counter, as if it was just waiting for him there, closed his eyes and in just a few seconds was holding my Rose in his hands.

"Mahan's Stone Rose ...' I can offer 50000 gold for the recipe right now or you can get 60–70 for it if you put it up for auction. What would you prefer?"

"Send it to the Auction House. I'm in no rush to get the money, so no point losing out on the extra 10000."

"All right." The scroll and the Rose created by the trainer disappeared and I acquired yet another agreement, this time about the sale of the recipe scroll at the Auction House. "I have no scrolls for someone of your skill level – you should gain at least 10 more levels and come back then. As for the sifting, this isn't that hard to teach. It would be more difficult to actually get any stones out of Ore. You may have a decent drop chance for beginner level precious stones and rare minerals, but getting a Sapphire would be near impossible. The percentage chance is just too low. But if you still want it, it'll cost you 10000 gold."

Your character has acquired a new ability: Ore sifting (requirement: knowledge of the Jewelcraft profession). There is some chance of getting a Precious Stone from the sifted Ore. During the sifting the Ore disappears. The chance of getting a precious stone depends on the Ore level and the level of Jewelcraft profession. Crafting stat. bonus: when sifting Ore you have an additional (Crafting/5) percentage chance of discovering a Precious Stone, corresponding to the Ore level.

Damn! Double damn, even! And here I was thinking that Crafting would grant an impressive bonus in this case as well, but it only increased the drop chance by a minute percentage ... Only one out of a hundred siftings might end in success – or might not, should the dice decide to roll the other way. So it looked like I would have to buy the stones for making the Dwarf Warriors after all. Speaking of which ... !

"Teacher, I have one more question. I did create the Orc Warriors, as you correctly noted, but when I began to make the Dwarf Warriors I came out with just copies – full and exact copies, but still only copies. Why do you think that might be?"

"What did you make the dwarves out of?"

"Out of Lapis Lazuli, as specified in the description."

"No, where did you get it? Did you mine it or buy it?"

"It was a gift."

"So there is your answer," smiled the gnome. "The Karmadont Set can't be made out of bought stones. The person recreating it must gather each stone himself. Either from a vein or from sifting or, as I see in your case, from smelting ingots. You do have Crafting, after all. By the way, as soon as you get a second Gem Cutter, you will be able to craft items that deliver up to +180 bonus to the stats. That's the limitation until you reach a third Gem Cutter. Anything else?"

"Thank you, I've found out all that I need to know," I heartily thanked the trainer. I now understood why I ended up with just copies of the dwarves. I had to gather the Lapis myself.

Anastaria's call caught me as I was about to reach the square, where I had headed straight after leaving the Jeweler.

"I'm in the square. Come over."

The solitary figure of the girl could be seen from afar under the lamp-posts. An occasional player running through the square might almost whistle as they spotted her, but they didn't dare to stop: Anastaria was known to be a cold and discerning beauty. Incredibly, she combined the qualities that most people all too often lack: brains, beauty and awareness of her abilities. This made her an incredibly dangerous opponent to anyone who might dare challenge her. As far as I knew, there were even special clans named 'We love Anastaria' and 'Anastarians', who were ready to shred anyone on her account.

"Looks like you were in no hurry," smiled the girl as soon as I entered the square "has being late for a date with a beautiful girl, as you put it, become the norm for modern men?"

"It's one thing if it's a date," I parried, "but there is zero chance of our meeting to arrange for my 'robbery' of Phoenix passing for a date. And anyway, you have so many admirers that being one of the multitude holds little interest for me."

"One of." Anastaria smiled once again. "I agree, there's little interest for a Dragon to be 'one of anything."

"Look who's talking, oh 'Gorgeous one', vanquisher of sirens." I returned Anastaria's smile, noting with some pleasure that the girl's eyes momentarily widened. "Oh yes! I completely forgot! When was your birthday? Or is it still to come? I've completely lost track."

"It's already been and gone – last week, in fact. Why?" Anastaria stopped, turned around and stared at me. "Did you decide to give me a present? Like those Cursed Chess Pieces?"

"Why do you think so ill of me? You're ready to

drag up those Cursed Chess pieces at the drop of a hat. That's not playing nice." I smiled and took the copy of the Dwarf Warriors out of my sack. "I realize I'm late with this, but it comes from the heart."

Anastaria was quite a sight. As soon as I took out the figurines, her face became a frozen mask and only the movement of her brown eyes indicated that she was still here. I decided not to reveal their properties, dragging out the moment of the handover. Stacey was doing her very best to hide her desire to snatch them out of my hands and have a closer look. She could see that these were dwarves well enough.

"Here you go!" I handed over the chess pieces to the girl and just had enough time to pull back my hand – so swift was the lady paladin's move to get them. Did these figurines really mean that much to her?

"COPIES?!" The girl's outraged voice seemed to shake the entire city. "You just palmed me off with copies?! You dared to think you'd be let off with copies?! And you call this a birthday present?!"

"What do you mean 'palm off'? I've made you a present and now you're screaming at me." I was rather enjoying watching the girl fly into a rage. When she was angry, she became so sweet that it was too easy to forget that one of the most dangerous players in Barliona was standing in front of me. "And you can quit play acting already. You may make a fine actress, but you're overdoing it a tad. You've been building an 'iron lady' reputation for yourself for too long to make the current hysterics all that believable."

"That's not playing nice!" It was like Anastaria was suddenly replaced. In the blink of an eye she regained a calm and slightly ironic demeanor. "You're not letting a girl savor the limelight! What if acting was my life's dream and you simply don't get my moments of inspiration? Do you know why you ended up with copies? I doubt this was what you were aiming for when you were making them."

"Yes, I figured it out."

"Mahan, we could make one hell of a team. Your inexplicable luck, my resources and analysts – it would a win-win for everyone. Look at how you grew in Beatwick – before the battle you were level 14 and now you've already reached 67. Players like this are highly valued in Phoenix. And what are the 'Seathistles'? Where did they come from? And where did you dig up such a clan, by the way?

"I didn't dig it up, I set it up. For now I'm its only member." I jokingly pushed out my chest, showing off the great hero that was standing there for all to see. "You said that you were interested in the position of a deputy in my clan. So, that position is now open. I'm inviting you to join me. But only after I get the four items off Phoenix. Come over – I've got cookies."

Anastaria's ringing laugh echoed through Anhurs.

"You are the first to try to poach me," chuckled the girl, "so you'd better tell me what it is you have that would make me consider your offer."

"That's easy. You already know about the

cookies, and they are far from trivial. Now you know about the copies of the dwarves too. What else can I offer you ...? I don't even know." I paused as if thinking. "Ah! This too! I've found the Dragons! But I won't be telling where they can be found to just anyone. I even got to know one of them. Well, you saw all that ... " On the one hand, if I was doing things by the book, I should have completely denied my connection with the Dragons – 'you were all just seeing things' – but on the other hand there were just too many witnesses to our little chat near Beatwick. "I think that's it. So give it a think – I don't offer cookies to just anyone!"

Anastaria walked next to me in silence for some time, probably gathering her thoughts. Of course I understood that inviting such a player into my clan looked stupid ... at the very least. It's not like she would ever leave Phoenix – she didn't become the head of the clan to swap all that for Seathistles. But one can dream for a bit ...

"It's not enough," finally came the girl's voice, "just a tiny bit more and you'd be there. What else do you have that would tempt me to leave Phoenix and become a Seathistle?"

"That's it!" I said in surprise. "Is everything that I've offered you so far insufficient? You truly are insatiable!"

"You have a think and perhaps I'll go for it," Stacey gave me a serious look. "We're here. If you offer me something else once we leave the Thricinians it's quite possible that I would agree. Think, Shaman!"

Is she hinting at the Karmadont Chess Set? On the one hand only an idiot wouldn't realize by now that I'm the one that made it. On the other hand, no-one has any proof. No, for now I wouldn't be showing the Orc Warriors off to anyone. I have a different solution.

Despite the late hour, the representatives of the Thricinian faction were still open for business. And really, it's not like NPCs had much else to do.

"How can we be of service, Anastaria?" a strange creature addressed the paladin. It had blue skin, two small horns, hooves and a tail – the Thricinian race was unknown to the wider public. At one point I spent a considerable amount of time trying to find out who they are. I discovered that they are called Danrei. Apart from that, who they are and what their history was remains unknown.

"I would like to buy four items of the highest quality I can access, which would suit this man." She nodded in my direction. "We need Shaman items. Please show us what you have. Phoenix will foot the bill."

"Please follow me." The Danrei addressed me and then turned back to the girl, "Anastaria, please wait here. Would you have some supper while you're waiting for your guest?"

What on earth did she do to earn such special treatment? We entered a small room and the Danrei asked me, "What are you interested in?"

"I need four items. Can you tell me if there is a set among the items of the level that has been made available to me? For a Shaman." I added, just in case.

"Yes, there is. Please wait here." The Danrei pointed me to a sofa in the room that we just entered. "The set will be brought out in a moment."

Just a few minutes later a young Danrei lady came out, holding Gloves, Pants, a Belt and, by the looks of it, Bracers. Well, well, let's see what we've got?

Shaman Pants of Danreic Inspiration. Durability: unbreakable. Description: +10 to the maximum level of Energy, +(Character level*6) Intellect, +(Character level*3) Stamina, +(Character level*2) Agility, +(Character level*4) to defense from all damage types. Item class: Scaling set. Level restrictions: No.

Set of two items: +30 to the maximum level of Energy.

Set of four items: +(Character level*10) to Intellect, +(Character level*10) Stamina.

A similar set of stats came with the Gloves, the Belt and the Bracers. I put the set aside and asked to be shown a few more items, but no combination of four ordinary items could ever approach this set. It looked like my choice was made.

"I'm taking these." I pointed to the Danreic Inspiration set and then asked my guide, "can you tell me why you hold Anastaria in such high regard?"

"The great warrior" replied the Danrei solemnly, "aided my people in gaining knowledge of our world. I cannot tell you more; you should ask her yourself. Thank you for making the choice so quickly. Some free citizens spend up to a few days inside our walls, trying to evaluate every item."

I put on the set and looked at my stats. Fear me, mere mortals! 1958 Stamina and 1958 Intellect. That's aside from my still unspent 265 stat. points. I was afraid to even think how much such a set might cost.

"Have you come up with something else to interest me?" asked Anastaria playfully as soon as we left the Thricinians, "or have you got nothing else?"

"Nothing?" I said with overplayed surprise. "Of course I have something to tempt you with. Like this thing, for example." I took out the Eye of the Dark Widow, which I'd shown off to Evolett, uncovered its properties and showed it to Stacey. "But that's just something I have among all the other bits and pieces."

After she saw the Eye's properties the girl's face once again turned into an unreadable mask.

"So, will you come over?" I asked. "I have a lot of stuff like this, I just don't have anyone who's able to utilize it."

"Two million gold clean – free of your tax – and the boosting of your entire clan to level 120, including all those that you invite. Half of the loot that we'll get in the raid will be yours ..." Stacey immediately found her bearings and started to bombard me with offers for buying the Eye. Strange, is it really that valuable? In that case I'm a damned fool for showing it off now and not after I reached level 100.

"It's not for sale. I've already declined Evolett and I will refuse you too. The Eye is only for the Seathistles clan, so you decide." I smiled once again. "The place of the deputy is free and awaits you."

"Send me an invite." Anastaria's calm voice stopped me dead in my tracks. What on earth is 'send me an invite' supposed to mean? Is she for real? Or is she calling my bluff?

I opened the interface of the invitation to the clan, selected Anastaria and sent her a clan invite, specifying the position of the 'Deputy Head'. The probability that she was bluffing was just too high, so I wasn't too worried. Leaving Phoenix for Seathistles ... Her own clan would shoot her on the spot ...

Player Anastaria has joined the Seathistles clan.

Rank: Deputy Head of the clan.

Clan achievement gained: A hundred's no limit.

Clan achievement gained: Two hundred in my sights.

Clan achievement gained: Three hundred's no myth.

Due to the presence of players that earned the First Kill of the Bloody Scythe Dungeon, the Seathistles clan gains:

The speed of Energy regeneration for all clan members, increased by 10%.

The speed of Hit Point regeneration for all clan members, increased by 10%.

These properties combine with other properties of other Dungeon First Kills.

Due to the presence of players that earned the First Kill of the Dungeon of Fear, the Seathistles clan gains: ...

And then followed the list of 25 First Kills, giving bonuses to all clan members.

"And now, Mahan, we will sign an agreement," purred Anastaria, looking pleased. "You can't have any secrets from your deputy. Otherwise it would be the wrong sort of clan... "

CHAPTER THREE
ANHURS

E VERYONE KNOWS THE EXPRESSION: 'Turn to stone'. Although it was something I thought impossible, it looked like this was a time for all preconceptions to come crashing down. Anastaria had joined Seathistles as deputy head of the clan. Aside from the fact that both Phoenix and the admirers of this sweet scoundrel will have my head for this, even if I wanted to, I wouldn't be able to remove her from the clan for the next three months: the leaders are closely linked to their clan, so they have to be chosen very carefully. From the moment they're appointed it isn't possible to disband the clan, not as long as it contains someone else holding the deputy head position. ... Something was telling me that my little joke had landed me in a whole world of trouble.

"Stacey, what are you up to?" I attempted to recover from the shock, regain my composure and try to wriggle out of the situation. Transferring from one clan to another was nothing out of the ordinary and players often switched their membership, which is why the leading clans introduced salaries and offered bonuses, such as places in exclusive raids, in order to keep their core team together. People are the most important resource in Barliona and can become the object of stiff competition. The structure of any clan is very simple: head, deputy, treasurer, castle owner and normal members. This standard set-up can be changed at any time after a chat with the registrar. I decided not to complicate things and left the standard structure in place. I could review it once other people started to join. Now then: because any player may leave the clan at any time, the clan founder, in this case me, would sign a temporary agreement with the hired players covering the exchange of information, joint exploits, leveling up, access to resources and other game-related things. Moreover, as far as I know, such agreements are not signed with everyone, but only with players of some importance to the clan. I was frantically trying to remember everything that I knew about clans, when Anastaria said, looking pleased:

"Deputy head ... you know, it's the first time this has happened to me – to be so dramatically demoted in the gaming social ladder: from the head of the best clan in Malabar to a deputy of a new and completely unknown clan. You owe me a cookie."

"Stacey, you didn't answer me. Despite the apparent recklessness of your decision, I don't believe you've made it on the spur of the moment. That's not the kind of person you are, so do please spill the beans on what's going on and why you accepted my invitation. And what's with the dirty hints about the absence of secrets between clan members and the disappointment of the Heralds? Are you trying to you call my bluff?"

"Let's go to the Golden Horseshoe for dinner and for a chat, 'bossling'. We will spend at least three months together, so it's time you put all your cards on the table. I bet you've never been inside the Horseshoe. I'll pay."

As soon as we stepped inside the Tavern we were dressed in the compulsory evening attire. I looked at Anastaria and was stunned: a glamorous, dark, figure-hugging dress showing considerable cleavage, an ideally matching necklace, the hairstyle ... I was looking at the embodiment of every man's dream. If she's anything like her gaming avatar in reality, all the top suitors in the world would be fighting over her.

"Can I be of assistance?" A waiter had materialized next to us but couldn't help staring at Anastaria wide-eyed.

"I need a table for my lady friend and myself," I said, beating her to it, and eliciting another astonished stare from the girl. What, something else you didn't know about? Surprise!

"Please follow me," the waiter directed us towards the depths of the hall. I don't know why, but I offered Anastaria my arm, which she accepted without hesitation, and we followed the waiter, like a model couple. The hall was almost deserted – only a couple of tables were occupied. There sat the tavern's patrons, surrounded by domes of 'Silence' and 'Distortion': the Golden Horseshoe looked after the virtual secrets of its guests.

I pulled out a chair, helping Anastaria to sit down and, having once again sent my silent gratitude to Clouter for his lessons, started to look through the menu. As I pretended to concentrate on choosing the dishes, I tried to think through the impending conversation. Arguing with Anastaria in the street would've been very bad form – it's not like we're little children or anything, screaming and stamping our feet all over the place. Brrr ... I realize that there are pros and cons for the clan as a result of the presence such a member, so first I would like to understand what it is that Phoenix wants and then decide which of these things I'm prepared to give up.

"You have access to the Golden Horseshoe": that was more of a statement than a question from Anastaria. When ordering I hadn't even looked at the names of the dishes in the menu and just picked the first thing at random, so I was now staring at some long, blue sticks that were wriggling for some reason. Had I not spent time in the mines, just the sight of them would have been nauseating, let alone imagining eating something like that. But after the monumental mass of green goo that we were fed at Pryke, any food would look appetizing.

"Of course. Why on earth shouldn't I," I

emphasized the last word, "have access to this place? Since we're talking now, please do explain the performance that you put on earlier and what I can now expect from Phoenix."

"Performance? Expect from Phoenix?" Anastaria pointedly raised an eyebrow, as if she had no clue what I was talking about. "You offered me to switch clans and I agreed."

She gets zero points for that. It really has been a difficult day today and it doesn't look like it's going to get better any time soon. And tomorrow I'll have to meet up with the guys and explain to them why I invited someone into the clan without giving them any say on it and why I immediately offered her the position of deputy head. "Stacey, let's talk plainly now! I do, of course, understand that you may leave at any time, but as head of the clan I have a whole day to flesh out an agreement with you, which will include a point about your compulsory presence in the clan for the next three months during which I cannot remove you. Care to refresh my memory on what's scheduled to happen in the next three months? If I remember correctly, this will be the period of preparation for the inter-clan competition, time which you will not spend within Phoenix. Are you prepared for this?"

"Blackmail really doesn't become you."

"And your words about the 'wrong sort of clan' weren't blackmail?"

"How I hate all these negotiations." The girl leant back into her chair. "It's a lot more interesting to solve the developers' puzzles, come up with plans for successful Dungeon runs or explore Barliona's history. Right now I'm sitting here doing my best to look all aloof and mysterious. No-one approved my leaving – Ehkiller has already contacted me and said he'll have my head if I don't return to the clan before the other players find out, so I'll be in your clan right up until the moment we leave the Horseshoe. Then I'll ditch you most unceremoniously. Why on earth did I do it ... ?" Anastaria fell silent and stared at her plate of food.

"Information," I completed her thought, "you need information. But why do you need information about a mere 67 level player? Compared to you I'm a total nobody and a noob."

"You want me to tick off the points on my fingers for you? I'll do it, I'm not too proud: The Karmadont Chess Set, the Cursed Chess Pieces, taking part in the Kartoss launch scenario, possession of information on Dragons, possession of a key to another world, inexplicable immunity to my poison ... Speaking of which – HOW? And access to the Golden Horseshoe, to top it all off! So there you are – the fingers of one hand were insufficient to count the ways in which you differ from a noob. I thought that in the moment of euphoria from getting such a player to join your clan you'd spill the beans on at least some of these things ... I'm sorry, I formed a mistaken opinion where your brains are concerned. I'm honest, as you can see. I really do want to get information on all these things, which is why I risked taking such a step. I simply improvised ..."

Player Anastaria has left the Seathistles clan.

The Seathistles clan loses the following bonuses from the First Kill: ...

Just a few seconds later the emblem of Phoenix appeared next to the girl's name. Anastaria returned to her clan.

"Key to another world – what are you on about?" I decided to clarify a point that had been bothering me.

"The Eye that you showed me: this quest takes place both in Barliona and in the world to which the Tarantulas departed. I could be wrong, but judging by similar quests, we would first have to kill a Priest who intends to bring back the Old Ones, then activate the Eye and jump to the other world, where we would meet up with the spiderlings of doom and show them the error of their ways. At the end of the quest each member gets an amulet that usually grants an extra 5–10 levels to a character and a certain amount of Reputation with the Emperor. And the First Kill, of course. The usual stuff."

"I see; thanks. Well, since we're off to such a good start, can you explain to me why you need the Karmadont Chess Set?"

"Aside from the fact that it's an exceptionally unique item in the game, it unlocks access to the founder of this world. According to the information we've obtained, the cave that contains the creator or whoever he left behind him also contains the very best bonuses in the game. This is somewhere I'd very much like to see, so I'm prepared to pay a lot for an 'entry ticket'. Until all the elements of the Chess Set are put together, it's of little use. Access is only possible when this takes place. The path to the place where the Chess Set can be activated is veiled in riddles contained in each type of chess piece. The first is contained in the Orcs. Have you solved it?"

"Why are you telling me all this?" I shrewdly deflected her question with one of my own.

"I'm trying to establish good relations between our clans. Would you have some pity on a girl already and give me a chance to solve the riddles? I'm not asking for the Chess Pieces, the riddles will be enough for me."

"Hold on. I still don't get why this performance, – all this drama with leaving Phoenix – was required. We could've just sat down and had a chat. But no, you felt you had to put on a show ..."

"Not everything that I do happens on your account," smiled the girl. "What I did ... it was something I needed to do ... it was personal and has nothing to do with you."

"It looks like it already does. At the very least the waiter has already seen that you're no longer in Phoenix, and because for everyone you are ... an ideal, an icon ... all in all, this could affect me as well, especially when your admirers find out about it."

"Some 'ideal'," smiled Anastaria. "Thanks for

the compliments, of course it's always nice to receive them, especially from someone who is doing all he can to resist my womanly charms," the girl smiled once again "but it's a pity you see me in this way. In truth, appearance is only a mask, what's inside a person is much more important. This is why I decided not to take part in the beauty contest this year. I've had enough of it. All these envious stares from other girls, the persistence of the men who try to find me in reality. ... They offer to shower me in riches if I agree to be theirs. ... It's all a bit too much, really. Although I'm already twenty-eight, I still haven't managed to find a worthy companion. ... But enough about sad things. I have a request: please don't divulge what I've just told you. There are many rumors circulating about it – starting from me supposedly being a cold-hearted bitch and ending with polyandry being my true preference – so it's not as if another rumor would make much of a difference, but ... if you don't mind, please forget what I've just told you."

"It's already forgotten. As far as your love for riddles is concerned, I have something for you. Here's the description. Perhaps you'll like it." I wrote down the formulas from the Orcs and passed them to Anastaria. Let her have some fun and I'll have a chance to find out how long it takes her to find the answer.

"The Pythagoras Theorem, the Fibonacci sequence and the formula for volume?" Anastaria became immersed in thought as she examined the formula descriptions: "Two multipliers, one equals sign and seven numbers after the dot? What is this?"

"An equation. You have to solve it."

"There isn't a solution here. These formulas have no meaning."

"You disappoint me. A solution exists and it's the only one possible. Find it."

* * *

The next morning I headed for the Jolly Gnoom tavern. It was unclear why it was called 'Gnoom' instead of 'Gnome'. The tavern was run by an NPC, so the name was the prerogative of the developers. Which of them came up with the idea (or perhaps made a typo) remains shrouded in mystery.

As I occupied a table and ordered some food providing +10% Intellect for 24 hours, I was still unable to quite recover from Anastaria's maneuver yesterday. What did she want to say by leaving Phoenix? Why did she join me? I had a gut feeling that this wouldn't end with the explanation that I was given and I had no idea which direction to dig in to get at the truth. I just didn't have enough information to hand.

"Hey there, 67th." A familiar voice sounded next to me, bringing a smile to my face. "Where'd you manage to level up like this?"

25-level Eric, 20-level Clutzer and 19-level Leite were standing in front of me. Judging by their levels, these guys had kept themselves busy in the past three months: if not for the Beatwick battle, they would've been well ahead of me in leveling up. Well done to them, all in all.

From the way the group was standing, it looked like they'd chosen a leader: Eric. Clutzer and Leite were standing a little behind him, as if giving room to the one in charge. Or, which is just as likely, I was overthinking things and they ended up standing like this by accident, or perhaps it's a habit from having the tank stand at the front, or ... why am I sitting here lost in thought instead of greeting the guys properly?

"Am I glad to see you!" I jumped up and gave each of them a hearty handshake. Whatever turn our subsequent conversation might take, I really was happy to see them. It mattered little that we'd only played together for a week and then spent the next three months at different ends of Malabar. "Sit down, why are you standing there like lemons?" I pointed towards my table.

"No prisoner headband and the gear – judging by its appearance – is of a Rare quality at the least, 67 levels in three months and the ten thousand that you sent us:" said Clutzer using normal speech (in the sense that it didn't contain a word of his usual slang) "are you still a prisoner or have you already been released?"

"No, I'm still in a capsule, like the rest of you." His question was pretty understandable. In the past three months they had had a chance to get to know each other, get used to each other and find common ground, and now it was time to accept someone else into their small group – someone they had been acquainted with, but hadn't seen in a good while. Moreover, this acquaintance looked very different to them now. "I've been through so many misadventures in the last three months: you get what you see right now. But I haven't stopped being the person who you got to know at the mine. Guys! Come off it already! Have a seat!"

Leite looked at Clutzer and Eric turned as well, while I mentally conceded a point to Anastaria. She was right that Clutzer's brains had ensured that he would become the leader amongst these three. It certainly wasn't Eric.

"It won't hurt to talk, I guess," he concluded. "Let's see what tune Mahan's gonna sing us."

No, he did still drop into slang from time to time. Well then, let's make it clear that I can do some analyzing as well.

"Clutzer, tell us where you're from. From the way you were speaking at the mine, gangster lingo is your native language, yet you're quite capable of speaking normally so that everyone can understand you. Where did you learn to speak like this?"

"Paris, one of its less popular districts. Everyone talks like that where I'm from; I picked it up as well, so as not to stand out." A smile flashed across Clutzer's face for the first time. "Reading is not too popular with my homies, but everything else ... so tell us what happened to you and how you lost the headband. Especially the latter – for us that's the main sticking point."

"The sticking point?" I asked.

"The PK-ers have really gotten to us," Eric spoke for the first time. "When we refused to join Phoenix, we became the targets of organized hunts, either by Phoenix members or some other idiots. You can't get away from the fact that as soon as we would try to leave the gates, the PK-ers would be waiting for us. We only managed to leave town properly a couple of times and were only able to gain a couple of levels at best. The rest of the leveling took place in town, with assignments, socializing and delivery quests. And all under the close watch of bounty-hunting enthusiasts. As soon as it rained, we were immediately sent for respawn if we happened to be outside a safe zone. At the same time, we were constantly bombarded with offers: to join Phoenix or to join the Dark Legion. ... "

"Eric is right," Clutzer took up the conversation "we were expecting a beginner twenty-level Shaman, but now you're sitting here in front of us with your 67 levels, excellent gear, without the red headband and already a member of a clan. Have you forgotten that we intended to make a clan together, or has that totally slipped your mind?"

"I see. Right, about the clan. Yes, I am in a clan, but I am its only member since I created this clan last night to save time doing it today. I created the clan for us."

"Seathistles?" chuckled Leite. "You've got to be kidding, right?"

"On the contrary. "If you hate the name, it can

THE SECRET OF THE DARK FOREST

be changed – I picked the first that wasn't downright terrible. The other names on offer, like 'We love Barliona, we play Barliona" and "Dark-eyed Cows of the West' didn't quite fit." I mentally gave myself extra points when all three of them chuckled. So, they're beginning to thaw. Good. "So you don't need to worry about the clan, I was never going to ditch anyone. Moving on to the headband, how much do you need to take yours off?"

"For me it's a hundred thousand ... what about you?" said Eric and looked at Leite and Clutzer.

"Two hundred and twenty," threw in Clutzer.

"A hundred and fifty," said Leite after a pause. "Why do you ask?"

"I call upon a Herald, I require your assistance!" I said, in place of a reply.

"You called me and I came. If your summons was a false one, you will be punished," the Herald uttered the standard phrase as soon as he stepped out of the portal. The three 'Red Riding Hoods' froze. Little surprise there – it was their first meeting with a Herald in the Game.

"I would like to make a payment in order for these free citizens to be able to remove their red headbands. Please deduct the money from my account."

A window opened before my eyes asking me to confirm the deduction of the required amount. I chased the Greed Toad into some distant corner and pressed the 'Yes' button. Unlike the wait following Nurris' payment, the red headbands vanished from the heads of the three convicts almost instantaneously.

"Can I be of any further help?"

"No, thank you. We can take it from here," I said and turned to the guys. "Listen, if it bothers you that I created the clan without you, you have my sincere apologies. I arrived in Anhurs yesterday, sent you messages and created the clan to save time later. If you don't like the name, suggest another one, we'll talk about it and, if it's free, change it."

"Thanks for the headband, of course," said Clutzer, "but can you tell me one thing: where did all this gold come from? You just made a generous gesture and shelled out four hundred and seventy thousand gold. Three months ago you had nowhere near as much money. What's with the ostentatious habits you seem to have picked up in the meantime? I want to know everything before I tie the rest of my game life to you. From A to Z. Otherwise what do we need a clan for, if it will be you constantly rubbing shoulders with those at the top and us doing all the grinding while picking up crumbs that fall from the table? We can do that in any clan."

"Catch and sign the non-disclosure agreements," I opened the list of standard agreement forms, which included the non-disclosure agreement, changed a couple of points, entered the players' names and handed them to the three men. "It's time to start playing by the rules and not by 'the code of the underworld'," I pointed out, seeing Eric's glum face.

"Now listen to what's been happening to me all this time," I began, as soon as all three agreements were signed. "I will start from the very beginning. The Pryke Mine and Kameamia."

I told them about everything: the creation of the Kameamia, the Orc Warrior Figurines, which they immediately asked me to show them, the Crafting skill, the First Kill, Beatwick, the Totem, Dragons, the Cursed Chess Pieces, the Priestesses of Eluna, the map of Kartoss and its sale, Anastaria and her presence in the clan and the Treasures of the Dragons. I kept nothing back, even telling them about the Dress of Leara. When I told them about the Totem, I had to activate the standard invisibility barrier that was available in this tavern so I could show them Draco, because the guys had trouble believing it otherwise. I didn't think that it would take me quite so long to retell six months of my life spent in the Game and I was also surprised by just how eventful this time had been.

"And that's how I became such a brash 'big shot' throwing money around," I concluded, having revealed all. "Now you know what happened to me. My current appearance doesn't make me any better or worse than you. I'm the same. I just got lucky in opening up the Kartoss scenario and striking it big, as they say. Stopping is completely out of the question right now. You have to keep it up, or your luck will run out and it's back to the everyday grind. Catch the description of the High Priestess quest." I shared Beth's assignment with the others. "We'll have to set out towards the Free Lands for the search as soon as possible. We need some more people, but I have three reliable guys, with whom I've spent enough time adventuring in my day. So, are you in?"

"Why didn't you join Phoenix?" Clutzer was still trying to get to the bottom of things. "When Rastor, Phoenix's chief recruiter, found us, he spun the tale of how Mahan was already in the clan and couldn't wait to see us there as well. We even went through some tests necessary for being accepted into Phoenix, but then decided to wait a bit before joining."

"That's why I didn't join ... Hellfire – you probably know who that is – told me exactly the same thing: that you guys were already in Phoenix and were just waiting for me to join. I was pretty upset with you at the time. If Anastaria hadn't made the slip-up that I mentioned, I may have even bought it. To be more precise ... I'm a Shaman and function on the level of intuition. So my instincts tell me that I must avoid joining other clans at all costs. I know it sounds stupid, but in three months my instincts have brought me all that you can see right now, so I try my best to follow them. And why did you decide not to join if they were trying so hard to recruit you?"

"We're no deserters and don't go back on our words." Clutzer's face relaxed. "Other clans invited us only on account of the First Kill, they didn't really need us otherwise. Protection from PK-ers? That's a bit of a joke; besides, even more would've ended up hunting us if we joined Phoenix or Legion. There was little point joining a smaller clan and we simply lacked the gold to create our own." Clutzer turned to the others and asked: "Has Mahan passed the test? Are we with him or do we part ways?"

"He passed," said Eric. "No tricks and he's not sticking up his nose at us. He seems to be the same as he was three months ago. The clan gets my vote. Leite?"

"Mine too. I thought at first the bastard came to have a laugh at us, but I see that I was wrong. I'm in."

"Then send us the invite," concluded Clutzer. "Have you already decided who will be what?"

"Yes. If there are no objections, I will remain the head. I've picked up a good number of quests and as the head they'll spread to the rest of the clan through me. Plus I have Moneybags – take a look at the description – which is another big bonus for the clan. Clutzer will be my deputy. What do you say?" I selected each of the players and sent them an invite.

"I won't be the deputy." Clutzer declined my invite. "Perhaps Eric would take it, but I won't do it. Make me an ordinary fighter."

"Why?" I asked, surprised.

"It's just not my thing. Thinking stuff up, figuring out a way to get in somewhere – I'm your man – but I don't want to be in the limelight all the time."

"I won't do it either," said Eric. "Becoming a deputy after Anastaria is just too risky. What if she decided to come back and the place was already taken? No, I'll pass."

"All right then," I said, once Seathistles clan

sported three extra players. "Guys, you probably know each other quite well by now – can you tell me what you're doing time for?"

"Tell us about yourself first."

"I'm here for hacking." I briefly told them about the bet with Marina and the hacking of the Intellect Imitator and looked at the others, "What about you?"

"Hacking," Eric spoke first. "I hacked an Imitator of this shop and was syphoning money off them."

"If my memory doesn't fail me, Clutzer's here for theft, right?" I asked.

"Two hundred and twenty gold for the headband equates to a twenty two million debt. What on earth did you steal?" I asked, surprised.

"Have you heard of the painting called the 'Mona Lisa'? That," smiled Clutzer. "Although I had no time to carry it out before the police arrived. Later they spent a long time questioning me about how I got inside. I told them, so ended up with a 7-year sentence instead of a 15-year one.

"I'm here for bribery," said Leite. "I was working in the district administration office ... usually everything was fine, but one time things just didn't work out ... it was my fault and I had to take the rap."

"Then this is what I propose we do with our clan. I know you probably have ideas of your own, but hear me out first. Let's see," I glanced at the clan properties and was disappointed to see that the bonuses for the First Kill didn't stack. It turned out that just one person with such a buff was enough to get all the goodies. "All of us have to level up in our professions. The clan will focus on producing and selling items made with the Crafting skill. We will have to find a reliable free person, who doesn't have the 30% convict tax deduction, to deal with the sales. As I said before, I already have three old acquaintances in my sights. I'll try to take them with me to the Free Lands and see if they've changed much in the last six months. If they haven't, one of them can easily be made into the Treasurer: these guys are reliable – they won't let us down. Each of us has different terms to serve, so the aim of the clan for the next 4–8 years, however long each sentence is: to earn money and secure a comfortable existence after release. In the time we're spending in the capsules, the world isn't standing still, so we will find it very hard to return to our previous occupations. I don't want to end up unemployed after Barliona, and neither do you, I suspect. So, all in all, that's the plan for now. If there are no objections, our task for today is ..."

As it turned out, Clutzer's ideas were running along the same lines, so after providing everyone with the necessary cash, I first sent them all to the Bank to buy themselves a new purse and a Mailbox and then visit the profession trainers and unlock the maximum number of both gathering and production professions. When the guys left, I closed my eyes and tried to relax. Right. These were some tough negotiations. It's not that I expected them to run at me with open arms, but I didn't expect this either. But that's fine; we'll make it work. And then suddenly I jumped up like one hit by lightning: the Princess! I promised to visit her yesterday, but never found the time! Or to put it more bluntly: I forgot. I had to go to the Palace straight away, before I landed in any extra trouble.

"You weren't in a great hurry." It looked like Tisha's Imitator had finally come into its own as a highborn lady. Before I could meet the Princess I had to explain to a flamboyant-looking gentleman in a long blue jacket – a butler or a steward, who knows with these Palace NPCs – why I needed to meet the Emperor's daughter.

"Tisha, a thousand apologies. It was my first day in Anhurs yesterday, and by the time I got on top of all my errands it was night already. Who would've let me in to see you at night? So that's why I came today first thing, as soon as the Palace gates were open." My level of Attractiveness with her was still at 39 points, which was comforting. At least the Princess hadn't taken offence.

"Seathistle," smiled Tisha as she examined my symbol, "a lovely wild flower. In Beatwick I often picked flowers like these and put them around the house. A little piece of sky can look very beautiful in your hands. I like that. What are you planning to do in the near future?"

"Today or tomorrow I'll be heading out to the Free Lands on an assignment that Beth gave me. It should take about a month. After that I'm free. Do you need any help with anything?" As soon as the Princess uttered the words 'I like that', I immediately looked at my Attractiveness. 42 points. Wow! So there are some advantages in a floral name and a blue emblem! Getting +3 to Attractiveness just on account of a name is ... very nice. Now I had to see if I could get Tisha to give me a quest.

"Yes, but it's not for me ... it's for Slate ..."

"The Prince?"

"He's no Prince. Father cannot allow some lowly Werebeast to become his daughter's husband, so he ... so we need your help. Slatey needs the blessing of his parents to marry a Vagren. For that he has to travel to the very center of Malabar, almost to the Kartoss border, but Father has no intention of giving him an escort. My future husband has to make it to his family on his own or with friends, and he doesn't have any. ... We are forbidden from hiring a paid escort – the Heralds are keeping a close watch over that ... Mahan, we need your help ..."

Quest available: Escorting the Prince.

Quest type: Scenario.

Requirements: Reputation with the Malabar Empire: Respect+; Attractiveness with the Princess: 40+.

Reward: none.

Penalty for failing or refusing the quest: none.

Time limit for completing the quest: 3 months.

There was no reward or penalty, but on the

other hand this was a Scenario. As Beatwick had shown, you had to grab quests like these with both hands.

"Princess, I will help the future Prince, but after I carry out the task that the High Priestess gave me. I promised Beth I will get the Stone back, so it wouldn't be fair of me to let her down."

"I understand," said Tisha, visibly saddened. "We can't even see each other until he has a proper title. Father sent him to the far reaches of the Palace, which I haven't explored properly yet. We tried to arrange a meeting via an amulet, but the Heralds blocked all the doors. Everyone is against me here." The girl sobbed.

"What if Slate comes with us to the Free Lands and then from there we'll head straight to his parents?" I ventured, keeping my fingers crossed. Beth's description didn't state that the quest could only be undertaken by players. This meant that we could easily hire NPCs for it – it might be expensive, but was still quite possible. And here was an opportunity to get a decent Werebeast for free, a future Prince, no less, and even level up in Attractiveness with him. "What if we come across something that will help your Slate to gain the blessing of his parents?"

"Hold on, I'll ask him." The expression of renewed hope reappeared on Tisha's face. She took out the communication amulet and briefly explained the situation to her Werebeast. I had to intervene and open the quest description for Tisha, which she then read out to Slate, and after a few minutes of questions and answers the party heading out to the Free Lands had grown in number, having enlisted a level 128 Werebeast into its ranks.

"We'll meet by the Palace's main gates in five minutes," I instructed the new member of my group, "and decide what to do next there."

"Princess, would you mind accompanying me to the exit?" I politely offered my arm to Tisha. "The palace is so new that I'm afraid of getting lost."

The joy on the Princess's face when she saw Slate and ran towards him resulted in +5 points of Attractiveness with her. The Heralds that turned up could only watch in silence as the young couple embraced – they had the power to block their planned meetings, but stopping one already in progress was beyond them.

"You have to be more careful," I heard the girl's admonition as I left the palace. I felt a bit sorry for the bear-man: the lady Vagren won't get off his back until she drills every health and safety rule into him. I decided not to interrupt the reunited lovers. In an hour I would contact Slate once again and arrange another meeting, so in the meantime I sped off towards the main square. I had received a letter from Elenium, saying that he was ready to meet me right away.

* * *

Elenium, Dukki and Sushiho were glad to see me, but I had to tell my story to each of them, read the commiseration in their eyes and assure them that there was nothing they could do, that I was perfectly fine and that I don't have any next of kin that are in need of help. All three of them agreed to take part in the quest, warning me right away that they could only be online between 6 in the evening and 2 in the morning, game time. Far from ideal, but this couldn't be helped: work and family were sacrosanct. The level numbers looked as follows: Elenium, 118; Dukki, 122; Sushiho, 127. Taking Slate into account, the total level came to 622, so the conditions of the High Priestess had been met. We agreed to meet at 6 in the evening by the temple of Eluna. I formed a group, met with the future Prince, described the situation to him and headed for the place that I'd wanted to visit for a while, but had little chance to until now: the Dating House.

"Biological age verified," came the voice of the Imitator responsible for admittance as soon as I stepped through the arch of the Dating House. "Limitations detected: no more than 24 hours a week. Time still available: 24 hours. You may enter. Welcome!"

I found myself in a small room, piled high with plush cushions and a single sofa on which a beautiful lady NPC was sitting and leafing through a magazine. Nothing had changed since my last visit: my sight still goes slightly blurry, the NPC still stays quiet until you speak to her or until 10 minutes goes by from the moment you enter the room – no pressure of any kind or any prickly comments. The room was generated individually for each player – the Corporation did everything to make sure that players didn't feel ill at ease. The task of the NPC placed in the room included providing advice on choosing the player's object of desire or, if the Imitator managed to correctly assess the player's tastes, manifest the direct embodiment of their preferences. I had another look at the girl: she was a human, quite cute, but not tawdry, with a slightly up-turned nose, bright blue eyes, which I saw when she shot me a glance, and luscious white hair. Why on earth had the system suddenly decided that I like blondes?

"Pretty Lady, would you help me choose a girl?" I finally ventured to make the request.

"Of course, have a look at what we've got." Several 3D holograms of elves, humans, gnomes and other representatives of Barliona's females appeared before my eyes. "Choose a race."

"I think I've already chosen," I said and smiled at the NPC girl sitting in front of me. The longer I spent looking at her the more I liked her. The Imitator had guessed correctly. "You are magnificent and I wouldn't change a thing."

"Thank you." The blonde girl blushed and a message flashed in front of me asking whether I was prepared to pay for the Dating House services worth 2500 Gold an hour. ... Nice prices they have here, I chuckled. Very democratic. Still, I pressed the 'Yes' button and embarked into a fantasyland of my own.

The allowance of 24 hours per week needed to be utilized ...

Three hours had gone by before the Dating House released me from the spell. I didn't think that my lengthy abstinence would have led to such an explosion of energy, but it would seem that my desire for intimacy had reached its peak. Right now I was walking aimlessly along Anhurs' streets killing time before the meeting by the temple and enjoying the sights of the city. Anhurs is almost the only place in the game not built following a template. Each house was custom-made and a separate design company was responsible for each street, every one of which they tried to make into something exceptional. I had no idea why it was necessary, but it made the place a wonder to behold. I would close my eyes and completely immerse myself in my surroundings as I cruised on autopilot along the streets that I had run around for two years before my prison sentence. When I was a Hunter, I had usually tried not to depart too far away from the capital, which was the scene of the most interesting happenings and which I knew like the back of my hand.

Without a thought that I could get lost or become a victim of PK-ers (the weather was great and the city was a safe-zone), I found myself next to a painfully familiar place: the Rogue training grounds. Subdued shouts from players doing various agility exercises, their happy exclamations when they got something right and bursts of laughter from the crowd when someone fell down ... this place brought back so many memories. ... My heart missed a beat, a lump came to my throat and I turned and entered the training grounds. At one time I spent at least two months teaching myself to complete the first stage of the obstacle course, so I felt completely at home in these training grounds. Since I ended up in this area, why not try to go through the course as a Shaman? Let's see if my body still remembers the movements that I'd honed for such a long time.

"Look – what do we have here?" said an unpleasant and jarring male voice. "There's a Shaman on the course, everyone stealth now! Ha-ha-ha!"

I managed to find the source of this mocking voice in the crowd of Rogues preparing to go through the obstacle course. He presented a standard image of a hero with a square jaw, a pack of muscles (why would a Rogue need muscles?) and a billowing cape. ... This was no player, but some comic superhero. I didn't even bother reading his name, since I immediately lost any interest in this person. Using an auto-generated game avatar wasn't forbidden, but it was considered bad taste amongst most players. Why choose a template when you could run around as yourself?

A word about the obstacle course. The main stat for Rogues is Agility, so that's what they level up in first. It can be increased not only with marksmanship exercises, but also by overcoming various obstacles. If you jump over a log you get +4% Agility, if you jump over two that would already be +5% and so on. The Rogue training area was stuffed full of various devices, but the crown was the main obstacle course: it was an enormous stretch of ground, about 500 meters long, peppered all over the place with swinging blade-pendulums, flame jets, hanging chains and other features that made progress through it a rather complicated affair. Hunters often came here to do some additional leveling up in Agility, because their training grounds contained little else other than shooting targets. Rogues welcomed such visitors and the reason was quite understandable. Often this kind of neighborhood gave rise to Hunter-Rogue PK group formations. Destroying such a group single-handedly was almost impossible: there was just too much crowd control, poison and additional force in the form of the Hunter's pet. It was three against one. The obstacle course was broken up into five parts, 100 meters each, and the task for each contender was to complete them all, one after another. Completing each of them granted titles that were seen as a mark of high honor among Rogues, but were completely useless to other classes. At the time, after a long period of preparation, I was able to complete the first 100 meters on autopilot, with my eyes closed. But that was the limit of my skills and I didn't know any Rogues that were able to complete the entire stretch. It was impossible to die on the course, since as soon as your Hit Points reached 1, you were teleported to the beginning with the length of the covered ground highlighted. A hundred meters corresponded to the title 'Dodger', which was the first step in the Rogue hierarchy.

"What'd you forget here, you miserable bastard?" The maladjusted player continued to have a laugh. "Get back to summoning your spirits, there's nothing for you to do here."

"Lloyd Redoombsky." One of the NPC's Rogue Masters appeared next to me. "Three laps around the course. On the double!"

"But why, Master?"

"Four laps with three stone weights! Now!"

"Yes, Master!" Mumbling something under his breath, the player ran up to the wall that surrounded the Anhurs Rogue training grounds, picked up three stones from the neat pile lying near the wall and sped down the track. Four laps equaled to almost ten kilometers, with weights that gave you +3–5% towards Agility and +2–4% towards Stamina. Despite all his grumbling it would do him good.

"How can I be of help to an Elemental Shaman?" said the Master, stressing the last word, my class, and hinting that there was little for me to do here.

"I would like to go through the obstacle course." I tried to speak with a degree of pride, but my last words were drowned out in the laughter of the Rogues and Hunters. Suddenly an idea popped into my head: why not put these snobs back in their place? That would be some joke. Who would expect a Shaman to complete a course that Rogues spend so much time trying to perfect? No-one. This could play in my favor. I had no idea if I could pull it off or not, but I still remembered every move in the first hundred meters. I wasn't deterred by the fact that back then I was a Hunter with maxed out Agility. I knew all about rings and had the ability to change stats on them too.

"Anyone is free to go through the obstacle course." I was grateful to the NPC for not dropping even a hint of a smile when he heard my proposal. "Shaman Mahan has never gone through this trial. I, the Master of Rogues, can confirm this. Give me a sign when you're ready."

"I'm ready," I grinned, as I watched the reaction of the players. They stopped doing their exercises, surrounded the strange Shaman, without blocking the way to the obstacle course, and kept making pointed remarks about my sanity and or total lack thereof.

"I bet five hundred gold that he won't get through even 20 meters!" finally came a shout that I was eagerly expecting. Bigheaded snobs shouldn't just be punished, but hit directly in the pocket – that's the only way they'll learn that putting people down randomly can result in unpleasant consequences.

"I'll take that up!" I shouted. "Five hundred for 20 meters. Anyone else?"

The place descended into chaos. I barely had time to sign the agreements that flashed before my eyes. First came the agreements for 30 meters, then for 50 and then even a handful for 90 meters, staking just over 3000 gold each. As soon as the bombardment of agreements had ceased and the players started to exchange pleased glances – clearly thinking that they were about to clean up as a result of a seriously nutty Shaman – I walked up to the start of the course and looked at the final total: a hundred and twenty three agreements amounting to 52000 gold. Not bad; now I just had to earn it. There were swirling cylinders and pendulums ... everything looked and worked the same as before. ... Let's see. I changed the bonus on my rings to Agility, closed my eyes and took the first step. The test had commenced ...

Jump forward, putting the weight straight on the knees. Immediately roll left and jump up, as a blade slashes under your feet. Two small steps ahead, head ducked, then stop for two seconds and make another two steps forward. Jump up, head still ducked, feel the air being sliced by blades just a centimeter away, lie flat and make a sharp roll to the right. Then jump straight up and five quick steps forward ...

I suddenly felt that something wasn't going according to plan. I sensed a threat coming from the right ... I soon lost track of time, so I couldn't say exactly how many meters I'd covered, but judging by the silence around me, only broken only by the squeaking of the mechanisms, I've covered enough: the players were very quiet. That'll teach you to cross a Shaman! All of this took just a moment to flash through my head, as I forced my body to make an awkward movement to dodge a probable line of attack. As soon as I fell down I got the feeling that I had to run from this spot. I rolled sideways, opened my eyes and looked around. 112 meters. Having covered the stretch that I had learned by heart, now I was in unexplored territory. I didn't have a clue how to get through here, so what the players were expecting to happen from the very first moments of the trial finally happened – I was hit by a pendulum … and flew out of the obstacle course. …

I came to myself by the start line. My Life Bar froze at 1 point, but soon began to slowly climb back up – having a healthy amount of Energy was helpful. Going through the obstacle course gained me +15 Agility and +5 Stamina. Although these weren't stats that a Shaman would need, I'd find a way to make good use of them too. I got to my feet and looked around. The silence of the players, who had just witnessed a miracle, was the best reward – even better than the extra 200000 gold I just earned.

"That's quite something," finally uttered one of the Rogues, and the crowd of players exploded with noise. As the enthusiastic buzz surrounded me, I began to be bombarded by messages – just as I had received agreements previously – that this or that amount had arrived to my account from some player or other. A minute later I only had five outstanding agreements, worth 3000 gold each.

"Some people still haven't paid up on their agreements." Without a moment's hesitation I tried to outshout the crowd of players. My ear caught a rather interesting scrap of conversation: "Are you sure you filmed everything? We have to put it up on the site today, no-one will believe it unless they see it."

"I haven't paid up," came the voice that had taken a swipe at me at the very beginning. "I won't pay. You cheated!"

"What?!" Such an accusation made my jaw drop. "What cheating? What are you on about?"

"No-one can cover that stretch on the first attempt. You trained especially in order to rip players off. You're a thief! I'll drag your ass through the courts! You'll be kicked out of Barliona for a trick like that! Hand over the money or I'll lodge a complaint against you with the Heralds!"

"Have you gone crazy, pretty-boy?" I took a few deep breaths, trying to regain my cool, but wasn't exactly succeeding. The urge to punch this idiot in the face was so strong that I barely restrained myself. Players weren't permitted to attack each other in the city, but on the training grounds fighting was allowed. As in the case of the obstacle course, a player couldn't be killed: their Life Bar wouldn't fall below one point while their attacker wouldn't be branded with the red PK-er mark. This was the training grounds, after all.

"The money, now!" The 'superhero' was really screaming by this time, probably trying to use the volume of his voice to affect my decision.

"I call upon a Herald. I request your assistance," I uttered the summons phrase. The buzz in the grounds immediately died down and camera pictograms appeared above the heads of the majority of players.

"You called me and I came, if ..."

"Please confirm that I have fulfilled all the

necessary conditions of the agreements signed with these free citizens." I waved my hand around me, indicating the crowd, five members of which still owed me money. "Then please deduct any sums owed from their accounts, or, if they don't have it right now, from the coffers of the Empire, you can settle this matter with the indebted individuals yourselves afterwards."

In Barliona you always had to pay anything owed under an agreement. If the player didn't have enough money to fulfill his obligations, the Corporation would come to his aid, paying the debt and then proceeding to settle the matter with the debtor. I had no idea what it was that they did, but I was sure they recouped their funds in full.

The Herald's eyes clouded over for a moment – he was probably looking through and analyzing logs – then he said:

"Confirmed! All agreements signed with Mahan on completing the obstacle course must be honored without exception. He broke none of Barliona's laws. The funds to be paid under the agreements have been deducted from the accounts of the five free citizens in question and transferred to your account. The fine for refusal to fulfill their obligations, amounting to the size of the bet, has been deducted from the guilty parties and paid to the Empire. Is there anything else I can help you with?"

After thanking the Herald for his help, I saw the messages concerning the remaining funds arriving in my account, and then headed back into Anhurs at a leisurely pace. The 'superhero' was silent and followed me out with a very unfriendly stare. I realized that I'd gained yet another enemy ...

Well, to hell with him! I'm a Shaman! Let him fear me. I've had enough of hiding and running away from every shadow. It's time for me to show some claws.

As soon as I left the Rogues, I knew where I should head next. I was familiar with the Rogue and Hunter training grounds and have visited them in the past, but there must be one for Shamans as well, where one could meet those who have chosen this challenging class. Why not get together with others like me?

After asking for directions from a squad of guards patrolling the city, I headed for the Anhurs Shaman retreat. Like all training areas, the Shaman training base was located close to the city wall. Externally it didn't look any different from the others – a wall, a covered training hall, arched gates: everything was the same as with the other classes. When I walked under the arch I beheld the inner layout of the grounds: one training dummy, same as the one Kornik set up for me, one dummy for mass spirit summoning and a great deal of greenery. Grass, trees, bushes and even a pond, which, although not green, was still a completely unexpected thing to find in a training area. Around twenty Shamans were summoning Spirits, under the guidance of an NPC Master. Another two- or three-dozen players were simply lying on the grass and chatting to each other. All they were missing was a basket of food to make this look like a real picnic. I think I like being a shaman more and more!

"Greetings, Elemental brother." A Master appeared next to me. Have you come for knowledge, skills, expertise or rest?"

Wow! The full Professional Training Package you're handed at every college, but with the offer of rest on top! This is no training course, but one big pleasure ride.

"It's knowledge I'm after, Teacher." I bowed to the Master. "I'll hone my skills and expertise elsewhere and I have no time to rest, so all that remains is knowledge. That's the thing I always seem to be lacking."

"Come with me, brother." The Master wasn't in the least surprised by my choice as he pointed towards the training hall. "There is a library inside the hall and that's where you have to go to obtain knowledge."

The library astonished me in the sense that it turned out to be a modest-sized room without any windows, covering no more than 10 square meters and lit by two flickering candles. The room contained a table and on it was the only book in the library; next to it a chair held a dozing NPC. The book was being closely studied by a girl whose name I couldn't immediately see in the room's subdued lighting, but when I did I froze. Antsinthepantsa: level 263 High Shaman. You could only level up to a Harbinger above that and by the looks of it she was expanding her knowledge in order to gain that rank.

"Listen, I need a couple more minutes with the book, all right?" said the girl in a rather hoarse voice. "It's a communal book, so we have to wait our turn to read it. I have to run in a minute anyway, so you'll have it soon enough."

"Yes, of course I'll wait. By the way, thanks for your advice – without it I wouldn't have become an Elemental Shaman."

"Advice?" The girl tore herself away from the book. "I've never laid my eyes on you before. Wow, First Kill at level 67? Impressive stuff. Nice flowers too. Seathistles, right?"

"Yeah, seathistles. About that advice – when I was going through the trial with the four rooms to pick my Totem, your guidance on the in-game forum came in very handy. I still follow it often: 'Forget that you have a brain. Thinking is for mages, Shamans feel.'"

"And how did you do in the trial?" The girl completely turned away from the book and stared at me.

This was no special secret, so I told her how I got through all the four rooms and about being given the chance to choose my Totem, without saying whom I got in the end.

"Exactly the same for me," whispered the girl. "How did you know how to do it correctly? Where did you read it?"

"Nowhere. That's what I'm saying – I did it thanks to your advice. On the second attempt, that is. I followed the standard path the first time, as you will read in the forums."

"And whom did you get? The Totem, I mean."

"I got the one I chose. While he's small I don't really want to show him off too much, I'm sorry. I don't know yours either, for example. When he grows up a bit, I'll show him to you."

"That makes sense. As for my Totem, I also wasn't given her, but chose her. I wanted a Dragon at first, but I felt nothing towards him, so I chose her instead." Silence descended on the room and then someone else joined us. It was a Black Panther, a meter and a half in tall. Beautiful, graceful, sleek and shimmering in the candlelight, she seemed the very embodiment of strength and power.

"Hey there beautiful." The words involuntarily flew from my lips and, surprising even myself, I went to the panther and put my hand on the back of her neck. Yeeesss ... the panther's fur was so pleasant to the touch, that I closed my eyes in enjoyment and scratched her as I ran my fingers over her skin. Completely losing any sense of propriety, I put my other hand under the cat's head and started scratching her neck. A few seconds later thunder-like purring echoed through the library.

"You're the fifth person to have earned the right to touch Bussy," smiled Antsinthepantsa. "She's a fussy girl and won't let just anyone near her."

After looking me in the eye the panther dissipated right in my hands – the lady Shaman had dismissed her.

"So, what's your Totem? You've seen mine now,

so it wouldn't be right if you weren't to respond in kind."

Dammit! She's got me there! Should I try to wriggle out of it? What would be the point? As soon as I reach level 100 I'll have to get Draco out in the open anyway. All right, why not?

"Hi. Come over."
"Coming."

"For crying out loud!" The NPC, a librarian by the looks of it, finally spoke up. "This is no place for showing off your Totems! This is a library, people come here to read the book and not get up to God knows what! Get that Dragon out of here, now!"

Antsinthepantsa stared at Draco, entranced, and didn't seem to hear the librarian. She walked over to my Totem like a zombie (is that what I had looked like as well?), stretched her hand and put it on the Dragon's neck. About ten seconds went by and Draco started to buzz with pleasure, stretching out his neck.

"All right, you can go now. I'll call you a little later," I told my Totem jealously. Here was me thinking that he responded to me alone, but the ungrateful reptile was very ready to volunteer his damned neck to be scratched by this Shaman girl.

After licking Antsinthepantsa on the cheek (something the panther failed to do to me), Draco dissolved in the air.

"A Dragon." It took her about a minute to regain her composure, as she stood mesmerized after the Totem disappeared. "So it looks like you're a kindred spirit if he decided to be yours ... and you already managed to embody him as well. How long have you been playing as Shaman?"

"Half a year."

"That's fast, but you haven't beaten me: I got your rank after four months. Right, I have to run now. Catch the invitation – let's meet tomorrow. I want to have a proper chat with you. What if you know where Kornik is?"

"It won't happen," I declined Antsinthepantsa's invite. "I'll write to you when I get back to Anhurs. I'm off to the Free Lands today and have no idea how long I'll be spending there. It could be a day or it could be three months. As soon as I'm back, I'll be sure to write to you. I have questions for you as well. And I can tell you this much about Kornik: he ended up in the claws of Geranika, the new super-Shaman. I don't know whether he's alive or not, my information is over a month old."

"I've heard about Geranika, although I don't understand where he gets his power. According to the information that the Corporation supposedly leaked into the net, Geranika is a Shaman who somehow side-stepped working with Spirits. The Spirits of the Higher and Lower worlds have declared war on him but he's just laughing at them. I thought Kornik might provide an answer, but no-one's seen him in the capital for a good while. And now you say he's been captured by Geranika. What on earth are those developers cooking up? Anyway, I'm really out of time and have to run. Be sure to contact me when you get back. I am spending lots of time in Anhurs at the moment."

"It's a deal."

"Bye."

Antsinthepantsa's eyes glazed over and her gaming avatar became transparent and disappeared. A player had exited Barliona. Man ... I should have found what clan she belongs to. The emblem in the shape of a tree wound with a ribbon didn't belong to any of the leading clans, so there was a small chance I would be able to tempt her over to join mine. We need Shamans like that. I'll be sure to speak to her about this when I'm back in Anhurs. But for now, it was knowledge I was after ...

"Honorable Sir, I would like to touch the wisdom of the ancestors." I bowed to the librarian, who had calmed down as soon as Draco disappeared and gone back to sit in his own chair with a melancholic expression.

"What's there to touch? Here's the book from which you can gain all the knowledge about Shamans you may ever need."

"All?" I asked in overplayed surprise "even what happened during the fight between Prontho and Shiam? Or how to get Kornik out of Geranika's clutches?"

The librarian froze for a moment, staring at me with his gray eyes, and then slowly said:

"No, the book doesn't contain those things. The truth of what happened during the fight between

Prontho and Shiam is known only to the two of them. You're free to ask either. As for getting Kornik out of Geranika's clutches ... someone will have to take a risk and venture into the lair of this lunatic. But I cannot entrust such a task to you. Only the Head of the Shaman Council can send heroes on such errands, so he's the one you need to speak to. I'm not sure that Shiam would send anyone out to fight his own brother, but you can give it a try."

"So what's useful about this book?" I decided to ask the librarian.

"It contains wisdom that Shamans have been gathering for centuries. Read it and you'll understand."

The librarian once again turned into a statue, so there was little else I could do but walk up to the table, open the book and immerse myself in reading:

A Shaman is a sentient gifted with special abilities to communicate with Spirits and supernatural forces; upon entering a state of ecstasy ...

When just two hours until the meeting remained, I managed to tear myself away from the book. It made for strange reading, really. I may not have understood half the words, and often the meaning of entire sentences eluded me, but I grasped the main point. That is, what this book was for:

Skill increase:
+3 to Spirituality. Total: 24

+ 1 Rank to Water Spirits. Total: 3

This book helped to level up in things necessary for Shamans: Spirit ranks, Spirituality, perhaps something else that I may not yet have. I only managed to read a little more than two hundred pages out of around two thousand, so I could see that I would be making visits here for quite some time.

I thanked the librarian and hurried to the place I should have visited first. It didn't really dawn on me until now that I was heading for the Free Lands, where finding mines would be a bit of a problem. In order to level up in Jewelcraft and Smithing I had great need of Ore, preferably in unlimited quantities. I also had to buy traveling bags both for myself and for the guys – they probably still had the standard ones with just 8–16 slots. I also had to think of getting a tent, since sleeping on bare earth would be far from ideal. Looks like I've become a bit too slack – it was time to get more organized. After silently berating myself with every kind of unpleasant name and disregarding all propriety, I ran as fast as I could to the gnomes, since these were the NPCs in charge of the Auction.

The Auction House itself consisted of a smallish pavilion, with an individual phase for each player. It was located on a small square, about 500 meters from the center of Anhurs. Inside it sat a gnome who provided players with the entry point for their offers and accepted their bids. The square where the pavilion was located was unofficially called 'The

Market'. This was where players offering goods directly hung out, side-stepping the Auction House, which took off 3% profit from every deal.

"WTB 4 sacks with 200 slots each," I shouted before entering the Auction House, in the hope of catching a deal on what I needed among the local peddlers. Bags tend to be in demand, but ones for 200 slots, which a year ago cost 30000 gold, were not among the readily available goods. I was unlikely to get any of my own Tailors in the clan in the near future, so I would have to stock up at the Auction House.

"Why do you need them so large? Get four with 50 slots." A player immediately popped up next to me, looking me over from head to foot with his shifty eyes. He was probably trying to figure out how much money I had and how big he should make his markup. "I'll sell them at 10000 apiece."

I shook my head and shouted again for the larger sacks before following up with several for the Ore – starting with Tin and ending with Gold. The hawkers, stared at me with annoyance for interrupting their normal trade, but I took little notice. Every player was free to shout at The Market. Ten minutes later there were still no offers forthcoming, so I headed for the Auction House.

"Good day," the gnome registrar greeted me. "Do you wish to buy or sell?"

"Buy. Could you give me a selection of all the clothing on Auction with Crafting stat as the required feature? The type of clothing is unimportant.

The gnome's eyes clouded over – he was probably conducting a search – after which he said in a disappointed voice:

"Your search produced no results. There are no items with Crafting bonuses at Auction."

Right. So it looked like they were either entirely absent or had been immediately snapped up by players. Little surprise there, as such items could completely pay for themselves in the space of a month.

"Then let's look at bags. Search parameters: 150+ slots, sorting by price – low to high, filter by number of slots." I made the initial request to solve the storage problem right away. Each player can carry up to 3 bags, so buying at least one large one is a top priority task.

"Your search request has turned up 2042 lots, sorting by price has been applied," reported the gnome and a list of bags appeared before my eyes. The prices for 150 slots began at 18000, those for 200 – at 30000 and for 250 (which I didn't even know existed) at 50000. After quickly weighing up all the pros and cons I bought a 250-slot bag for myself, and 200-slot bags for the others. In total this purchase cost me 149000 Gold, but I was happy: now neither my fighters nor I had to worry about where to store things. As soon as the gnome handed over the bags, I put mine on and made a search request for Ore. Things didn't look all that great in this area: Copper Ore – 20+ Gold per stack (1 stack = 40 pieces of Ore), Tin – 100+, Silver – 180, Iron – 290, Gold – 500 and

Platinum – 1000. I didn't even bother looking at the rest to save myself the disappointment. One bag slot could take 10 stacks, so I stocked up quite well: 80 stacks of Tin Ore, 200 of Iron, 300 of Silver and 100 Gold. As a result of this ruinous errand I only had just over 330000 gold left, but I wasn't worried: with Jewelcraft and Smithing professions I would be able to make a good return on these investments. I made a search for rings for level 50 with the maximum stat bonuses and found out that a Gold Ring of something or other with +13 to Intellect and + 7 to Stamina was worth 3500 Gold. Precious Stones, such as Lapis Lazuli cost upwards of 3000 each, so I whistled when I added up how much Hellfire had spent when he sent me 50 stones. ... Some gift he wanted to make Anastaria ...

"And one last thing. I need a Frontier Ranger Tent. How much is it?"

The gnome's eyes again became glassy and then he said:

"Tents like this sell for 60000 and above. In total there are three such tents for sale."

"I'll take the one for sixty thousand." I barely uttered the phrase when a window popped up to confirm the transaction. After pressing the 'Yes' button, I saw the most sought-after item for any intrepid traveler lying on the gnome's table:

A Ranger Tent.

Description: the best piece of kit for travelers setting out on a long journey.

Spaces in the tent: 10.
Comfort level: 6 out of 10.
Visual detection radius: 1 meter.

I stuffed the items I had got from the gnome into the bag and ran off towards the Temple. Now I was ready to head for the Free Lands.

CHAPTER FOUR
DEPARTURE FOR THE FREE LANDS

"SINCE WE'RE ALL HERE, LET ME do some introductions. All of you know me, so I will skip that part. Let's start with the ordinary residents of Barliona. Please give a warm welcome to Slate, the uncrowned Prince of the Malabar Empire. He's run into some family-related trouble: catch the quest description – we'll be doing it together. As soon as we complete the High Priestess's assignment, we'll all head off to a rather interesting place. I hope his family issues get resolved and he ends up marrying the Princess. The Prince is a decent Smith, Repairman and Warrior and will be very useful in our mission. I'm starting a group: accept the invite."

The longer I spent introducing Slate, the more astonished everyone's faces grew. In the end it was a scene worthy of a painting titled: 'a herd of deer staring at the headlights.' Only Clutzer gave a nervous laugh:

"Prince of Malabar?"

"Your Highness," muttered Leite. All, including the non-convict players, bowed their heads and bent their knees, complying with the standard etiquette for greeting a monarch. We won't get very far if they continue treating Slate this way. Had they never had any contact with members of the Imperial family before? Although there was one exception – Clutzer didn't bend his knee, but briefly bowed his head as a sign of respect before immediately straightening up. Well done to him. But the rest ... they gave the impression of messenger boys in a huge corporation suddenly facing the managing director who has dropped in for a party – sporting a can of beer, lack of tie and plenty of determination to have a good time. It was a similar type of reaction, what with their obedient stances, lifted, or in our case bowed, heads and readiness to carry out any command ... such an awkward attitude didn't bode well.

"Right, guys! Relax. Take a few of deep breaths. So what if he's a Prince? Eric, Leite, snap out of it already! You'll have to appear before the Emperor to be honored for your First Kill in two months' time – is this the way you plan to react to him as well? "

"I thought you were fibbing before," mumbled Elenium. "The Emperor, the High Priestess of Eluna, the Heralds ... it just didn't sound real ... and now we have a Prince in our group ..."

"Please get up," said the future Prince, somewhat red in the face. "Just call me Slate, I'm not a Prince yet and if you don't help me I may never become one. So please, don't kneel every time you want to speak to me. Just think of me as the group's blacksmith."

"Slate is right," I tried to talk some sense into my stunned team "you better start getting used to the idea that our group has another member. Forget about his status. And in general, you should get used to the fact that from now on your standing in Barliona will change: I don't know whether it will be for the worse or for the better, but change it certainly will. We'll mix with Princes and Princesses, and even the Emperor will no longer be some distant unapproachable figure. Let's get on with the introductions. This is Clutzer. Like me, he made it out of a mine and now we're in the same clan ..." I started to introduce everyone in turn, recounting when and how I came to meet them. "What relationships develop between you guys is your business, it's not like I can force you all to become friends, but while we're on the quest I ask that you maintain normal professional relations, setting any emotions aside. Put off any arguments and so forth until we return. Everyone, I'm sharing both quests with you: that of the High Priestess and of the Prince."

"Mahan, we have a problem," Clutzer's voice came almost straight away.

"What do you mean?"

"Look at the quest description, namely at the limitations section. We don't cut it level-wise."

"What the heck?" I exclaimed, as I dug up the

quest description. The overall level of the group amounted to 622, but it came up as 494(128) in front of the required 600-level limitation. 494 was the combined level of the players, while 128 levels were Slate's. It looked like our NPC didn't count towards the total group level and so Beth wouldn't give us the quest. ... Where did it all go wrong? "If we are lacking in levels, we'll have to invite someone else. Any of you know someone who could take off to the Free Lands for a couple of weeks right this minute?"

"I'll have a look," was Eric's businesslike reply "I did play as a tank for quite a while and my contacts should all still be there." Judging by his appearance he went into mail-sending mode and was quickly jotting down messages.

"What about you?" I asked my friends from my former gaming life.

"I don't have anyone," came Elenium's honest answer "as soon as my son was born, I left Barliona for a long time – even got kicked out of the clan as an unreliable element, although I gave them my reason. You wouldn't want to invite people like that on an expedition.

Following Eric's example Sushiho and Dukki began writing letters to their acquaintances.

"I don't have anyone to invite either", said Clutzer. "I would be categorically against inviting any of my old acquaintances ... that is assuming they even managed to get out of the mines ..."

"I have a candidate," I said thoughtfully, weighing up all the pros and cons. "I'm not a hundred percent sure of them yet, but it still might be better than hooking up with a total stranger."

"Do it, invite anyone you can think of," said Eric quickly "I've already had three declines. Supposedly they don't have any time. Bastards. They know that I've been in the can and don't want to associate with a convict."

I made up my mind and started to write a letter.

'Hello Marina.

I know that I just recently wrote to you saying that we may only meet up in three weeks' time, but circumstances have changed. I urgently need a player with 106+ levels. As far as I remember, you've reached level 107 in Beatwick, so you meet the requirements. In essence, the quest is to make a trip to the Free Lands and find a precious stone. The assignment was given to me by the High Priestess of Eluna. I'm attaching a link to the quest chain. We're gathering in Anhurs right now and we have to decide quickly. Quest duration could be around a week, from 18:00 to 01:00 in the morning system-time each day."

After a little while Eric shook his head disappointedly to show that his search for extra players was unsuccessful. It was the same story with Dukki and Sushiho – there were no candidates prepared to suddenly take off for an indefinite length of time. Now we only had to wait for Mirida's decision ...

"Hi Daniel,

I'm quite far away from Anhurs at the moment, otherwise I would've happily accepted your offer. I don't have a portal scroll and riding Fluffy to the capital would take about two weeks.

Sorry."

"No-go on my front either," I said and sat down right on the temple steps, crestfallen. Can someone explain to me why the developers thought you actually had to be looking at another player before you could add him to the group? Why no long-distance invites? Is cutting us some slack with this against their religion or something?

"All we can do now is shout in the group-finder channel," concluded Eric. "I have done this often in the past and, in all honesty, I have to say that I always ended up with total third-raters. So it's a double-edged sword, really."

"Do we have any choice though? The person I had in mind can only be in Anhurs in a couple of weeks. We can't wait for her until then."

"Her?" Clutzer latched onto the word.

"Yes, 'her'. She's a Hunter, level 107 Beastmaster. We fought together against the Kartoss forces in Beatwick." I provided a neutral explanation, reluctant to reveal Marina's true face. I would have to have a chat with her first and only then would I tell the others who she really is. "All right – I'll start searching. Let's hope we get lucky. Clutzer, I have a little task for you. Can you look through standard Clan Agreements: we need to formulate a proper Agreement for our clan, one that will cover everything: joining, leaving, loot allocation, roles, structure and everything else you see fit, right up to the monthly salary for the players of a certain level."

"Why me?" Clutzer asked, surprised, although you could see by his expression that he was extremely pleased.

"Because you could only get to the Mona Lisa if you were able to think through all the possibilities. No-one could arrange everything more correctly and prioritize better than you. Guys," I turned to the others, "please help him. It's time we made this a proper clan."

After handing that task over to the team, I opened the group search channel and started to shout throughout Anhurs:

"Looking for a competent 106+ level DD for a trip to the Free Lands. Duration: at least two to three weeks; must be available in-game between 18:00 and 01:00 system time. We're starting a quest chain, details in the mail.

As soon as I sent this announcement, I was hit with an avalanche of letters:

"I cannoot from 18.00, hwe about 12:00 to 14:00? 64-level Rogue."

"I'll boost you through the Patris Dungeon. Cost – 10k gold."

"153-level Mage. Will accept 2020 gold per day.

All the loot is mine. Have an agreement ready."

There was so much of this junk that I sensed people were failing to read the original text of the message and simply sent replies to anyone that popped up in the channel. There was little else I could do other than delete the letters or, if they sounded completely mental, stick the senders straight on the blacklist.

Attention! The official blacklist of the Dark Legion clan comes into effect in the next 5 minutes. Please confirm that you have read this message.

This came with a huge 'Yes' button that covered most of the view. Damn ... I didn't think that putting a team together would take this long. I was running the risk of ending up in real hot water. ... All right, not much I can do about that, I thought as I pressed the button, and continued to look through the letters. I urgently needed a competent player.

"Hi,

I'm a 147-level Druid. I have a few questions about the group: What's the loot allocation? What's the make-up of the rest of the group? Why aren't you using NPC mercenaries? Send me a link to the quest, so I can see what I need to take with me. What are the gear requirements? How do we get to the Free Lands? I propose we discuss all this first, before deciding whether I should join or not."

Ten minutes later I had finally managed to dig up a message written by an experienced Druid – or rather, a Lady Druid, since Barsina was clearly a female name.

"Hi,

We haven't discussed loot allocation yet, but I think we'll follow the standard route. Gold is divided equally among all and gear goes to whomsoever it benefits the most. If it suits several people at once, we'll let Lady Luck decide. The group is made up of 7 players between level 20 and 150, with 90 as the level average, and 1 NPC. We can't get mercenaries because the quest has a requirement for the level of the participants and so any NPCs' levels do not count towards that (already checked). Here's the link to the quest. There are no gear requirements; I'll trust you to be sensible. We'll be ported to the Free Lands. I think that's it. We are currently gathered by the Temple of Eluna. You may join us – I'll explain everything you want to know once you get here."

Keeping my fingers crossed, I sent my reply to Barsina. Judging by her questions, she was a competent player – of the kind I really needed right now. The main thing was for her not to have any hang-ups or additional demands, or it might turn out that although she was asking for one thing now, in actual fact she was after something else completely.

"On my way. I'll ask you straight away – do you have the means of transport taken care of, or will the group depend on its level 20 members who wouldn't be able to afford a normal horse?"

I read over the message one more time and realized that I probably owed Barsina a present. Would some flowers do the job? Whether she decided to join us in the end or not, mentioning the mounts from the start was very much the right thing to do. It looks like she might have had a bad experience with a group in this respect, if she brought it up straight away.

"I think I found one," I told the others sitting next to me, "she'll be here in a minute. By the way, what are your transport arrangements? Does everyone have mounts?"

"I don't," Clutzer quickly answered. "Why? Are you saying there might be other options?".

Eric and Leite also didn't have anything, but Dukki, Sushiho and Elenium had better news. This meant that we would only have to buy four horses – preferably not the cheapest kind to avoid traveling at the speed of a sightseeing snail.

"Other options should and must happen. Sergei, do you know where they sell horses? Take our mount-less lot to the stables. Here's an Agreement indicating that the gold for the horses should be taken off my account. Try not to get the most expensive ones, but not the worst quality either, all right? I can't go myself, since I'm waiting for Barsina. Move it, people, we're catastrophically running out of time!"

"How come?"

"The Dark Legion clan stuck me on their blacklist, the official one, and open season was declared on me a few minutes ago. Look at the way the passersby are eyeing me. They're probably seeing the message that there's a reward on my head and are considering whether to go for me or if it's best not to get involved."

"A reward? Why can't we see any of that?" Sushiho said in surprise.

"That's because we're in the same group. At least that's my best guess. Let's check this – Dukki, can you leave us for a couple of minutes?"

"Five thousand for each kill," he said almost straight away, as he was reading through the text. "You can be attacked even inside the city without any fear of the PK penalty. You must've seriously rubbed Number Twos the wrong way! How did that happen?"

"Sure thing, I'll tell you as soon as you join the clan," I replied. "Rejoin the group. And, Sergei, you'd better be off to get the horses."

It should be said that when I met up with my old gaming buddies and invited them to join the clan they refused at first. They said that they would have to see who the other clan members were, what the clan policies looked like, the loot allocation and so on, and only then would they decide. Although they knew me well enough, they would have preferred to play it safe at the time, because each of them had been receiving a certain salary-shaped bonus from their own clans and were reluctant to lose the additional income. My proposal to sign Agreements right away was met with approval, but it was finally agreed that could be done after we completed the quest. When I asked about the bonus, which was something new to me, it turned out that from level 5 10% of all the money a player received from quests or mobs went to the clan treasury. This amount wasn't deducted from the player, but was an additional payment made by the Corporation. So certain clans chose to provide a degree of financial support to their members. According to Dukki, because of this he was receiving 10000 gold a month. A pretty healthy sum – considering that he was getting it pretty much for nothing.

The matter of clan levels really piqued my interest, so I sent Dukki back to 'reality' for additional information. The situation with levels was far from simple: the more group quests, Dungeons, or crafting projects clan players completed, the more clan points – of some kind – the clan collected. As soon as the clan accumulated 20 million of these points, the clan gained its first level. The second level required 60 million and 40 million more for the next level, and so on. The maximum clan level was held by Dark Legion, which beat Phoenix on account of its extremely large membership. At least in this regard they weren't 'Number Twos'.

Attention! You have been discovered by a player from the Dark Legion clan. They are under obligation to attack you. Prepare yourself!

I barely had time to read this short text before a 5-minute Stun debuff landed on Dukki and Sushiho. Rogues! I immediately jumped up, looked around and kicked myself for not buying any stealth-detecting elixirs. A Stun could only be applied to 122 and 127-level players if the opponent was of the same level or higher. Otherwise Dukki, also being a Rogue, would've detected the attack and had time to react. And now I was left to face two or more players all on my own. There was little hope in relying on Slate – as an NPC he wouldn't interfere in the fight even if it were happening right around him.

Damage taken.
Hit Points reduced by 14533: 16314 (Critical Kick) – 1781 (Physical defense)
Total Hit Points: 5106 out of 19640
Attacker: Lloyd Redoombsky, level 172. PK restrictions have been lifted.

I was flung about two meters away and slid down the temple steps. The worst thing was that I could feel very well where that kick had landed – the part usually used for sitting. Bastard – if I ever get my hands on him, I'll kill him! As I got up, I just glimpsed a flickering in the air a few meters away – Lloyd stealthed once again. As soon as a Rogue attacks from invisibility, he drops back into vision for 5–10 seconds. One of the abilities of that class is that they can stealth several times in a row, perhaps three or four times all together, though I don't remember the exact number. Such a sneak-attack always inflicts extra damage. In general, it's a pretty unpleasant class in a solo fight. On the other hand, if you manage to survive the first two or three attacks, the Rogue is as good as done for – you can do what you like with him in the time it takes for his invisibility to recharge. It's a pity that our level difference was so great – 105 levels. Otherwise I would've taught him a lesson, as I did Reptilis. But why was he hitting me with his foot rather than his daggers? After all, I did spot fairly decent gear on Lloyd earlier!

The Shaman has three hands ...

It took me just over four seconds to call up the Spirit Summoning Mode. The Tambourine and the Emperor's Boots did their job. I summoned a Healing Spirit and cursed myself for failing to put things in order earlier. I got a third Spirit rank, which meant that now I could include three spirits in one summoning, but I hadn't selected that in the settings yet. It's not like I had much time for that. ... All this went through my head in a flash while I was restoring my Hit Points. It was strange that no new attacks came as I was healing myself; it was as if Lloyd intended to allow me to heal myself. Had he decided to play around with me for a bit?

"Peed your pants, eh, you little shit?" Lloyd's pleased voice came from nowhere. "There's no obstacle course here to hide behind! You'll pay for that six grand you cost me!"

"Guards!" I shouted frantically. "An attack in the city!"

"The PK-restrictions have been turned off for you, you idiot," Lloyd's voice came from somewhere to the right, so I rolled to the left and caught another Critical Kick from a foot belonging to Mlish the Magnificent, level 154. He was another player who had refused to pay the money he lost on the bet. "You stupid turd. You went and pissed off the entire Dark Legion!"

The Rogues remained stealthed, so I couldn't select them and start to bite back with Water Spirits. As I flew through the air I saw that, like Lloyd, Mlish appeared for 5 seconds after the hit and then vanished once again. This meant that both he and Lloyd only had 2–3 stealth-dives left. After that, for the next 5 hours, I could do with them what I liked. The main thing was that I hoped they would keep to kicking and not switch to sticking pointy things into me. Any hit with a weapon or even a shuriken throwing star would land me at the respawn point. So then ... Mlish is to the left and Lloyd is to the right, but there's no-one in front of me and the way into the temple is clear. I hope Beth will save me ...

A direct hit to my chest completely winded me and sent me flying about twenty meters. The system happily informed me that a third bounty-hunting enthusiast had joined the fight. Another Rogue – one of those that tried to go back on our bet. I hit the corner of a house with my back and my vision began to swim: birds started to fly around my head and, alongside the message that I now had a 20-second Stun debuff on me and a critically low number of Hit Points (145), I was beginning to hallucinate:

Player Plinto has invited you to join a group. Do you accept?

I knew that fighting hallucinations was useless, so I pressed the 'Yes' button. This can't get any worse, so why not take the chance?

As soon as the Stun expired, I got back on my feet again, healed myself and looked around. So we had three Rogues (I really hoped there weren't more) who had decided to play cat-and-mouse with me and slowly trample me into the ground. They could've sent me for respawn several times over as I was lying there, but they opted not to, preferring to remain invisible. As did Plinto. His see-through outline, visible only to members of the group I had just joined, was a couple of meters away from me. Plinto was intently examining his surroundings and when I looked at him, put his finger to his lips, indicating that I should keep quiet. All right then; keeping quiet was just fine by me. But what was he up to?

A little more time went by before the former leader of the Dark Legion Clan seemed to come to a decision of some sort. He pointed towards a small alley about twenty meters from me, and did all he could to indicate that I should go there. The guards that had run over at the sound of the fight were standing about forty meters from me and were very busy doing nothing while looking various passersby over. All the local NPCs quickly dispersed, shops shut their doors and a crowd of onlookers began to gather along the edges of the street where the fight had taken place. These were mainly players below level 100, but from the shouts that reached me they were having a heated discussion about how many level 50s one might need to bring me down and get the Dark Legion's reward. How kind and considerate of them.

I tried to stop myself thinking as I followed Plinto's instructions and dashed towards the alley. As I was running past a house, another kick from Lloyd caught me below the belt and provided me with the acceleration required to get to my destination even faster. I ended up tumbling the last stretch like a football that had been kicked, but one that came with an added speed bonus. I ran around a corner, leaving my pursuers behind, purposefully summoned a Strengthening Spirit to give me added acceleration and ran forwards as fast as my legs could carry me. It was just as well that I had no time to change my ring bonuses from Agility back to Intellect. The extra speed would be pretty handy right now.

I only managed to take about a dozen steps before I came to a halt. A dead end! Plinto had sent me to a dead end!

"Looks like your luck's run out!" Lloyd

appeared from behind the bend. He was still in stealth mode, but I could see him well enough: a mark was hanging above him that allowed both of us to see him. The other two were still completely invisible – looks like Plinto turned up after they had started their leisurely attempt to assassinate me and he hadn't managed to mark them out too. In all truth I gained little from seeing where Lloyd was. Our level difference was just too big for me to do much damage to him with my Spirits. "I want you to see how we are going to cut you to pieces." Lloyd de-stealthed and just a couple of seconds later two more players appeared next to him. "I'm done playing around. We'll meet in 12 hours at the respawn point!"

As he was saying this, I saw how Plinto put marks on Lloyd's two buddies to keep them in his sights, pointed at Lloyd to me, then pointed at himself and at the other two players. Was he really suggesting I take on a 172-level player? And why the heck not? It's just a 105-level gap. That's nothing; I'll crush them all with my bare hands!

"Whoever hits him from twenty meters away gets a super-prize! I'll go first!" Lloyd shouted and then events went into overdrive ...

As soon as the first throwing stars flew towards me, Plinto entered the fight. His attack was quiet, fast and left Mlish zero chance of escape. I managed to duck, letting a shuriken fly past me and, at the same time, summoned a Spirit of Water Strike on Lloyd. I then surrounded myself with a Water Shield. Perhaps not by much, but it should have reduced any damage that would come my way. The second star cut through the shield as if it didn't exist and seemed to veer off course, but the system happily informed me that my Hit Points went down to 300.

"The super-prize is mine!" Lloyd managed to shout just before a sun seemed to flash under his feet, leaving the 'Blindness' debuff on all the attackers in its wake. Without stopping, Plinto took care of the second Rogue, leaving only Lloyd still standing.

"He's all yours." I finally heard his voice and a moment later Plinto left the group and stealthed.

"Why did you do this?" I shouted my question into empty air, but there was no reply. Plinto had vanished. And who's going to enlighten me on what just happened here? The 'Blindness' on Lloyd lasted the standard 5 minutes, so I decided not to give him a second chance and began summoning Spirit after Spirit onto him.

Achievement earned!

Elephant and Pug level 1 (until the next level: 9 kills of any creatures or players 50+ levels higher than you)

Achievement reward: Damage to all creatures and players 50+ levels higher is increased by 10%.

List of achievements to be found in character settings.

Even my Intellect went up by one point, giving a total of 106 – the difference in our levels was that big. As soon as Lloyd's juice had 'run out', Sushiho flew to my side, screaming "die you bastard!" In the blink of an eye, he threw a green bubble of some kind around me, which reduced damage by 20%, judging by the description. Perfect timing.

"Hang in there Mahan!" A dozen seconds later Dukki appeared, getting his daggers out as he ran and stealthing.

The crowd of onlookers staring from behind the corner vanished as soon as they saw what happened to the three attackers. Plinto might still be somewhere nearby and he was considered a dangerous loose cannon, although I was becoming less and less sure of that myself.

"Legion numbskulls," cursed Elenium, when the rest of the clan arrived on their horses to hear what had happened. "Where is this Barsina? Anhurs has so many people from the Legion running around it you'd think it was a queue for Anastaria's erotic show tickets. Maybe even enough for three queues."

"An interesting metaphor. Are you Shaman Mahan?" asked a beautiful female voice, slightly lisping her 'sh's. I turned around and saw a petite girl. A human. She was a head lower than me in height. Small – even miniature –, she could have been confused with a child from afar. The name Barsina hung above her head and she had an empty space where a clan membership emblem might've been. I glanced over her gear and noted that she looked pretty well-equipped. Rare or perhaps even Epic items together with a meter-and-a-half-tall tiger made it clear that the girl wasn't experiencing any financial difficulties. An involuntary smile crossed my face as Barsina walked under her tiger's head barely having to bend her own.

"Hello Barsina. Guys, let me introduce you to our potential partner on this quest."

"It's Barsa for short, if you like. Hang on, you're not the Mahan about whom there was an announcement from the Emperor a couple of days ago and on whose account all the gaming forums are buzzing after the events in Beatwick, or whatever that place is called? And how did you manage to upset the Dark Legion so much that they're now offering five grand for your head? Will this affect the completion of the quest? I'm sorry for all the questions, but I prefer to settle any matters as they arise, before signing any agreement. I can't stand flakers."

"That's all right," I replied happily and briefly answered all of Barsina's questions. Had we actually managed to get hold of a competent player? That would be some stroke of luck!

"All right, I agree. Do you guys mind if I join you?" The girl looked over the other players. "But let's make some things clear from the start: I don't want any amorous attention or flirting. This is my main condition. I'll have to disappoint you straight away and say that I'm a married woman and don't want any problems with my husband. Deal?"

The entire male population of the group nodded, so Barsina continued:

"Then I have no more questions – let's sign the

agreement. I have my own template that I usually use with all the groups that I join; here's the text. It's a little different from a standard group agreement: I added points about open flirting and show of emotions. They may seem like insignificant details, but these things can really do your head in when on a mission."

I carefully read the agreement and, not spotting anything unreasonable, I signed it and Barsina joined our group.

Requirements for the quest 'Restoration of the Holy Relic, Step 2 ,Searching for the Stone of Light' have been met. See the High Priestess of Eluna to be transported to the Free Lands.

"Wow, that's not exactly next door," sighed the girl as she read the description. A dot appeared on the map marking the location where we were heading, but that area was hidden to me, so I could only make a guess at the distance: it looked like around five trips between Farstead and Beatwick. That is, 10 days by cart, 15–20 days on foot or 6–10 days on a decent mount.

"Right you are. We have a long trip ahead of us. All right, guys, everyone ready? Barsina, we have one constraint – three of us can only be in the game from six in the evening until one in the morning, system-time. We have to set out right away so we can to cover as much ground as possible today. Do you need time to get ready?"

"No, I've been looking for a group to do some quests with for a couple of days now, so I've been ready for a while. Last question – where will we sleep? On the ground?"

"I have the Frontier Ranger Tent that sleeps up to 10, and will be very comfortable for 6, so that part is covered."

"In that case I'm ready. Let's go!"

"You did the right thing by listening to my advice and taking your friends with you," said the High Priestess happily as soon as we stepped inside the temple. Surrounded by her handmaidens, Beth looked very majestic, having completely regained her previous role. "I see that you've taken a Priest of Eluna with you. A very good choice. Have a look through the items that you left for me to bless earlier and wait here; I need to have a private word with your Priest. Come." My jaw almost dropped as Beth took Elenium aside. We were prevented from following them as a crowd of junior Priestesses surrounded us. They quickly brought a small table and arranged all the rings and ore that I had made and gathered in Beatwick on it.

"May I?" asked Barsina, as she turned one of the rings over in her hand.

"Yes, have a look." I looked over the ring that now granted an extra 5% to Experience, and uncovered its properties. There was nothing secret about the ring, so I wasn't worried that its properties would surprise Barsina too much.

"Nice band," concluded the girl, putting the ring back on the table. "Made by you, judging by the properties. Are you a Jeweler?"

"Yes."

"How far have you leveled up in Jewelcraft? I need to upgrade my rings and I'm prepared to buy if you can make any with +20 to Intellect."

"I'm sorry, but I'm restricted in this respect for now: maximum stat bonus is only +12. So, for the moment I can't help you."

"All right, how much would you sell one of these for? It's always good to have an Experience bonus."

"Barsina, I don't know. I honestly have no idea how much such a ring should cost. If I say 100000 it could be too little and you'll consider me a total sucker, or it could be too much and you'll think I'm a greedy idiot. It cost me nothing to make, so there's no point talking about a markup."

"Would a thousand gold suffice?" asked the girl.

"Quite." I handed the ring to her and got a message that I just received 700 gold. 30% of the sum went towards the Empire, as usual.

"Do you have many rings like this?"

"I don't know yet – you yourself saw them being returned to me just a moment ago."

"Can I dig around? What if I find more things I

could use in that pile?"

"Be my guest." I uncovered the properties of the rings. I could probably sell them for a better price at the Auction House, but good relations in the next couple of weeks were worth infinitely more. So I had no trouble sacrificing part of the profit. Barsina started going through my rings, looking at each of them in turn. Meanwhile I tried to figure out where Beth took Elenium. I would have to ask Sergei later why she called him aside.

"Also these two." Barsina highlighted two rings: for +10% to Intellect and +5% to Experience. I had no trouble letting go of the one with the Experience bonus, but the Intellect one ... I had 106 Intellect points at the moment, which meant that the ring would give me an extra 10 points. At the same time, I could now make rings with +12 bonus. The latter was a much better option, especially at this level. But if I spent all of my 265 free stat points on increasing Intellect, this ring would already give +36 ... then compared to that my +12 wasn't much to look at.

"Judging by your face, the Intellect ring has caught your eye as well," said Barsina, putting the ring back. "Then I'd like to take one more for Experience, all right?"

"We're back," declared Beth, who turned up just as I received another 700 gold from Barsina. "Mahan, I told you the aim of the assignment; here's the scroll with the return portal. Activate it as soon as you find the Stone and you'll be brought back to Anhurs. And now we should go, it's time."

After shoving all the blessed items into my bag, handing over the ring Barsina initially wanted to Elenium and giving the bags I bought to the other players, I followed the High Priestess. I'll ask what she was chatting with Sergei about later, in the absence of potential eavesdroppers in the form of the Heralds, who couldn't go to the Free Lands. By the way, there's a question – who ensures the law is obeyed in the Free Lands? Are there equivalents of the Heralds there? I'll have look into this. Our steeds turned into small bridles as soon as we entered the Temple. This was a rare, if not unique, concession to the players by the developers: you could take your mount into a building, upon which it turned into a bridle. And as soon as I left the building, I knew I would regain my stallion. Or mare. Whatever it was – it's not like I had had much time to look.

The neighboring room contained the shimmering transportation portal, kept open by three priestesses. Beth looked at us in a regal manner as the expedition was about to set out and I realized that there wouldn't be much point asking her anything at this moment. I nodded to her in farewell, gripped the bridle in my hands and dove into the portal.

* * *

"A nice little forest they have around here!" uttered Dukki as soon as he appeared next to us. I totally got him – the forest was really quite something.

Great, mast-like trees hung over us like some giants of legend. The cold wind, which only the convicts could actually feel, put a Chilled debuff on everyone, reducing all stats by 1%; the ground in the forest was covered by some kind of phosphorescent mist, puffs of which constantly seethed and bubbled, seemingly having a life of their own. There was no sign of any verdant plant life such as grass – instead bare gray sticks, dark brambles and a mass of hostile-looking shrubbery made the forest quite impassable. You could say it was created in the image of the best traditions of the antique horror movies. A small path, which one would have struggled to call a road, lead into the depths of this developers' fantasy and it became clear that our trip wasn't going to exactly be a walk in the park. I was the first one through the portal and, as the others arrived after me, I walked to the edge of the forest to get a better sense of the place – I was immediately immersed in a different world. Just before the forest there was an invisible boundary; crossing it took you to another location: there, the wind became even colder, some distant screams from what I hoped were animals started to reach my ears and odd whispers periodically floated at the limits of hearing. And, judging by the map, our 8 mounted treks would take us into the very depths of all this; we would not know whom or what we might bump into.

"The Dark Forest," said Slate. "There are many bad stories about it amongst my people. Terrifying and full of horrors, this is not a place from which you return ... the birthplace of Vampires."

"Vampires?" asked Barsina in surprise. "I thought they just stayed in their towns and didn't venture out much."

"Of course," he continued. "Those towns are for ordinary Vampires, the domesticated sort, you might say. But the Dark Forest is the place of the original, ancient ones, who put founded many a vampire clan. The Reardalox Clan, if that means anything to you. According to legend, this clan is ruled over by the oldest sentient in Barliona, the one who still remembers the Dragons." I pricked up my ears, but tried not to show it. If Dragons were mentioned, quests that feature them might not be far behind. If I summon Draco the clan head would be putty in my hands. The main thing was not to show my cards until the time was right.

"Right! Attention everyone! Our task is to get to the marked spot and find the Stone. If it was Reardalox's Vampires that did away with the priests, we'll have to do some thinking. But for now let's forget about Vampires – it's not like we can do much about them at the moment, even if they're actually hiding behind the next tree. Barsa, can you please check the forums and look up how to fight those things. Do we need stakes, garlic and other special gear or is the only difference between this and other mobs in the name?"

"All right, I'll look. But I should say that starting out by foisting tasks you could do yourself on others is bad form. I'm not against you giving orders, but don't get carried away."

"Hold on, don't go yet." I stopped the girl. "Here, take a look at my properties. I think that should make it clear why I can't look things up myself. The same goes for half of those present here." I opened access to the part of my properties where it said that I was a person of limited rights.

"I'm sorry," Barsina turned red, thus earning an additional ten points of Respect with me. "I ... I didn't know. ... Why didn't you say straight away?"

"Would you have joined us if I shouted 'A bunch of convicts are looking for a player ... Barsa, the fact that we've left the mines shows only one thing – we're reformed in the eyes of the law. I hope you have no issues with people like us."

"No, if you didn't say I would have never known. ... Please, once again, accept my apologies. ... So, are there any other disadvantages to your situation?"

"Pain: we feel pain. Otherwise we're just like other players."

"They also take 30% off all gold paid to us," put in Clutzer. I looked around and saw that everyone was listening in on my conversation with Barsina with some interest.

"Guys, I see that you've already finished the Clan Agreement, since you've gone into 'chill out and chat' mode. Can I have a read?"

"All right, I'll go and leave you to it," smiled Barsina, while the others looked down, slightly embarrassed. "A Clan Agreement is a very important thing. Be sure to cover everything." With that the girl's eyes clouded over and she left the game.

"Here." Clutzer surprised me. "We took a standard agreement and made a few corrections. We decided to change the structure slightly. The clan will have a Leader (that would be you), a Deputy, a vacant position for the moment and a Treasurer, also vacant for now. Then come the Officers, which would be the six of us, and then the Fighters and Recruits. A question arose about the Keepers – are we going to try to get our own castle like Phoenix, for example, or not?"

"Not for the moment. We'll cross that bridge when we come to it. What else?"

"We set out the duties and powers of each and all – we didn't really change anything there. And also we set down that 30% of the clan's monthly income would be allocated for paying salaries. These would be proportional to the profit generated for the clan and to the member's rank. Also ..."

Clutzer handed me the draft agreement, explaining all the amendments that they'd made in this time.

"Good work." I accepted the agreement. "There is only one point I disagree with: namely, the one about making decisions that touch upon the clan's best interests. Right now it says that decisions should be made at an assembly of members with the rank of Officer and higher, but I propose that we leave this privilege to the Clan Head. To me, that is. What if the Emperor summons me and offers to send the clan to a Dungeon or complete a unique quest? What am I going to tell him? 'Can you wait a little. We have to decide this as a clan'? Can you imagine what would happen to our Reputation in that case? No, the clan should and must be consulted, but the decision should be made by one person and it has to be its Head ..."

After five minutes of debating over certain points the entire Seathistles Clan accepted the agreement.

"I call upon a Herald, I need to register a Clan Agreement," I spoke into the air, summoning the official representative of the authorities. Currently we were right on the edge of Malabar, but still within the jurisdiction of the Heralds, so one of them should hear and teleport here. You didn't need them for signing agreements with players, but a Clan Agreement had to be confirmed by a Herald. It was the only way it could be done.

"You called me and I came. Please provide the text of the Agreement."

I sent the Agreement to the Herald and his gaze clouded as he checked the legitimacy of the changes, after which he said:

"Confirmed! Now and henceforth the Agreement of the Seathistles Clan is inviolable and can only be changed by an Advisor!"

Then came the clap of the portal and we were alone once again.

"If that's how it is, take me into the clan right away" said Elenium "I already saw the Agreement for myself and have a vested interest in the clan's speedy development. The more clan members that complete the quest the better it will be for leveling up the clan. So, I'm with you."

"Me too," said Dukki and Sushiho at the same time.

"Then, I welcome the new Officers to the Seathistles Clan," I mumbled, rather pleased, as I invited the guys into the clan. "But why did you decide to leave the post of the Deputy vacant?"

"Because the Head must pick a person whom he trusts more than his own mother. You'll appoint whoever you end up choosing, that's how we set it out in the Agreement."

"Right," Barsina was back before I could respond to Clutzer's words. "The Dark Forest is uncharted territory. Some maps do exist, but they cost a lot – up to a 100000. I even had a closer look at the small piece that was released for publicity: it was drawn from the air, most probably by a person flying around on a griffin and sketching what he saw. There's only forest and rivers – nothing that could be useful to us. There's not a word written there about Vampires, but I'm inclined to believe Slate. There is one legend on the official site that somewhere in Barliona there lives the oldest Vampire, the Patriarch, as he's also called. Very old, very wise and very dangerous. As for garlic and wooden stakes – Barliona has no such conventions. Vampires are simply very long-lived sentients who are forced to drink blood, or whatever it is we have inside us. The only warning was that they're very fast, about three times faster than any of us. That's it, I think."

"Then I suggest we get going. We've already lost a great deal of time. We have an exciting journey on horseback ahead of us, so summon your mounts. I would give a lot to know where this path will end up leading us."

"To the heart of the Dark Forest," Slate, who was doing an excellent phone mast impersonation up until this point, immediately volunteered the information. You had to give it to the developers for configuring the Imitators in such a convenient way. As soon as players start talking about the real world, NPCs appear to turn off or simply act as if nothing is being said. "All the paths in the forest lead to where clan Reardalox Vampires live."

"That's where we should head then. Mount up, people! Adventure awaits!"

Three hours of riding along the foggy path were completely demoralizing. You got the feeling that we were moving along a narrow deep canyon, carpeted with twigs and deadfall. Our horses easily hopped over any obstacles, but that did little to lift our spirits. We hadn't seen anything of the sun in all this time, hidden as it was by the thick canopy of the pines overhead. Thus we rode on, knee-deep in the mist, making the best guess of the direction in which we were headed and occasionally jumping over fallen trees. It was monotonous and tedious, but there was little to be done about it.

"Right, sorry guys," Elenium finally said "but it's time for me to call it a day. We just spent too long getting ready. If anyone decides to continue, I'll turn on Follow."

"I have to go too," Dukki said immediately afterward. "Will you keep going?" he asked me.

"Yes, it's not like we have anything else to do. Hook up the Follow to my horse. We may keep going for another two or three hours."

"In that case, you can tow me along as well," concluded Sushiho. "We will meet up tomorrow at 18:00 server time, is that right?"

The gaming avatars of three members of the clan flickered and became transparent, but didn't disappear altogether – the tethering was doing its job. This was quite a convenient feature when a group of players needed to get to a certain location. You select one poor sod to make the actual journey, attach a Follow to him and then you could be free to log out into the real world. This is the principle along which caravans function, transporting around players instead of goods. This is a very profitable business, when the distances are vast and people don't want to cough up the money for a portal.

"Why did you decide to stay, Barsina?" I asked the girl. "Throw us your tether and return again tomorrow. Not much point in you hanging around now. It's night already."

"I'll stay with you a little while longer. It's quite pretty around here," the girl said, surprising me. What did she find so pretty about this forest? "It's so ... oppressive, as it were. Makes you think. So I'm riding along, lost in my own thoughts. ... How long do you think it will take us to get there at this pace?"

"Hold on, I'm just finishing sketching out the map, it should become clearer then." I put the finishing touches to the map, not missing anything that we'd seen that day: fog, brambles, fog, trees, fog ... more fog. ... "Right. We've covered around ... according to the map we've made almost no progress. But three hours of riding isn't much. It should become clearer tomorrow, so I suggest you go and have a rest."

"I'll have time enough for that. How did you get this quest chain, by the way? I looked around in the manuals and it's a quest from the restricted section. That's not something you can just pick up any day. You've got the chain from the High Priestess too. In general, you're an interesting bunch: you haven't gained level 100 yet, but already have a First Kill under your belt. Can you tell me how that happened? Or is this a clan secret?"

"No, it's no secret. It's just ... as they say – it was blind luck. I ended up being in the right place at the right time. Where I lived there was a lady who, on closer acquaintance, turned out to be a former High Priestess of Eluna. According to the conditions of the scenario (and I'm fairly certain of this now) there were quite a few such High Priestesses around Malabar – in all the key points of the scenario, but only one of these points was set in motion – the one that was unlocked in Beatwick. This is where the current quest originates. Simple luck, that's all. And how did you ended up being a 'gun for hire'?"

"Didn't you read my agreement?" smiled the girl. "It just so happened that the same situation developed in all the clans that I joined. The Clan Head, Deputies or Officers would start to shower me with attention. I liked it at first, but once they'd crossed a certain line and taken complete leave of their senses, they'd begin to search me out in real life. ... So I had to leave and start everything from scratch. I don't want to join a women-only clan – those places have different aims to mine. All I want is to earn a comfortable living for myself and my family. So that's why I joined the ranks of the mercenaries. My goal in the next six months is to reach level 200 and officially register as a free fighter. It may not be the case with Phoenix, but other big clans such as Azure Dragons use the services of mercenaries."

"So, that's why you joined us," I said. "Did you do it in the hope that the Rare quest chain may bring you a lot of Experience?"

"Let me give you a piece of advice for the future: never ask a girl a question to which you already know the answer. Otherwise things will never work out between you and that girl."

"But you're not here in the capacity of a girl – just an ordinary member of our group. You yourself asked us to forget about your gender ..."

Thus we traveled on for another hour or so, until Barsina latched a Follow onto my horse and left the game.

"Guys, you can also put a Follow on me and go to bed. I'll spend a couple more hours riding, but there's no need for you to suffer."

"It won't work," said Eric straight away. "Wanted to turn on Follow a while back, as soon as we entered the forest, but we can't do it – just don't have the function. You can check for yourself. It gets turned on when you exit Barliona, but we don't have an exit button. So we'll be riding with you all the way."

I quickly verified Eric's words and cursed under my breath. That's right – no Follow option for prisoners.

"Then we'll set up camp. There's little sense keeping on going and we need to rest as well. It's nearly one in the morning already. Leite, you make a fire, Eric and Clutzer, put up the tent and I'll take care of the food." It was just as well that right at the last minute – straight after the Auction House – a food stall caught my eye, so I didn't just have a supply of prepared food, but raw meat too. This could be a chance to level up in Cooking as well ...

"Barsina is a decent player, by the looks of it," said Leite when the lively fire fought back some of the darkness and the smell of roast venison spread throughout the camp. What else would four guys talk about if not about the ladies? (Slate didn't count, as he immediately went to sleep in the tent.)

"I wouldn't draw any conclusions after three hours' riding," volunteered Eric. "When it's time to fight it should become clear who and what is riding with us. For now all you can say for certain is that she's a good traveling companion. She doesn't pester you with demands to explain every little thing, keeps quiet where appropriate and keeps up the conversation when needed."

"That's what bothers me the most," Clutzer couldn't help adding his two cents. "If she plans to work as a mercenary in Barliona – even get an income from doing that – her approach should be completely different. She should be trying to fish any piece of information she can out of us to gain maximum advantage from this trip, but she just rode on and contemplated the Dark Forest scenery. At the same time she doesn't seem to be a scatterbrain. The conclusion being that something's fishy here."

"Guys, I think you're overreacting." I surprised myself by suddenly coming to the girl's defense. "She's just an ordinary player, like so many in Barliona. The fact that she's not trying to drag any information out of us on the first day together speaks in her favor. And she did spend only three hours with us, after all. I agree with Eric – we can only make up our minds about Barsa after more time or after the first fight. She may well turn out to be a complete noob."

"Still, I'd keep a close eye on her," said Clutzer, still unconvinced.

After making the supper and getting my Cooking up to 6, I added our route to the map; then I took out the Smithing tools, walked a little way off from the camp so as not to disturb anyone and started to make ingots. I didn't feel like sleeping, so I decided to spend a couple of hours stocking up on ingots that I needed for leveling up in Jewelcraft.

"Do you have a lot of Copper Ore?" Eric came up to me after an hour. "My main profession is a Smith, and as you said it's probably time to start leveling up in it."

"Yes, I have some left." I took out all the Copper that I had: both the Ore and the ingots. "Here you go. Try to get as far as Tin – I have 50 stacks of it. I'll use up 10–15 of them now and leave the rest for you. What professions do you have in general?"

"Level 13 Smith, so I have 7 levels to go before I can touch Tin. Hopefully this Copper will be enough. And Level 16 Miner. These are the ones that I've leveled up. Otherwise we all unlocked Lumberjacking, Herbalism and Fishing. Although they're all level 1 at the moment and there isn't all that much you can do with these professions in this forest."

"That's fine – when we get back, I'll send you for speeded up leveling. Right now you should focus on improving your Smithing while you have some free time on your hands. Something tells me that we won't be getting all that much of it for professions around here."

On my seventh ingot a miracle happened: as I was making another Tin ingot a large blue stone was left at the bottom of the smelting pot. It was Lapis Lazuli. A stone I obtained myself ...

I left Eric where he was and returned to the camp, sat in front of the fire and opened the design mode. The images of the Dwarf Warriors hadn't gone anywhere, so I recreated the image of the stone I just got and smiled, feeling rather pleased. The Jewelcraft trainer was right: right now the stone exceeded the figurines in size by several times, which could mean only one thing...

Congratulations! You have progressed on the path of recreating the Legendary Chess Set of Emperor Karmadont, the founder of the Malabar Empire. Wise and just, the Emperor offered his opponents the chance to settle disputes on the chessboard instead of the battlefield. Each type of Chess piece was made from a different stone.

Pawns: The Malachite Orc Warriors (Creator: Mahan) and Lapis Lazuli Dwarf Warriors (Creator: Mahan).

Rooks: A Battle Ogre from Alexandrite and a Giant from Tanzanite.

Knights: A War Lizard from Tourmaline and a War Horse from Amethyst.

Bishops: Troll Archers from Emerald and Elf Archers from Aquamarine.

Queens: An Orc Shaman from Peridot and Elemental Archmage, a human, from Sapphire.

Kings: The head of the White Wolf Clans, an Orc from green Diamond and the Emperor of the Malabar Empire, a human from blue Diamond.

The Chessboard: black Onyx and white Opal,

framed by white and yellow Gold.

Numbers and letters on the chessboard: Platinum.

After the death of the Emperor the chess set was destroyed. Now it is only up to you and your skills whether Barliona will again see this truly great wonder of the world – the Legendary Chess set of Emperor Karmadont.

You have created the Lapis Lazuli Dwarf Warriors from the Legendary Chess set of Emperor Karmadont. While the chess pieces are in your possession, each minute you will regenerate 1% of Hit Points, Mana and Energy in addition to your standard regeneration, +1 to Crafting.

Skill increase:

+1 to Crafting. Total: 6

+2 to primary profession of Jewelcrafting. Total: 44

You created a Legendary item. Your reputation with all previously encountered factions has increased by 500.

Our makeshift camp turned into a great pillar of light with my hands at its center. Aside from this, as I looked around I was able to get a clear view of the surrounding forest– the light emanating from the chess pieces had dispersed the fog for ... I couldn't tell exactly how far, but it was quite far. I would have a better look in the morning.

The pure white light, together with an intermittently appearing rainbow and solemn music, was doing strange things to the surrounding world. The branches of the trees began to emit a black mist of some kind, which soon disappeared, dissolving into the surroundings, while the trees themselves ... they were being transformed. Right in front of my eyes branches took on the natural color of healthy bark, green shoots appeared, the black ground became covered with grass where flowers sprang up here and there. You got the feeling that the entire area had just been subjected to a Blessing. ... But I'm a Shaman! I don't know how to do things like this!

"What the heck have you done?" Leite flew out of the tent. "What's going on?" I might've been wrong, but I thought I heard a note of panic in his voice.

"Will you show us the Dwarves?" Clutzer asked after he read the announcement. "You just created them, didn't you?"

"Sure, have a look." I showed Clutzer the figurines, which I was still holding in my hands, after first concealing their properties. I'll be the first one to read the description of the second riddle!

"Mahan, duck!" came Eric's shout, after which the full weight of the chunky dwarf hit me at speed, bringing me to the ground. Three black arrows hit the place where I had just been standing but immediately began to melt in the light shining from the chess pieces.

"Clutzer, stealth now! Leite, put on your armor! Level-100 Vampires! Three of them!"

I rolled together with Eric behind a tree, got up from the ground and just caught sight of three pairs of red eyes dashing between the trees. They didn't enter the zone covered by the light, as if afraid of something, but they had an excellent opportunity to shoot us from afar.

"That was the first warning." The surrounding space was filled with a voice – a terrible voice. It seemed to come from every tree, branch and newly emerged blade of grass. It vibrated, making you shake and causing a resonance that covered the body of your gaming avatar with goosebumps. Bypassing the brain, the effect of the voice made you want to fall to the ground, wrap yourself in a blanket and whimper – just as a result of being spoken to by someone who was infinitely more powerful. "If you fail to heed it, my warriors will not miss the second time. Leave my forest!"

The red eyes of the Vampires dissolved into the Dark Forest and then there was silence. The pillar of light and the solemn music faded and darkness covered the surrounding world once again. The three black stains in the place where the arrows hit were the only reminder of the attack.

"I get the feeling that the next time our choice of camping spot should be carefully planned in advance rather than picked at random," said Clutzer, speaking up. "That Patriarch has an interesting voice. Shakes you up enough to give you goosebumps. I don't think I would like to run into him one-on-one."

"I'm afraid you'll have to," the Prince came out of the tent. "Only such a sentient could have captured a Great Priest in possession of a Stone of Light."

"Good travelers," another voice sounded nearby as each of us were thinking over Slate's words, "please allow me to touch the purified ground before I die!"

I looked in the direction of the voice and was stunned: it was a Woodwothe! The meter-wide fur ball was floating above the ground at the border of the dark and pure forest, hesitant to cross it. And I could clearly see why that might be – only scraps of its fur remained now; dark lines of it with rotting flesh were hanging in long shreds that reached the ground, feathers from a dozen black arrows were sticking out hedgehog-like all over its body and waves of darkness emanated from the Wothe in every direction. The warning from the Vampires had clearly been insufficient, so the Cursed Woodwothe of the Dark Forest had decided to pay us a visit.

CHAPTER FIVE
THE GUARDIAN OF THE DARK FOREST

"WILL WE BE HARMED IN ANY WAY if you enter this ground?" I carefully asked the Wothe as I very quickly tried to think of what to do next. It was such a pity that all the free players were currently off-line. I was desperate for information from the forum – the real forum and not my truncated version – that I wanted to howl in frustration at being so helpless.

"I cannot harm the Guardian," was the hoarse reply of the Wothe, which by now had descended nearly all the way to the ground. Aside from the waves of darkness, which couldn't penetrate the cleansed area, it also had thin streams of dark liquid dripping off it – probably the creature's blood.

"What 'Guardian'?" This word from the fur-ball unsettled me.

"The Guardian of this ground: you. As long as you stay in this zone, no dark creature will be able to cause you or any of your group any harm. Even the Vampire's arrows would have simply bounced off your body and immediately disappeared. Inside his territory a Guardian is invincible."

So there you have it. Now I've been roped into being a Guardian too. I just wish I knew what on earth this was, what you do with it and, most importantly, why me?

"I grant you my permission to enter," I replied. If the Wothe sees me as a protector of sorts, perhaps I can fish a quest out of this NPC. After all, there must've been a reason behind the developers putting it here.

"I thank you, Guardian." The Wothe floated, or rather rolled, onto the cleansed plot and a sigh of relief sounded throughout the forest. "Yeees! It's so good to be on pure ground once again ..."

A black puddle began to form under the furry sphere that had now fallen to the earth, but the Wothe took no notice of it. It looked like it altogether lost interest in life and really was preparing for its final rest. Like hell it would! Where's my quest? And what about a bonus for my help?

I selected the Wothe, spent four seconds entering the Spirit Summoning Mode and engaged in vigorous resuscitation. The 120-level Cursed Creature, with a crazy amount of Hit Points (over 500000) of which barely 10% remained, and burdened with some unintelligible debuff, which every ten seconds took the Imitator of the fur-ball 10000 Hit Points closer to its well-deserved rest, was silent, taking little notice of my efforts. No, you're not getting away that easy – I'll get you to do a thing or two for me before you head off to the Repository, or wherever it is Imitators are kept. You're not going anywhere until you give me a quest, and even if you do die, I happen to have a Necromancer on my team. He'll get you back up no problem, if need be.

"Leave me, Guardian," croaked the Wothe five minutes later. "Your efforts are futile, they are only prolonging my agony. It is beyond your power to remove the curse – you've already done much more than anyone could imagine. You gave me a chance to leave peacefully."

"You got that wrong, you woody wonder!" I wheezed as I continued to summon Spirits on the Wothe. The other three, along with Slate, stood nearby, shifting from foot to foot, not really knowing how to help me.

"Mahan, can we do anything or will you manage?" said Clutzer, as if reading my thoughts.

"I'll manage! On second thoughts, no! Guys, get those arrows out of the Wothe! Wothe, don't do them any harm, even if it hurts. Don't touch the arrows with your bare hands! You'd better use the pliers – Eric, they will be amongst your Smithing Tools. Hop on it, everyone, we have to get this fluff-ball back up!"

I continued to demolish my mana reserves without a moment's pause, but had little to show for it. All that I could do was keep the Wothe's Hit Points from sliding further downwards.

"The arrows are out." Eric broke the happy

news a minute later. "Though I'll have to throw away the pliers now. They've rotted! Imagine that – an item that can only be used for crafting corroded away completely!"

"Guardian, I beg you to let me go," whispered the Wothe after another five minutes. As soon as the arrows were pulled out, the debuff on the fur-ball started to take off only 5000 Hit Points a second, which allowed me to heal the suffering creature back to almost half its total Health. "You can restore my health, but you cannot remove the Curse. As soon as you stop healing me, I will die. Make a decision, Shaman!" for the first time the Wothe didn't address me as a Guardian, but emphasized my class. "A Shaman's spirit must be firm. His entire life a Shaman must make hard decisions, which will make some perish and save the lives of others. You too must make a decision!"

"I! Will! Get! Through!" I was almost shouting, whilst trying to drag the Wothe back to life. The Spirit of Cleansing was powerless against the debuff. Healing did nothing to it, and I began to get the sinking feeling that the system was rubbing my nose in the fact that not everything in this Game was within the power of the player by the name Mahan. There were things he couldn't change and the sooner this player realized this the better. Yes, I left the mine very fast, received the Totem in a spectacular manner and ended up at the center of the scenario that unlocked Kartoss ... but I couldn't even heal an ordinary Wothe ...

A minute later my shoulders slumped. I managed to heal the Wothe completely, but the stupid debuff hadn't disappeared – as I hoped it would if I managed to restore all the Hit Points – and methodically continued to destroy the creature. I turned away in anger and frustration, wishing to see nothing, but the silence that descended was soon broken by Clutzer's voice:

"Why did you call Mahan a Guardian? When did he become one?"

"He was the one who cleansed this area of the forest from the taint," replied the Wothe. "The forest might have been called 'Dark' before, but now it could be more correctly titled 'Cursed'. This pure area needs a Guardian in order not to disappear, so Eluna appointed Mahan. He may not see it himself, but creatures like me can see the Guardian's halo above his head."

"Why did the forest become Cursed? Is the Patriarch behind it?" Clutzer continued his bombardment of questions, gradually helping to bring me back to normal. Why hadn't it occurred to me that even a dying Wothe could be questioned?

"The Patriarch has nothing to do with this. He has locked himself away at the heart of the forest and is doing all he can to fight off the Cursed Ones. The Dark Forest was cursed ten years ago, why or how I do not know. The trees whisper that a group of people came into the forest and brought the taint with them. Then came others who wanted to stop them, but they perished and a curse fell on the forest. For ten years I resisted it, but the curse was too strong in the end."

"We've taken so many arrows out of you. If they didn't come from the Patriarch's Vampires, who on earth shot you?"

"The Fallen. These are the ones who were captured and turned by the Cursed Ones and their Leader. You – and later I – were attacked by the scouting group of the Sergeant of the Fallen, the weakest Vampires of the Cursed Ones. May Eluna keep you from coming across a Lieutenant or a General ..."

"So where is this Leader and who is it?" I blurted out, but no answer followed. Even though the Wothe's Hit Points hadn't yet gone down to zero, it became clear that its Imitator was making clear that it had enough and had now departed for some well-deserved rest, so it could enter a new NPC later on.

Update of the quest chain 'Restoration of the Holy Relic, Step 2: Search for the Stone of Light'. Priest Midial's party has been destroyed. You must go to the settlement of the Clan Reardalox Vampires and find out from the Patriarch what really happened.

"So it looks like he really does exist," mumbled Eric. "Our non-con team-mates would skin us alive if their quest doesn't get updated too."

"It's a quest mob, maybe we should bury it," said Clutzer five minutes later, pointing out that the Wothe's body hadn't despawned. "It could stay lying here for a week. ... It just doesn't seem right ... polluting such a clean place, as it were. What do you say, Guardian?"

"I agree. Let's bury it right where it's lying. Unfortunately we have no spades, so we'll have to use our picks. You haven't forgotten how to swing them yet, I hope?" I tried to cheer up the others, though my own heartfelt heavy. What does it mean to be a Guardian? Why didn't I get a message about it? What responsibilities have just been foisted on me? What if burying a Cursed Creature in a cleansed zone is against the rules? Bah! Why is it when you need those non-con players the most they're nowhere to be found?

"Now I understand what you meant when you said that all kinds of rare stuff tends to gravitate towards you. We had next to zero chance of running across this Wothe," said Eric as soon as we started digging a hole. "This is a whole hidden branch of the quest progression and it doesn't even matter if we complete it or not, we're sure to get more rewards than before."

"We'll see," I brought our daydreaming tank to earth, "we have to make it to the Patriarch alive and it's not like I can create Chess Pieces like these every night to defend us from such scouting parties. And remember that the Wothe mentioned a Sergeant, a Lieutenant and a General. If the voice of the Sergeant made us tremble, can you imagine what will happen when we came across his superiors? We'll have to keep guard every night, even with four of us being periodically absent. We'll have to have a chat with Barsina. What if she's actually able to live inside the Game for an odd week: who knows with these girls? My gut tells me that we have some tough going ahead of us, so we'd be getting ahead of ourselves if we were to start thinking of bonuses. We might even end up losing levels if we're not careful!"

When everyone headed off to sleep, I decided to make a Malachite Jewelry Box with Lapis inlay, so that I would have somewhere to put the newly-created Chess Pieces. Jewelcraft didn't go up by a lot – just 35% along the progression bar – but with my 44 points this was quite enough. Before putting away the figurines, I took a look at the Dwarf Warrior riddle. There sure was enough there to wrack your brains over:

If you fail to provide the correct answer to the question on your second attempt, the clue of the Dwarves will vanish forever.
[Entry field]
Number of answers submitted: 0 of 2.
bnwtrufeoxrrzdmqsrzdgcrvyigowlqn
7 + 1 = 8
4 + 4 = 8
5 + 2 = 7
5 + 1 = 7

It was good that I found the warning about the two answer attempts in the first Dwarf I looked at, since that stopped me from putting in random numbers as I tried to guess the correct answer. Judging by the parameters of the question, this was one of the versions of a cypher and you had to determine which type of cypher was used, find the key – if that's what was needed – decipher the text and type it into the entry field. For the time being I had no idea what to do with the four equations, one of which didn't add up at all. What if this was the key to the answer? I would have to give it a real think, otherwise there wasn't much to do here – it was so 'easy' I'd be done in five minutes ...

In my dreams, that is. ... It looked like solving this one was definitely beyond me. Here you either had to know the key to the cipher or use powerful deciphering Imitators, which would pull this line apart into its components. It looked like I might have to end up going to Anastaria for help, something I really preferred to avoid. It was strange that she hadn't contacted me after I created the figurines to offer her congratulations. Either our Lady Paladin is getting slow or she was out of the Game. No matter, I bet one of Phoenix's logged-in members is already writing Stacey a message with the news. This level of information would be relayed to her as a matter of the utmost priority ...

"Leite!" Clutzer's frantic shout shook all the sleep out of me. Before I could even open my eyes, I flew out of the tent to see what had happened, although I could already make a pretty good guess. Leite's frame became gray: he had been sent for respawn. A quick assessment of the situation told me what happened to my fighter: just a couple of paces from our little glade three arrows were sticking out of the mist – three black arrows of the Fallen Vampires.

"You have chosen to ignore my words." The terrible vibration of the forest again shook me up, giving me goosebumps. Something had to be done about that otherwise the Sergeant would give us all a fit by just using his voice. "For this you will be destroyed."

"Bloodsucking bastards!" cursed Clutzer through his teeth. "Leite decided to have a look for what was out there in the forest and caught three arrows the moment he stepped out. There are three 100-level archers and a Sergeant of some higher level. They can down the three of us with a sneeze, and you won't fare much better. What if we set Slate on them? He is level 128, after all. Otherwise we'll have to wait until evening when the rest of the team turns up – which would be very far from ideal – and then hunt these things down, getting rid of them once and for all."

"Slate is the future Prince, we can't risk him." I gave myself a good shake, chasing away any residual sleepiness. "I'll try to pop out in a minute and see what's going on. And you can stop looking at me like a total idiot! I'll pump myself full of Spirits, make a bunch of scrolls and give you half, which you can use to hit them with from a distance. We'll see who comes out on top and who gets a kicking. I already have the third rank, and with the cloak I can summon Spirits of the fifth. ... Right, forget all that." I smiled as I saw

Eric and Clutzer looking at me with a silent question in their eyes: 'what the heck are these Spirit ranks and how do they work?' "The main thing is that we know that the scrolls will hit them hard and with precision. Eh ... If I only knew where this damned forest had its respawn point ... Leite could've been thrown a hundred kilometers away, which means we may never find him. Eric, can you check if you can use the scrolls that I make? Here," I opened the scroll scribing mode and penned down one with a Healing Spirit "the level difference between you and the scroll is less than 50, so it should be fine, but it's still best to check."

"Is the Spirit scroll used in the same way as one with a normal spell?" asked Eric right away. "I won't have to run around with a tambourine and sing songs, will I?"

"No, you won't." I smiled. "You just select and use it. Well?"

Eric and Clutzer could use the scrolls I created just fine, so I sat down to craft a pile of them and the world ceased to exist for about an hour. Scrolls are a tremendously useful thing in the world of Barliona, but they did come with a number of limitations that you had to take into account. Firstly, you couldn't use scrolls whose level exceeded yours by more than 50 points. Otherwise you'd end up with avid enthusiasts who would roll up level 1 characters, buy a bunch of scrolls of Armageddon and start nuking cities. Secondly, a stack of scrolls took up one slot in your bag, you could only hold one stack in your hands, a scroll put down on the ground immediately disappeared and – most unpleasantly – you could only put 4 scrolls into one stack. If I hadn't had the large bag that I received back at the Pryke Mine, I wouldn't have had any place to put the scrolls I got from Anastaria. This is why before large raids players would call entire meetings dedicated to choosing which scrolls would be indispensable and which could be replaced by a mage or a healer.

You got the paper for the scrolls from the Cartographer's Set, although it should be said that the Corporation tried to make some profit even on this front: for each white sheet of paper, which could only be used for making a spell scroll, a silver coin was deducted from your account. You could also buy a normal piece of paper to leave a message for another player, like Hellfire had done in Beatwick. But this sheet of paper would set you back 500 gold, without any visible benefit. If you had a Personal Mailbox, it was much easier to simply use that for mailing letters and items.

"Here you go." I handed Eric and Clutzer a hundred scrolls of Water Strike Spirit and fifty scrolls of Water Healing each. I had no idea what turn things might take and really didn't want to have to spend time on healing myself. "Eric, you were a tank, so you'll be a healer. You know the drill, so try not to let me down. Clutzer, with you it's easy: you see a Vampire, you use a scroll and then get the next one out. The scrolls contain 67 level Spirits of the 5th rank, so you'll keep the 100-level bloodsuckers happily occupied, despite the difference in levels. Ready? Let's roll ..."

The Shaman has three hands ...

I knew perfectly well that any song would do for activating the Spirit Summoning Mode, even a bunch of random sounds would work, but I had begun shamanism with this one, therefore ... truth be told, I've become attached to it. As long as the spirits are still summoned I won't change anything, following an old rule of programming: if it ain't broke, don't fix it. I cast Strengthening and Water Shield on myself; I stepped into the mist and immediately rolled forward, in the hope of missing any potential arrows.

Damage taken. Hit Points reduced by 6445: 8236 (Arrow hit) – 1791 (Physical defense). Total Hit Points: 13195 of 19640.

I was ready to feel pain, but not of such magnitude. ... My vision began to darken, but even through the pain I forced myself to roll to the side. ... Two black arrows hit the place where I had just been. Great! Now, I'll have to try and make sure I get caught by as few of these as possible – then we'll be fine and I won't turn into a screaming bundle of pain. Eric cast a scroll of Healing and I began to roll randomly from one side to another, trying to get at least one Vampire in my sights. If I spot that pretty boy, I'll place a mark on him and that's that – there will be one less Imitator in Barliona. My guys will unleash all those scrolls on him and I'll give them a hand too. ...

Damage taken ... Damage taken ... Damage taken ...

I came to myself when I was in the middle of the flight into which the three arrows had sent me: I take my hat off to Eric. My tanking-wizened dwarf did his job by throwing in a Healing between the second and third arrow. It mattered little whether his timing was intentional or completely accidental. More importantly, during my flight through the twilight of the foggy forest I caught the glimpse of a rushing shadow: 102-level Vampire. I slapped a mark on him that could only be seen by players – those that were part of the same group – and rushed back to the cleansed zone, dodging from left to right like a rabbit. I'd marked the target, so there was little sense in putting myself at any more risk.

The chilling scream of a Vampire hit by two Water Strikes at once were music to my ears and a reward for the painful acquisition of +10% to Endurance. The targeted Vampire was still in our sights, so I could see well enough that, of his 120-and-a-bit thousand Hit Points, 10000 were shaved off with each hit by a scroll. And because my fighters were working together, using one scroll every two seconds, the Vampire simply had no time to get to a safe distance. ... I wondered whether he'd drop any fangs after we were done with him. That's still loot, after all!

Soon Eric and Clutzer were surrounded by light, which lasted for a couple of seconds and told the rest of the world that they had just leveled up. Both gained +2 levels from one Vampire and gained the 'David and Goliath' achievement to boot. They did have an 80-level difference between them and the mob, after all. The downside was that they killed the mob with the scrolls, which meant that they didn't level up their main stats. Progressing through levels and gaining skills are different things, to which you must pay most careful attention.

"One down, now I'm off to get the second. This time there should be less damage, but don't let your guard down."

"Does it bite hard?" asked Eric, probably meaning the pain from the arrows.

"Yeah, a bit, but I can handle it. Compared to a certain turtle that I once ran across, or turning into a Dragon, as I've told you earlier, these arrows are more like mosquito bites."

"You'd better watch that those bites don't send you into pain shock, or you'll freeze like a statue and we'll have to think of a way to get you out ..."

We managed to handle the second and third Vampires following the same plan of attack: I came out, caught a few arrows, howled in pain, spotted the bloodsucker, slapped a mark on him and then ran back to the protection of my turf, letting Eric and Clutzer continue to level up. It looks like these NPCs have a rather unsophisticated Imitator inside them since they fell for the same trick three times in a row. Too bad that Leite was sent for respawn. Getting 4 extra levels from three Vampires – as was the case for Eric and Clutzer – to top up his 19 levels would have been just great.

"Hey, Sergeant! Is that the best your mongrels can do?" I shouted into the Dark Forest when a further foray out of the protection of the cleansed zone brought no result. "You were going to destroy us, so you'd better get on with it! Or don't you have the guts? Well?! I'm waiting! Will I have to scream so loud that the entire Dark Forest can hear that you're a wimp?"

I did all I could to get the last mob to attack me, but by the looks of it this Imitator did his homework when he went to school, since he was much smarter than his subordinates. He completely failed to fall for my taunts and stayed quiet, as if he had never been there. Emboldened, I checked over the three mobs that we killed, picking up forty-two and a bit gold off them. I also became the happy owner of three pairs of Vampire-fighter teeth. Judging by the lack of description, these were items for some quest that we would now have to find and to gain. The third bloodsucker we brought down dropped an Uncommon level-80 cloak, increasing Agility by 30 points. That should come in handy – I can give it to Clutzer when he levels up enough. But where did the Sergeant go? I didn't want to continue our journey while leaving such a powerful enemy at our back. We should also wait until Leite returns. We should write to him just as well that we had the Mailbox – and get him back.

"Right!" I said to get everyone's attention. "We have several possible courses of actions, but they can basically all be reduced to two: we either continue on our way or we stay here. Personally, I'm in favor of staying. Firstly, we need to wait for Leite to get back and, secondly, for the rest of the team."

"Agreed," replied Clutzer. "The rest of the team is all above level 100, so they won't be so easily ..."

"Guys, you'd better take a look at this," said Eric, breathing out slowly and looking wide-eyed at something behind me.

I turned around and saw what had surprised our tank so much: a tree was vigorously growing out of the Wothe's grave. What had at first been a small shoot – that was probably first spotted by Eric – was now a young tree busily growing, both in height and in width. But the biggest surprise was yet to come. The glade – the territory of which I had recently been made Guardian – was rapidly starting to grow in size. The tree was sucking all the taint from the Cursed Forest and in some mysterious way converting it into the nutrients it needed for growth. A thought flashed through my head that by consuming blackness the tree might itself become black, but it soon evaporated. The healthy look of the oak bore witness to the opposite. Where the two zones met, the mist was being absorbed into the ground, as if by a giant vacuum cleaner: black stains fell off the trees, revealing healthy bark underneath, hit the ground and were immediately absorbed into it like a sponge.

The strongest resistance came at the places where we destroyed the three Vampires, but soon even those spots fell under the fierce advance of a miracle being born. The purified area was also undergoing changes: all the trees on it were rapidly shrinking back into the ground, as if time had been set in reverse. The mast-like pines became smaller and smaller, turning into small trees, shoots and then disappearing altogether, clearing space for a meadow. These transformations had been going on for only ten minutes when we found ourselves under the canopy of an enormous oak. It covered the entire purified area with its shadow, which increased to no less than three hundred meters in diameter.

"The others will be sure to kill us when they see all this in the evening," I muttered the first thing that came into my head. "We should say that we found this glade already as it is and not created it ourselves ..."

"Guardian," Slate, who had just come out of the tent, bowed his head. But bowed it towards the oak instead of me! So is this oak the Guardian now? And am I just a dispensable 'place-holder'? Or am I indispensable after all? Damn, why is there always such a dearth of information?

"You may approach, Mahan." Judging by yet another attack of goosebumps, all the NPCs in this forest spoke in high resonance mode: the sound came from everywhere, but it was clear that it was the oak speaking. Or rather, the Oak, which was alive and wanted something from me ...

I stopped a couple of meters from the enormous trunk and, doing all I could not to give in to my nerves, tried to imagine how many players it would take to encircle this giant. If I take up this much space then, supposing that the trunk is a perfect circle, we'll need around ...

"Seventy-two sentients with the same arm-span as you," the resonating voice sounded again through the glade. "What you're thinking is quite evident on your face, so have no fear: I can't read your thoughts. You have my thanks, former Guardian of the zone, for not letting yourself be destroyed and finding a way for me, the Guardian of the Dark Forest, to be reborn."

"I was not alone," I quickly managed to add, in case we were about to be handed many bonuses, or punishments – whatever luck had in store for us. "Everyone currently in this glade helped to bring about the birth of the Guardian. Even the one who isn't here right now, but will be back soon."

"I know. The Free Citizen who has been sent to the Grey Lands will reappear in my glade in ten hours. He will also receive a reward, just as all those present here will. But you were the Guardian of the zone and you sacrificed this gift granted you by Eluna so that I could be reborn. I know full well the extent of your sacrifice and what it was you gave up, so I will try to compensate you for your loss. Stretch out your hand ..."

Very carefully, as if fearing that it might hurt me, a branch stretched from the tree, touched my hands and immediately drew back, like a frightened dog. Taking no heed of the branch's strange behavior, I looked down and saw a small wooden object, whose properties were eloquently 'illuminating':

Left Earring of the Guardian of the Dark Forest. Item class: Unique.

That's it. No bonuses, no achievements, no ... nothing at all, in fact, except for this piece of wood and an incomplete piece of wood at that. The Right Earring was still out there somewhere. It was, of course, a unique and interesting object, probably with a story of its own, but this would be of more interest to real lore-fanatics of Barliona, like Anastaria. I'll sell this earring to her; she'll be sure to put it to good use. The gaming avatar allowed you to put on various earrings, bracelets or whatever else a player could think of, but these were purely decorative. Even a second neck-chain would give you nothing save an extra weight around your neck. Items that improved player character stats were quite strictly defined.

"I thank you, Guardian, for such a rare gift." Being polite to NPCs, especially those with whom you have Attractiveness higher than 80, should be a cast-iron rule for every player. Otherwise you're no player, just a total noob. As for the gift ... what gift can a tree give? Just a piece of wood like this, so it'd be pointless being upset at the Guardian.

Eric and Clutzer were in turn given wooden daggers and Slate a disc or a shield of some sort, which made him so happy you'd think he received an invitation to be the groom at Tisha's wedding – handed to him personally by the Emperor. We'll have to ask him what that giant coin-like thing was.

"That is not all, former Guardian of the zone," the Tree addressed me once again. "Although you have laid down your powers, I will permit you to use the reward to which you are entitled, especially because its time to come forth is near. But first I would like to ask you to perform a service. The Dark Forest must be saved. It has to be cleansed of this taint! I don't know where it came from, but it has no place here."

Quest available: Cleansing of the Dark Forest.

Description: Barliona's Dark Forest, which stretches many hundreds of kilometers on the East side of the continent, is facing a calamity. A curse has been put on it. Its Guardian was destroyed and its Sentinels defiled. After rekindling hope in the forest when you helped the Dark Forest's Guardian to be reborn from a dead, but unbroken, Sentinel, you have been given the impossible task: to destroy this taint. Where it came from and how one should fight it remains unknown.

Quest type: Unique scenario.

Limitations: only you can pass this quest to other players.

Maximum number of participants: not more than 2000.

Reward: The second part of the Dark Forest's Guardian's gift (if the first part is already in your possession), +500 Reputation to all encountered factions, +40 to any main stat, +10 character levels.

"In its current state the Dark Forest holds many dangers, so you must bring others to aid you. But you shouldn't bring all of Barliona here, or the taint might get a fright, vanish and reappear in another forest. Find the golden mean, Shaman! The Dark Forest must be cleansed!"

After accepting the quest and sharing it with the rest of my group, I sat down right under the Tree, leaning my back against it and, not knowing where to put the new gift, stuck it into my ear. Yup, I'll be running around with just one rough wooden earring on, looking like a complete dolt. This way everyone will see the kind of presents you get from Guardians of giant forests.

"I had a bit of a think." Finally Clutzer started to make good on all the praise heaped on him by Anastaria. He was finally putting his brain to work. "And it occurred to me that this scenario and the one we're doing for Elizabeth should be completed together. If we find the Stone of Light and find out what happened to the Priests, we will find the source of the taint. I'd bet my boots that these quests are linked. I also think that the local Dark Ones will declare open season on us and our small group will get pwned by a certain fluffy polar beastie.

"You don't say ... how the heck can someone from Paris be familiar with swear words all the way from what used to be Russia before the unification?" I chuckled. "'Fluffy polar beastie' – a.k.a. 'arctic fox' – is from there; there's no such expression in modern lingo."

"Bah! All the best swear words come from there, 'moi droog'. They're beautiful, melodious and let you use the same word to express a multitude of meanings just by varying intonation ... like a song. If you just want a sing-along, you can use any old pop tune, but if you want to become a great singer, you have to study the classics, modern innovations and all the other key genres. I'm a good singer, not a great one – German swearing is a little beyond me – but I aim to do a good job of it."

"All right, we'll hear what you've got later, when we're somewhere more suitable," grinned Eric. "So what are we going to do? Whichever way you look at it, we'll never be able to complete this quest on our own. The Guardian said right from the off that you need a group, which means gathering a large crowd and doing that quite soon. I agree with Clutzer – we're going to be hunted now. We let the Sergeant slip away and he'll be back, angry and nursing a grudge. He'll probably bring a Lieutenant along too, for backup."

"So tell us what you've come up with. I can see that you've got something." I looked at Clutzer, who appeared to be thinking something through as he rubbed his chin.

"We'll have to get mercenaries, like Barsina,"

put in Eric, but Clutzer immediately corrected him:

"That won't work. A mercenary's aim is to make money, not gain reputation. They don't give a damn about the latter. This quest doesn't have a monetary reward, so mercenaries won't do. We need to invite those for whom the words 'Reputation with all factions' mean a lot and who would be prepared to hand over half the clan treasury for +10 levels and +40 to all stats. Damn, I've just let slip about the clan part: I would've liked for you to figure that bit out for yourselves. But you can see what I'm getting at, right? Hellfire, Anastaria and others from Phoenix. Undigit from Azure Dragons, Etamzilat from Heirs of the Titans ... players who have gained level 300 and for whom each new level is a reason to celebrate ..."

"Clutzer, you're a genius! We could earn so much cash this way that it'll last us for the rest of the Game and then some!"

"I don't know about 'genius'," smiled Clutzer, "but the idea does have merit. Now we need to draft a proper agreement, which will limit the rights of everyone except members of the Seathistles clan. I can do that and when Leite, our most bribable official – I mean that most affectionately, no need to look at me like that – gets back, he'll check it over and amend where necessary, as we did with the Clan Agreement."

"How do we connect the High Priestess scenario to it all?" I asked Clutzer. "We should try to make sure that no-one (or only a very limited number of people) knows about the existence of the second quest. At the same time, the sharing of that quest should happen only via myself or it will spread like a virus through all the clans. It could easily end up being completed in the blink of an eye, altogether without us."

"But how do we even tell the high-level players about the Guardian's quest?" put in Eric. "We're here and they're all the way in Anhurs. Do we send them letters? They'll never believe us."

"I'll handle that part. I have a communication amulet for contacting Anastaria. I'll start with her and then we'll see. I'll invite Plinto as well – his behavior was just a little too strange when I was attacked. I have a communication amulet for contacting him too, so we'll have a chat. I have nothing to lose and something tells me that debts like that have to be repaid. Although, stop! Guys, we're getting a bit ahead of ourselves! We've decided everything between the three of us, but what about Leite, Dukki, Sushiho and Elenium. Even Barsina, if you think about it! I think it would be wrong to take any steps before discussing things with them! We should wait until the evening and only then start offering the quest to everyone. Is that all right with you?"

There were no objections, so I closed my eyes for a nap. It felt like only few moments later when I opened them as Clutzer was shaking me like a doll.

"Mahan, wake up! You have to see this!"

I quickly checked the clock and was surprised to see that almost six hours had gone by and then looked to where Clutzer was pointing. A Copper Vein. A Large Copper Vein. A Tin Vein. A Large Tin Vein. A Marble Vein. A Silver Vein. A Large Silver Vein, Iron ...

all the veins were standing next to each other, taking up about a third of the glade. The other two thirds weren't exactly empty either: one was full of herbs, where Eric was already vigorously grazing, and the other was full of small trees, probably intended for Lumberjacks.

"And how are we in the middle of a resource El Dorado all of a sudden?" I couldn't help saying. I noticed that as soon as Eric picked a flower another identical one sprung up in its place a moment later.

"I have no idea what's going on here, but our professions are being leveled up, which is the main thing," said Clutzer, sharing the happy news. "I've got my Herbalism up to the maximum, so I'll start on the Lumberjacking now. Eric will be finishing with the herbs soon as well. His main profession, Smithing, has been leveled up pretty well, so he'll get further than me with Herbalism. No matter, I'm a Wood Carver, so I'll be getting some materials for leveling up in that. Look how much wood is growing around here. Right, I've got you up, now it's up to you what you want to do next – I'm quite busy at the moment. I wanted to wake you straight away when it started, but the Guardian wouldn't let me. He put up a dome of twigs around you, but as soon as that was gone, I shook you awake to fill you in. But now, I'm off." Clutzer ran off towards the trees and soon the surrounding area was filled with the sound of the axe and Anastaria's amulet exploding in a torrent of swearing.

"And good day to you too, beautiful!" I greeted

the girl, activating the amulet. At least I hope it's her and not Ehkiller or Hellfire. That would be a bit awkward!

"Where the heck are you?" Instead of a normal 'Hello', something between an agitated and a shouting voice hit me from the amulet. You never know in Stacey's case. "I couldn't connect to you for five hours! The amulet went mad and kept telling me that you were outside the reachable zone! That can't happen in Barliona! Amulets can be accessed at any point in the Game, even in other worlds that unlock for special quests! But you were completely out of reach! I even contacted the developers, asking why the amulet was behaving so strangely, but their reply was that everything occurring was in accordance with game logic. How did you manage to hide?"

"I was asleep," I had no idea how to respond to this barrage.

"Asleep? The amulet should have been screaming like mad until you woke up."

"Stacey, why were you calling in the first place?" I decided to quickly change the subject to dampen Anastaria's onslaught. If I started responding in the same tone, I could easily blurt out where I was, what I was doing and how to get the quest. I think not. I needed a 'time out' to gather my thoughts and set out my conditions.

"What's that? Someone's chopping wood in the background? Are you in the middle of a logging camp? How did you manage to hide from the communication amulet?" The girl continued to dig for information, so I went on the offensive:

"Stacey, give me the password for full access to the Phoenix clan treasury."

There was a sudden silence on the other end of the amulet and then Anastaria said in a happy voice:

"Great! I was beginning to fear that you'd spill all the beans to me now. Still, I had to give it a try, no?" This was followed by a little laugh on the other end of the line, as if she was savoring every moment of this conversation. "I wanted to congratulate you. Looks like you've somehow managed to get hold of some Lapis Lazuli on your own, right?"

"Look, here's my standard answer: what makes you think that I was the one that created the Dwarves? It's not like I even need them."

"I didn't say a word about the Dwarves. I congratulated you on getting hold of the Lapis, that's all."

"Damn! Stop trying to confuse me already! Instead tell me what's a 'zone Guardian' and what one does with it?"

"A zone Guardian?" her voice sounded surprised, as if she'd never heard of such a thing, but I felt with every fiber of my being that Stacey knew full well what it was. "It sounds familiar, but I just can't remember. Where did you hear this expression?"

"Well, you see, I have no idea how, but I managed to remove the taint from a small plot of a cursed forest, after which a half-dead local Woodwothe crawled over to me and named me a Guardian. But I haven't received any announcements about it. So now I'm sitting here and working out what's to be done next. Because something tells me that I shouldn't leave this place."

"Which forest are you in right now?"

"Stacey ..."

"Mahan, do you want the information? If you do, let's both share."

"Yeah, right. So this is the bit where I tell you where I am and instantly get landed with a hundred-strong Phoenix strike-force flying around the area and getting in the way of me completing the quest. I've been there in Beatwick, when Hellfire destroyed my wolves because he happened to be passing through and was bored. I can't tell you my location."

"All right, I'll look up what a Guardian is and how a player can end up being one and get back to you. But remember, you'll owe me."

Just a few minutes later Anastaria called back.

"Looks like you've gotten caught up in something big over there!" came the girl's cheerful voice. "When I get kicked out of Phoenix, I'll be sure to join you. Interesting things keep happening to you and I want in. Would you accept this newbie girl into your clan again?"

"Only if you make it through the selection process," I replied, mirroring Anastaria's tone. " The cookies were a one-time-only offer. To enter the clan a second time you'll have to try very hard."

"Oh, I will, to be sure. So, what are zone Guardians and what do you do with them? There isn't all that much information out there, because even though Guardians periodically appear in Barliona, the logic behind their appearance hasn't been completely understood yet. You weren't given an announcement for the simple reason that you would only have been a Guardian until you get sent for respawn. After this your zone would disappear and be absorbed back into the surrounding world, in your case, a forest. No-one can cause you any harm in the zone of which you are a Guardian and, essentially, this is it. We can only guess what the developers meant by this title, but, personally, I think that this could be connected to some hidden quest chain. You'll have to dig a bit deeper. I don't suppose you need the aid of a mercenary? We could sign an Agreement stating that I would be acting purely as a hired hand for the duration of your quest and ensuring there wouldn't be hordes of Phoenix players running around. It would be quite interesting to finally get to the bottom of this Guardian business. Often players themselves don't realize that they've been made a Guardian and only find this out once they've been sent for respawn and the relevant message pops up. But here we have a unique case of you being told who you are. You haven't died yet, I hope?"

"No, I haven't died and I don't need hired help right this moment. Let's be in touch in the evening. I may have a thing or two to tell you."

"Mahan, I gave you the information you needed, so you owe me! If you want to stay on good terms, learn to share!"

"Stacey, the information that you just gave me

isn't worth me granting you access to anything. Check your mail for the description of a certain quest – sorry, I won't be adding a proper link to it, since it will show you where we are. Once you read it you'll see for yourself that I'm right." I opened the Mailbox and copied the conditions of the Guardian's quest, while deleting any mention of the Dark Forest. Let Anastaria turn on her brain and try to figure out for herself what this is all about.

The silence from the amulet seemed to last an eternity.

"For a day after a plot of land chooses you as its Guardian, it will produce rare ores, trees and herbs. Some of them will match the level of your gathering profession, but the majority will be much higher. In a zone like this the leveling up in all professions happens at double the normal speed. I wanted to find out where you are in order to send a team of gatherers there. There have been cases of a Diamond Vein, Redwood or Emperor's Bloom appearing in such places. Do I need to tell you how much all of this can be worth? The resources appear 12 hours after the event, and judging by the chopping sounds in the background, you already know about that. This is my full answer about the Guardian."

"And why couldn't you tell me this straight away?"

"And why couldn't you tell me about the quest straight away?" Anastaria replied with a question of her own.

"What's with the habit of answering a question

with a question?"

"And what's with the habit of driving a girl nuts?"

"You're not married by any chance?" smiled Eric, who had finished gathering the herbs and was listening to our verbal sparring with some interest. "You bicker like you're a seasoned couple."

"Is that Eric you've got there?" asked Anastaria, showing off her good memory.

"The one and only. Let's try the following: you've already seen the description of the quest. I will call you in the evening and invite you to do it with us. My clan comes first, so if anyone objects, there'll be no quest sharing. Stacey, I will need more than just the Phoenix people. Get hold of Undigit, Etamzilat and other high-level players. The more people there are from different clans, the lower the price for taking part will be. Yes, you heard me right – anyone who wants to take part in this quest will have to pay. The phrase that I am the only one who can pass on the quest is no exaggeration, but comes straight out of the original quest description. Think it over, gather some people and we'll speak in the evening. Deal?"

"All right. Until then." When the situation called for it, Anastaria was quite capable of speaking plainly and briefly, without any jests or chuckles.

The girl disconnected and I sat down on the ground, holding my head in my hands. As much as I had wanted to wait for the others, I failed to keep shtum about the quest and, essentially, made the decision for the rest of the clan on my own. Never mind, the rest of the team should be here in three hours and I'll explain to them that I had little choice.

"Hello everyone, I'm a bit early today." About ten minutes later Barsina appeared in the glade. "Wow! This is some nice place you've found to make camp! How did you manage to find this? And what's this quest update?" I breathed a sigh of relief: the High Priestess's quest had updated for everyone in the group. "Mahan, would you tell me what happened here while I was away? How come Leite's dead?" Barsina asked after noticing that his frame was grey.

"Well, there's been a bit of a shoot-out," I replied for us all. Eric and Clutzer were lost to the world with wood chopping as they leveled up in the Lumberjacking profession, so I had to do all the talking. After I told Barsina of our misadventures she asked a reasonable question:

"You won't mind if I do a bit of gathering of my own? Our agreement doesn't seem to prohibit it, but I wasn't involved in the business of bringing this about."

"Be my guest." I flexed my shoulders, got my pick out and headed for the Veins. "Just don't be too surprised by what you see.

"See?" asked the girl, but I didn't reply, having already thrown myself at an Iron Vein. With my level 52 in Mining, I just had 8 more levels to go until I could mine Gold, but the main profession limitation wouldn't permit me to gain more than +2. That's a pity ... should I perhaps focus on leveling up my Jewelcraft instead?

"It renews itself!" Barsina's astonished voice came from somewhere to the right, as she saw for herself how a new flower sprung up in place of the one she had just picked. She did have a surprise after all, I chuckled, as I continued to strike at the Vein, despite me warning her and everything!

After increasing my Mining to its current possible maximum (which was limited by my maximum level in Jewelcraft), I sat down under the Oak and began to make rings. Eric and Clutzer followed my example and started to level up in their main Professions, since they had plenty of crafting materials to hand. When Leite appeared two hours later, the Guardian handed him a wooden sword, same as the others, and I sent him off to gather herbs, chop wood and mine veins. Leite's main profession was Alchemy, so he was only able to get it up to 10 with herbs, after that you needed special ingredients like Rat Tails, Spider Legs and Field Mole Whiskers. I had no idea where to get all of these in the Dark Forest, so Leite's leveling up wouldn't get very far. Never mind, the main thing was to lay the foundations – it would be easier after that.

Anastaria was right: the speed of leveling up in the professions doubled and at times even trebled. In just three hours, until the rest of the group showed up, I got my Jewelcraft as far as 50. Eh ... if I could only get to the trainer now ... he had so many recipes for this level that subsequent leveling up would have been sheer pleasure ...

"Listen up, everyone!" After I crafted the last

ring for the day, I addressed all the industrious herbivores. The players were flying at the herbs as if they'd never seen or gathered them before in their lives. That side of the glade was periodically filled with surprised exclamations and happy shouts whenever someone gained yet another level in Herbalism. "Guys! Stop grazing like a herd of hungry cows. I need you here for ten minutes; it's a serious matter!"

It's true when they say that as soon as a player sees a freebie, he completely loses his head. *"So many herbs ... Aaaahh! We need to gather them! Gather them all!"* It never even occurred to anyone that their bags would never be able to fit this much hay. They would stuff their sacks full of Daisies, increase their Herbalism to the point where they could gather Yarrow, then chuck it all out and start gathering Yarrow. Why they couldn't throw things away as they gathered them remained a mystery to me. Probably it broke some religious statute of their greedy inner zoo.

"So that's how it is." I finished my retelling of the quest and the potential Agreements with the leading clans. "What do you say?"

"It makes sense to me", said Barsina thoughtfully, after Sushiho, Dukki and Elenium expressed their approval. "But would this affect our agreement? We signed it for four weeks and at the moment there's a risk of it not being fulfilled. Ten levels and +40 stats points, in essence comes to almost +18 levels, which is a very nice, but ..."

"Barsa, I totally see where you're coming from, so I can offer only this: I'm sending you the

Seathistles Clan Agreement. Have a look at it and if you find nothing else amiss, we could add the restrictions on open flirting. When you complete quests with us, this one and any others, you will receive as much as any other member of the clan. The degree of the reward will be proportional to the part you take in the quest – it's all there, have a look. I have nothing against simply paying you something for making extra use of your help, but right now I have no idea how much we will earn in the end. It could be a million or a couple of coppers. To avoid these problems, simply join Seathistles, at least temporarily. I think this will give us a fair way to distribute future rewards. What do you say?"

Barsina stayed silent for a moment, probably reading through the text of our Agreement and weighing something up, and then looked at me and at the other Fighters awaiting her decision and said, "Send me the invite. You have a great Agreement – you can see straightaway that whoever drafted it knew what he was doing. Was it you?"

"No, but we have a guy in the clan who, one might say, is a specialist in this area." I invited Barsina into the clan as a Fighter and pointed out a pleased-looking Leite: "that's him over there, beaming like he's just won a prize. If no-one else has any other proposals, let's talk about what we'll be asking from our dearly desired top players."

When the discussion was coming to an end, Barsina proposed something else that could gain us additional profit. Why waste resources by throwing them away when you can invite high-level gatherers and allow them to graze on the glade for a certain percentage of the profit? Both they and the clan will benefit. So, looks like fresh blood was good for the clan. Well done, Barsa. She thinks like a true mercenary: how to spot a cash cow and milk it for all it's worth. We could use pragmatic thinkers like that in the clan.

"Speaking!" Anastaria's cool voice came from the amulet. How had she managed to get upset with me? Doesn't seem like her.

"Hi, this is Mahan ..."

"We're not ready yet, we need more time. Call back in three hours."

"This is about something else. Do you have a couple of high-level gatherers of herbs, ore and wood to hand? The glade will soon disappear and it seems stupid and wrong to lose a chance for profit because of excessive greed."

"Then why didn't you invite people in the first place?" Anastaria briefly raised her voice, but immediately calmed down. "The Guardian's resources appear only for a day and we've already wasted so much time. My people are ready and await your signal. The Mages will make a portal – you just have to give the coordinates. You can look them up if you ..."

"I know how to look up coordinates. I'm sending you an agreement, stating that aside from the gatherers not a single Phoenix member will show up in this territory without my permission in the next 5 hours. I'm sorry, but I don't want to be trampled over by your Fighters until we settle things properly. Finally, I want half of everything you gather."

"Ten percent maximum," the girl immediately replied. "I realize that you're on a roll now, but even 10% is too much for a beginner clan, if you consider that you will be profiting without lifting a finger."

"Forty percent, but that's only out of respect for you," I parried. "Stacey, there's little sense for me in sharing my location for just ten percent. Nothing would be better than such a pittance. Forty! I'm giving you too much as it is!"

"All right, twenty. Think about it: consider the labor of my Fighters and the fact that for you herbs will be little more than something to hang from the ceiling – something that you wouldn't have any idea what to do with. A fifth of what's been gathered is a reasonable price for access to the plot. Just think of the expense we'll incur by opening a portal to you. We have to recoup it somehow."

"Thirty, and that's final. The portal will cost you nothing, in total. You just said yourself that your players will be opening it. So what if your Mages will be without mana for a day or two – it will do them good. They'll level up their Intellect."

"Agreed," came the reply from the amulet after a little while. "Thirty percent of what's gathered will go to Seathistles. Send your agreement."

"The Dark Forest ...," she said in a thoughtful voice after the agreement had been signed and I gave her our coordinates, "I wouldn't have thought."

"And also ..." I managed to remember an important point for the clan before the girl turned off the amulet.

"What now? I agreed to your conditions! Everything's been signed!"

"It's not a condition, but a request. While here in the zone I leveled up my Jewelcraft to fifty, but I have no recipes with which to continue leveling up. Can you ask someone from the clan to send me some of the recipes sold by the profession trainer specifically for this level?"

"All right, they'll send it to you with the bill and you can just pay them back later."

"Then, since my foot is off the brake, I might as well try my luck further: can you do the same for Smithing, Wood Carving and Alchemy? In the case of Alchemy I need non-herb ingredients. And the recipes need to be from level one to a hundred inclusive, for all four professions. I'll repay the money, with commission on top, if needed, and I'll owe you a cookie for your help."

"You're one brazen Shaman, I can tell you that. Bork here heard you. He'll get everything done before the end of the day and send all the required recipes and ingredients in a letter. And don't forget about the cookie; I'm only helping you because you promised me one. Right, we'll be with you in a couple of minutes."

"We? Whatever; we'll figure it out. I need to make another call now."

"What?" You couldn't mistake Plinto's rough voice for anyone else.

"Greetings to the self-styled Robin Hood," I said, "the rescuer of the poor and needy. It's Mahan bothering you, if you didn't catch on yet."

"Where'd you get my amulet? Ah! I was the one that handed it to you ... Mahan, put the amulet on a stone and smash it hard with a hammer. If I catch you, I'll send you to a respawn point and keep you there until the Heralds intervene."

"While you're trying to think of more original ways to kill me, take a look in your Mailbox. I've sent you the description of one little quest, which I reckon will pique your interest."

"Did ya bang yer head real bad today? Get your ass to Anhurs in an hour and I'll show you just ..." Plinto suddenly fell silent. He had probably read my letter.

"Yes, exactly." When the silence from the amulet became worrying (what if Plinto was so overjoyed he had had a heart-attack?), I decided to give the Rogue a nudge back towards the conversation.

"Who else will be there?"

"I don't know. I offered it to Anastaria and suggested that she gather all the top players. Let's talk again in a few hours and discuss terms."

"I can't afford it," he said and I noted that when the need arose Plinto could speak without playing the 'demon on a rampage' just fine. "I don't have that much cash since I got thrown out, nor do I have any gear that would suit you."

"What has money got to do with it? You helped

me and I'll help you. And then we can go back to hating each other and killing each other at every meeting. Or, rather, you'll do the killing and I'll do the running away."

"So what do I have to do to get to you?"

"We're quite far away at the moment, so please contact Anastaria and tell her that I have personally requested that you take part."

"You do of course realize that I'll owe you for these ten levels?"

"Exactly. Having the third-highest level player in my debt is a very nice and useful thing."

"I'll get in touch with the b*tch," Plinto assured me and put down the amulet. So who's going to tell me what the heck that was about? Why did we have one Plinto before he read up on the quest and a completely different one after? Is everything he does purely for the benefit of an audience? It's like he's created an image and is following it to the letter. So why was he kicked out of the Dark Legion? Perhaps ... what if he simply didn't want to move to Kartoss? I'll have to try to talk to him later.

I put aside Plinto's amulet and waited for the Phoenix team to show up, but I was feeling uneasy. There was something I hadn't done ... something I hadn't thought of ... if that crowd turns up here now as it is, no matter how big or small, we won't complete the quest ...

"Hello Antsinthepantsa! This is Mahan. We showed off our totems to each other in the Library. I

urgently need your help – your help as a Shaman. I'm attaching the description of a quest. I have no idea what link it might have with Shamans, but my gut tells me that if you're not with us, we will fail. I can't explain it. If you're interested, please contact Anastaria, the head of Phoenix, right now and say that it is my personal request to add you to the team."

As soon as I sent the letter, I breathed a sigh of relief. I couldn't explain why, but without a High Shaman – one who was doing everything possible to become a Harbinger – there was no completing this quest. And Antsinthepantsa is the only Shaman of the right rank that I knew.

"I'll be there. You owe me a training session between Draco and Bussy."

"Hello everyone!" Five minutes later a portal appeared next to the Oak, out of which stepped Anastaria. "Guardian." The girl bowed respectfully to the tree and to my great surprise the branches began to move, touching Stacey's head, and a green sphere immediately began to shine around her. The Oak put some kind of a buff on Anastaria! So why didn't it do anything like that to us, its creators? Heartless piece of timber! That's what you get if you've leveled up in Reputation with everything and anything! "Two on the ore, two on the trees and Rick and myself will take the herbs. Off we go!"

Well, well! Aside from being a favorite of various

Guardians, she also happens to be a high-level gatherer! I was really itching to access her properties and have a good dig through everything in there!

"Mahan," Anastaria paused from picking some kind of a shiny herb, "I've handed over the amulet to Ehkiller; he's now the one gathering people at our castle. Plinto and someone named Antsinthepantsa will also be there. By the way, why them?"

"I owe Plinto so it's time I paid him back and we won't get anywhere without Antsinthepantsa." My answer should have made Anastaria very thoughtful. Let her wrack her brains about how on earth I picked up such a debt and what this lady Shaman could have that Anastaria herself does not, and without which the quest is doomed to failure.

"Are you sure about Antsinthepantsa?" Stacey's voice sounded clearly interested now. "The quest description that you sent me made no reference to Shamans. Or did you just neglect to send me the full description?"

"No, that was the full version. Since you're here already, there's little point concealing it." I sent Anastaria the full link to the Guardian's quest. "And why aren't you working? Want to leave my clan without its due income?"

Anastaria gave a hearty laugh and returned to resource gathering. I spent some time watching various herbs being picked by a girl who was exceptionally splendid in every respect. It never occurred to me before why gathering herbs took such a long time. I'd thought that all you had to do was walk over, pick one and move on to the next. But things were not quite so simple. In order to gather herbs fit for use, and not end up with trash that even traders wouldn't accept, you had to diligently measure the height and width of the stalk, then figure out their ratio and times that by the herb type, measure the resulting distance from the ground and thus find the only point at which the herb could be cut. This wasn't resource gathering, but an exercise in mathematics. It was so much easier being a Lumberjack or a Miner – you just stand there and swing an axe or a pick, without a second thought. Although ... I recalled how my pick ricocheted during my initial training at Pryke ... in the end every trade came with its own difficulties ...

I got infected by the Phoenix fighter-gatherers' industriousness and brought my Jewelcraft up to 55 (going any further would've just been a waste of resources) and then moved on to conquer the Iron and then Gold Ore Veins. I wasn't about to miss out on earning my own share of the loot.

"'Killer says that everyone's gathered now", said Anastaria four hours later. "He's ready for your call."

I took a few deep breaths – preparing for strenuous negotiations between a small fry and a bunch of hungry sharks – and made the call. Previously, the guys and I had decided that we could begin negotiations at one million per participant, gradually lowering it to six hundred thousand.

At the same time, I set the maximum number of players to thirty. I had little desire to make this into a free-for-all and eighteen million gold would give the Seathistles clan a good start, even with player salaries taken into account.

"Hello, Mahan. This is Ehkiller." Our conversation began in an official tone, putting everyone in a businesslike mood. "As you requested, I've gathered thirty-two players of level three hundred or above. This includes players who expressed an interest and were currently in the Game and also the two players who say that you personally requested their participation in this venture. Please confirm this. Everyone has seen the quest description that you gave us; now, over to you."

"Good day everyone." You had to admit that taking part in negotiations at this level over a communicator was somewhat easier that face-to-face. You didn't have to worry about watching the finer points of your own body language. Although ... I did have Anastaria sitting right next to me; having by now completely abandoned herb gathering she had, like the rest of my team, begun to carefully listen to the conversation. "No point beating about the bush, so I'll get right to business. I confirm that Plinto and Antsinthepantsa must take part in this quest. Their terms have already been agreed. As for the others, according to my modest estimates, for a 300+ level player gaining an extra 10 levels are priceless, so I've valued them at a million and a half per player. It's not like I'm forcing anyone to take part," I added when I heard outraged exclamations from the other end of the line.

"We'll call you back in five minutes. We have to discuss your conditions," said Ehkiller, turning off the amulet.

"Not forcing anyone?" Why is it that every time we speak, Anastaria looks more pleased than the cat that got the cream? What's so funny that each time she speaks with me she chuckles so much? "After all, I already know the location and have seen the quest description, so I could just step out and return with around four hundred thousand players. Then we'd see how you are 'not forcing anyone'."

"You have leveled up your Reputation with me to the required level, so you won't be doing anything of the sort," I replied in a similar tone, not wishing to show her that I wasn't in the mood for jokes at the moment. "And you also hinted that you will be joining my clan once you're thrown out of Phoenix, so it's not like you would want to upset your future employers. So be it, I'll take you without putting you through any trials. You've convinced me."

"Thank you, oh benefactor! What would I do without you?"

"Exactly! Who are you in Phoenix? You're just Anastaria, the head of this clan and just coincidentally officially the most beautiful girl for the past few years," I ventured, not wishing for Anastaria to have the last word.

"Absolutely. There's no way could I miss the opportunity to become the most important and powerful first deputy leader of the great Seathistles clan, which has managed to scale the great heights of level one. That really is food for thought."

"Just think faster" – man, she sure has a sharp tongue: she can twist those words so well that you'd spend half an eternity trying to catch up – "or Ehkiller will call now and start demanding that discount. You don't know everything yet, my beauty. Prince! What are you planning to do at night if you spend all day asleep?" I shouted into the tent.

"I'm not asleep." Slate's head emerged from the tent. "It's just that this wonderful dwelling can, among other things, keep out all unwanted noise. I've had quite enough of the sound of mining picks back in Beatwick, so I decided to hide for a bit. Bah, they're still at it!" Slate made a face as if suddenly beset with toothache. "Right, I'm going back in."

Slate dove back into the tent and I turned again to Stacey.

"You see, there's still much you don't know ... " We had discussed this point with the entire group, so I wasn't winging it. Whichever way you look at it, going up against the Vampires would be very difficult, the Sergeant's squad was proof of that. If we come across a Lieutenant, we're dead meat. We needed additional muscle, so why not Stacey?"

"The future Prince of Malabar, right? The fiancé of the new Princess?"

"Yup."

"And he's in your tent miles away from Anhurs."

"Yup."

"Where he's hiding from the noise ... because

he's had enough of the sound of striking picks ..."

"Yup."

"Quit it with the 'yups'! I'm trying to figure out how you got him to come with you and why the Princess would let him go, and you're just throwing yups at me. Spill the beans already!"

"I know some more words, as it happens: in your dreams!"

"You have another quest!" Anastaria lit up and her changeless smile spread across her face. "It's not like you were naive enough to hand over another quest to the top players! And here's poor me all ready to lament the fact that the promise of money had suddenly made a normal player out of you – that you've suddenly acquired a brain! You gave me quite a fright there, Mahan! You owe me a cookie for the recipes, but please answer me just this one question: do you have another quest connected to the Prince or to the Dark Forest? I'm not even asking what it is, just tell me whether you have one or not."

"No, I do not have one more quest." I gave the girl a completely honest answer. And why not? It's not like I lied in the slightest. "I don't have ONE more quest." As the glint of excitement started to die away in her eyes and she was already beginning to turn into a Snow Queen again, I added: "I have TWO!"

CHAPTER SIX
THE FIRST BATTLE OF THE DARK FOREST

"MAHAN, IT'S EHKILLER." THE VIBRATING amulet saved me from Anastaria, who had already taken a deep breath and was ready to tell me what a bastard I was. Putting my finger on my lips, I indicated that exploding in indignation right this minute could seriously jeopardize her 'Snow Queen' reputation and breathed a sigh of relief. I managed to avoid the most dangerous first flash of anger – in a moment Stacey would regain self-control and be thinking of how to use the situation for her own profit. I just had to make sure some of that profit went my way as well.

"You have my undivided attention!"

"You must realize that a million and a half per player is too much. We've gathered around fifty potential participants, some of them couldn't make it to the meeting at such short notice, but indicated that they want in. To be more exact, we've got fifty-three players, excluding Plinto and Antsinthepantsa."

"Then it should be fifty-two – we've already come to a separate arrangement with Anastaria." I looked at the girl who had raised her eyebrow in surprise. To be fair, aside from her, my entire team were sporting rather surprised expressions: this was not something we had previously discussed. Leite, who was still drafting the Agreement, looked up at me, emphatically shaking his head, and said, "I'll include that too. I'll be including every little thing" before re-immersing himself in correcting the text. Some people really don't need all that much to keep them happy. ...

"Mahan, are you sure you know what you're doing?" whispered Clutzer, who happened to be standing closest to me. "I don't seem to recall us discussing this."

I put my finger to my lips once again, showing that now was not the time to distract me and returned to my conversation with Ehkiller. How could I explain to the guys that Anastaria would work much better for free than for money? For her the concept of being indebted was not just some random collection of sounds, but the worst possible curse, one that, once placed, would have to be lifted as soon as possible. If I took money off her for the Guardian's quest, Seathistles wouldn't be getting a mercenary, but the leader of the Phoenix clan. Despite this being one and the same player, in fact there were two different people in there. Knowing this, how could I share the

High Priestess's quest with her? It's just not gonna happen. So, she either joins us for free or we'll have to do without her.

"Then it's fifty-two," continued the shadow leader of the Phoenix clan without any change in tone, as if he'd counted on this from the outset. "We are offering you twenty million gold for everyone."

"That boils down to less than four hundred thousand per head," I said after some quick number crunching. "That's a laughable amount!" The scenario has no time limit, therefore I can wait a couple of years, gain some levels and complete it myself just with my clan. That'd be more profitable."

"So tell us your conditions. Just stop going on about a million and a half – you give the impression of someone with more sense than that."

"All right, I realize that getting that much money wouldn't be realistic." I was dragging out the conversation until I saw with some relief that Leite looked up at me and signaled that he was done with the Agreement. Finally! We had discussed almost all possible options earlier, so now it only remained to turn our decisions into a well-worded text, the task that Leite had taken upon himself. And there was me potentially getting it all muddled up with the bit about Anastaria joining us for free ...

"Mahan, are you still here?" Ehkiller gave a polite cough, returning me to the negotiations.

"Sorry." I quickly scanned through the text, taking note of all the main points. "Let's talk everything over in a proper, business-like fashion.

Five hundred thousand gold per head is too little for what essentially amounts to 18 levels. I believe that the most reasonable price would be a million gold each. There's little sense in going any lower. Any gold looted during this assignment will be split equally amongst everyone in the group. In this quest my clan will be carried and there's just eight of us, so you won't even notice our presence. We'll divide all the loot through an Imitator – it will do it better than any of us – but I will retain the right to claim any eight items that drop irrespective of the norms of sharing loot, including rolls of the die and class suitability. Any quests acquired by any member of the group while completing this scenario will be shared with all other members of the group. Each player will have to make a decision concerning the amount of time they are present in the Game during this scenario. However, I take no responsibility if you happen to be logged out during a key event or during the completion of the scenario. In this case I ask that no claims are made against the Seathistles clan – this point will definitely be included in the Agreement. There is another point of considerable importance to me: there should be no members of the Dark Legion clan in on this quest. I have nothing against them, except for the fact that they're obliged to send me for respawn on sight. I think that's it for now."

"No, it's not," came Hellfire's voice. "Who's going to run the raid? Who will be the leader and who will be calling the shots?"

"I will be the one making the decisions, after

first consulting Anastaria. She will be the one leading the raid, no-one else would do it better." I glanced at the girl, who immediately composed herself. Whatever happened to that playful fire that was dancing in her eyes a few minutes ago? I was now looking at the real Anastaria: focused, capable of making split-second decisions even with limited information, clever and incredibly beautiful. Right, that last point has nothing to do with anything.

"Anastaria, can you hear us?" Ehkiller asked the girl.

"I'm here and agree on all the points except the one on making decisions. Undigit, are you planning to bring Donotpunnik with you?"

"Yes," the voice of the Azure Dragons leader, which I recognized from the time of the Beatwick battle, came from the amulet.

"In that case, I propose that, aside from me, you should also add him as an advisor. Is my recommendation sufficient for this?" Anastaria asked me.

"Sure. Leite, add him to the Agreement." I passed this on to my bureaucrat. "I'm prepared to share out the quest under the terms we've discussed. I'll hand the Agreement over to Anastaria and she'll send it to Ehkiller and everyone else for examination. Now we just have to settle the price and write in the full list of the participants." I sent the amended Agreement to Anastaria. It now contained just a few blank sections: the price, names of those taking part and the destination coordinates.

"I see," Ehkiller responded thoughtfully. "We'll need a couple more minutes to talk over your words and come to a decision. I'll call you back."

The amulet fell silent and, exhausted, I slumped to the ground. If sweating were possible in Barliona, I would've been sweating buckets from all the tension. I'd never had to conduct negotiations at such a level before, so completing my very first attempt with this enormous profit would be quite a feat. And I think I managed to pull it off, so I could only hope that a million gold was a reasonable price for the respective clan heads and the like.

"Mahan, are you sure about a million?" Clutzer crouched next to me, staring into the distance. "I remember us agreeing that six hundred thousand was a good price. Especially if we'll have that many people on board. And what if they don't go for it? What then? Agreeing to a discount a second time is lame – they'll start taking us for fools. And what's the deal with Anastaria doing this for free?"

"Clutzer, go chop some trees." I'd barely had time to reply to this very reasonable remark from my fighter, when Anastaria appeared next to us. "I need to talk to Mahan. Please," added the girl when Clutzer didn't flinch.

"You might have failed to notice, but I'm also talking to him right now."

"You'll have time enough to chat later."

"The same goes for you. If someone butts in on your conversation with Hellfire, just how far will you send him flying?"

Anastaria stood there for a couple of moments, trying to stare Clutzer down, and then turned to her fighters and shouted: "Rick, what's with this idling about? Did you forget what we've come here for? Let's get back to the herbs so that the Seathistles can get their chit-chat over and done with."

"I think you're letting this lady have her way a little too much." Clutzer turned back to me as soon as Anastaria left us. "The times of going it alone are gone. Now you're the leader of a clan, for which you are responsible. You're also starting to let the wrong part of your body do the thinking. Forget about the gold we might be losing on account of Anastaria – if all goes well we'll make it back from the higher price you've demanded, but I am asking you not to act so rashly next time."

"But we do need her. All of us did decide, after all, that we'd take her along for the High Priestess's quest," I pointed out in my defense. "We won't be able to get past the Vampires without her and if she ends up paying to take part, we won't just get her, but the entire Phoenix clan. Is that what we really want?"

"That's why I kept quiet when you came out with all that nonsense to Ehkiller. The sooner you understand that you're not on your own and that the clan is there to back you up, the better. Right, I should get going or she'll incinerate me with her eyes. Just remember, you're a clan leader and not some lone 67-level player. If you roll over now, you'll be rolling over for the rest of the game."

"I can see you've got some fierce fighters there,

quite hair-raising." Anastaria sat next to me as soon as Clutzer was gone and, unlike him, used a Scroll of Impenetrability, concealing us from the rest of the world. No-one could hear or even see us; our senses were in no way impeded as we continued to watch the others at work. A convenient thing for those who want to hide, the only drawback being that it couldn't be moved once activated.

"*Mahan, are you under a dome?*" A message from Elenium immediately appeared in the clan channel.

"*Yup, Anastaria put it up,*" I replied to the guys to stop them worrying. "*She's being terribly mysterious!*"

"*Remember our chat,*" came a message from Clutzer, "*And why didn't we talk like this before? It's very convenient when others are far away.*"

Leaving Elenium to explain to the others why clan chat is accessible to clan members only, I returned to Anastaria.

"They're worried, eh?" asked the girl with a smile. "Afraid that I'll eat their leader?"

"No, rather, they asked me not to do anything bad to you," I parried. "After all, this is none other than Anastaria we're talking about here: I could end up doing something stupid and then spend all of five minutes regretting it. Was it so obvious that I was using the chat?"

"Yup. Damn! I caught that stupid word off you! Were those your first negotiations of this caliber?"

"There's also this other word: yer."

"Good for you, you handled yourself well. I remember when I was taken to a similar meeting for the first time. 'Killer was negotiating the purchase of a key to another world, same as that Eye of yours. That was so long ago! Almost ten years now! I was just a foolish little girl, who had just joined Phoenix. I was watching wide-eyed how serious grown men were haggling over the purchase of an artifact worth three million. I just didn't get it – how can you hand over so much money for a bunch of numbers in a database? At the time I had just started university and had a generous monthly allowance of a thousand gold – if you converted it to Barliona currency – which allowed me to survive in relative comfort. And you can stop sniggering! That money gave us an entire month of truly magnificent dinners of ramen and corned beef. Someone who's never been a student wouldn't understand. For example, are you familiar with the special skill of persuading a teabag to produce something resembling tea at third brewing? I am! The funniest thing was that everyone brought their kids to the dorms in limos or expensive convertibles ... yet the taste of a piece of bread toasted under a gas grill, washed down with a freshly-opened carton of milk, will stay with me forever. It was then that I understood that it's not the money or the status of your parents that makes you who you are; you're the only one responsible for how people really see you."

"Why are you telling me all this?" I asked the suddenly nostalgic girl.

"Because you also managed to level up your

Reputation with me and ... that's just it ... so you know. All right, enough memories for today. Tell me instead whether you managed to solve the riddle?"

"Riddle? What riddle? Aaahh! The one with the three formulas? It was pretty easy!" I lacked Anastaria's skill of switching conversation topic at the drop of a hat, so felt a little lost at first. Perhaps I should get her to give me a master class in this? She sure could teach me a thing or two ...

"You don't say. My troopers spent ages wrestling with it. We had to do a good deal of digging before we came up with a possible answer. It's beautifully put together, wouldn't you say? How did you stumble upon the solution? I'll never believe that you simply solved everything in five minutes."

"I had the swearing filters on, then a certain player swore in front of me and the system corrected him ... in a helpful way. Before that I also spent a long time grappling with it, you might even say it began to haunt me in my dreams, but eventually something clicked and I realized what had to be done. I need your help now though. I'm sending you a line of text." I sent Anastaria the cipher I got from the Dwarves. "There's no key or any information on what type of cipher is used, so I'll never solve it by myself. Could you run it past your deciphering team?"

"Of course, I'll send it to my guys. They'll pick this line apart into all its constituent elements. So, you trust me so much now that you're not even demanding an Agreement?"

"I have to trust someone in this game, so why

not you?"

"And yet the Karmadont Chess Pieces are still a no-go zone?"

The girl's question caught me completely flat-footed, so I had to close my eyes and silently count to ten as I tried to keep my emotions in check. All I wanted to do right now was grab Anastaria by the shoulders and shake all the baloney out of her. How long can she badger me with these chess figurines? I opened my eyes, looked at the grinning girl and counted to ten once again, but slower and more thoughtfully this time. No, things can't carry on like this. The matter of the chess pieces has to be settled once and for all, or I'll spend the rest of my life looking over my shoulder, to see if Anastaria was there, waiting to make her move.

"You're a strange one, Stacey. Sometimes I get the feeling that you're not even human, just some soulless machine bent on pursuing its aim, oblivious to anyone or anything else." The girl was silent, so I couldn't think of anything better to do than to take out all the Orc Warriors and put them in her lap. "If these things can make you risk your character by misusing the Sirens' Poison and you can't help constantly bringing them up and teasing me about them, then clearly your life isn't complete without them. They're yours. Your peace of mind is worth more to me than a collection of algorithms. Take them and do what you like with them."

That's it. The die had been cast – as one of the ancients said, there's nowhere left to retreat, the bridges are burnt. As soon as I spoke the phrase 'they're yours', the owner of the figurines changed and I no longer had any claim over them, except authorship. Now, even if I came to my senses and decided to take the Orcs back, my fingers would go right through them. To be honest, I was playing it far from straight with her by giving her only the Orc Warriors, staying stubbornly silent about the Dwarves. She could think that's because I did it in the heat of the moment. I made my move, now it was Anastaria's turn. All our future relations depended on what would happen next.

"One of the Orc Warriors from the Karmadont Chess Set," said Anastaria thoughtfully, turning the figurine around in her hands. "You have no idea what I would've been prepared to do to get my hands on them, and here you just gave them to me, without any conditions at all. ... Not so long ago I wouldn't have given a second thought to immediately throwing them in my bag. But now ... I had to know for sure that the Chess Pieces did in fact exist – that it wasn't some error in the Game code, which spread this announcement throughout Malabar. Here," Anastaria handed the figurines over to me, "they're yours. No-one in this game apart from you has any claim over them. There's a reason I was remembering my student days ... as corny as it may sound, you've made me respect you and not just the results of your crafting. Whatever you may think of me, for me a relationship of trust is more important than gold or the Karmadont Chess Pieces. You can buy everything except that ...

thank you!" The girl leant over to me and did something completely unexpected: she kissed me. Intensely, passionately, unforgettably ... there were no words.

"All that I ask of you is that no-one else finds out about this kiss." When Stacey drew back, my head was still floating in the clouds amid beautiful dreams. I have no idea how, but an ordinary kiss gave me so much pleasure that, compared to it, any visits to the Dating House seemed to pale into insignificance.

"Judging by your expression, you're not exactly immune to the magic of Delight after all." Anastaria's laughter sounded inside the dome, "I'm sorry, I just had to check. Now I just need to find out why my poison had no effect on you. How do you know about it, by the way?"

Like a giant cold shower these words shook me out of the pink clouds and sent me crashing back down to earth. She really is such a ... woman ... Wothebugs take her!

"I think we've had enough revelations for today." I tried to regain composure, which, despite Anastaria's last phrase, was an uphill struggle: the pink clouds were refusing to let me go and my face still sported a stupidly happy smile that I just couldn't shake off.

"Will you tell me what the other two quests you have are?"

"Will you tell me what you're prepared to give me for them?"

"Without even looking at their descriptions first? The correct answer would be – nothing."

"All right, let's take a different approach. Do you know who the Patriarch of the Vampires is?"

The girl's silence, as well as her wide-eyed surprise, were a clear enough answer to my question. She knew who that was, all right!

"Mahan, this is Ehkiller." The call of the amulet interrupted my intimate meeting with Stacey, allowing her to regain composure and start trying to figure out whether I was bluffing or not. "We've discussed and accepted the Agreement that you've sent. We'll pay the price of one million per participant and will be sending you the list of players in a moment. Please confirm that the location coordinates will appear in the Agreement as soon as it is signed and the money arrives in your account."

"Confirmed, but it shouldn't be my account, rather the account of the Seathistles clan. Thank you for reaching a decision so quickly," I thanked Ehkiller. "I have another question – do you want to start the quest today or tomorrow morning?"

"We will settle the formalities today and start the assignment tomorrow," the Phoenix representative assured me, "Anyone who wishes can join you today, but we'll set out tomorrow morning."

"You know, the more time I spend with you, the more I think that you're a spy for the Corporation," said the girl, now quite recovered, the moment Ehkiller disconnected. "There are just too many coincidences for a simple prisoner, don't you think?"

"No, I can call the Emperor as a witness (although I have no idea how he would be able to check); I have nothing to do with the Corporation. I did work for it once, before the mines, but only odd-jobs here and there."

"You do know that the Patriarch is as legendary a figure as the Dragons? Or that no-one has seen him in the entire 15 years of the Game? But it looks like you're already acquainted with him and all ..."

"I'm afraid I'm not. I have a quest that involves finding him and having a chat about what's going on in the Dark Forest. Can you see the connection with the scenario that I've shared with the top players? The other quest is focused on the Prince and has nothing to do with this place. So, have you decided if you're with me?"

"In the search for the Patriarch? Like you need to ask!"

"Then let's make things clear straight away – you'll be joining us as a mercenary alongside my clan and not as the head of Phoenix. I don't need any extra hangers-on on this quest."

"*Mahan, what's taking so long? How many times have you scored already?*"

"*One more joke like that and I'll dock you 5% of the loot. The Agreement is being signed: the 53 million will soon arrive in our account.*"

"It's a deal," said Stacey, staring with some puzzlement at my clan, who had started to run around the glade in sheer joy. Even Barsina, who was usually still somewhat reserved, was unable to restrain herself and was embracing Clutzer. I just hope that wouldn't be interpreted as violation of her non-flirtation rule. "You told them that the Agreement's been signed? Look at them. Happy as kids at Christmas. What's your loot allocation amongst the clan?"

"The same as the one I'll be offering you: 70% of all the money gained goes into the clan treasury, 30% on salaries, depending on the level of participation. Loot is allocated by an Imitator. If you're happy with these conditions, with the fact that you'd be a mercenary and not the head of Phoenix, and with not sharing the quest with anyone else, I would be happy to discuss your joining us.

"Reasonable clan demands – I'm ready to sign an Agreement. Who else do you plan to invite, other than your clan?"

"Antsinthepantsa. We'll fail without her."

"You don't like her very much, do you? Why tell one girl that another is indispensable? I'll eat her alive and not bat an eyelid. As if I'd let her hang around my Shaman, when there's not enough of him for me as it is. ... All right, I'll deal with her later. Where's the Agreement?"

"When did I become 'your' Shaman?"

"Quit nitpicking. Send the Agreement."

"What's the point? It's not like there are any Heralds around to validate it."

"Why do you need the Heralds? They uphold the law only in Malabar; in Kartoss that's done by Magisters and in the Free Lands by Guardians. ...

What, didn't you know?"

"To be honest, I'm not exactly an expert on these things. But that isn't important. The Chess Pieces have shown that you wish to lay claim to the title of 'Madam who can be trusted'. Catch the Agreement. Its main feature is the loot allocation, it has no other restrictions."

"That 'Madam' will earn you a slap in the face. While we're on the subject, it's 'Miss' to you – while standing to attention. And say it like you mean it, please. Let's dispense with Agreements altogether – see who's who in all of this."

"Here it is, then." I shared the High Priestess's quest with Anastaria. "I think people will start arriving in about twenty minutes, so let's wrap things up. They'll get here and what will they see? A huge opaque dome concealing a man and a woman: that leaves too much to the imagination. ..."

Instead of an answer Anastaria was silent for a few seconds while looking directly into my eyes and then, whispering, "I'm being such a fool!" she planted her lips on mine once again. And, for the record, she got no protest out of me. Whatever this Delight was doing, it was working 100%! It felt like gaining five or six levels in your main profession in one go, with Endurance turned off. I'll have to get to the bottom of what this magic was and what one was meant to do with it.

Clan achievement gained: 'Clan of the Oligarchs'

Conditions for Procurement: conduct transactions worth over 40 million gold with the clan treasury within 2 game hours.

5% discount with NPC merchants for all clan members. Now all your trade negotiations with NPCs will end in the words: 'Of course, with a clan like that!'

"Oooh! Adamantium!" Just a minute after Anastaria took down the dome, players began to arrive at the glade. Everyone had the same sequence of reactions: surprise, greedy stares, the growing realization that, unlike the bunch of noobs standing nearby, they had the relevant professions sufficiently leveled up for gathering the high-level resources and, finally, a befuddled expression after walking up to a vein / tree / herb and discovering that the pick hit the ground – the axe went straight through the tree – and that working out the mathematical equation for finding the right point to cut was the only thing they were able to do with the herb. You could only gather something in the Guardian's glade if you had the relevant permission, which I had no intention of handing out for free. Of the ten early arrivals only four agreed to hand over 30% of the resources they gathered to my clan, the rest refused.

"Judging by your pleased expression," Dooki came up to me once players had stopped appearing, "Anastaria had good reason to put up that dome. It's too bad that it doesn't really grow dark in this forest or we could've used you as a giant torch. You're positively glowing! I do, of course, understand that two million each is a good addition to our retirement fund, but even this can't make a guy look THAT pleased. Are you gonna spill the beans?"

"What the hell?" As I was trying to think of a sharp comeback for my second Rogue, a surprised shout echoed through the glade. I didn't immediately realize where the sound had come from, but when I did, we were a player down: one of those who refused to benefit the Seathistles clan with his labor had decided to go sightseeing and had stepped out into the mists of the surrounding forest. Judging by the map of this area, the Dark Forest was a location for 100-level players, so supposedly high-level players had nothing to fear around here. Yeah, right! It was hard to imagine what forces were lurking in the surrounding twilight if someone with level 288 went down in close to ten seconds.

"YOU HAVE CHOSEN TO OPPOSE ME." The forest once again shook with reverberations, but this time an hour-long 'Fear' debuff was slapped on us, which reduced all stats by 5%. Looks like that Lieutenant had finally dropped in for a chat. I don't remember the Sergeant having such abilities. It was a completely different voice too. "I WILL DESTROY YOU!"

"Mahan," Anastaria took a break from the herbs and stared at me, just as all the other players that had arrived in the glade were doing, "is there something you want to tell us?"

Realizing that keeping things to myself was no

longer an option, I recounted everything about the Cursed Wothe, its warning about the Vampires and its assurance that in this zone neither I nor any of my group had anything to fear. Speaking of the group ... I immediately sent an invite to each new arrival, even the gatherers, mentally thanking the Fallen for not flooding the glade with arrows just yet. The local NPC-minions probably didn't think that I could be so ... imprudent, I think that's the word. If only I had thought about the group straight away, Anastaria would've been able to get the player out on pure reflex, simply by seeing his frame. She would've thrown a bubble over him or would've cast something on him. Hmm ... altogether too many 'wouldas' here. In the end we have what we have, so all the 'shoulda woulda couldas' are a bit pointless.

"So it looks like the area is being patrolled by a squad of Vampires of indeterminate level, headed by some sort of Lieutenant, who are quite capable of taking down an unprepared 288-level mage in 13 seconds," Anastaria mumbled thoughtfully. "I might have been able to get him out, of course, but the speed at which he was killed was something else. Now we must wait for the rest of the group, especially the tanks and a couple of healers – we can't enter the Dark Forest without them. Let's see what they'll do with Hel around. ...."

"Guys," I addressed my free fighters as soon as all the other high-level players returned to resource gathering, "I have a question. Can you take a holiday for about three weeks from tomorrow morning? From the financial point of view, you've already got your salary covered for the next three years, if not more, so you can afford to take some time off. It would be a pity if the top players complete the quest, but you don't."

"Well, aside from the fact that we haven't been paid our salary yet, since the Imitator will only transfer it in a couple of weeks," said Elenium, "the idea of a holiday is a good one. I'll let you know tomorrow. Right, I'm turning on 'Follow' – time for me to get some rest."

"When are we planning to set out?" asked Barsina as soon as all the other free players in my clan left the Game. "Time is not an issue for me, so I can simply stay from now on. You said something about a tent before, got space in there?"

"I have five with me, so if purely male company isn't a problem for you, you're very welcome to join us."

"Good: that can be a test of whether you guys can be trusted," said the girl. Before disappearing into the tent, she turned and blew me away with a question: "So what's with you and Anastaria, then?"

* * *

The next morning began with a commotion that even the tent couldn't keep out: the noise of the rest of the arriving players.

"Mahan! Up you get! It's time to form the

groups!" You'd never tell from Anastaria's cheerful and alert voice that she spent the entire night communing with high-grade herbs. Who would've thought that the second-highest player on the continent, totally unfettered by concerns for her dignity, would be crawling around on her knees and measuring the length of a stalk with a ruler? Everyone who turned up last night watched this spectacle and, judging by a few camera icons, some of them even filmed it.

"Do you ever actually leave the game?" I mumbled as I crawled out into the fresh air. The resources were still there, but no-one took any notice of them anymore. Everyone was focused on one thing only – the upcoming battle. The player who was sent for respawn was already back with us, indicating that the usual 12-hour absence is a limitation that only affected newbies. If you leveled up your Reputation with the Empire to 'Exalted' and added to that around a million gold on top, the time you had to spend outside the Game after dying was reduced to 6 hours. In Barliona everything becomes a question of money, and in almost all cases it's a million gold. Do you want a flying pet? A million gold, please. You want to halve the respawn time? Just pay a million. Do you want to take part in a scenario? Please be so kind as to hand over a lump sum to keep those Seathistles happy.

"Hel, take your team and very carefully try stepping outside the glade." As soon as I had invited the rest of the thronging crowd into the group and shared the quest, Anastaria started to put things in order. "You know the situation, so put the defense up right away: there's some very unpleasant rabble loitering out there. Don, what would be the best place to try to lure them out, in your opinion?"

"Let's say three o'clock. The sun is on the right and Vampires can't look at it directly, which means they'll get a 10% miss chance," said Donotpunnik, who turned out to be a level 303 Death Knight, clad all in black. His two-handed sword was surrounded by a cold blue aura – probably part of the visual design of this class. From what I could see he was just another fighter, like Hellfire, but if Anastaria has no qualms about asking his advice ... and why hadn't I heard anything about him before? "It's best to set out in ten-strong recon-units (two tanks, three healers and five fighters), range 6, and put it up right away. The black arrows, if I remember correctly, do AOE-damage in melee. The first ten are yours, I'll be on the right and Etamzilat on the left. Twenty should be the backup with scrolls, the standard Alpha support. ..."

"I disagree," Anastaria interrupted him, "Alpha is good in open ground. We have trees here, which won't allow the Mages to deploy their skills fully and things will be more difficult for healers too. Let's modify Delta, look ..."

This was followed by an untranslatable volley of words between Anastaria and Donotpunnik. The interesting part was that they appeared to be using normal language, just in a completely incomprehensible way. It was all Alphas or modified Deltas ... the high-level players immersed themselves in their favorite activity: preparing for a raid with tough mobs.

"Maybe we could just get other people here and flood the whole forest?" Barsina couldn't help adding her two cents, which provoked smiles from the raiders, while Anastaria turned to her and explained, as if to an inexperienced schoolgirl: "My dear, if you start running as a healer, how long will the 'Steel Skin' buff stay on you?"

"That's nonsense," said Barsina, perplexed. "How can you even cast Steel if you're in healer form, let alone run around? Do you even know how to play Druids?"

"You see, you've just answered your own question." Anastaria once again smiled at the reddening girl before returning to the laughing raiders to continue discussing the plan. Right ... something tells me that it's time for me to intervene, or my clan will be pushed so far to the edge that getting back into the heart of things would take me the rest of my prison term.

"What have you decided?" I came up to the group of raid-leaders who were just finishing their meeting.

"Listen, small fry," Etamzilat looked at me condescendingly, "go and chop some wood or something, eh? You yourself said that your clan is going to be carried on this quest. This stuff is completely out of your league."

"Let's pretend I didn't hear any of that and I'll ask you once again: what have you decided?" Although I was fuming on the inside, I tried to retain the appearance of calm. Small fry! On the one hand, fair enough, but on the other ... the 'grown ups' had just tried to show me my 'proper place'. In their dreams! Either I'm the head of the clan and of this expedition, or I might as well give up on leadership right now and throw myself into crafting. These sharks would swallow me in one gulp. "And, by the way, Etamzilat, I don't remember your name among MY advisors. Anastaria and Donotpunnik do happen to be included in the Agreement, which was signed by all, yourself included. The Agreement very clearly lays out everyone's roles in this scenario. So maybe you should be the one who should be doing the wood-chopping while I'm making decisions?"

"The fact that you found this scenario doesn't make you ..."

"Enough!" Anastaria intervened. Now here was someone who was an indisputable authority among other players: Etamzilat immediately fell silent. "Etamzilat is right, Mahan. I'm sorry, but you don't have experience of leading raids. Now is not the time to quibble over who has higher stats and thicker armor. We have to get on with things now and you're getting in the way."

"That won't work. With all due respect, the events in Beatwick showed very well the extent of your experience. You have ten, twenty, perhaps even thirty clan raiders, each of them tried and tested in more than one Dungeon. And that's all. As soon as raiders from other clans turn up, you'll be a stumbling mess. People, either we start working together properly from the outset or I'm returning your money, cancelling the Agreement and you can hang out in the Dark Forest on your own, dancing around the Guardian in the hope that he'll give you the quest."

"We've decided to leave the glade on the west side in three ten-strong groups," said Anastaria after giving it some thought. "Who or what awaits us out there, remains unknown. The three Rogues sent out on stealthed reconnaissance were discovered and attacked. We barely managed to get them back in one piece. We'll have to scout with a fighting party, so we modified one very well-known formation, where the tanks take the first and fifth place, shielding five players each. The distance between the players ..."

Under Etamzilat's reproachful stare, Stacey began to explain the tactics of the planned battle. Suddenly a certain feeling, which hadn't popped up for quite a while, started to flash within me like a red light. Well, hello there, you incomprehensible beastie!

"Stacey, we can't go west." I closed my eyes for a moment and tried to interrupt the girl's logical exposition. "We'll get shafted. We have to go east and head towards the center of the forest from there."

"Explain." Donotpunnik spoke in place of the still silent girl.

"Do you remember the bubble on Hellfire in Beatwick?" I continued to look at Stacey, ignoring the

Azure Dragons raid-leader. "It's the same situation."

"Mahan, you do understand that based on all logical accounts Donotpunnik is right?" the girl finally uttered. An announcement popped up before my eyes informing me that I'd got a letter from Ehkiller. Strange.

"I completely understand," I replied, "give me a couple of seconds, please." Realizing how it must look, I opened the Mailbox and read the letter. Why couldn't Ehkiller just say something, especially when he's standing only a couple of paces away and is listening to the whole conversation?

"Mahan, stay quiet about this. Anastaria asked me to send you a letter to say that if you're sure that standard logic shouldn't be followed in the Dark Forest, you'll have to prove it to the rest of the players. Respawn hasn't really hindered anyone in the past and the loss of 30%of Experience is a fair price for a mistake. Accept what they've decided. Anastaria will try to stay alive."

Well, well. I have a long way to go to reach the stature of these veteran players. After taking a split-second decision to wipe out thirty, or at least twenty nine, players – including nine members of her own clan – Stacey had secretly written a note on the inter-clan chat asking Ehkiller to pass on this message to me. This girl sure knows how to play hardball. I have no idea how she'd had time to do all this!

"All right guys, let's do it your way. But I will

say it once again: we cannot get anywhere except by the eastern route, but I guess you can't argue against logic, eh?" I decided to follow Anastaria's advice. "Go for it – let's see how far you get." After that I turned around and went back to my clan. Judging by my fighters' expressions they realized full well what had just happened – I'd been pushed to the side, utterly and completely. What kind of a leader am I, if I give up so easily under pressure from high-level players? My only remaining hope was that my intuition wouldn't let me down. I think I'm beginning to place too much trust in it – what if I've missed the mark this time?

"The first group is ready." The entire glade turned into an anthill. Here and there flashes of buffs being cast lit up and immediately faded, players were diligently drinking elixirs and eating stat-boosting food – normal raid preparation was in progress. Even Antsinthepantsa was dragged into the support group. Only the Seathistles clan was standing idle, watching what was happening from the sidelines, not knowing how to make themselves useful. Reluctant to show any emotions, I opened my Mailbox and began to learn all the Jewelcraft recipes that I'd been sent at Anastaria's behest. Iron Ring of Strength, Silver Neck-chain of Balance, Gold Ring of Intellect ... nine recipes that were a perfect match for my level and resources. After learning all the scrolls and sending all the Alchemy materials to Leite and the profession scrolls to my other fighters, I sat myself down on the grass. I didn't feel like doing anything with Jewelcraft, so whether I liked it or not I would have to witness this high-level-player fiasco. I don't know about the rest, but personally I had zero doubts about the outcome of the coming battle: 0:1 to the Dark Ones.

"Are you sure that east is clear?" Plinto came up to me. Like us, he wasn't included in the ten-strong fighting groups.

"It's not clear, but there we have a chance to break through." I had no idea why I answered the way I did.

"Break through? From where?" Plinto's surprise was a clear indication that I just said something stupid. And really, why would we need to break out of here? We could just make a portal and we'd be golden. Or we could get on our flying mounts and fly to any point of the Dark Forest. Not a bad idea, that, by the way!

"Ready to roll, one minute countdown." At this point I discovered that there was inter-raid chat on top of the inter-clan chat too. This I had no idea about, since during the raids in which I took part as a Hunter we communicated by normal speech.

"Center, move forward," Hellfire announced, using his normal voice, and the Phoenix raid group stepped out into the Dark Forest mists.

"The wings are off!" The tanks of the Heirs of the Titans and Azure Dragons announced their departure.

"The support is ready!" Ehkiller and twenty more players came up to the edge of the glade, scrolls at the ready.

"I think I'll go and have a look at what's happening on the east side," said Plinto, who stealthed and hurried in the opposite direction to the main group of players.

The battle for cleansing the Dark Forest from the taint had begun. ...

"The center is clear!"

A whole minute had gone by from the moment the raiders moved out into the Dark Forest, but the mobs were in no hurry to bestow extra Experience on the players. No-one was attacking or running around or even moving. It was as if this wasn't the same forest from which just ten minutes ago the scouting Rogues had to be rescued.

"Center, keep moving!" Hellfire gave the command to Phoenix to follow in his steps, as he had departed from the glade by more than a hundred meters. "Wings, spread out! There are no mobs here!"

A couple more minutes of tense waiting yielded nothing: the forest was dead. All thirty players had walked a hundred meters away from the center, trying to provoke the mobs into attacking.

"Something tells me," said Ehkiller, rolling up a scroll and putting it back into his bag, "that Mahan was wrong and we have nothing to be afraid of. Anastaria!" He shouted into the forest, any ideas what's going on?"

"No!" came the girl's shout. "Try to come out in twos or threes! Keep those scrolls at the ready! Maybe they'll attack smaller groups! Rick! Drop the herb-gathering and come out as well. We have to maximize the search area.

The three ten-strong raid groups went out even further, the wings began to circle, searching for the Vampires, and the remaining players, splitting into groups of two or three, started to leave the Guardian's glade.

"Mahan." Antsinthepantsa came up to me. Aside from myself, she was now the only one who hadn't stepped out of the glade. Even the guys from my clan had gone out in search of the mobs, supposing that low-level players, as easy prey, would lure them out. "I ... we mustn't go there."

"I know, but I failed to convince the others."

"It will happen right now." The girl suddenly went pale. I began to get that sinking feeling too and it became clear that in the next few seconds there would be a big 'Boom'!

"Stacey, BUBBLE!" I screamed at the top of my voice into the twilight of the surrounding wood. "Everyone back!"

"Back to the glade! MOVE IT!" Almost simultaneously, an internal raid announcement came from Plinto, whose frame had rapidly begun to melt away. Someone was giving him a kicking, and a pretty hard one at that. *"Ash, 4 seconds! Glade +400!"*

For me Plinto's message was total gibberish, but I saw the reaction of Ehkiller who was standing about twenty meters away from the Guardian's zone. At first he'd looked surprised when I shouted about the bubble, but his eyebrows flew up when he read Plinto's message, then he bolted for the glade like mad, then, finally, disappeared. In fact, everything disappeared: trees, branches, twilight ... players. Aside from mist and about fifty see-through figures that were once high-level players, the enormous circle with a 400-meter radius contained nothing at all. There ended up being two neat-looking glades: one was a perfect circle, the glade, and the second was a slightly cut back circle, which touched the Guardian's zone, but was unable to subdue it. The scene was completed with two stunned Shamans whose gut instincts prevented them from stepping out into the mist. Although – wait! Anastaria! Surrounded by a bubble, though now strangely darkened, the girl was frozen about twenty meters away from us.

"YOU ARE TOO WEAK TO WITHSTAND ME." Another resonating voice spread throughout the glade and I realized that every voice we'd heard before was just a weak parody of something truly terrifying. Our entire bodies began to shake: you got the feeling that your teeth were about to jump out and head off into the forest just to stop experiencing the full 'charm' of this voice. ... "I AM DISSAPOINTED. IS MALABAR TRULY THAT WEAK? MY FIGHTERS WILL DEAL WITH YOU NOW."

Perhaps there were other words, but at that moment the surrounding world began to swim and I slipped out of consciousness. ...

"Wake up already!" Through the comforting, and very quiet, haze I could hear the demanding voice of Antsinthepantsa, so I tried to concentrate and open my eyes. I only managed on the third attempt, but the darkness didn't go anywhere. Pictograms of buffs and debuffs appeared in front of me instead of the Guardian's glade. A message flashed past me that my Endurance increased to 138 and quickly vanished, reluctant to lift my spirits with any extra light. One of the debuffs, Blindness, wouldn't be gone for another ten minutes, so the system diligently ensured that I remained incapacitated until then.

"I dispelled what I could from you, but most of it is beyond me. You'll have to manage on your own. Try to summon the Spirit of Restoration," the girl's hoarse voice came from afar – by the looks of it the Stun debuff was also enjoying the opportunity of spending some quality with this player.

"How long has it been?" I croaked, surprised at my own voice. My senses were telling me that I'd spent two days walking under a burning sun, got completely desiccated and then finished off my vocal chords by singing a few songs: my throat felt as rough as sandpaper. That must have been the Dumbness debuff. All these debuffs were really a bit much: they'd camped out in a neat row of twenty-three nice icons before my eyes, varying in duration from 10 minutes to 2 days. And that was after Antsinthepantsa managed to take some off me.

"About ten minutes. I'll tell you again; summon the Restoration Spirit. You may even try one of a different rank to you, as long as you summon it."

"But I didn't learn ..."

"So what? Do you really think a Shaman needs to be taught in order to communicate with Spirits?

Are you not the master of a Dragon?! Now!"

The girl's outburst was so sudden that I even managed to sit up. Why is she so sure that a Shaman can communicate with any Spirits even without proper training? This goes against Game logic, where you have to learn first and only then use a skill you've learned. I was about to let the lady Shaman know what I thought of her words, but then recalled a certain episode from my life in Beatwick – my teacher's order: "RUN, YOU FOOL!" At the time I did manage to summon a communication Spirit without even suspecting that it existed. So perhaps the same could be done for Restoration. At least in theory.

"Are you going to sit around all day?" Antsinthepantsa hurried me along: "My scrolls will soon run out, my Mana's at zero and Anastaria is still outside the glade. Hurry up!"

Anastaria is alive? Ah, I'm being slow now – she was shielded under a bubble. But then why isn't she back in the glade? I just don't get it. I quickly have to get back to normal, but how do I do that when my head is throbbing like a locomotive and the driver keeps pulling the whistle? Practically every second. What did the Guardian say? 'No-one can cause you harm in this glade'? When I'm back on my feet, I'll go over to that block of wood and politely ask it why the heck I ended up with a ton of debuffs. I'd like to see it get out of that one, the unfeeling log. ...

"Mahan!" Antsinthepantsa's voice once again broke through my staggered thinking "Do something already!"

'Do something?' What is she on about? I was heading to the Guardian ... Anastaria! She's dying and I'm sitting here dawdling, getting all ready to chop down the Guardian. ... With some effort of will I forced myself to concentrate, enter the Spirit Summoning Mode, free up an active slot and start a summons. I needed the Spirit of Full Restoration, the one that would restore not only myself, but other players too. So, where can you be hiding?

"What's taking so long?" A few minutes of summoning finally allowed me to find the right Spirit, which led to the immediate removal of all my debuffs. Looks like a pretty useful thing, this Full Restoration. It doesn't affect Hit Points, since healing deals with that, but it does return a player to his initial state: it removes curses, debuffs and poison. This Spirit can be summoned if you're Stunned, but – if I understood the description correctly – under such conditions, the next summons would only be possible in 24 hours. This means ... that Antsinthepantsa had first restored herself, dispelled those debuffs from me which could be dispelled with normal cleansing, shook me awake and forced me to learn Restoration. I'll have to have a thorough chat with this girl. How come she was so sure that Shamans are able to work with Spirits this way, without any teachers? All this is rather unorthodox. And in general, chatting with her would be very helpful in order to find out more about my class.

"Yeah ... I got a little held up. What's up with Anastaria?" The girl's frame indicated that her Hit

Points were on a steady journey towards zero. Antsinthepantsa took turns in using her healing scrolls and Spirit summoning, trying not to waste Mana, but she was unable to remove all the debuffs from Anastaria. And Stacey had ... I selected the girl and whistled: there were 32 debuffs on the 'Cursed' Anastaria. Wow! They managed to land a curse on her too! It wouldn't be for long, of course, just until the first respawn, but the very fact that you could curse such a high-level player ... if my memory didn't fail me, it could only be done by someone with double her number of levels. Anastaria was currently at level 331, therefore, she was cursed by someone who was at least level 662. If you took into account that even Emperors were only level 500, I was liking what was happening less and less.

"Take all the debuffs off her." Once again Antsinthepantsa brought me back to reality. Perhaps I have a concussion and that's why I keep freezing. That's the last thing I need. "My Mana and scrolls are running out, get a move on already!"

"Stacey!" I couldn't help shouting as I took all the debuffs off Anastaria and, instead of running for the glade, she fell to the ground like a broken doll. It was only now that I noticed that summoning the Restoration Spirit takes 40% Hit Points off me. That was almost a half of what I had and without so much as a warning. I immediately summoned a Healing on myself, solemnly promising to finally put together an altar and make a sacrifice to the Spirits and, without thinking of the danger, ran to the place where

Anastaria had just been standing. The phantom players were no longer around – by the looks of it, they had not been permitted to depart until the local Lord (or whatever we were supposed to call him) had said everything he had to say. But as soon as he did, they were free.

"Some place you found to have a nap." I jumped to Anastaria and tried to lift her, but she sagged in my arms like a dead weight.

"So I have ..." The girl tried to smile, but instead her face put on a strange expression of bared teeth. "Don't keep me here, let me respawn ..."

"Yeah, right! Like I'd lose the pleasure of being in your company for six hours with practically no-one else around ... I'd be the laughing stock of Barliona's entire male population!"

"Mahan, what happened? Why hasn't she come to herself yet? I have only enough Mana for two more summonings and I'm out of scrolls!" came a shout from Antsinthepantsa.

"Mahan, I give you my word that we'll definitely meet later one-on-one. But now, please let me go." Anastaria tried to get up by leaning on the ground, but the arm of her gaming avatar broke with a quiet crack, as if it was made of glass. Uh-oh! The avatar could only break in one case – if a quest or a scenario demands it. I sat right down in the mist and carefully put Anastaria's head in my lap. Lifting and dragging her to the glade wouldn't work – she'd break completely, but leaving her here on her own ... I just couldn't do it. You can't just leave a girl in distress like that. ... So all I could do was sit and wrinkle my brow at the unpleasant feeling I got from this new version of Anastaria. For some reason her skin had darkened, had become slimy to the touch and constantly bubbled. I shuddered to think what would happen if I ended up with skin like that. It was a good thing that she was just an ordinary player. This looked painful.

"Stacey, what happened? Do you think we won't make it? So help us, we'll get you back on your feet in no time! So what if you've turned to crystal. I'm sure you've been through worse in your time."

"Turned to crystal! It HURTS!" the girl screamed so loud the entire forest seemed to hear. "My senses have been turned on by 30%! Can't you see what's happening to me? Let me die! I can't even leave the Game right now. If I do, I'll return to the same cursed body! I must go through respawn!"

Antsinthepantsa froze in the middle of summoning another Healing Spirit. I was so shocked by this news that I didn't even notice that the Hit Points of the lady Paladin had run out and her gaming avatar flickered, then disappeared. I hoped that at least now she could leave the capsule and scream all the pain out of herself. Or get drunk to forget the feelings of the curse. To go through what she just went through, without so much as a groan ... I wouldn't have been able to do that. Whether I could trust Anastaria or not no longer mattered. By her actions Anastaria deserved to be ... respected. Yes, that's the word. I really started to respect her as a person and not just some girl with a cute face. Now I just needed to be careful not to let this respect grow into something more. Our weight classes were just too far apart, after all. ...

"Mahan, let's go." Antsinthepantsa once again brought me back to myself. I'll have to remember to do something nice for her after all this. "Anastaria will respawn as good as new. We have to get back to the glade."

"Antsinthepantsa, can I ask you something?" I said as soon as we were back under the protection of the Guardian.

"Just call me Natalie. My gaming name is a bit of a mouthful, so those who know me use the other name. So – shoot."

"Can you tell me how you found out that the Shaman's initiation could be completed in a non-standard way? I'm asking because before I thought that the inexplicable feelings that arise within me on various occasions were something only I experience ... but it turns out that you felt something too. I wish I could get to the bottom of all this, otherwise I'm feeling a bit lost ..."

"Hold on ... you, the owner of a unique Totem, who has an acute perception of the surrounding world, have no idea what it means to be a Shaman?"

"Before your rather emotional exclamation just now I thought I knew what it meant to be a Shaman. Now I'm not so sure. Will you tell me about it?"

"Do you know Kalatea?" The girl was on a roll. "No? You should! And you're not a member of the

Order of the Dragon, are you?" She continued to bombard me with questions.

"Not a member of what? Listen, I think I told you that I only became a Shaman half a year ago, having spent half of that time in a mine where I didn't really use any of my Shaman skills. I have no idea who or what you're talking about now. I asked you because you really helped me out when I was going through the initiation. Now this incomprehensible matter with this stupid intuition or premonition remains. I thought you might know what this is. And now you're trying to scare me with some Galanterea and Orders of the Dragons."

"Kalatea."

"What's the difference? Who the heck is she, anyway? Or 'he', even?"

"It's a 'she'. A lady Shaman. Level 360. She's not in Malabar, but in Astrum, the Empire that lies on one of the neighboring continents. The Order of the Dragon is an association of Shamans headed by her."

"An association of Shamans? I thought this wasn't a particularly popular class ..."

"That's right. On our continent, that is. But in Astrum players choose it quite often. It is part of their cultural heritage, after all, and it's held in high esteem there."

"I think I've lost you there. Can you start again, but in more detail?"

"I can start again," smiled Antsinthepantsa. "No-one would believe this if I told them: a three-month-old Shaman, who managed to get a Dragon and can make active use of his abilities, has no idea about the Order of the Dragon. So. The Shaman class appeared in Barliona just over ten years ago, precisely because players from both the Americas started to petition the Corporation to introduce it. For the first two years Shamans could only be created in Astrum; Kalatea was the first player who managed to complete the initiation in the Path of the Shaman. Essentially this class was especially created with her in mind. Kalatea was actively involved in the design of the abilities and development of the class quests. She was offered a job in the Corporation but refused, preferring to remain an ordinary player. But even now the developers often ask her for advice on various aspects of Shaman gameplay. By the way, she's the only player Harbinger in Barliona."

"Hold on. I read the manual – there are no Harbingers."

"Not in Malabar. The manuals are focused only on the continent from which the information request was made. So, we have Kalatea. That gal founded the Order of the Dragon (the association of Shamans), joining which is every Shaman's dream. I was only accepted there on my third attempt to join. Twice I've failed my initiation, and each time I had to delete my character and start all over. Only after I was given the chance to choose my Totem, did Kalatea agree to take me in. By the way, she's the one who receives new members personally, not one of her officers."

"You've deleted your Shaman twice in order to complete the trial correctly?"

"Yup. When I created the third one, I didn't think I'd make it through, so I gave her this name. When I did complete it, my first impulse was to delete again and re-create with a normal name this time, but ... Bussy turned out to be such a sweetie I didn't have the heart to delete her. So I had to stay as Antsinthepantsa. Oh, by the way! Let's level up our Totems while no-one's around. They will grow faster wrestling with each other than hunting down smaller mobs."

"I think that's a great idea," I agreed and summoned Draco. I told him what was up and sent him to fight the Black Panther. I just hoped he wouldn't leave too many burn marks on her with his acceleration. "So, what happened next? Kalatea founded the association and became a Harbinger. What has intuition got to do with it?"

"A lot. As I said, in both Americas there is already an established image of a Shaman: this trickster with a tambourine who is tuned-in to the surrounding world. I can't tell you all that much, since it is forbidden, but I can give you a rough idea. Did you notice how the premonition only works when you interact with the surrounding world and not with other players? Today, for example, when we were choosing the direction in which to go. Aside from the east side, which contained those who summoned the 'ash', all the others were blocked. And blocked at the level of scenario, at that. So, our class was lucky with its founder. Kalatea managed to convince the developers that the Shamans should also be given a slight, almost imperceptible feeling of disquiet when they are doing something incorrectly. After all, this is possibly the only hybrid class. The developers scratched their heads and together with premonition added the Spirit Summoning Mode – not to make things too easy for us. At the same time they have calibrated the perception of the system warnings in such a way that if you don't use them or ignore them they become weaker and weaker, until one day they disappear altogether. Every six months the Order of the Dragon carries out a re-examination of its members, to find out whether they follow their intuition or not. This was the Corporation's gift to Kalatea for her contribution to the development of the Game. Aside from Shamans, only Paladins have anything of the sort, but I don't know much about it. You should ask your girl, she would know."

"My girl?" It was a good thing I was already sitting down, or I would have dropped where I stood. "Whom do you mean?"

"Anastaria, of course." Antsinthepantsa gave me a strange look. "Am I wrong?"

"No, it's not like that." I would have been lost for words to express how I felt. Bloody hell! Someone actually thinks that Anastaria is my girl! A year ago I would have given half of all I owned to hear that! "We are just good acquaintances who have mutually beneficial dealings with one another. But a couple ...? Let's get back to Shamans."

"Well, that's all I have, pretty much. I'll tell Kalatea about you today. I'm sorry but I must do that,

that's in our rules. So you should expect an invitation to a meeting in the next couple of weeks."

Natalie fell silent and began to watch our Totems dueling. Despite being three times smaller than Bussy, Draco won every fourth battle. By the looks of it, as soon as his intensification cooldown expired, he activated his ability and flooded the poor cat in fire. It was interesting to watch a Dragon letting the panther ride on his back while trying to bite one of her legs, but I was preoccupied by a different matter. In particular what the girl said about intuition – that these feelings that popped up on various occasions were triggered via the system. And there was me thinking that I was something else, that I was on the path to becoming a 'super-player' ... but it turned out that there were more of these players in Barliona than you could shake a stick at ... that there were even Harbingers out there. ...

"Natalie, can you tell me if your intuition has ever let you down? Have you ever had instances when you trusted it, but the result was not what you expected?"

"Of course! This was the main requirement of the Corporation in order not to end up with unstoppable monsters instead of Shamans. Usually about eighty percent of the premonitions don't have any meaning behind them. Moreover, aside from being beset with this 'white noise', we also have incorrect instincts generated for us. These begin from level 100, so you shouldn't worry about it yet. Otherwise yes, about half of what we intuit is wrong.

With situations like today, you can see straight away that it's the real deal, so that's straightforward. But the rest ... you constantly have to level up in Spirituality, in order to keep things on the right level. I hope that's one of the stats that you chose, yes?"

"Yup."

"Good, it'll come in very useful. Listen, I have a question for you now. Why do you need me on this quest? I wouldn't argue that it suits me very well, which is why I dropped everything in Anhurs and headed out here, but I don't get what Shamans have to do with it. It was clear that today a spell was used against us, not Spirits, so it's not like we can really make a difference here."

"How can I explain this ... if I let myself be guided by your words – the system whispered in my ear that this is categorically impossible without Shamans. I would even summon Kalatea here, if I could, to have a fuller team. When you write to her, say: "Mahan is inviting you to join him on a quest". I can't explain it, but it cannot be completed without Shamans. You do know about Geranika, the new Lord of Shadow? He's a Shaman."

"So what? What do Geranika and the Lord of the Dark Forest Cursed Ones have to do with one another?"

"Who knows ...? But I can guarantee that they are connected in some way. Guardian!" I addressed the silent tree. "I have two questions! Would you mind answering them?" I took the silence to be a sign of agreement and continued: "Why was I struck down with debuffs if you said that nothing can harm me on this ground. And do you know Geranika?"

"Ten years ago, a few days before my death," replied the Guardian after a few moments, using its favorite vibrations, "a sentient by that name came to the Dark Forest. He asked me to teach him about Ishni, but I refused him. The Shaman left, but two days later a caravan entered the forest that brought the curse with it. I've heard nothing more about Geranika."

"What is an Ishni?" I asked straight away, ignoring the fact that the Guardian failed to answer my first question.

"Ishni is not a what. Ishni is the heart of my forest. She is my Unicorn."

CHAPTER SEVEN
THE BLACK AND WHITE

"NATALIE, CAN YOU TELL ME IF THIS IS the right way to level up my Totem?" I asked the lady Shaman, as soon as Draco's allotted time in this world had run out. In a couple of hours of fighting with Bussy, the Dragon's level had increased by an entire point, reaching 38. At this pace I'll be leveling him up till Chinese Easter, whatever that's supposed to mean. I'm doing something wrong and a fellow Shaman might have an idea what that is.

"What do you mean by 'the right way'? Do you mean fighting? Of course," replied Antsinthepantsa with surprise and then continued, sounding less sure, "Although I might be mistaken. Why, do you have some ideas about this? I don't think I can remember any specific articles on the subject from Kalatea. Hold on, I'll be a moment," the girl's eyes glassed over, indicating that the player had logged out.

I returned to my program of ingot-making when I realized just how alone I was once Natalie left me with no-one but the Prince around. I had used the two hours during which the Totems were vying to see who was stronger on crafting. When I bought the ore, I didn't really think of the fact that leveling up in Jewelcraft would require ingots and that I would still have to make them. My level of Smithing allowed me to smelt Tin and I didn't have far to go until Bronze, but that 'distance' still had to be covered. Keeping in mind that I could only level up in Jewelcraft by making things out of Silver, Gold and Iron and that Silver Ingots only became available from level 60 in the profession ... something told me that I was looking at a toilsome and vigorous grind ahead of me to level up. I could only place my hopes in the boost the Guardian's glade would give me – in the two hours I had left before it was due to expire, that is. Once again cursing myself that I omitted to switch on my brain in Pryke and level up Smithing virtually for free there, I continued to wear out the smelting pot.

After explaining who Ishni was, the Guardian had clammed up and was now completely refusing to talk. As soon as his Petrification debuff wore off, the Prince, who was dutifully sitting inside the Tent when it had all happened, came out and asked me to remove all the other debuffs from him. I summoned a Restoration Spirit and felt like going over and banging my head against the Oak for completely forgetting about Slate until now. Earlier, when the high-level players began to arrive and I was re-forming the group, the Prince completely slipped my mind. I sent him the invite and tried to talk him into temporarily returning to Anhurs. I was really reluctant to risk a life that was so dear to the Princess. Even if Slate wasn't a standard NPC – you might even say he was a key scenario mob – something irreversible might still happen to him, such as his Imitator unexpectedly hitting early 'retirement'. For that Tisha would lynch me, then reanimate me and lynch me again. The future Prince of Malabar carefully listened to my arguments, even agreeing with some, and then gave me such an earful that if he were Tisha's real husband I would have been immediately kicked out of Malabar. So I had to take the risk and keep him with us, making a note to ask Anastaria to secretly look after him just in case. ...

"Mahan." Natalie returned after about thirty minutes, giving me enough time to raise my Smithing to 36. And that was with the current speed of professional leveling up ... still too slow, really. The system looked favorably on my diligent ingot smelting and rewarded me with six pieces of Lapis. That meant three thousand gold for each, if I remembered the prices right. Not bad at all, but I was rather downcast upon consulting the manual. The next set of chess figurines needed Alexandrite, obtained by smelting Silver, which, as it now became clear, was still a long way off. I had to find a way of speeding up.

"The Order of the Dragon has no guides on leveling up Totems and Kalatea simply chuckled when I called her and asked about the correct way of working with them. This can mean only one thing: I've been using the wrong method to get Bussy to level 120. Damn!" cursed Antsinthepantsa, "why didn't I think of this before? Right, it will take around nine more hours for everyone to respawn, so I'll log out for a bit – need to have a chat with other Shamans. I'll find out how they do it. I've mentioned you to Kalatea, by the way, and she asked you to contact her. Here's her visor number, you can contact her there, she's expecting your call."

"Eeehh ... I can't give her a call," I said, noting down the number just in case in my notebook. "It just so happens that I have no access to visors for the next eight and a half years."

"Then use the phone, what's the difference?" asked Natalie, surprised.

"You don't understand. I don't have access to phones either. You see ... I'm currently in a prisoner capsule, my rights are restricted and I won't be free for quite some time yet."

As soon as I uttered the key word 'prisoner', Antsinthepantsa's face froze. Seems our society has instilled certain attitudes really well in us: it's good to be good and it's bad to be bad. And to hell with the tautology, you can't hide the truth: people aren't too tolerant of prisoners in our world. The dregs of society, social outcasts, the disgrace of the human race ... I've had enough chance to hear all kinds of labels in my time.

"I'm sorry," uttered Natalie, after she finally finished wrestling with her prejudices. "I didn't think

... I didn't mean to offend you ..."

"Listen, just hold off slapping me on the ignore list. Let me tell you who I am and what I'm doing time for and then you can decide what to do. So, it all began when ..."

I painted a colorful picture of how I ended up in Barliona in this capacity and tried to emphasize the fact that I had an agreement with Marina, that I thought I was working with a test Imitator and that I handed myself in as soon as I found out the consequences of my actions. It was a really good thing, after all, that my fighters and I had our red headbands removed. Judging by Antsinthepantsa's reaction, the majority of the players see convicts purely as convicts, law-breakers and not as people who had been successfully rehabilitated at the mines. It was even surprising that Elenium, Sushiho and Dooki took the information that I and the other clan members were ex-prisoners from Pryke so well. To be honest, I expected worse.

"I'm sorry," muttered Antsinthepantsa, this time looking embarrassed. Was I wrong, or did she go red in the face? "It was just so unexpected ... the 'Terror of the Collectors' ... I will be sure to read up on you today and tell Kalatea that you ... are somewhat out of reach."

"Natalie, before you run off, can you tell me if your senses have also been turned on? You looked embarrassed, your face reddened and this ... this can't happen with the filters on."

"Of course they're off." Antsinthepantsa looked

perplexed: "Who would agree to spend over three or four hours a day in this world without feeling all it has to offer? Taste, smell ... I'm not Anastaria, of course, and wouldn't set pain at 30%, but I've raised even that to 10%, to keep my reactions sharp. I was even permitted to increase my neutral and positive sensations to the full 100. Are you saying that before prison you played with all the senses turned off?"

"Yup," I said, trying to keep my jaw from hitting the floor. "I read about the senses and several times almost went to the center to unlock them, but each time I was stopped by a reluctance to feel pain. Nowhere did I read that you could split the activated senses between pain and pleasure! I used to follow the topic quite closely; this wasn't the case six months ago!"

"You're right about the division of senses. This is a new feature introduced by the Corporation. Just three months ago all the capsules were replaced, practically for free. Until that time the senses were combined, feeling pleasure and pain came as part of the same package. But now it's all been separated. Why are you blushing?" asked Antsinthepantsa, when my gaming avatar went rather red in the face. Anastaria ... that time she tried to use the Sirens' poison on me and I explored her all over with my hands, thinking that she couldn't feel a thing. So it looks like the revulsion expressed on her face at the time wasn't from what she was seeing, but from what she was feeling. ... Damn! I've made such a fool of myself!

Until the Guardian's glade stopped providing the professions bonus, I managed to get my Smithing up to 42 – I couldn't get any further on Tin alone. To make Bronze ingots I needed Copper, all of which I had handed over to Eric. No Eric, no Copper. The Copper Vein, which was doing its best to attract me and get me to swing my pick at it, failed to generate much enthusiasm: I had no desire left to work whatsoever. After I repaired all the items I could, leveling up Repair to 5, I lay down under the Guardian and started to read Theodore's book. One shouldn't leave a source of free stats like this untapped. ...

"Hello Mahan. Listen, we need to talk." A little later Elenium appeared in the Guardian's glade. The players that were sent for respawn were going to start turning up any minute now, so it was good that my solitude should be broken first by someone from my own clan.

"Of course, did you manage to take that long holiday?"

"Yes, I will be in the Game in the next two weeks. This is what I wanted to talk to you about. You see ... I did something stupid, really stupid."

"What do you mean?"

"Do you remember the High Priestess taking me aside?"

"Of course I do, I just haven't had time to corner you and get you to tell me what that was about. You were given some kind of a class-based quest, right? Since you've brought it up already, do tell. Although, stop. Are you saying that you've already managed to break some condition of that quest?"

"No, the conditions are just fine. It's just ... damn, I'll have to tell you this one way or another. I shared it with Phoenix and they offered me good money and a place in their clan for the quest," blurted out Elenium and then sighed in relief. "I'm sorry, but I have to think about my family, so potential big money in the future is worth less to me than good money right now."

"Come again? I'm not getting you at all." I shook my head in incomprehension. Sergei had said something using apparently everyday language, but the meaning was completely eluding me.

"I ... offered ... the quest ... to Phoenix ... got an offer to join their clan," said Elenium slowly, trying not to look me in the eye, "and I accepted."

"When ...?" As it finally sunk in that what I'd just heard wasn't the fruit of my fevered imagination, my brain went numb. What does it mean that he gave away the quest and went over to Phoenix? Does this mean he's ditching me? It just doesn't make sense ... of all things, you wouldn't expect a stitch-up like that from Elenium. ...

"Last night, when Anastaria got here and you hid under the dome with her, I came over to Rick and showed him the quest description. I told you, I messed up. I should've talked with you first, but it's Phoenix, after all. ... Rick passed it on to Raster, their head of player recruitment, who contacted me today and asked me some questions. ... To be honest, I never thought that something like that could happen, but you know what being in Phoenix would mean to me, so I answered honestly about the circumstances under which I got my quest chain and then agreed to go through their tests. The test results were reviewed by Hellfire himself and he's offered me a place as a support group Fighter. Not a recruit – a Fighter right away, but ... he did it under the condition that I should leave Seathistles today and in no way give the description of my quest to you. He's right; it's only open to Priests and I can't share it with any other class, so ... phew ... I'm sorry, but this invitation means far too much to me."

"Sergei, didn't we want a clan of our own ...?" I had to force the words out. "How can all this crazy talk be true?"

"Dan, I completely understand what you're trying to say, but you have to understand me too. There's my wife and kid and a stable salary for four compulsory hours online with Phoenix on the one hand and you, a bunch of convicts, and some unintelligible salary from my contribution to the clan on the other. There's no way that I can sit in Barliona twenty-four seven, so my contribution to the clan would be minimal. This means that I wouldn't earn enough even to pay the subscription, let alone enough to keep a family. I'm not prepared to leave reality for Barliona completely, so Phoenix's offer to me was ... I need hardly say ..."

"Sergei, are you sure? Look how the top players

are dancing around Seathistles, handing over piles of money. We have enough additional quests to earn us a whole load more. It'll all work out."

"I know all that very well! Stop trying to persuade me like I'm a little kid. It's not the clan those top players are dancing around, it's you. Once you're gone, everything else is gone too. The risks are just too great. What'll happen to the clan if you end up back in the mines? Do you know how hard it was for me to make this decision? But that's the decision I've taken and I'll stick with it, come what may. My entire life as a player I've been dreaming of being accepted into Phoenix and now when I've finally been given the opportunity, I can't let it slip away."

"Do you realize that what you're doing is called a 'common stitch-up'? I was counting on you and you quit the moment a lucrative opportunity beckoned. Sergei, I never expected something like that from you. Perhaps, Dooki or Sushiho, but you ..."

"Well, since you brought them up ... I asked Raster if there's a chance they would be accepted into Phoenix too. If I'm right, they're going through testing as we speak."

"WHAT?!"

"That's right," said a deep chesty voice that for some reason women find so attractive. Although for me it became the embodiment of everything that was bad about Barliona: Hellfire – in the flesh. "But Elenium's got it wrong. They have ALREADY done the tests. Their results weren't as good as those of the Priest, so I'm not prepared to offer them the role of

Fighters. But Raster said that they'll do fine as Recruits and will go through a second round of testing after proper training. Elenium, have you made your decision?"

"Yes, I agree to your terms."

"Then no point putting things off. I need you to call on the Emperor as a witness that you haven't given Mahan the description of the quest. After that I'm prepared to accept you into Phoenix. Those are the rules."

"Let the Emperor be my witness," Elenium called on the ultimate arbiter in Malabar, "that I haven't given the description of the class-based quest chain I received from the High Priestess to anyone other than members of the Phoenix clan."

A cloud of light immediately formed around Sergei, and quickly dissipated without causing him any harm. The Priest hadn't lied – the Imitator confirmed that. They say that the developers have learned to use capsules as lie detectors, so that if you blabbed a secret outside the Game – in reality – the system would still figure it out. But in all likelihood these were probably just rumors. Otherwise players would've kicked up a fuss a long time ago, protesting against such an intrusion in their private life.

"Welcome to the Phoenix clan, Fighter," uttered Hellfire, when – just a moment after the official confirmation – the symbol of the flaming chicken clan appeared above Elenium's head. "Our Head Priest will contact you today and set out a leveling-up schedule for you. Now let me talk to Mahan."

"So what is it you're trying to achieve here?" I asked the hateful dwarf as soon as Sergei walked away. "Just don't bullshit me with a story about how you suddenly had a revelation that these three were prime examples of priestly, rogue and necromancer genius."

"Why? Elenium really is a talented Priest – it's a surprise that he hasn't tried to take our tests before. Mahan, you're wasting your time looking for some malicious ulterior motive where there is none. My task is to make the Phoenix clan stronger and poach the very best players from all the other clans. Preferably doing as much as possible to destroy these clans in the process, leaving them no chance of catching up with us. Seathistles have been getting too much limelight all of a sudden. Every other person seems to be saying that a clan has emerged with none other than Johnson himself as a member. But I'm sure that you aren't him. This would be just too petty for him. You're nothing more than an ordinary player, who's managed to get hooked into one scenario. And, as you've been riding that wave, the developers have managed to use you and all those near you for the subsequent scenarios so that they can have a sure shot at launching the update."

"That's all very informative, but it still doesn't explain what possessed you to start poaching my people."

"It seems that you didn't hear me: Mahan, please understand, this is not personal. For the Phoenix clan you represent the potential threat of losing out on good profit. Therefore I've taken certain steps to counteract that."

"You do realize that now I'll stop involving Phoenix in any new quests?"

"What quests? Mahan, get it through your head already! If you are removed from these scenarios, you will stop getting any more of them. Your decision to invite all of us to the Cleansing of the Dark Forest was downright stupid. I concede that you've made a very good gain financially, but with subsequent developments ... the times of Beatwick are over, now other continent-wide scenarios will be coming into play, one of which was given to Elenium and, consequently, to Phoenix. Of course, I could've given you a blank face and simply told you to take a hike, but I decided to explain everything to avoid any misunderstandings. That's something we can do without. People can take offence and start doing stupid things. You just can't be allowed to return to the mines right now. The Guardian's quest is tied to you, so for the time being you're useful. But I'll tell you straight away, I will do everything I can to make sure Phoenix takes this quest off your hands. Perhaps you should quit being obstinate and accept my offer? The place of the Master of Phoenix is still waiting for you."

"No." I couldn't think of anything sufficiently offensive to unsettle Hellfire, so my answer was monosyllabic. My apologies, Anastaria, but from now on Phoenix is going on my ignore list. The whole clan.

"As you wish. Ah! There's Dooki and Sushiho.

Are you ready to accept my offer? You can see that Elenium has already made his decision," Hellfire said to the other players that'd just arrived, and then turned to me and moved in for the kill: "not much point in me going after the three convicts – those guys follow the code of honor amongst thieves and won't leave Seathistles. I respect that, but you should know that I intend to talk with Barsina and take her with us as well. Mahan, I won't let your clan get off its knees."

As the Seathistles clan lost two more players, I finally understood that my previous life as a Hunter had ended for good.

Hellfire stood next to me for a little while, probably expecting me to explode in anger, but I remained deathly still. Snorting, the top dwarf of Malabar left me alone as I lowered myself to the ground.

Can you describe pain? Can you describe complete disappointment? Can you describe the realization that no matter what you did it would all be fruitless, because someone like Hellfire would turn up and simply buy all your fighters? If everything is so bad, what's the point in continuing to struggle and trying to make it to the top?

My eyes closed, cutting off the colors of this world. I wished I had some way to block sound as well, but I had no scroll for doing that, like Anastaria. What if there's a Spirit that can separate you from the surrounding world? I should dig around for one ASAP. Right now I didn't give a damn that Hellfire was savoring his victory over me and, consequently, my complete defeat at the hands of his legendary and unparalleled might. Right now I needed to find a way of being alone. Spirit, where the heck are you?!

Are you sure that you want to leave this world and be transported to the Astral Plane?

Astral Plane? Well, what's the difference? If it's got to be the Astral Plane, the Astral Plane it is. I really didn't care anymore, even if I got sent back to the mines. What's the use of making plans for developing your clan if you have no way of ever getting them off the ground? I was counting on the free players so much that I was completely unprepared for such a move on their part. It was hard to wake up to the fact that the guys with whom you've played for well over two years are first and foremost people who could simply be bought. And then most likely sold on and thrown away, like useless junk, after all their potential is used up.

Stop!

How about I stop feeling sorry for myself? Maybe it's time for me to start showing my teeth and fighting for what's mine? Am I a Shaman or a shy mouse, when push comes to shove? Why am I behaving like a complete pushover? Oh noes! Someone took a shit on me! Enough! I need to pull myself together and take this on the chin, or fight back with everything I've got. So Hellfire wants to destroy my clan, eh? He can dream on! That flame-grilled chicken douchebag is due for one hell of a comeuppance!

Having made up my mind, I opened my eyes. There's no returning the ones who left, but Barsina will stay with me. You have to fight for your clan members. I don't get it ... what happened to the Guardian's glade?

The surrounding world had transformed. The trees, the mist, the other players and the Guardian had disappeared. Everything had vanished, even the ground! I ended up at the center of a sphere divided into two: one part consisted of unbearably bright Light and the other of frighteningly pitch-black Darkness. Those designers sure know how to do visuals – looking at just one of these half-spheres was enough to give you goosebumps. The only thing that didn't cause any discomfort was the gray line dividing the light from the dark and that's where my gaze came to rest. The main thing was not to stand there wide-eyed, but figure out where the heck I'd ended up.

"You dared to enter our world, Elemental One!" thundered the Darkness, enveloping me in a terrible coldness.

"You aren't ready yet, almost Great One," whispered the Light, caressing me with its warmth.

"Where am I?" I whispered, stupefied, and blinked a few times in the hope that all of this would stop and I would find myself back in the Dark Forest.

"You have entered the abode of the Supreme Spirits of the Higher and Lower Worlds, Elemental

One!" thundered the Darkness again, sweeping another wave of cold over me.

"You have entered a place of answers, almost Great One." The gentle sounds of Light pushed back the dark and rekindled my desire to keep playing – what if them voices come with a nifty buff or two?

"Mahan, where did you go? And, more importantly, how?" An internal raid message from Ehkiller popped up in front of me, but I waved it away like some annoying insect. I had more important things to do than chat to those who would shortly be going on my ignore list. I finally had an opportunity to get some answers. But the unpleasant part was that I had no idea which questions I should be asking. ...

"You don't belong here, yet, future Great One," whispered the Light a couple of seconds later. "We were watching our best student in Malabar and were not expecting to meet another Shaman entering the Astral Plane – unprepared and uninitiated. You should not have ended up here and ... we will be more careful in the future, but we must atone for our mistake. You will receive an answer to any question. Ask!"

"An-," I began, but regained control of myself just in time and fell silent. If I asked 'Any?' now, the answer I'd get would be 'Yes, but now you've used up your question'. Now I could see who Almis and Kornik took after in the 'how to be a pain in the neck' department: none other than these Supreme Spirit dudes. But back to the matter in hand: if I have a chance to ask a question, there's no way I can let it slip away. I just have to decide what interests me the most. Should I ask about the Karmadont Chess Set? Like, 'Can you give me the exact coordinates of the cave?', for example? But what if it's not a cave or if you need a key to enter, that key being the chess set itself? Not much sense in asking this then. I'll find that out from Anasta- ... damn, from Barsina or any other player. To hell with Phoenix! Should I find out how to complete the trial to become a Great Shaman? I can ask Antsinthepantsa that. Where hoards of gold might be hidden in Barliona? I'll be sent off to such a distant middle-of-nowhere that no amount of gold would make up for having to trudge there. And in any case, I have those two Dragon treasures waiting for me, so I'm sorted on the loot front. What then? What does it mean to be a Shaman? What happened during the fight between Prontho and Shiam? Is Kornik alive? So many questions to which I'd love to get answers, but I can ask only one ...

"What is the source of Geranika's strength?" I finally managed to articulate the question that was continuing to bother me. Antsinthepantsa said that there was no answer and Kalatea is unlikely to spill the beans, since she probably enjoys watching players explore various features she'd helped design for the Shaman class, so this was a highly relevant matter. Keeping in mind that Geranika promised to do all kinds of 'pleasant' things to me, any information on his capabilities would come in very handy. I could even trade it with Natalie on mutually beneficial terms.

"O Supreme ones, are you still here?" When over a minute later no answer was forthcoming, I politely reminded them of my existence. Either the Spirits have no idea, or ...

"We cannot tell you this, because we do not know it ourselves," growled the Darkness. Looks like getting to the bottom of Geranika's strength is connected to some scenario quest, so the Imitators can't 'leak' this information before it's time. The developers wouldn't permit this. Very interesting. A negative result is still a result. "The last time Geranika summoned a Spirit was twenty years ago, from then on he has been using something else. We didn't answer your question and you cannot ask us another, to our regret. In the whole of Barliona only the Patriarch is able to help you, but he is out of reach. We cannot touch the dead ones; neither can they enter our world. It is time for you to go. We will transport you back without imposing penalties for your lengthy stay in the Astral Plane. A Shaman is able to speak to us for no more than three minutes, after that Spirits stop responding to him for a long time. Remember this until our next meeting. When you decide to become a Harbinger, you will find yourself in our presence once more. Until we meet again, Elemental one," concluded the Darkness. The sphere surrounding me began to spin, slowly at first and then faster and faster, until, finally, reaching a crazy speed, it blurred into continuous gray. There was a quiet clap, as if someone had shot a gun with a silencer attached, like in one of those antique films, and the sphere dissipated like a cloud of smoke, returning me to the Guardian's glade. The first thing I saw when I appeared were the surprised eyes of Antsinthepantsa. So, she's already back.

"The gusts of wind have brought us mist, our Shaman hiding in its midst," Natalie greeted me with a rhyme and a chuckle. "Judging by the visual effect, you've just had a meeting with the Spirits of the Higher and Lower Worlds. Only High Shamans are able to do that and only a couple of those exist in the entire continent. Are you sure you're just 'Elemental'?"

"Can all Shamans appear out of the mist?" Some other player decided to join our conversation. "Stunning!"

"You haven't seen the arrival of a Harbinger yet. When I saw her for the first time, I had to scrape my jaw off the floor. If you want a definition of 'stunningly beautiful', that is it."

"Guys, let's not mope around. It's time we knuckled down but now you've started with all this Shaman talk." I put a stop to all the chitchat, showing a total lack of desire to continue the conversation and trying to get people into a working mood. "Anastaria and Donotpunnik! We convene to discuss plans in five minutes! Everyone else – get ready to step out into the forest, we have another fight ahead of us! Plinto! Where's Plinto? Not here yet? When he appears, send him to me straight away. We have to find out what it was he saw and what this 'Ash' is. Let's get to work!" I didn't care how ridiculous an under-level-100 player ordering about level-280+ players might look, that's just how it was. We had to complete the clearing of the forest and find the Patriarch as soon as possible, so I could forget this bad dream. I couldn't exclude the deserters from doing the quest, but removing them from the group and leaving them to complete the quests by themselves ... no, if we started together, we'd finish together. Let Eluna be their judge, but I had no intention of turning into Bat from Pryke. Had all my additional stat slots not been taken, right now the System would have offered me the Meanness stat for sure. Like I needed it. By the looks of it, Elenium only got the current quest because he was in one group with me. If I kick him I have no idea how he would complete it or hand it in – there's a risk that he wouldn't be accepted, and I wouldn't want to stitch him up, potentially. Although ... if it's a scenario, what difference does it make to the High Priestess who completes it? The main thing was the result. In this Hellfire was right – while I'm at the center of attention quests will keep falling into my lap, but as soon as I get sidelined this flow of bonuses will stop.

"Mahan, would you permit me to have a chat with you," said Ehkiller graciously, in an almost fatherly tone. "Anastaria, do join us. Put up a dome please," he asked the girl as soon as she walked over.

"Well ... as disagreeable as it is to admit it, a very delicate situation has arisen between our clans, which the both of us have to try to resolve."

"You call poaching players in the middle of a quest a 'tricky situation'?" I chuckled. "In that case what would be a 'negative' or an 'unpleasant' situation? Killer, this was a stitch-up, pure and simple. This sort of stuff warrants a black eye, or two."

"You are letting your emotions do the talking." Ehkiller refused to be provoked and continued, firmly sticking to his agenda, "You must realize that if you found yourself in a similar situation, you would've acted in exactly the same manner. I'm quite sure of it. But let's not talk of what could've been, let's return to the players that crossed over. I have to admit that they will have to remain in Phoenix: I doubt you'd take them back if I excluded them from the clan and I don't want it to become known throughout Barliona that I am not a man who keeps his word."

"Will you tell me what it is you want from me now exactly? You already got your hands on pretty much everything you wanted: the Guardian's quest, Elenium's chain quest, whatever that is, and also ... I can already see that I've made a mistake in sharing the Patriarch quest with Anastaria, especially in doing it for free and without limitations on sharing it with other players. I fell for this word called 'trust'. These things happen. Hellfire has shown me exactly where I can take and shove this particular word ... I get it already and I'm done. What's with the current circus performance?"

"Emotions, Mahan: you're allowing yourself to be ruled by emotions. What Hellfire and Raster did was in line with Phoenix policy, so their actions are understandable. But they didn't have all the information. For instance, they didn't know about the Patriarch and the Eye. And our dearest Anastaria only supplied this information today, just as Hellfire was already making the transfer offer. Such offers are common practice for any clan, not just our one. As a side note, I only found out about all of this today, which is why this usually active young lady is staying very quiet now, and that I emphatically forbade her to pass on the quest to anyone else, until we settle this matter with you."

"How nice ... 'Killer, I'm really not with you on what exactly it is that you actually want. It's not like I can demand Phoenix not to accept anyone else from the Seathistles clan. No-one would ever join us if it meant that their way into Phoenix was permanently barred after that. Whichever way you look at it, you really are the best clan in Malabar. What can I say about the (now official) clan membership 'realignment'? Only one thing – if fate once again smiles on me and I get hold of another quest, Phoenix will have no part of it. I'm sorry, but this is a necessary measure."

"This is exactly why we are talking right now, to avoid any need for such measure. You are quite right – what's done is done. You are also right that an agreement between our clans would be the kiss of death to yours. I would like to offer you compensation. For example, you have no Priests, so Elenium's quest is of little use to you. So I could offer you, temporarily of course, one or two Priests who will complete this quest with your clan. That way

Seathistles will get the First Kill."

"And as soon as the quest is finished these players will go back to Phoenix, taking any bonuses from their achievement with them. What's the point in getting the First Kill if those who have it will end up back in Phoenix? Just to tick a box for clan status? I don't need it."

"What do you want in that case? Money? Gear? We can provide that too."

"People, I already told you what I want. Or, rather, what I'm going to do. As soon as these quests are completed, the Seathistles clan will have no further dealings with Phoenix. You're a high-flyer all high and mighty; good for you. We'll keep our feet firmly on the ground and do what we do best: sit and wait for our prison sentences to end. If I've got you right, the gist of this conversation runs something like this: 'Sorry, Mahan, we have started to destroy your clan a bit too early. Jumped the gun and all that. But you should know that you're finished the moment it becomes convenient'. Although, wait, 'sorry' hasn't even come into it. Dear Phoenix representatives, I am telling you again: once we complete these two quests we will go our separate ways and our paths will never cross again."

"I hear you. It's a pity that we've failed to find common ground on this. I propose that we postpone this conversation and return to it later. I can guarantee you that we will not approach Barsina and if she contacts us herself, you will be informed. Anastaria will not share the Patriarch quest without first gaining your approval. Will you remove the players who crossed over from the groups for both quests?"

"What's the point? Just to show what a bastard I am? Let them stay."

"All right. I have only one small point to clarify. If you aren't disbanding the group, I would like to compensate you for the participation of our new players in the current scenario. Their level barely exceeds 100, so I'm prepared to offer you a hundred thousand for the three of them. What do you say?"

"A hundred for three? That's not even funny. They might as well stay for free."

"So how much do you want?"

"A hundred and thirty," I paused, watching the faces of both Phoenix players, baffled by such a paltry increase in the price, and then added: "each!"

"All right, I'll send you the Agreement in a minute. Then the matter of the transferred players can be considered settled," concluded Ehkiller. "Now we must return to the matter of apologies. I have a feeling that words alone will be insufficient, so I thought of something else: Anastaria. What do you say?"

"Quasiproton," I shrugged.

"What do you mean 'quasiproton'?"

"And what do you mean 'Anastaria'?"

For a while Ehkiller looked at me somewhat perplexed, but then his face lit up in a smile and the shadow leader of the Phoenix clan continued: "I understand. I didn't express myself very well. You see,

Anastaria broke ..."

"'Killer, I insist that you tell Mahan the whole truth," Anastaria spoke for the first time, interrupting the mage. I'd nearly forgotten she was with us. "The scenario with the punishment will look stupid now. I'm against it."

Ehkiller froze for a moment, chuckled and then, apparently having come to a decision, looked at me cheerfully:

"Well, well, Mahan ... getting Anastaria to go against my decision ... if you were my son I would be proud of you. Good! Here's a Confidentiality Agreement. I'm sorry, but we can't do without it. There's just too much at stake."

As soon as I signed, agreeing that the information I was about to hear would not be passed on to third parties, 'Killer commenced with his explanation:

"I apologize in advance for digressing into history, but you may struggle to understand everything without it. Forget everything I just told you – none of it has anything to do with the real state of things. Aside from the money: that you'll get in any case. So ... the Phoenix Clan was founded on the very day that Barliona was launched – you could say it's the oldest clan in the game. We've had our ups and downs, but by about ten years in we'd gathered the core group of players on whom I felt I could rely. I poured a huge, no, an insane amount of money into the Game (being fortunate enough to be able to do so), set out the clan development strategy and methodically began to weed out the competition. Alongside Phoenix, the Dark Legion began to emerge as our clear virtual enemy. After all, aside from the best clan in Malabar, there had to be a clan for all the players rejected by us to join. Otherwise Phoenix would have been trampled underfoot a long time ago. But this way everyone could enjoy watching our battles. Evolett steered things in the right direction, not allowing his players, like Plinto, to bring down our Crafters freely, and focusing attention on Fighters and Recruits instead. This went on for a long time, until the Corporation decided to unlock Kartoss. Knowing that such opportunities couldn't be passed over, we flipped a coin to see which of our clans should move to Kartoss. Evolett won. When you appeared, with your unique collection of Reputations, Evolett chose you instead of one of my fighters and is now sitting in Anhurs and quietly celebrating such a fortuitous turn of events. This is a brief overview of what's been happening in the past ten years of the Game."

"Right, but what do you want with me in all of this?"

"Take it easy; let the old man have his say. It's been a while since I've had the opportunity. Sooner or later the rot creeps into any established organization. It becomes stilted, starts to suffer from complacency and an overinflated sense of its own unique place in the world. ... Around a year ago Rick raised his Crafting to 10 and fell into a state that can be easiest described as a 'superiority complex'. Knowing full well how important he is to the clan, he started demanding various kinds of preferential treatment, which often breached the bounds of common sense. ... For example, did you know that Rick is one of only three Phoenix players who are able to declare war on behalf of the clan? Me, Anastaria and him – a simple head of the Masters. Even Hellfire and Castle Keepers don't have such privileges."

"So why don't you simply kick him out of the clan?" I asked in surprise, struggling to grasp Phoenix clan's internal problems.

"Because a player who has gained 14 levels in Crafting is very valuable for the clan in the financial sense. Items that he creates are a source of stable income, so kicking him out would deprive the clan of a golden goose. It would be foolish and wasteful."

"In that case you'll continue to have a malcontent in your clan who will keep laying down increasingly unreasonable conditions all the time. You'll just have to deal with it."

"This is why I decided to make a knight's move. Who is 'Anastaria'? She's not just a name, she's an entire brand now. She is so closely identified with Phoenix that everyone takes it for granted that whatever she does I would never kick her out – because this would cause great damage to the clan. This is exactly why I started to hatch a plan to make an example of Anastaria by publicly throwing her out of Phoenix."

."..?"

"Don't look so surprised. Yes, I intend to solemnly and dramatically remove Anastaria from the clan, to make it clear that no-one is irreplaceable. Under my close supervision, for several months now, she's been committing all kinds of terrible outrageous acts within the clan: she doesn't submit reports, periodically leaves the clan, fails to inform anyone of what she's up to, provokes arguments and uses clan resources for her personal ends. And everyone just accepts it, because she's the leader. Everyone sees the clan rules being brazenly flouted, but does their best to turn a blind eye. Today's situation was simply a boon to us in view of all this. I'm sorry, but your players did approach us of their own accord, and because Raster is the one who deals with admitting people into the clan, I found out that Elenium had passed all our tests and had already been offered a place only after the fact. Hellfire outdid himself. It seems that he's taken a dislike to you, and quite a big one at that. However, as sad as it is, the transfer of your players to Phoenix made a good trigger for putting my plan into action. Anastaria raised hell, called everyone – including myself – idiots, self-absorbed morons and other equally endearing names, and demanded that the Agreements with the three new players to be torn up. She threatened to leave the clan if her conditions were not met. No-one in Barliona, except Evolett, and now you, knows about our close cooperation. The clan is currently awaiting my reaction to Hellfire's actions, which go against the spirit of cooperative questing, and to see how I handle the situation with Anastaria. After all, everyone now automatically associates Anastaria with the word

'Phoenix'. This is why she'll be kicked out of the clan today."

"A neat series of moves, what can I say?" I concluded, when Ehkiller paused. "And there was me trying to figure out what Anastaria joining my clan was all about. Makes sense now. But 'Killer, your plan resulted in three people leaving my clan! Three people with whom I ran around the Game for two years!"

"Look at it this way," Anastaria intervened for the second time during this meeting, "we did not try to lure them over, they switched to Phoenix of their own accord, at the first opportunity. I don't want to say anything bad about your friends, but think about this yourself, Mahan: what would've happened if they'd left you six months later, for instance, after becoming an integral part of your clan in many ways? It could be just guesswork, but the risk that they would've ditched you in any case is very high."

"Yes, I can see that, but ... fine, the matter with those three is now settled – they'll stay with you in any case. However, tell me why am I being told of the Phoenix clan's internal problems right now?"

"I need your help. I really do. At first we simply planned to cut Anastaria loose and make her wander about Malabar listless and disgruntled, but after today's developments I quickly thought of another plan. In order to make up for this misunderstanding I thought of loaning Anastaria to you – let's say for three months. This would be good both for her and for your clan."

"And how did you intend to pull that off?" I

couldn't help asking.

"That's simple. I was going to tell you how Anastaria started breaking the clan rules, that she had become uncontrollable, then summon the Guardian and officially exclude Anastaria from Phoenix. To be honest, my plan was based on a 90% probability that you would have invited Anastaria to join your clan. She would've spent two or three months with you, until just before the big clan competition, and then resumed her place in Phoenix. It would have made for a magnificently choreographed move, falling completely within the logic of her hysterics earlier today. But now that thanks to her you know everything ... since we've put our cards on the table ... you have my sincere request that you accept Anastaria into your clan. The advantages for the clan are quite clear – I don't think I need to go through them, since you've seen them all for yourself. The downsides ... there are more than enough of those too. Firstly, Hellfire and Rick will develop considerable dislike both for you and for Seathistles, exacerbated by the fact that Anastaria ended up in these unfortunate circumstances on your account. They will stop creating problems in the clan and will start looking for a way to get even with you instead. Secondly, there's the reaction of the rest of Malabar. As I already mentioned, Anastaria is a brand and everyone's gotten used to associating her with Phoenix, so Seathistles, a first level clan, won't have an easy time of it. Anastaria's fans will start trying to get into your clan and threaten you if you refuse to take them in. Thirdly ...," Ehkiller fell silent, as if struggling to find the right words to express his main point, so I beat him to it:

"Thirdly, Anastaria will not be just an ordinary member in my clan, but a representative of Phoenix , even if she's not officially its member. A spy, level ... can't even think of a good comparison – a supersonic jet among crop-dusters. And you're suggesting I forget everything that's happened before? Like the Siren poison that was used against me. You still expect me to welcome this girl with open arms? A very lucrative proposal, especially after three of my fighters went and joined your clan."

"This is why I thought that we should tell you the whole truth and not try to outmaneuver you once again," replied Stacey. "This really is no joking matter now – Phoenix could be facing a split and we can't let that happen, at the least not until the intercontinental clan competition. The only way to preserve the clan now is to make a sacrifice. I'm ready to be that sacrifice. But if I were excluded now, I would automatically be excluded from all scenarios. As soon as we finish with the Guardian and meet the Patriarch, the clan leaders will take charge of the scenarios and freestanding players will be left out in the cold. I really don't want to miss out on this, because for me this is ... important ... I want to find out what it is the developers have come up with, what possible workarounds they've included. ... Of all the clans present here only Seathistles and Azure Dragons would be able to accept me without raising suspicions with Rick and his team. But the Dragons have Donotpunnik, who would be certain to draft an Agreement in a way that would force me to stay in that clan for five years at the least."

"So, I'm the fool that can be suckered into doing this, taken for a three-month ride and then dumped when appropriate?" I grinned. "I mean, it's not like I'm Donotpunnik, who knows how to draft Agreements properly."

"Mahan, I ... you're free to take whatever decision you want, but I'm asking you to please help us ... to help me ... I would get kicked out in any case, but losing the scenario ..."

"All right, let's suppose – suppose, mind – that I take you into Seathistles. Since we're talking openly now, I would like to share an interesting piece of information with you: it's about to become public knowledge anyway. When are you planning to get kicked out?"

"Today."

"Great. Then listen. In exactly ...," I went into the quest description and looked at the date I received the quest from the Emperor, ."'.. three days and two hours, a certain individual known as the Emperor of Malabar will appeal to all 200+ level heroes, saying that he is in dire need of help, the poor old thing. Moreover, he will also issue a similar summons for craftsmen with level 100 and above in a profession. This is a continent-wide scenario, not a normal one, like the Guardian and the High Priestess' quests. The Emperor will also announce that any player can take part, including those previously banished. They will be granted a pardon, I suppose. Just to prove I'm not making it up here's the quest description that I was given." I sent Anastaria the text and watched for any change in her emotions. "And now a question for the experts: who would have the ability to complete this quest, but with the words 'find and bring' instead of 'craft' in it?"

"Damn it!" said Anastaria and descended into a censor-worthy cursing spree.

"Are you sure that the information about what will occur in three days is correct?" 'Killer asked me, ignoring the enraged girl.

"Yes. The Emperor really will issue this summons, so we have to wrap things up here as soon as possible. The sooner we finish with the Guardian, the sooner we can start looking for the Holy Relic."

"You do realize," Ehkiller addressed the girl, "that if Phoenix completes this quest without you no-one would ever suspect our bluff now? Everyone knows how mad you are for all things unique."

"'Killer, there's no way I can miss this!" Stacey was almost shouting. "This thing is continent-wide, not locked to a particular class! You can then use it to get ..."

"Anastaria!" the mage sternly interrupted her. "Time to decide! Either you leave and Phoenix do the quest without you – showing everyone that the threat of punishment is real – or we scrap all our plans and forget what we've been trying to do for the last four months. From what I can see, Rick should get the quest for creating the Holy Relic. He wouldn't be able to complete it outside the clan, so he'll be facing a clear choice: either he follows in your footsteps or falls in line, signs a new Agreement – seriously curtailing his rights – and continues crafting for the good of the clan. Hellfire will focus on you and going after Mahan. Stacey, decision time!"

"Damn it all to hell!" the girl continued to curse, "'Killer, you can't force someone to choose between duty and passion! That isn't fair!"

"Guys, maybe you'll stop arguing and explain to me," I interrupted the bickering players, "why in hell should I accept Anastaria into my clan, only to become a target for her fans and Hellfire? Nice future to look forward to; a dream come true, for sure. No First Kill bonuses can compensate for being constantly kept at the respawn point."

"I do have something that can persuade you to cooperate," assured the mage. "Now I know for sure that you are the creator of the Karmadont Chess Pieces. You have already solved the first riddle and right now we are ready to give you the answer to the second. It's already been deciphered. We are prepared to help you with other riddles as well, but that's beside the point right now. The important part is that you will get a description of what the Chess Set is, what it's used for and what limitations and special features it has. There is a special scroll with all this information at the Emperor's palace and I'm prepared to obtain it for you."

"Some reward that is. I happen to have Respect

with the Emperor. When I reach Esteem I'll be able to read this scroll myself."

"That's all very well, if not for one little detail. There is only one version of this scroll: no copies can be made of it and currently it happens to be in the firm grip of a certain Assassin's green paws. Even if you were at Exalted and a 100 in Attractiveness, you'd still never see it. I can make sure this scroll ends up in your hands. I call the Emperor as my witness that I'm telling you the truth about the scroll."

"So that's how it is ... but what has Attractiveness got to do with this?"

"Our Reputation with the Emperor and other elite entities simply opens certain doors to us, but Attractiveness is the key to quests," answered the girl, who had run out of curses for the time being. "For example, I have Exalted Reputation but zero Attractiveness with the current Emperor, so I would never be given any unique quests. Not a single one."

It was now clear why Tisha and the High Priestess sent me on these missions. They simply liked me as a ... to put it plainly, they just liked me.

"Stacey, what have you decided?"

"It's not like I really have a choice, is it?" growled the girl. "It's clear as day that this is an ideal situation: the clan will be subdued so we can ride this wave and re-draft Rick's Agreement. But ... dammit! A continental scenario!"

"Mahan, it's up to you now. Do you agree to take Anastaria into your clan in exchange for receiving the Emperor's scroll with the description of the Karmadont Chess Set in three months' time?"

"Yes; it looks like I don't have much choice in the matter either. You've really got me cornered. Agreed. Anastaria can be one of my minions for three months. Got any preferred position?" I asked the girl slyly.

"Of course! Only the deputy, only hardcore," she replied in the same tone.

"Then quit and I'll accept you."

"It's not quite so simple," Ehkiller intervened with more 'good' news. "Now, when the decision has been made, we need to put on a show for the clan and other players. We'll do most of the acting, but right now you need to leave the dome looking angry, grumbling and bad-mouthing me quite thoroughly. Something along the lines of 'Phoenix have gone completely crazy and want to buy up my entire clan'. Stacey will kick up a storm, as she has done on plenty of occasions, so it won't really surprise anyone, and then it will be my move. Everyone got it? Then let's do it."

My role turned out to be simple enough: I entered the dome looking angry and left it just as angry. All good. After asking the others once again about Plinto, who still hadn't returned, I called over Anastaria and Donotpunnik and told them that our strategy meeting would have to be postponed until the Rogue gets back. As soon as I stopped talking the girl began typing something into the clan chat and Ehkiller, who was sitting not far off, periodically shouted, "What are you doing? Stop that immediately!"

"That's it! My patience has reached its limit!" the mage shouted after some time. Plinto still hadn't reappeared (his respawn timer probably had one or two hours left to go), so there was no need to hurry. This gave Anastaria and 'Killer time to have more fun with their performance. "Guardian, I require your assistance."

"You called me and I came. If your summons was a false one, you will be punished," the glade vibrated.

"Agreed! Guardian, I ask you to confirm my decision!" Ehkiller addressed the Oak. "With the power bestowed in me by the Agreement of the Phoenix clan, I remove Anastaria from the clan for breaching the Clan Agreement! All her clan leader responsibilities will be assumed by me. From this moment on Anastaria has nothing to do with the Phoenix clan! I ask that all the interested parties are informed of this, including the Emperor, the Thricinians and the Lords of the Air."

"Accepted!" The tree's vibrations went through the glade, which had now descended into silence. "All the free citizens and faction leaders have been informed and Agreements with Anastaria have been transferred to Ehkiller."

Attention, residents of Malabar! For breaching the Clan Agreement free citizen Anastaria has been excluded from the Phoenix

clan! All Anastaria's responsibilities as head of the clan have been transferred to Ehkiller.

The sign of the flaming bird above the girl's face faded and she looked up at me with eyes full of tears. What an actress! She even managed to tear up!

"'Killer, you can't!" she shouted.

"I can and I did! Enough is enough!"

"In that case I'll ... Mahan!" Anastaria shouted in my direction. "I ask you to accept me into Seathistles! You were stripped of three players, so I offer myself as compensation."

."..?"

"I'll repeat for those who are slow on the uptake! ... I'm! ... Asking you! ... To take me! ... Into your clan!"

"Anastaria, I ...," I tried to look completely bewildered by such a crazy request from the best girl in Malabar. "Ehkiller, talk some sense into her!"

"I've had enough of Killer and his ilk! Either you invite me or I'll go elsewhere. Donotpunnik will be happy."

"Fine! But I should warn you right away, that there's no democracy in my clan, just the harsh totalitarian system headed by a tyrant; that is, yours truly. If you're prepared to sign an Agreement that you will remain in my clan for at least three months, I'll take you in," I replied.

"Deal! Send me the Agreement!"

"Stacey!" Ehkiller intervened. "Do you understand that there'll be no way back after this?"

"I don't give a damn about your threats! It won't take a week for Phoenix to go stale without me! ..."

I had little desire to land a bigger part in this performance, so under the shocked gazes of other players, I selected Anastaria and sent her the invitation to my clan.

Player Anastaria has joined the Seathistles clan. Rank: Deputy Head of the Clan.

Due to the presence of players that earned the First Kill of the Bloody Scythe Dungeon, the Seathistles clan gains ...

"Holy shit," Etamzilat, the head of the Heirs of the Titans, exhaled next to me, a camera pictogram flashing above his head. Looks like the banishment scene had been caught on tape. "Back in a couple of minutes," he said, after which his gaming avatar became transparent and disappeared. He probably went off to upload the video.

CHAPTER EIGHT
THE PATRIARCH

"**I**F THERE'S ONE THING I DON'T GET it's why you took that bitch in," summed up Plinto as soon as he appeared in the glade and was told the news.

"What's your problem with her?"

"I have enough problems with the flaming chickens for a year's worth of respawns, and for this 'lady' I'll make that three. If you hadn't initially included the condition that you couldn't waste other players, I would've rubbed her out ages ago. And you too – my hands are still itching to do just that."

"Then why the heck did you help me in Anhurs?"

"Because I didn't want to give those bastards the pleasure. You'll become my personal punching bag as soon as this quest is over. The pawn of Number Twos ... get ready for a meeting with a Herald – no-one else would be able to get you out of that one."

"Sure thing; I'm already shaking in my boots and looking for a place to hide. Before you start thinking up a more effective way to bump me off, tell me what you saw, what this 'Ash' is and how's it made? And by the way, have you ever considered that in chess a pawn is a rather formidable figure? Especially after it takes six moves forward."

Plinto mumbled 'mm-hmm' and 'froze' for a few moments, probably thinking over my words.

"Quit messing with my head," he said, finally reaching a conclusion. "The eastern side where I went was completely stuffed with ..."

"Hold on, let me call my advisors first," I interrupted Plinto. "I'll have to tell them everything anyway, so they may as well ask you all the right questions. Anastaria! Donotpunnik! Come over!"

"I'm not talking to that bitch," Plinto almost hissed. "Mahan, I'm grateful to you for access to the scenario, I had no money for the ticket and all, but dealing with her ...."

"Listen, cut the drama crap, eh? That's the last thing we need now! It's bad enough trying not to think about what Hellfire & Co will do to me for taking Anastaria into the clan, now you go ballistic every time her name is mentioned. Why don't you show me how to get them off my back instead of brandishing your trigger-happy side."

"Are you trying to recruit me or something?"

"Call it as you see it! Right, people have started turning up, so let's save this chat for another time.

Think about what I said, though. I'm in dire need of protection from Phoenix and no-one would handle that better than you. If you have a bone to pick with that clan, let's use it to our mutual advantage. Anyway, we'll talk later ...."

"I see you've been chatting with our bad boy," Anastaria couldn't help quipping as soon as she came over. "But I should say that he surprised me. Writing down the words 'Back' and 'Ash' correctly and without resorting to spellcheck ... even I could have barely managed that. Did you practice in advance or something?"

"Anastaria," I interrupted the girl. "I'm asking you, as your boss, not to aggro Plinto while we're completing this scenario. At the end of the day, he's the only one who has managed to gather any kind of useful information. The three ten-strong raid groups, the twenty-strong support group and the specially trained scouts screwed up most spectacularly (and that goes for you too), while one 'bad boy', as you put it, could've saved you all if you hadn't wandered off quite so far. Don't you think you're being more than a bit unfair?"

"Do you need him?" A message popped up in the inter-clan chat almost immediately. It was just as well that the 12 hours hadn't elapsed since the battle, so none of my Fighters were present yet. This way the chat had ended up being private. But how can she write in such a completely surreptitious manner?

I barely nodded in answer to her question and then continued: "now that we understand each other,

I suggest we begin. Plinto, please tell us what happened on the eastern side and how you were not detected?"

Flashing an angry stare at Anastaria, the Rogue began his report: "I'll begin by explaining what 'Ash' is. Everyone here knows what it is, except you, by the way. In all the most recent Dungeons the developers have tended to use a new type of spell, called 'Ash Tempest'."

"Not in all, but just the last four. It's as if they're preparing us for something," put in Anastaria. She behaves rather strangely when Plinto is around. I must speak to her about this later today. Why do they keep fighting like cat and dog for no apparent reason?

"Do you want to do the talking?" snapped Plinto.

"Maybe I do. This Ash, as raiders have dubbed it, is a very unpleasant spell. Unlike Armageddon it cannot destroy gear, but there's no way of evading it except with a bubble. This is why all the latest raids need so many Paladins and Priests for resurrecting fallen players. By the way, resurrection from Ash, into which your gaming avatar disintegrates, looks very beautiful. It comes together, forming a thin film, and then your body starts to take shape as if it were rising out of the surface of water, covered by a fine silk sheet."

"Women," Plinto spat for emphasis, showing that only a girl would start enjoying special effects in the middle of a fight.

"The 'Ash Tempest' can only be used once per

Dungeon and burns up enormous amounts of mob Mana, so the main task is to survive the blast with at least one Priest alive. I followed the same tactic here – put a bubble over myself –, but failed to take the special characteristics of the Dark Forest and the Scenario into account. It says that the first attack in the wrong direction would result in failure and that no players would survive even in a bubble. The curse was cast on me two seconds after the Ash, which means that the Imitator outdid itself in getting around that defense. That's how I became 'Cursed Anastaria'."

"That's what you were to begin with: no use pretending." Plinto wasn't about to miss this opportunity for a jibe, which finally made me lose patience with their back-and-forth.

"Plinto, Anastaria! One more dig from either direction while we're completing this scenario and I'll quit being so reasonable. I've had enough of you! You're acting like a pair of little kids!"

"And you've never seen them going at each other in Anhurs", grinned Donotpunnik. "The whole of Malabar's been laughing at these two – not that they care."

"Like I give a fig about all that! Plinto! As the head of the Seathistles clan I'm inviting you to join me as a Fighter."

"What, be in the same clan as this ..." the Rogue began, but I interrupted him.

"No! To be in the same clan as me! Phoenix will declare open season on me because of Anastaria coming over and I need protection. While in the clan you'll be receiving a salary, calculated in the standard way: 30% of the entire income of the clan, divided among the members depending on the rank and contribution to the clan. I'm also prepared to negotiate the sum that you'll be paid for preventing attempts on my life made by Phoenix members. Anyone else wouldn't bother if they see you around, but Phoenix, on the other hand, would get even more aggro. Do you remember what I said about the moves? You made two moves forward when you left Legion, Anhurs was another move and the next would be agreeing to join. You have just two squares left, this is one of them."

"I have a condition," said Plinto thoughtfully after some time. "I will have the opportunity to send you for respawn at least twice. You owe me and I won't rest until I do this."

"Agreed. As soon as we finish with the Dark Forest, you will have such a chance. Anything else?"

"Anastaria." (Wow! He actually used her name!) "What rank does she have?"

"She's the Deputy."

"I will answer directly to the head and no-one else. Neither the Deputy nor the Officers will have any authority over me."

"All right, this will be included in the Agreement. Anything else?"

"Five million gold, right now, for personal use," Plinto blurted out after a pause, all the while looking at Anastaria for some reason."

"And what would that be for?" I was beginning

to lose track of what was going on here, because at this point Anastaria lowered her gaze.

"No! A thousand times no!!!" The clan chat exploded with the girl's screams.

"Just a personal whim", was Plinto's short answer and I suddenly understood where this money was going. It would go to the girl. But for what?

"I accept. As the head of the clan I guarantee you five million gold for joining Seathistles. However, in that case I have some conditions too: you will spend at least a year in the clan or until I personally exclude you; and you will accept the clan rules."

"Agreed." A smile spread across the face of the usually serious Rogue. "Guardian, I ask you to witness our Agreement on my joining the clan before we sign it!" shouted Plinto.

"The conditions have been recorded!" the glade immediately declared with its vibrations.

"Then send me the invite," concluded Plinto, "I'm prepared to join the Seathistles under the agreed conditions and will diligently carry out all responsibilities this lays on me."

"Eh, Mahan ... thanks a lot, what can I say? ... "

Player Plinto the Bloodied has joined the Seathistles clan. Rank: Fighter.

Due to the presence of players that earned the First Kill of the Silver Scream Dungeon, all Seathistles clan members gain +2 to Attractiveness with all Malabar NPCs. ...

This was followed by another list of bonuses for the clan, but this one only had seven items on it, compared to Anastaria's twenty-something. So it looks like Dark Legion did complete some things before Phoenix after all. ... I started to look through the achievements that I got via Plinto, so didn't immediately notice how the Guardian's branches began to grow around my sole (for the moment) Fighter and around my, likewise, only Deputy. I don't get it, what's going on here?

"Plinto the Bloodied!" roared the Oak. "According to the Agreement, you must pay a monetary reward worth five million and four hundred thousand gold to free citizen Anastaria. Anastaria! According to the Agreement, once this amount is paid to you, you are obliged to hand over the final part of the phoenix reins!

"I'm ready to transfer the money," said Plinto immediately. "Please take it off my account and the remainder from the account of the Seathistles clan, according to the conditions under which I was accepted into the clan."

"Mahan," thundered the Guardian, "I ask you to give the final confirmation of the conditions of accepting Plinto the Bloodied into the clan."

"Confirmed!" Five million is a huge amount and it would take me forever to explain myself to the others, so I'll have to find out what I owe and to whom. And, most importantly, why?

"Anastaria! Plinto has fulfilled the conditions for acquiring the final part of the phoenix reins. Are you going to hand them over?"

"They're in my Personal Room," said the girl, discomposedly. "I give my permission for them to be taken and handed over to Plinto."

"The Agreement has been fulfilled and is considered closed," concluded the Guardian and descended into deep thought once again.

"You know Nick, I'll bury you for this", said Anastaria after some time. "I'll even complain to your wife that you've upset me. She'll have your head."

"Stacey, then you should have thought twice before making the bet. I did say from the start, that I'd get my hands on them, sooner or later. Now my flame-wing will be the fastest in all of Barliona! This year I'll finally get the prize! The game's on!"

"Are you done yet?" I interrupted this fascinating conversation. I'll find out later what this is all about – right now, with Donotpunnik giving us a rather cryptic look, it was time to get back to work. "Plinto, do continue. I get the deal with the Ash. What happened on the eastern side?"

"Yes," added Donotpunnik, "you can also tell us how you managed to get through where other scouts were discovered."

"Who are you calling 'scouts' exactly? Lanterius and Fogger? Their arms should be ripped off and sewn onto their asses, which they've been using for thinking anyway. You think I didn't see how they were 'discovered'? Any dumbass would've realized that mist, which covers every part of the ground must conceal lots of alarm-traps. Why the heck did they go on the ground? Are they so low on Agility they couldn't use the trees? Hopeless idiots ...."

"Let's not get distracted!" I told my Fighter.

"In short, it's simple: we were toast in any case. There were three barricades to the east. First came level 100–150 Vampires. I counted forty, but I might've been wrong, they kept moving all over the place and my line-of-sight radius wasn't very big. It was the trees, damn them. They had no special attacks, just physical damage and speed. About half of them had bows and black arrows, which probably land you with a curse on hit. We'll have to be careful and make sure the Priests keep their eyes open and cleanse any cursed players. The Vamps were waiting a hundred meters from the glade and had a boss with them: the Sergeant. Level 200, nothing difficult at the first glance, if you discount the 'Regeneration' buff: it restores 2% of total Hit Points every five seconds. The second barricade, a more serious one this time, came a hundred meters further out: three level-300 Elementals, five 350+ mages and one boss, concealed by black mist. According to his properties he was some sort of Lieutenant, level 400. There was no information on his race or abilities. While I was logged out I tried to look him up on all available databases – nothing. The Elementals are interesting too: there was fire, water and an earth one. There should have also been an air one, but it was probably somewhere else at the time. They have no special abilities, but they're no pushovers, because these three stand very close to each other and we won't be able to pull them one by one. You'll have to figure out how to bring them down. The third cordon wasn't even a cordon, but the camp of the final boss, and is two hundred meters further out. There we had another mist-covered boss, a General of some kind, level-450, and six Necromancers, who were busy summoning the Ash. There was nothing else there. Catch the video and the stats that I managed to get off the mobs. When Ash started to form, I tried to interrupt it, knowing where this was going ... but ... as soon as I came closer, the General took me out straight away. Just three hits and I was pushing daisies. He only used a physical damage attack, so while I was under 'cloak' I managed to warn you about the Ash. That's it, I think."

"Plinto," said Donotpunnik a couple of minutes later, after he reviewed the info my Fighter sent. "Listen, I'm lost for words. ... How did you do this?"

On some level, I agreed with Don. It made for engrossing viewing: to watch Plinto jump from tree to tree, Tarzan-like, all the while managing to assess his surroundings, not allowing the trees to sway, and looking through the properties of each mob that came into view.

"Mahan, as soon as the rest of the clan gets here," Plinto turned to me, ignoring the question, "I'll take charge of them. I see that you have two Warriors and one Rogue, all of them around level twenty. I won't touch the Druid, but these guys ... it's time they stopped faffing around and started leveling up properly. I'll take it upon myself to ensure that happens."

"Then wait for them to turn up – should be about an hour – and you can begin straight away. Later you can put me through my paces as well."

"Sure! No problem! You covered a hundred and twenty meters of the Rogue Obstacle Course on your first attempt," chuckled Plinto, "no going easy on you with that record to beat?"

"A hundred and twelve," I corrected him, but Plinto was no longer listening; he'd stealthed and started roaming around the glade.

"We'll have to give our scouts a good talking to," said Anastaria the moment he left us. "Who would've thought that a douchebag could provide such a thorough scouting report? Levels, descriptions ... did you see that on the second minute he even pointed out the movement trajectories?" she said to Donotpunnik.

"Yeah ..." muttered my second advisor, looking somewhat at a loss. "This day is just full of wonders. ... Mahan, maybe you should take me into your clan as well? Just to complete the set. We could invite someone from the Heirs of the Titans and that'd be it – all the leading clans of Malabar will have transferred one leading player to the Seathistles clan. It's mindboggling. Stacey, how many First Kills do you have? About forty? Plinto should have about a dozen. Mahan has one as well. Seathistles is light years ahead now. There's also some NPC sitting in Mahan's tent: Slate. ... Will your leaving Phoenix affect your taking part in the quest?" he suddenly asked the girl.

"No," was Anastaria's firm reply, "I joined up of

my own accord – no-one paid for me – so I don't owe anyone anything. Let's decide what to do now. I propose we start with a brainstorming session. ..."

"Before we start, I'd like to bring something to your attention. I already knew about the three bosses, but Plinto didn't say anything about the Lord of the Fallen, who was shouting announcements to the whole glade after the Ash hit. So there should be a fourth cordon, even though it was never scouted. ..."

The attack plan was for the most part fleshed out by Anastaria and Donotpunnik, while I simply stood by, acting as a litmus test of sorts. If I went red – if I started to become unsettled – the plan was a bad one. If I stayed silent, the plan was good and worth considering. A worthy and solid role of a frog in a jar used to predict the weather. At least they weren't intent on making me croak.

"On the whole, our knowledge about this territory is sparse," I finally heard Anastaria utter words I could easily understand. All these formations, raid add-ons, saves, pots, pre-pots, flasks, masks, casks ... brrr ... ."In the 15 years of the game not a single quest was discovered here. There is a map made by Newtonovich, but he drew it from atop a griffin, so it isn't much help to us. I've found nothing about Dark Forest Guardians, and nothing pointing to scenarios dealing with the cursing of the entire forest."

"Same here: just the map and lots of unexplored territory. You know, I had a bit of a think. ... There's something that immediately jumps out in all of this ... why on earth is a player, who is hunted by the entire Dark Legion clan, roaming around thousands of kilometers away from Anhurs? All the way in the Dark Forest, which supposedly doesn't contain a single quest. And the place isn't exactly bursting with resources either – if you don't take the Guardian's glade into account. And then this mysterious Shaman, who's been dubbed a son of the Dragon, turns up and offers us a quest from a place that isn't supposed to have any quests at all. To top it all off, in the space of just an hour he gets to recruit the second and the third highest-level players on the continent. Guys, is there something you'd like to fill me in on, perhaps? It's a bit difficult to construct a chain of reasoning on the basis of incomplete data."

It's tough to deal with people who have a habit of using their heads instead of their emotions. Stacey cracked me right from the start and Donotpunnik too ... and here was me thinking that I was terribly unreadable and mysterious.

"Right, so you don't feel like sharing, then," the Azure Dragons player summed up a few moments later, then looked at Anastaria, pursed his lips and smiled. "No, I really must take some lessons from you. You probably knew what was up even before Seathistles. ... Did the small fry get his hands on some other quest? And you're not going to tell me anything about it, are you?" Donotpunnik 'froze' for a minute. "Let's play a guessing game then ... the Emperors can be ruled out as the source – they're new and need at least a week before they assume their roles properly. The Princess ... I'm not sure, it seems highly improbable. That leaves only the High Priestess. Judging by what happened in Beatwick, Mahan has leveled up in Attractiveness with her almost as far as 100. And then there was the poaching of the three Fighters by Phoenix ... most likely in order to take charge of a quest. ... No, there just isn't enough information. ... Raster wouldn't have taken players into the clan if they didn't come with some benefits. ... That means ... it wasn't Mahan who had the quest, but the Priest! He was the first to be accepted into Phoenix and the others just hopped on the bandwagon – the level difference is just too big. Then it could be those with whom ... yes, of course! Mahan is a prisoner and he probably spent time running around with these three when he was a normal player, but they ditched him and decided to offer the quest to Phoenix. How nice of them. What can I say? And you ...," Donotpunnik looked at Anastaria, "you're a known champion of justice. ... That's it, the puzzle comes together."

No, dealing with someone who knows how to use their head isn't 'tough': it's downright dangerous! The slightest gesture can be used to read you and prepare ten different ways of responding! Perhaps Donotpunnik has a point and I should take a couple of lessons from Anastaria, while there's time ...

"You were saying something about joining my clan," I tried to concentrate and forced out a chuckle. "Let's talk it over, I'm ready to hear your conditions."

"I think not," laughed Donotpunnik. "Not much

point in me crossing over – Phoenix has that quest now."

"Making logical deductions based on incomplete information is an unforgivable mistake when it comes to this player," volunteered Anastaria, pointing to me. "As long as I've known him, he's had the ability to respond to any sound logical argument with one or even two completely illogical actions or quests. So Mahan is right, Don. You should think about coming over ..."

"This isn't a clan but a den of nutjobs!" Eric panted out as he finished running his tenth lap around the glade. Plinto had called for a break, so all three players dropped to the ground. "Like hell I'll do any more dying! I'll write a message to the developers and say that as soon as the clan is sent for respawn its head completely flips out and starts doing crazy things and ask them to give me complete immunity to every kind of damage. Perhaps that might get you to see reason ..."

A little while earlier, if my swearing filter had been turned on, the first phrase I would've heard uttered by Clutzer when he came back from the Grey Lands and saw the Seathistles emblem above Plinto and Anastaria might have sounded something like: "What the "flying snail" is going on here?! Well I'll "quack a duck" from such a "cluster bunnies"! This is total "bunny hop," "noble lady's socks" take you ..."

When in a couple of words I'd explained to the agitated players why we were now three players down (but also two players up), pointed out the First Kill bonuses and other advantages in protection from PK-ers, everyone seemed to calm down. That lasted all of two minutes – until Plinto came up to us, formed an additional training group and got my Fighters to run laps around the glade. He'd explained to me that it was high time these guys leveled up in Agility, Strength and Stamina, and that anyone not wanting to level up, would have his ass mercilessly kicked. It is impossible to die within a training group, so when the guys were about to protest, Plinto's knives reduced their Hit Points to one and all arguments stopped. It became suddenly clear that increasing your stats was extremely important ... and the clan leader had told them not to slack in any case. ...

By the time the last players arrived (Antsinthepantsa and Barsina), the second attempt to leave the Guardian's glade had commenced. There were again three ten-strong groups, each with its own support group, although there were some changes to the Phoenix-led ten: an Azure Dragons healer replaced Anastaria, while she remained by my side. She wanted to have nothing to do with Hellfire and Ehkiller and they weren't too eager to spend time with her either. Plinto continued to make my Fighters run around the glade, making it clear that he had no intention of taking part in the battle, should one commence. To his credit – glancing at Leite, Clutzer and Eric's stats – I saw that in just an hour they increased their Agility by +3, Strength by +2 and Stamina by +4. Plinto didn't limit himself to running – there were jumps, rolls, sprints and rolls again. ...

And it should be noted that as soon as the first leveling up took place any grumbling ceased. The result could be clearly seen and felt, which meant that it was worth the sweat. ...

"Vamps spotted! Three of them, moving fast, no bows," a message from the central group of ten came up in the raid chat. "Wings, close in on the left and right, chase them towards us. Hellfire, get ready ..."

The first cordon, if it could be called the first, was wiped out in just a couple of minutes. To 280+ level players a bunch of level-100 Vampires weren't even good for target practice, so the scouting Rogues took them out themselves. Only the Sergeant presented any real challenge. The level-200 warrior furiously attacked Hellfire, restoring his Hit Points with every attack. All three groups had to focus on this mob at the same time before they could send its Imitator for a rest. By the way, it was just as well he didn't attack me when we were luring out the Vampires that time. He wouldn't have even noticed my Spirits.

After the battle at the first cordon each player got thirty-two gold, twenty-four Vampire Fangs and one Sergeant's Circlet. It looked like both the fangs and the Circlet dropped for each player separately, like the loot at the Dolma Mine. Even though they took no part in the battle, just for being in the same group my three low-level Fighters gained three levels each, but Plinto completely forbade them to allocate their new free stat points. I didn't manage to level up, but I had only a measly 140 Experience Points to go.

From then on, however, we ran into a problem. The second, third and, according to my logic, fourth cordons were nowhere to be seen. The scouts found the place where the Elementals were (there really were four of them) and they found the place from where Ash was cast, but there wasn't a single mob in sight. They retreated, leaving us only the Sergeant for slaughter. Much to my disappointment, we failed to find a probable location of the Lord of the Fallen – it was as if he'd never existed. Either there was no fourth cordon or he'd managed to hide himself really well. After assuring the others that the search for the vanished mobs would restart first thing in the morning, I told the players they were free to go home. Anyone wishing to stay could stay, while those who had business back in reality could leave. I saw little sense in entering the Dark Forest during the night.

"Eric, how much Copper do you have on you?" I asked my Fighter as soon as the glade was mostly clear. Of the free players, there remained only Plinto, who continued to inflict vigorous training on my Officers, Anastaria, who was energetically debating something with Donotpunnik, and Barsina, who was watching the guys being trained.

"About thirty pieces. What do you need them for?"

"Did you get as far as Tin?"

"Yup. I've been saving it up for Bronze. ..."

"Consider it a failed save. I only have eighteen levels to go until Silver, which I must do all I can to get through."

"Damn, what am I supposed to do after Tin, then?"

"Just keep up with the running, what else? Plinto! I think Eric's slacking off here, his Energy's all recovered now ..."

I spent about an hour making ingots, but unfortunately the thirty pieces of Copper was only enough for +9 to Smithing and three pieces of Lapis. In an ideal world, right now I would hop over to Anhurs, buy some Copper Ingots and Ore and raise my Smelting to 10% and Gem Cutting to level 2, but where would I get a portal here? And it would cost so much money that the subdued amphibious / terrestrial wildlife inhabiting the depth of my soul would kick the dust and bite the bucket. Or the other way round. Whichever way you turn it, they wouldn't be feeling very well. Do I really need this? No; so the portal idea can be ruled out. Where can I get more Copper? What if I ask Anastaria for help?

"All right, I'm off. Until tomorrow." By this point Donotpunnik had stopped arguing with Stacey, turned into a transparent silhouette and vanished.

"Me too," said my deputy. "Time to go and scare my family with an unplanned visit. I finally have a chance to spend some quality time at home and I'm not letting a chance like that slip away."

"Hold up," I stopped the girl. "Listen, is there any way you can use some of your old connections to buy and send me some Copper Ingots? Or even just the Ore. I really need them. ..."

"Gimme a sec," Anastaria opened her mailbox

and started writing a letter. A couple of minutes went by and her eyebrows shot up – she probably got a reply. "So that's how it is ..." muttered the girl and started to write again. Two minutes later there was another reply, which again did not please the girl at all, since her reaction was one capacious word: "Hmm." "How much do you need?" She finally asked.

"About 10 stacks."

"I'll get them," the girl assured me. "You'll have the Copper in the morning." With these words Anastaria became transparent and a moment later melted into thin air.

After another twenty minutes Eric, Leite and Clutzer's Energy once again hit zero and Plinto and Barsina left us. As soon as Donotpunnik left, the lady Druid joined my running and jumping officers, wishing to do some leveling up in Agility and Stamina herself. She didn't seem to mind that Intellect was the main stat for her class: it was good to level up on all fronts. Good for her: she thinks like a true mercenary – never failing to take advantage of potential gain for her own dear self. If only everyone was like her.

"And now tell us what went down," as soon as the three former red-head-banders got their breath back, they crowded around me. "How did you manage to get Plinto and Anastaria into the clan and what was the real reason Elenium, Sushiho and Dooki left...?"

I would have never thought that a tale retold by yours truly could come out so colorful and rich in events and drama – with villains and heroes, betrayal and friendship, feelings and ice-cold logic. I didn't conceal the truth from my Fighters, honestly admitting that Anastaria was with us for only three months and Plinto for a year (and for a payment at that), but the way I relayed all this was really something! Mihail Demov, a skilled spinner of tails, would surely see a worthy colleague in me.

"Peace to you, brave storyteller and his listeners," said a heavy deep voice barely a moment after I finished. It was night in Barliona by this time and just a few meters away from the Guardian's glade two red dots were shining in the darkness. A hostile mob! A level-200 Vampire with red eyes, indicating that he presented a danger to us! "Permit me to enter the Guardian's circle!"

Eric and I looked at each other. He understood as well as I did what the Vampire's red eyes meant and what would be the result of his entering the glade: respawn for us and inglorious death for Slate.

"No thank you, we're kinda fond of staying alive," was my strained reply. "To what do we owe the honor?"

"I cannot harm those who have become objects of interest to the Patriarch," uttered our night guest, compelling me take a closer look in his properties. Level 203, a Vampire-scout, Hit Points ... and not a single word that the NPC standing before us was cursed. However, his red eyes indicated the opposite. "My Lord wishes to speak with one of you. He would like to know the aim of your visit to his forest."

"His forest?" I couldn't help myself at this point. "This forest has been flooded by the Fallen and their leader, while your Patriarch has barricaded himself up in his castle, or wherever it is. And yet he continues to call this Cursed Forest his own. We came to destroy the taint, a quest that was given to us by the Guardian. You can go and tell the Patriarch this." I was probably taking a risk in being openly rude to the messenger, but I'd run out of niceties for the day. I was too tired. I knew that NPCs had to be buttered up, but not today.

"My Lord has ordered that one of you be delivered to him and I will do this," said the Vampire, unperturbed. "The Guardian's glade is not out of bounds to me. Only respect for those who have managed to turn the eyes of the Fallen away from our castle and onto themselves – giving us the first respite in ten years – has stopped me from going any further." With these words the Vampire did something completely unexpected: he entered the glade and nothing happened to him. He didn't start writhing in agony, no pillar of fire appeared around him and even the Guardian continued to doze, as if nothing had happened. But the red eyes of a hostile mob ...

"I will meet the Patriarch." I finally found my bearings, realizing that if the Vampire didn't attack, despite being fully capable of entering the Guardian's glade, we had nothing to fear. At least for the moment: later we'll figure out who was indebted to whom and by how much. ... Except that Stacey, the moment she's back in the game, will kill me as sure as day. ...

"Touch my hand," the Vampire appeared next

to me in one imperceptible movement. He's so damn fast! "I am linked to the castle with a transfer portal. You will be taken there in the same manner."

The Vampire forced me to look at him from a different perspective! Well, I'll be! So it looks like mobs around here aren't as simple as they may seem at a first glance. Ordinary messengers are supplied with anchored portals, which usually cost crazy money. It's a convenient thing to be sure, but you'd have to dump so much gold on the anchor and the summoning scrolls ... yet here we have simple scouts running around with anchored portals like this was the norm. They are probably used as a security measure. If the Fallen were to catch such a Vampire, he'd just fly off in a flash. Nice fail-safe, for sure. Realizing that I didn't have much choice in this, I touched the Vamp's hand and the world around me blinked, indicating the transfer to a different location. When my vision was no longer blurry, I beheld a monumental structure in all its glory: the inner court of the Vampire Patriarch's castle.

What immediately struck me was the total absence of the mist, otherwise ubiquitous throughout the Dark Forest. There was a cobbled square, which contained a massive stone castle-palace, and several small buildings, which were probably there purely for decoration. In any case, no-one lived in them, because great piles of various weapons and armor blocked all the entrances.

"Our spoils of war," explained my guide after noticing my gaze. "First they filled up the entire armory, then the barracks, and then we just started to pile them up outside. We cannot leave the weapons on the battlefield, as they will return to the Fallen, nor can we use any of them ourselves since they're cursed. So that's why they're gathered here in these useless piles."

"Can I have a look?"

"That will depend on the result of your meeting with the Patriarch. Perhaps I won't even have to take you back. Free Citizens know how to return from the Grey Lands, so you could be returning to the Guardian's glade on your own. Whatever the Master commands. Follow me."

My guide headed inside the castle and I, trying to keep up, continued to take in my surroundings. High stone walls around the castle perimeter, reaching up to ... whatever their actual height, you couldn't see the trees beyond them. I might give them six or seven meters, but there's no way to be sure. There was nothing else. The castle covered about the same area as the Guardian's glade, but contained nothing except the four buildings. It looks like this was home to the wrong type of Vampires – a bit too ascetic, as it were. If you'd seen any antique films, you'd think these guys love luxury, since they lived a very long time. But here they were being downright Spartan. Vampires stood along the entire wall perimeter and kept sending arrows somewhere outside. Then the question occurred to me: where do the local Fighters get their weapons and food? There was no sign of a smithy or trees from which to make arrows, for starters. Did the developers depart from the game logic in this and permit the NPCs' weapons to renew themselves and for the arrows to just 'pop out' of the quivers? And the replenishing of the ranks of the original Vampires was also begging for an explanation. They should've all been killed off in the last ten years: where could they be born around here? So, all in all, I had many questions, which, in all probability would never get answered. It's a scenario, that's all there is to it. ...

"Greetings, traveler. What brings you to my forest?" The Patriarch of the Vampires had a surprisingly beautiful voice. It was so ... I don't even know how to describe it. Confident and kind, it made you feel that you could trust and rely on it, that all your problems had been long-solved, leaving you without a care in the world. The local boss, dressed in a bright red mantle that covered him from head to foot, was sitting on a throne made of skulls and watching me, like all other Vampires I encountered here, with red eyes. His throne was truly 'cosmopolitan': heads of humans, orcs, horned kobolds (if I wasn't mistaken) ... almost all the races of Barliona were represented in this frightening creation by the developers.

"We are on a quest from the Guardian of the Dark Forest to cleanse the forest of the taint," I replied to the elderly Lord of the castle. His snow-white hair and pale skin made such a strong contrast with the bright red eyes that surrounded the Patriarch that a few times I caught myself in the process of averting my eyes. Damn! There were no buffs or debuffs, but the NPC's influence could be felt very clearly. Was it Charisma? Or did he have something more interesting about him? I had to get to the bottom of this. "I would also like to find out what happened to the Great Priest Midial and his group" – I made sure I didn't forget the second quest too – "and who destroyed him."

"Destroyed him?" smiled the Patriarch. "I would have given much to destroy the sentient you just called the Great Priest Midial. After all, the Lord of the Fallen and Midial are one and the same. ..."

"Faster!" Midial was increasingly impatient, as he tried to hurry his team ahead. "We have to get to Ishni before nightfall! Only she can tell us where to find the Tear of Eluna! Onwards, brothers!"

"Don't run your people into the ground, Priest." A blindingly bright light chased away the deepening shadows of the Dark Forest as the Unicorn stepped out of the trees. It was the heart of the Dark Forest – Ishni. The expedition sent by the High Priestess froze, gazing in wonder at the flawless white skin, the resplendent horn and huge eyes full of unearthly wisdom. "I will give you the Tear of Eluna, I have no more need of it. Take it and carry the Light with honor!"

The Unicorn lowered her head and the group

saw that a small chain with a drop-shaped pendant was hanging from the tip of her horn, the lost amulet of the High Priestess. Everyone sighed in relief; the expedition had ended in success and a great reward awaited everyone upon their return. The group relaxed, many started to smile and Midial bent to his knees and said: "You have my thanks, o great Ishni, for helping us find the lost relic. We will be able to achieve much with its help ..."

"Much? Priest, it seems you do not know that the Tear of Eluna is incapable of bringing Light. How can the Goddess's grief, her pain and loss carry Light? For centuries the High Priestesses guarded the peoples of Barliona from the effect of this amulet and the time has now come for the new Priestess to take this burden upon herself. The Tear cannot be used, it can only be guarded."

"I beg your pardon, o great one, I misspoke. I will not use the Tear: it is beyond my power. My innermost desire is to deliver the relic to the right place."

Midial rose up, walked over to the Unicorn, and took the pendant from her. He looked at the amulet for a few moments and then a malicious smile spread across his face: "And isn't it just my luck that the right place is right here? Geranika!" The Priest suddenly shouted into empty air, "I obtained the prize that you sought! The Dark Forest is ready to fall at your feet!" After uttering these words Midial tore the Tear off the chain and stuck it into the ground.

"Stop, you madman!" Ishni managed to utter

before the world came to a halt. The priests who sprang up to stop their leader, the Unicorn, who lowered her head to run at the enemy and even the wind, which previously had been hardly noticeable in the Dark Forest, froze in an elaborate swirl. Everything paused.

"You did it!" said a man, dressed in a tailored suit, who appeared next to Midial. "I have to admit, my apprentice, I started to doubt you, but you managed to live up to my hopes. From now on I name you the Lord of the Dark Forest. Very soon it will become Cursed and you will supply me with a ..."

"Who dares intrude into and desecrate the Dark Forest!" Although time had stopped, the projection of the Oak appeared not far from Geranika and Midial. The Guardian had come to defend its forest.

"You still haven't dealt with this problem?" Geranika looked at Midial in surprise. "Apprentice, you begin to disappoint me. How did you manage to do such a good job on the one hand and botch it on the other so spectacularly? Prepare to be punished."

"You will be destroyed," the Guardian continued with his denunciation, "nothing will save you and ..."

"Silence!" A tambourine appeared in Geranika's hand, the Shaman closed his eyes and the surrounding world was shaken by several resounding bangs.

"You dare tell me ... . What?! What is happening?" shouted the Guardian, as dark mist started to swirl around him. Its touch first wilted leaves, then branches began to fall off and just a few moments later the Oak vanished, having disintegrated into dust.

"Apprentice, this is your punishment: until you destroy the Patriarch of the Vampires who lives in this forest you shall have no place at my side. That is all." Geranika looked at the bowed head of the Priest, walked up to the Unicorn, broke off its horn and, after a pleased chuckle, vanished.

The surrounding world moved once more, but now Midial was its Master. He lifted up his hands and, as with Geranika earlier, dark smoke started to stream out of them. In a snake-like movement it twisted around all those still alive in the glade, including the Unicorn, and lifted them above the ground.

"I appoint you Sergeant," said Midial to one of the priests. "You the Lieutenant and you the General of the Fallen. The rest will come in handy for the initiation. As for you," the Priest turned to Ishni, "I have great plans for you. ... Argh! The damn thing burns so much!" Midial took a small frog statuette from somewhere inside his robes and threw it to the ground. "Useless trinket!"

* * *

"As you can see," said the Patriarch, "for ten years now Midial has been trying to return to his teacher, but without success. The Reardalox clan will never capitulate before the invaders."

While I was recovering from what I'd just been shown, a string of messages flashed before my eyes:

Quest 'Restoration of a Holy Relic, Step 2: The Search for the Stone of Light' completed. Reward: +35000 Experience, +500 to Reputation with the Priestesses of Eluna, +100 to Reputation with the Goddess Eluna.

Level gained!

Quest available: Quest 'Restoration of a Holy Relic, Step 3: Return of the Stone of Light.'

Step 3 description: The lost Stone of Light was dropped somewhere in the Dark Forest. With time, an oasis of goodness and peace has formed around it. Return the Stone of Light to the High Priestess.

Requirements: Reputation with Goddess Eluna: greater than 0; Reputation with the Priestesses of Goddess Eluna: Friendly or above; combined group level: 600.

Quest chain class: Rare.

Reward for completing Step 3: +1 Level, +500 to Reputation with the Priestesses of Eluna, +100 to Reputation with Goddess Eluna.

Reward for the quest chain: Hidden.

Penalty for failing/refusing the quest: none.

The quest chain will be updated for all the members of the group.

Update to the 'Cleansing of the Dark Forest'

quest. Source of the taint: the Tear of Eluna planted into the ground.

"I can see that my words have shocked you," the old Vampire returned me back to the game. "I understand that it's hard to accept betrayal, especially from a Priest, but that is the story of my forest. You will now be taken back. I've found out all that I wanted to know: I have no interest in helping you, but my warriors will not hinder you either. You will be allowed to pass through our lands unimpeded and take the Tear of Eluna out of the ground yourselves.

"Then why ..." I started, but then fell silent. At first I wanted to know why the Patriarch's Vampires wouldn't pull out the amulet themselves, but why ask a question to which I already knew the answer? The Tear was probably stuck in the ground at the place where the Priests were initiated into being Cursed Ones. This means that's where the Lord of the Fallen, who is Geranika's apprentice, will also be located. But then another question immediately arose: how could a Shaman teach a Priest? Formally they deal with different entities ... although ... if I remembered the words of the Supreme Spirits of both worlds, Geranika hasn't been using Spirits for a long time now: ten years or more. And yet he used his tambourine when destroying the Guardian ... I urgently needed Antsinthepantsa. ...

"Thank you for your help, we will walk this path to the end. I have a request and a question. The question is simple. So that we don't spend ages roaming the Dark Forest, can you please tell us where Midial stuck the Tear into the ground? The request is a bit more complicated. You have a lot of Cursed Weapons lying around your square. I am a Blessed Artificer and have the ability to change Cursed weapons into Blessed ones." I may have been slightly economical with the truth here, since I'd never actually done this, but I had to give it a go! What if it worked? At the very least I could always take them to Beth and she could help me remake them. "Can I take a few of these items, since you aren't using them?"

For a few moments the Patriarch was lost in thought – probably his Imitator was calculating possibilities and analyzing the piles of metal for anything useful – and then he answered:

"I will not mark the spot where my enemy is located. The fight between us is an internal Dark Forest matter, not something free citizens should concern themselves with. If you want to get involved it's your business; my Fighters will not stand in your way. But don't expect any help from them either; you have to solve your own problems yourself. As for the weapons and armor ... yes, we really don't have anywhere to put it, but I cannot just hand it over without knowing for sure what you will do with it. Prove to me that you are indeed a Blessed Artificer. You will be brought a sample: change it. If you succeed, I will allow you to select around ten objects. This will be my personal gift to you. If you fail ... you will have to make your way back to the Guardian's glade via the Grey Lands. Do you agree to my conditions?"

So that's how it is! That's some twist Mr. Head Vampirello put on things! And in general, our meeting didn't seem to have come out quite right. Firstly, the Patriarch didn't appear in the list of encountered factions, so leveling up with him in Reputation was a separate story. Secondly, he had no intention of helping us and there was nothing to be done about that. Thirdly, he was about to send me for respawn, because I was no Priest when it came to switching polarities. And I couldn't decline either; my Reputation with the Patriarch could easily plummet, which was the last thing I needed. What to do?

"I agree," I answered the impossible question, mentally preparing myself for a 12-hour rest, although for me it would rush past in the blink of an eye, and at least my body would get a break from Barliona.

"You will be brought one of the simple objects suitable for your profession," said the Patriarch, snapping me out of self-castigation mode. "Suitable for my profession" meant that I would have to work either with a ring or a neck-chain, in other words with a piece of jewelry. All I needed was an hour of time and ...

Cursed Ring of Driall.
Item class: Epic, Unique.
Minimum level: 320.
Stats: +12800 to Intellect, +5400 Stamina,

+80 Energy, +1400 Agility, +1400 Strength, when casting a spell you have a 30% chance of an instantaneous free repeat cast. 2 Gem Stone sockets. Upgradable (the cost and level of upgrade can be confirmed with an Advisor/Master).

Cursed Ring's special properties: when worn, -20 character levels (the effect is applied no more than once to any player wearing the ring; total stat point reduction: -100); when placed in inventory, -30% to all stats (temporarily).

Its properties were quite mind-blowing. Prior to this I thought that the most expensive and amazing items for players were those made by the Thricinians. The armor I was now wearing would be quite decent even at level 300 ... but now that I'd seen the properties of a 'simple' – as the Patriarch put it – Epic ring for level 320, I realized that I was wrong. Very wrong.

"This is the ring of the first Lieutenant. Three years ago we managed to destroy him. Midial initiated a new one, but his level and experience are not the same. You have an hour, as of now." With these words the Patriarch froze on his throne, showing that for the next sixty minutes I didn't exist for him. That's fine by me. The main thing now was to figure out what could be done with this ring. ...

After twenty minutes of fiddling with the ring it finally dawned on me that I was unable to recreate it in the design mode. The ring constantly turned out deformed however I tried to imagine it: either the gem sockets were bent or the ring itself became square or its surface looked corroded, as if by acid. It looked like the level difference between my profession and a 300-level object was just too large. Was giving up and preparing for respawn all I could do? I would've dearly preferred to avoid that, but by the looks of it ... although ... what if ...

I went to the Shaman abilities and started to read. It's true what they say: everything new is just the well-forgotten past. If I couldn't use Jewelers' skills, perhaps I could use my Shaman skills instead? Essence of Things and Change of Essence. ... Let's hope that this ring doesn't have the 'Shield' spell active on it ...

Revulsion. Rage, pain, fear and again revulsion. As soon as I applied the ability to the ring, I was engulfed by a great torrent of negative feelings. I don't know how I managed not to chuck the ring and wash my hands of it there and then, but I'm pretty sure that the look of disgust on my face was reminiscent of someone who'd just fallen into a cesspit. The ring wanted to be revolting, wretched, evil, and terrifying. The list could go on, but I tried to detach myself from the sensations that the capsule was trying to feed me and went back to the ring. So, are you a piece of filth hell bent on being that and nothing else? I see. But what if I try to force you to become a happy and harmless lump of metal?

My first attempts at Change of Essence resulted in nothing except a headache and, most surprisingly, a nosebleed. I glanced at the Patriarch, who was still sitting statue-like on his throne, and realized that he'd sensed the blood too. His nostrils widened slightly, as he inhaled its sweet scent, but the Vampire himself remained motionless. There was little else to do than sit there and try to guess what was going on: was this due to the properties of the location, which happened to be the abode of blood-loving Vampires (similar to the Shaman Initiation Cave) or was it specific to changing the Essence of the ring? Forty minutes had already gone by, but I saw no clear way of solving the problem. Time to give up? What else is there left to do ...? Like hell I will! I'm a Shaman and no ring is gonna make me give up!

Once again I closed my eyes and called up the design mode. There was black empty space where items that I had created were sorted on their own special 'shelves'. Kameamia, with the note 'cannot be repeated', the images of the Orcs, the Dwarves, the thirty-two players from Phoenix and the Dark Legion clans, the stone button, a ton of rings and neck-chains ... a good collection of crafted items, for sure. Now I just needed to add another ring there, which was completely refusing to appear. What if I'm doing it all wrong? What if I shouldn't be trying to re-model this ring, but just skip the first stage and create the ring that I'm aiming to make? I am a Blessed Artificer, and not a Cursed one, after all, someone who makes blessed and not cursed items, so why do I need a 'black' item on my shelves?

The template of the ring appeared straight away – round and shining, molded from a single piece of metal, with two gem sockets (I should experiment with designing such rings, as well as with the number of sockets – why should there only be two?). The ring I created looked very similar to the one that the Patriarch had given me, but no waves of light were emanating from it. If I crafted it now, I would simply get a bronze cast ring of something or other. There had to be an extra ingredient to make the ring change, but how?

"Hi, come over, I need your help," I called my Totem. I saw no other means of correcting the ring other than bathing it in Dragon's breath. This was probably stupid, but I was out of options: I had only ten minutes left.

"I'm here. What do you need? Is it normal for you to have a dark ring hanging in front of your face?" Draco asked, almost breaking my concentration. It turned out that if I relaxed even a little, the ring in my imagination immediately started to melt and deform.

"Take no notice. Now here's the job: the ring must be burned. Do it, just try not to fry me as well."

"I'll be careful," Draco roared at me and warm air began to blow in my face. "Nope. It's not working."

"Accelerate."

"But ..."

"Draco, I realize it will hurt, but do it!"

"All right, I'll jump to level two ..."

"No. If the second level won't do it, go to third and fourth. ... Something tells me that you should jump straight to six."

"I've never gone that far! It will hurt a lot!"

"If you don't do it, I'll be destroyed. I won't force you, it's your choice." Even if he were just an NPC, but this is Draco ... I'd become attached to him and I wouldn't make him do something he doesn't want to do, even if I really needed it. What's 12 hours of sleep? Nothing, gone in the blink of an eye ...

"I will do it, brother," said my Totem in a hollow, heavy-sounding voice and then warm air again began to blow into my face. "Entering the second," Draco reported and strange things began to happen to the ring in the design mode: it started to melt, like a piece of butter in the sun. Was this really the result of the Totem's breath? I should've been happy that it was working, but a feeling of foreboding rose up within me: something wasn't right. I had to prevent the ring from melting entirely; it had to remain whole. ...

"Entering the third," said my Totem through gritted teeth – or rather fangs in Draco's case – when I started to fight for the ring to stay whole. Its form had to be round, two sockets for the gems, a perfect surface ... a few seconds went by, but the ring continued to melt. Either I was lacking concentration and experience, or I was doing everything totally wrong. Stop! Didn't I just ask my Totem for help? Why don't I make use of my Shaman skills? The three seconds it took me to enter the Spirit Summoning Mode seemed an eternity to me. I freed up one of the active slots without even a glance at what I was chucking (I'd get it back later) and began to summon the Spirit of Petrification. I had no idea whether one even existed, but I really needed it right now. ...

You have summoned the Lesser Spirit of Petrification. ...

This was a great relief. I didn't even have to summon Spirits – by the looks of it the design mode combined beautifully with the Spirit summoning mode, so the newly-summoned bodiless entities started to circle around the ring, returning it to its initial shape. That's it – it's as good as done now: Draco will finish frying the ring and the Patriarch will give me my reward. I even managed to sigh in relief until the next piece of news tore all my plans to shreds.

"Fourth!" shouted the Totem and the Spirits that I'd summoned evaporated as if they'd never been there. I summoned them a couple more times, but as soon as they flew to the ring, which started to melt again, the Spirits vanished. They weren't the right level. ...

You have summoned the Spirit of Petrification.
+1 to Spirituality. Total: 25.

Now I could clearly feel an inferno raging around me, and periodically a message flashed before my eyes that I'd lost 1–2 Hit Points on account of the blowing hot air. A Totem's fire cannot harm its master, but the air that he heats up is oblivious to the fact that the Totem means me no harm. The summoning of the ordinary Petrification Spirits did not come easy to me; I felt my head growing heavy, some strange hum spreading through my ears (on second thoughts, it might have been the Dragon's fire) and there was an unpleasant metallic taste in my mouth: the ring became whole once again.

"Fifth!" If the hoarse voice that just sounded was any indication of his current state, Draco wasn't feeling too great right now. The worst part was that I could do nothing to help my 'brother', because the ordinary Petrification Spirits also began to disappear. The Dragon's fifth acceleration level took them out even before they reached the ring, which once again started to lose shape, so there was little I could do other than ...

You have summoned the Great Spirit of Petrification. ...
+2 to Spirituality. Total: 27.

I waved away the announcement that I would be losing 10% of my Hit Points every five seconds, because the summoned Spirit was beyond my rank, and tried not to breathe, because breathing fire was no picnic. The 'No Air' bar appeared before my eyes, helpfully telling me that I had 63 seconds before living would become difficult. The penalty for the summons only had the chance to appear three times (the second of which had me thinking that I was about to lose my concentration and scream), when Draco squealed more than howled: "Ss-s-s-i-i-i-x!"

I don't know what the Dragon had started to breathe at me, but the system told me that I was now in a lake of molten rock and losing 100 Hit Points a second. Obviously the initial figure was much higher, but I really liked the footnote: my Totem had made the lake, so I received only 0.1% of the damage. This brought little comfort, considering that even Great Spirits were unable to come near the ring, with the Dragon now breathing fire of sixth level of acceleration at its original physical form. Or not at the original – it mattered little: the Spirits couldn't manage it. As far as I understood there was no-one higher than the Great Spirits, apart from the pair who'd earlier told me how small and unready I was. The ring started to melt once again, the Dragon was growing hoarse, the fire was roaring, the Patriarch had probably left such a shocking scene (he may even hand us a bill later for destroying his hall), so I gritted my teeth and, disregarding all the warnings, both from the system as well as my own brain, started yet another summons. Supreme ones, I kinda need you right now.
...

You have summoned the Supreme Spirit of the Lower World. ...
    +4 to Spirituality. Total: 31.
    + 1 Rank to Water Spirits. Total: 4.
    Your Totem has gained a level.
    Your Totem has gained a level...

"We have come, Great one. You have passed the trial. Henceforth you will be able to call us, but no more than once a week: you are not a High Shaman yet. A penalty is incurred by anyone who spends time in our world; you can find out about it from any Shaman trainer. And now, release your Totem, brother. It is time he had a rest."

Character class update: Class Elemental Shaman has been replaced by Great Shaman.

+10 to Reputation with the Supreme Spirits of the Higher and Lower Worlds. This Reputation cannot be increased on account of the 'First Kill' Achievement.

You have received the new rank of Blessed Artificer. Current rank: 3

Item acquired: Holy Ring of Driall.

Item class: Epic, Unique.

Minimum level: 320.

Stats: +12800 to Intellect; +5400 Stamina; +80 Energy; +1400 Agility; +1400 Strength; when casting a spell you have 30% chance of an instantaneous free repeat cast.

2 Gem Stone sockets. Upgradable (the cost and level of upgrade can be confirmed with an Advisor/Master).

Holy Ring special properties: +200 to Faith; +200 to Reputation with Goddess Eluna (these effects are applied to the first player to wear the ring, after which this property of the ring will disappear).

Restriction: Only usable by Priests and Paladins.

Quest 'The Path of the Shaman, Step 3.'

The trial to become a Great Shaman is completed. Seek out a Shaman Trainer to be given the next step.

As soon as the messages stopped flashing past me, I dismissed Draco and opened my eyes, finding myself in a two-meter-wide melted crater. Its entire perimeter was crowded with Vampires, their weapons pointed in my direction: bows, spears, swords. ... Around ten level-200 bloodsuckers stood around me and it was clear that only an enormous feat of willpower stopped them from attacking me.

Your Reputation with the Patriarch of the Vampires has fallen by 24000 points. Current level: Hatred.

"The Master of the Enemy," said the Patriarch from his throne in a heavy, terrible voice, full of hatred. "Only because you have fulfilled my conditions will I forego sending you to the Grey Lands. You will be taken back to the Guardian's glade after which I, the Patriarch of Vampires, head of the Reardalox clan, shall declare you the enemy of all the Vampires in Barliona. You may take the ring with you and I shall also give you a certain scroll, because that was the will of the victors. You shall not receive the ten cursed objects for which you asked earlier, let

Tartarus be my judge. Leave us," the Patriarch told his Fighters, "the Master of the Enemy will not do me any harm."

This NPC sure came with a strange script: he's prepared to incur the wrath of the dark god just not to hand over ten cursed items to me. And there's my new title as well: 'Master of the Enemy'. Did he mean Draco? By the looks of it, the encounter between the head Vampire and the flying lizard didn't leave the best of memories behind if it had dropped my Reputation all the way to Hatred. Now Anastaria won't just lynch me, but will make sure my next hundred million years are filled with pain and suffering. Destroying her chance of meeting such an NPC is an achievement in itself. Although, on second thoughts, the Patriarch only spoke of me, so maybe his wrath would not extend to those accompanying me. ...

"I care little for the enmity between you and the Dragons," I replied to him, "they have left Barliona long ago and will never return. My Totem is not a Dragon, but an incarnation. I realize that it's useless to try to explain this after my Totem's destroyed part of your hall, so I'll skip any explanations. You can take me back now."

"For two thousand years Vampires were at war with the Dragons. For two thousand years they destroyed, burned and persecuted us ... we managed to bring down only three Lords of the Air, but afterwards each death was revenged. Their vengeance was meted out furiously and mercilessly; entire clans were eliminated. When, of all the Vampires, only my clan remained, the head of the Dragons came to me and demanded that I yield. Either I bowed my head and accepted his power or all the remaining Vampires would be destroyed. I subdued my pride with fetters of steel, and bowed before the victor, because I had to think of my people. I was handed a scroll that I had to give either to a Dragon or to his Master. Then the Dragons departed ... departed forever from our world. Some Vampires never accepted our submission before the flying serpents and left my clan, founding their own clans throughout Barliona. And I remained here, to remember forever the lesson that we were taught by the Dragons. When you summoned your Totem, which turned out to be a Dragon ... for the first time in ten thousand years I remembered what fear was. Fear before the inevitable. ... I did not enjoy this long forgotten feeling, so I will do all I can never to feel it again. This is for you." A scroll appeared in the Patriarch's hands, which then floated towards me through the air. Well, well! Even personally handing over an item to me was no longer possible for this red-eyed NPC. He was prepared to use a crazy amount of Mana for levitation so as not to approach me. ... Maybe he should see a shrink or something? It's as clear as day this Imitator is beset by a whole bunch of complexes.

As soon as I took the scroll one of the Vampires appeared next to me, his face full of revulsion, offered me a hand and I found myself in the Guardian's glade. The Vampire disappeared, the guys were nowhere to be seen – having probably gone into the tent to sleep – so I sat under the Oak and began to examine the Patriarch's present. I removed the wrapping and stared at the paper scroll:

Item acquired: The Treatise on a healthy diet for Dragons.

Description: Dragons kept a close watch on their figures: if they were to eat one too many cows or sheep, indigestion was guaranteed. For this reason the High Dragon developed a diet that would allow Dragons to enjoy their life to the full.

On use: you will learn a unique cooking recipe 'Dragon Porridge' (required Cooking profession level +1), which will increase the growth of all Dragon stats by 100% for 24 hours.

Restriction: only for Dragons.

'Dragon Porridge'?! They've got to be kidding me!

CHAPTER NINE
THE LIEUTENANT

D ING!
The sound of a letter arriving in the Mailbox cut through my sleep, and returned me to Barliona. I'd have to dig around in the settings and switch off these annoying sound effects. I could easily ignore it when awake, but when asleep it sounded like a loud gong hitting me on the head. Who the heck is after me?

With sleep-ridden, and thus totally clueless, eyes I selected my mail and opened the first letter that popped into sight.

"Hi! I'm a 219-level Warlock. I'm prepared to discuss conditions under which I would enter your clan. I require ...

The sheer impudence of it shook me completely awake. What the heck was 'conditions' for entering your clan supposed to mean? Wasn't he getting something mixed up here? I read over the message one more time, and raised my eyebrows in surprise. I just wasn't getting the meaning of this text. What did he want? As soon as I deleted that letter, another popped up in front of me:

HI! HI!! ! MY NAEM IS DROOLF THE HANDMAN!!!!!1 I WANT TO JOYN YOUR CLAN!!!! I'M ALREDY 17, CAN DO PVP SOON!!!!! LWTS MEET AT THE ANHURS SQUERE TOMORROW!!!!

Full of mistakes and all in caps – probably trying to create a bigger impression or something. What's happening? After deleting this nonsense and putting the sender on the blacklist, I skipped reading the third letter and went straight to the root folder of the mailbox. Once there, I ended up staring in incomprehension at the happily glowing '847' – the number of unread messages.

"Awake now?" The painfully familiar voice made me glance over my gaming avatar to check that my lower half was still under the blanket. Anastaria. ... "Good! I asked Plinto not to let anyone into the tent and sent Slate out for a walk. Everyone is gathering in thirty minutes; here's some food, eat it and don't let anything disturb you," the girl handed me an appetizing piece of meat. "Tasty?" asked Stacey once I'd finished and then sat right next to me. "Cooked it myself, especially for you."

"Thank you, of course, but why are you

suddenly taking the trouble?" I probably still hadn't quite woken up, since I didn't understand what was going on in the slightest.

"Did you receive the letter with the Copper Ore?" asked Anastaria, ignoring my question.

"I have no idea! I have eight hundred unread messages, so if there's one with the Copper Ore, I'll need to dig for it."

"Just eight hundred?" Anastaria's eyebrows flew up. "My admirers are a shadow of their former selves, by the looks of it ..."

."..?"

"Yesterday there was only one topic of discussion on the forums – my jumping ship to some unknown Seathistles clan headed by a certain Mahan. At the same time many took note of the fact that the player's name is short – just a couple of syllables long – and that his level is under a 100. Everyone thinks that you mothballed this character a long time ago and finally decided to return to playing him. If you think of how many declarations of eternal love, oaths of loyalty and other rubbish I get every day, it would've been foolish to think that some of those players wouldn't try to join our clan. After all, it's not that easy to get into Phoenix, while here you are, some unknown low-level Seathistles – sorry to be blunt about it. But eight hundred in one night ... not all that much, really. ... In any case, your next two or three days are going to be pretty lively. I advise you to configure your mail and turn off the sound. Trust me, those pings could easily drive you nuts."

Ding! You've received 14 new messages. Do you wish to view them?

"All right, you can sort out the letters as we travel. Now let's decide on the best way for me to help the clan. Plinto had taken the stat training upon himself (and the spaztard is quite welcome to it) so I propose that Clutzer is trained in analyzing situations and Leite, if I'm not mistaken about his disposition, in drafting various agreements. After all, real life agreements and game agreements are totally different things. I'm sorry, but our Clan Agreement has so many holes in it that you may, for instance, freely get into the clan treasury and not worry too much about the consequences. No need to look at me like that, I remember the phrase 'operations with the clan treasury require the approval of the Head or the Treasurer' well enough. It's just that you probably don't know that operations worth one copper coin aren't subject to clan registration, but are written off as minor errors. In the course of a day any player can carry out over ten thousand transactions and if he sets an Imitator to withdraw just one copper coin per transaction, he could end up siphoning four gold off the clan's account each day. It may seem like pennies, but think what would happen if you had a thousand players like that. Neither you nor the Treasurer would have any idea where the money was going. We pointed out such a loophole to the Corporation at one time, but they suggested that we clearly set out the permitted transaction amount for the clan treasury and use that to close the loophole. By the looks of it, this oversight has a prominent role in the operations of the rogue clans, which specialize in theft. There's a ton of details like this in the Game. Like Elenium's defection to Phoenix and his taking that quest with him, for example. I can help Leite keep the clan safe from such things."

"That'd be a great idea!" Once again Anastaria had managed to surprise me. And here was me naively thinking that I had an ideal Clan Agreement, which even Barsina praised – you'd think she would have a good grasp of these things being a mercenary. But that wasn't the case at all. ...

"There is one 'but', however." Anastaria immediately brought me back to earth. "If I will be acting as your real deputy for the entire three months I'm with you, I would like to be treated as your deputy and not as a spy and an enemy."

"What do you mean? Who's treating you like that?"

"You, who else? Last night both quests got updated and if we decide to stay true to our roles of Head and the Deputy, it would make sense for you to tell me what happened."

"Stacey ..." I started, but immediately checked myself. She really has set it up rather beautifully – she was prepared to invest real effort into developing the clan, help with closing the loopholes and with training, and then completely push me into a corner. If you want help, hand over the information. And what was I supposed to do now? Tell her to take a long hike? That's probably what ninety-nine percent of men with, erm ... avatar dolls of steel would have done. But I must swallow my pride: I'm not a lone hero, but someone with a clan, albeit a small one, behind me. So, I'd have to share the information. But how much of it I should share was something I'll have to think over carefully.

"You haven't fallen asleep, have you?"

"No, I'm not asleep, I'm thinking."

"What about?"

"Where I should begin my tale. So much happened yesterday that I don't know where to start ..."

"Start with Beatwick and the Dragon's words that you are his son."

"What's that got to do with anything? We're talking about the Dark Forest now."

"Something tells me that it all began there," smiled the girl.

"Not exactly, but fine! He's what all the fuss is about." I paused and summoned Draco. The time has come to show him off: he's big enough now and in need of constant levelling up, but I keep hiding him like some poor relative.

"Hello everyone," said Draco happily, but with one look at Anastaria, he did the last thing I'd have expected: he entered fighting mode. "Brother! A Siren is here! I'll hold her off, run!"

"No!" I shouted when the first ball of flame flew towards Anastaria. You had to give it to the girl – she managed to put a bubble on herself just in time, so the Totem didn't do her any damage. ... "You can't attack her!"

"She's a Siren! An Enemy!" shouted the Totem, flashing his eyes at the girl, but stopped his attack. I'd never seen Draco so agitated; I must find the time to read up on why Dragons were at war with Vampires and Sirens.

"Right! Back you go," I dismissed the Totem, "I'll summon you later and we'll have a chat. And remember, no attacking anyone until I tell you to. The war is over!"

"But you'll be careful, right?" Draco warned me as he began to fade. "Sirens are treacherous ..."

"A Siren?" I looked at my Deputy with some interest after my Totem disappeared. If the word 'shock' could be applied to this girl, Anastaria was definitely in such a state as she stared at the place that had been occupied by my Dragon just a moment ago. "So it's not that you've learned to control the poison, you simply changed your race? A Siren-paladin. Sounds nuts ..."

"A Dragon ... son and brother of a Dragon," uttered Stacey slowly, staring into space. "Did you go through modification too?"

"What do you mean?"

"You speak of a change of race so calmly you'd think you've come across this phenomenon before. Let me give you the good news: your case is the second in the entire incomplete eleven years of my playing the Game. Only the re-creation of a character allows you to change your race – at least that's what players are supposed to think. Six years ago I became a Siren and have now met my bitter enemy ... you are aware that our races were at war?"

"What's the difference what our races were to each other? I became a son and brother of a Dragon when I incarnated my Totem, in Beatwick I came across a scenario that ..."

"No need to continue," Anastaria interrupted me, "I get it already. In Beatwick you stumbled across one of the launch points of the scenario, made good use of it, became acquainted with the local copies of the High Priestess and the Princess, managed to befriend them, then the battle ... . In Anhurs the Princess gave you the quest with Slate (you still haven't shared it with me, by the way) and the High Priestess gave you the quest for the search of the Stone of Light. And here the legend about the Patriarch and the Dark Forest pops up. They've probably been wanting to launch it for some time, but no occasion presented itself. ... This is why the Guardian turned up, who gave you the quest and then you invited us. ... That's clear enough. But what happened yesterday remains a mystery to me. The present quests have been updated, but no new ones appeared, a possibility clearly mentioned in the Agreement. So it looks like you didn't get anything ... how could such an NPC fail to give a quest? He's not been put into circulation for nothing ... . So it looks like you messed up ... a Dragon-Shaman ... the Patriarch of Vampires and a Dragon!" Anastaria nearly screamed the last words, "You summoned your Totem in the presence of the Patriarch? Please don't tell me you've gone and done that!"

I didn't even know what to say to the girl's onslaught. It'd been a while since I've seen Anastaria this worked up. Truth be told, I'd never seen her like this.

"Arrrgggghhh! How?! Didn't you know that Vampires and Dragons are enemies? What kind of a Dragon are you if you don't even know the history of your race? Right, hang on a moment! I'm dawdling! Why the heck did you even need to summon your Totem in Patriarch's presence? Mahan?!"

"What?!" Anastaria's agitation transferred to me now. "Don't you think you're going a bit OTT with all this? Yes, I have Hatred with the Patriarch, but this concerns me alone as the owner of the Dragon. It doesn't affect other people. What else do you want? Did the quests get updated? Yes they did! It's easy enough to find the location of the Lord of the Fallen's base and as for the Stone of Light – you have the High Priestess's quest: it's marked by a dot on the map. I'll bet you any money that this is where we need to go. That's it! We're as good as done, everyone gets bonuses and there's general jubilation! Stop jumping down my throat already! If you hadn't logged out yesterday you could've gone to the Patriarch yourself! You would've managed to get at least a hundred quests out of him, sure as day. So the entire raid – because, as you said under the agreement the quests spread to everyone else – would've been sitting and scratching their heads at what 'Bring ten pine cones of doom to the Patriarch of the Vampires' was supposed to mean."

"Well, you've got me there," said the girl, who had immediately calmed down, "And there was me thinking you wouldn't figure it all out, but I just get worked up and you spill the beans. I guess it didn't work. Fine, tell me what happened next."

"Tell you what? Are you sure you haven't gotten confused, pretty lady?" I asked angrily. I'm just no good at switching so fast between emotions and I have a habit of finishing what I started. "What do you mean 'tell me'?"

"Exactly that: I'm all ears," the girl's smile grew even wider. "Mahan in the last few weeks you've demonstrated such unique survival abilities in the world of big money, that you've attracted attention. And not only that of clan heads, but a multitude of scam artists, for whom swindling a successful player is their main purpose in the Game. The avalanche of the letters you received is a drop in the ocean of what's in store for you. You have to learn how to communicate with players of every level and here we have two possibilities: either I help you, or you'll be learning from your own mistakes. It is, of course, your choice, but if you choose the former, we have to agree from the start that you share any information (and it is information I need) with me immediately and in full. I can't give you sound advice based on fragments of sentences."

"Judging by the way you're offering your help,

you're not even considering the possibility that I'll choose my own mistakes, are you?"

"No," the girl shook her head, "you seem to be a sensible person, capable of listening to a woman's point of view, rather than one of the 'alpha-males', for whom there are only two types of opinion: theirs and the wrong one. For example, go outside and try Donotpunnik."

"What's he got to do with this?"

"What indeed. He is your second adviser. Like the rest of the raid, he had his quest updated and, according to the Agreement, has a right to know how it happened. And fishing everything out of you, down to the smallest detail, isn't that much of a challenge for him. Especially if you're unprepared."

"Yeah, right, so you, being so kind and magnificent, are willing to prepare me to face the monstrous Donotpunnik, eh? I can't call what you're doing right now anything other than a scam. So what do you want for the great honor of training me, then?"

"Nothing extraordinary. We agree that I will have the opportunity to ask you any question, to which you will give me the fullest possible answer. That's it. For that I am prepared to help you."

"Just a question? And not to transfer or hand something over? Just information?"

"Exactly. Items are not my highest priority ..."

"Tell that to the Chess Pieces," I muttered and tried to think hard: what could Anastaria ask that I would really prefer not to tell her? How to find the Dragons? That's stupid: she's a Siren, so it would make little sense for her to go visiting Dragons. They'd go into 'Patriarch mode', blocking any attempts to speak to them and chuck her out of their world. What else? How to become a Shaman? Total nonsense, since there's probably plenty of information about that out there. The Chess Set riddles I was going to throw to her anyhow, because I need the answers. And that's it; I can't think of anything else. So, on one hand I should win in this exchange, but knowing Anastaria ... she's being just a bit too approachable, something isn't right here.

"Fine", I finally forced out a reply, "I will answer your question, only let's be clear on what exactly you're going to do. 'I can help' is too vague – it could mean just about anything, down to tying my shoelaces. And nothing more useful than that."

"Sending you an agreement, it covers everything. At one point I signed a similar one with Ehkiller, so I still have the template. If the wording suits you, you can proceed to tell me exactly what went down yesterday."

"When the majority of the players returned to reality, I told my fighters the reason that Elenium left and why you joined the clan. I stayed within the limits of the confidentiality agreement, but I gave them the basic idea." I signed the agreement and then gave an accurate account of what happened last night. "In the morning I woke up to the avalanche of clan applications and then saw you snooping on me."

"So it looks like aside from Hatred you managed to get a 320-level ring for Paladins and

Priests out of the encounter ...," said Anastaria thoughtfully. "Why are you so damn lucky? Even I don't have anything higher than 300 ... all right, we'll return to the ring later. Would you mind if we invited Clutzer?" the girl asked me, "It's time he started learning."

"Agreed. I'll call him over."

"Clutzer. Come into the tent, there's stuff we need to talk about."

"I wonder – will Plinto stop him or obey your order?" muttered the girl musingly. "I did ask him not to let anyone into the tent ... . One point to Mahan," she added, when she saw Clutzer come in, "Plinto's your man, congratulations. All right, let's begin. The majority of the players have only one question now – what happened during the night? Our aim is to produce a decent explanation for yesterday's events, without revealing any secrets, because under the Agreement Donotpunnik will be demanding full information. And he will be within his right: the quests have been renewed and people like him are real sticklers for details. So we have to figure out what we can tell him and what we can't. Here's what I'm proposing to do in view of what happened on account of Mahan's Totem and, most importantly, why I'm proposing it ..."

"Attention, everyone! General meeting in five minutes!" I shouted as soon as I came out of the tent. "I have information that I intend to share under the conditions of our Agreement! There is no need to surround me now – I'll be telling everyone everything a little later in any case." I immediately stopped the players who had begun to approach me. It was Anastaria's suggestion that any attempts to refer to non-compliance with signed documents had to be shut down. This was quite dangerous, because there was no telling which way the Imitators' brains would spin if it came to any disputes. But if I made a clear announcement of my intention to comply with my own Agreement conditions, it would be hard for them to find fault. Moreover, as the raid leader, I had to draw attention to my good self and ramp up interest in [anticipation of] the meeting. Simple psychology, nothing unlawful.

"So, yesterday, when the majority of the players logged out to reality," I began with the requisite reference to the fact that it was their own fault, letting it slip that I didn't mean all of them – just the majority. Let them look at each other and wonder which of them was around and is withholding information. Few know that only those unable to log out had stayed behind. "A Vampire-scout entered the glade. One that had not been changed. Yes! Aside from those we've come across, this forest also has unchanged Vampires. He used a portal and brought me to the camp of the local partisans and I spoke to their leader. You can all see the result – the quest was updated. I managed to find out the cause of the taint and what it is we have to do. The Boss refused to tell me the place where the Tear was stuck into the ground, insisting that the war between them and the Fallen was an internal affair of the Dark Forest. They will neither help nor hinder us."

Anastaria had laid out so many arguments why we shouldn't tell the others about the Patriarch, that in the end I agreed with her. I may have Hatred with him, but she, when she goes back to Phoenix, will have a chance of finding him and getting some quests out of him. When I voiced these suspicions, Anastaria smiled and proposed an agreement whereby Seathistles would get ten percent of any loot that Phoenix could manage to get out of the Patriarch from the moment this promise is made. This agreement was made on Ehkiller's behalf. Of all things, I've never heard of such a method of signing agreements on behalf of another clan, so after swapping a couple of phrases with Clutzer and raising our profit to 15%, I agreed. The text of the agreement appeared before my eyes, sporting Ehkiller's signature just a minute later. He signed under the girl's words – and that was that. The door to the Patriarch was now closed to me anyhow. ...

"I summoned my Totem during my meeting with the Vamps: him." With these words I summoned Draco. I had debated this point quite furiously with Anastaria: she was very insistent that I should show off my Dragon, switching all the attention from the Vampire boss to him. I kept refusing, arguing that he was still too small: if people were to see him now they'd start hunting and killing him, bringing his level down by 10 levels per death. All in all my arguments were quite childish, while Anastaria contended that I'd have to hurry up with leveling my Dragon, and that this would be pretty difficult if I kept hiding him from everyone. And I also had to give some kind of explanation for the increase in my rank: yesterday everyone had left an Elemental Shaman behind, but they were suddenly seeing a Great one. Ranks don't go up just like that; you have to do something extraordinary for that to happen. In the end I'd agreed to show Draco, so now I was watching the reactions of the players very closely. There had been all kinds of creatures in Barliona in the fifteen years of the Game, but no-one had come across a Dragon before. Before the events in Beatwick no-one had even believed they existed, and suddenly here's a Shaman with a pet Dragon! "With the help of the Dragon I've fulfilled certain class-based conditions and become a Great Shaman, but I also learnt of a certain Dragon trait: Hatred with Vampires. I discovered this last night, when the local partisan boss almost sent me for respawn, so I'm not a suitable contact for this group. If we should run across any more unchanged ones, I propose that we send Anastaria and Donotpunnik, my deputies, to communicate with them. What I just described is exactly what happened during the night. Let the Emperor be my judge if I lied!" I waved away the message informing me that I was summoning the main Imitator in Malabar as a witness too often and that from my next summons I would start receiving terrible penalties, and looked at the players. As Stacey had pointed out, I wasn't facing a bunch of gamer kids, who had just seen a Dragon for the first time, but the top managers of the largest Game corporations: they would not take even their own word at face value unless it has been verified in writing and certified by a notary. After I'd honestly retold last night's events it would be impossible not to believe me. You couldn't deceive the Emperor. He doesn't check just the formal side of things, when something unsaid is equated with the truth, oh no. If you wanted your words to be verified, you had to tell enough of the truth to pass the test. Any play on words counts as a lie for him ... .

In a few hours' time, having gathered into one big group, we ventured out from the Guardian's glade. According to our scouts, there was no-one for a radius of a couple of kilometers around, so the raid wasn't in danger of running across another Ash. The option of using flying pets to travel was ruled out after one of the players mounted his griffin and flew up. As soon as he rose ten meters above the ground, he immediately disappeared. According to the map – upon which the player was indicated by a small dot – and the swearing in the raid chat, he was thrown right back to the entrance to the Dark Forest, where we'd been initially teleported by the High Priestess. The player tried to fly back to us from there but as he got close to us he disappeared again upon landing. He was back at the start of the Dark Forest and once again there was much swearing. It became clear that only travel on foot was possible in this location. According to the unlucky player, he needed two hours to get to where we were. So we would have to wait ...

"Elementals, two hundred meters, 300+, eight

heads, two full sets: twenty meters apart. Mage support, twenty, 350+: zero meters apart." Plinto's economical report appeared before my eyes in the raid chat. As soon as our raid group was back together, we moved towards the center of the forest. All possible paths vanished within an hour of walking, so after sending the scouts ahead, we started to beat our way through the trees, leaving a narrow path behind us. The mages, to give them their due, managed to burn a hundred meters of the forest in less than five minutes by using their Mana prudently, allowing the raid to keep moving. No-one was keen on trying to fight through the thicket. In the end, after three hours of this kind of movement, we'd put quite a distance between the Guardian's glade and us as we searched for Midial's troops. Now finally Plinto had run across them. I couldn't help feeling pleased that I'd managed to understand at first glance what that potentially incomprehensible text actually meant. A sure sign that I was getting the hang of it.

"The Rogues take the mages, keep half stunned and interrupt the casts of the rest," Anastaria said as soon as we called a council. "Elementals are more difficult. One tank won't be able to handle a full set; he'll get mowed down. But the distance between the mobs will allow us to pull them one by one, so it shouldn't be too bad. Then we ..."

"Elementals and mages fifty meters. ETA to raid – 30 seconds. You've been spotted." Plinto's next message interrupted Anastaria's lecture. The girl spent a couple of seconds looking at Donotpunnik,

somewhat lost, but then the spark appeared once more in her eyes and my Deputy began to muster the raid:

"Phoenix, drive Alpha, Hell you're on the fire ones! Undigit, the water ones are yours, Etamzilat, get the air ones. 'Killer, try to stop the earth ones. We hit single-target only! If I see anyone using AoE spells, I'll rip them a new one! All Rogues, to the mages! Stun them! Small fries – three hundred meters back into the forest, now! All the Priests twenty paces back and get anyone who's down back up! Here we go guys, this is gonna get messy!"

"Visitors – 20 meters. Hitting you in 10 seconds. Moving very fast, I can't manage to ..."

With a wild crash the trees twenty meters from us fell down and for the first time in my gaming life I saw a Fire Elemental. Before, in pictures, holograms and video this mob didn't look all that big or scary, but now ... it was a nearly two-meter tall pillar of fire, moving in the air about a meter off the ground and burning off even the mist from underneath it. The players were engulfed in a wave of warm air. After bursting into our clearing the Elemental halted for a second, looked around and, with a strange screech, headed toward us. Behind what was presumably its back pillars of water, earth and air started to appear, figures of human mages flashing between them. The 'guests' had arrived.

"I'm taking the flaming ones!" shouted Hellfire, throwing an axe at the impressive spectacle and pulling another with his tanking ability.

"I'm on Hell and Undigit," shouted Anastaria, starting to pour healings into the Tank, whose Health started to slide. "Plinto, the mages! 'Killer, slow the earth! Don – help with the mages! Mahan! Why are you still here? Get back, now!"

"Minus two! Five are in stun! Crowd-control on the rest! ..."

"Elenium, get Brast up! Some Priest, damn you! Move it!"

"Mahan, get out of the way! Beat it already! Hell, I'm running out of Mana! Hunker down, I'll recharge! Everyone hit the mages – Elementals have immunity slapped on them!"

Unlike in Beatwick, right now the raid was functioning like a single organism. Six of the Elementals were being held off by the tanks, and the two remaining were constantly crowd-controlled by the mages. The healers were pouring healings into the Tanks, without sparing any Mana, and the main body of the players were focused on the group of level 350+ mages. Not wanting to be the odd one out, I started to summon Spirits, but all of them had pretty much zero effect. The difference between a 68-level Shaman and such a high-level mob was just too big. All that I could do was summon strengthenings into the tanks and restorations into the healers.

"Minus Undigit! Hell, take the mobs! Priests – resurrect on cool down! Plinto! Switch to the Elementals; try stunning them! Get those mages down already!"

"Mahan," Antsinthepantsa appeared next to

me, downing some restorative potion. "It's not the mages who are keeping the shields up around the Elementals!"

"What?"

"The mages aren't the ones keeping up the shields on the Elementals! Someone else is doing that!"

"Plinto, did you hear that?" I didn't doubt the High Shaman's words for a second. When you have twelve players already sent for respawn, while the enemy's lost only ten mages, doubts can go hang. "Find him!"

"On it!" After putting a 20-second stun on another Elemental, the Rogue stealthed and rushed into the forest at top speed.

"Damn, we're doing something wrong," whispered Antsinthepantsa, wincing at the unpleasant squelching sound as one of the Elementals tore away from Hellfire, flew over to a group of our mages and smashed into them. Four players lost. "Elementals are counterparts of the Spirits, so why are they on the side of the Fallen?"

"The Lieutenant, 300 meters. Dark Priest 400+. I'm gone." Plinto's frame went down to zero in less than two seconds and became gray. The Rogue had gone for a 6-hour rest. There were only two Priests in the raid and they could only resurrect one player every five minutes, so given that almost half the raid was already lying dead, Plinto's turn wasn't going to come around any time soon.

"Natalie, what do you know about Elementals?

You're supposed to be a Shaman, no? Out with it! Quit dragging your feet, we're running out of time!"

"'Killer, chuck the Elementals, we can't do anything to them. Destroy as many mages as you can!" came the order from Anastaria.

"Nothing special." Antsinthepantsa finally snapped out of it. At this point all four Elementals had surrounded Etamzilat and only twenty-three fighters remained alive. "Elementals are warriors of the elements, while Spirits are the souls of the elements. They're like brothers. At level 100 you will gain the ability to summon an Elemental for a few minutes, depending on your rank. Similar to a Totem, but temporary."

"How do you communicate with them?" A crazy idea popped into my head. If you could talk to Elementals, what if it were possible to strike a deal with these ones?

"Through the Astral Plane," said Antsinthepantsa slowly and suddenly her eyes lit up. "That's it! We can subdue them – just give me a minute!" With these words the girl sat in lotus pose and – what surprised me the most – began to rise above the ground. Not very far, but … looks like Shamans are quite the high flyers, with a special relationship to gravity and all that … . Strange that when I ended up in the Astral Plane, there was a message from Ehkiller that I'd disappeared. But now this girl simply rose up … is that because each Shaman has a different way of entering the Astral Plane or did I disappear in the Guardian's Glade because I ended up there by mistake?

"Stacey, bubble over Antsinthepantsa!" I thought it right that the lady Shaman be protected from being interrupted by any mob that might suddenly break loose.

"I can't! I threw it on Hell recently, it's still in cool down! What did you guys think up?" Only after Anastaria's reply did I realize that the bubble lasts merely a few seconds and wouldn't be much help. She may as well throw it on Hellfire in this case. I was being a bit slow on the uptake. ...

"There's a chance of gaining control over the Elementals. Antsinthepantsa is checking it out."

"All right, try using the scrolls that I sent you ..."

"Mahan!" Antsinthepantsa's baffled shout interrupted Anastaria's. "Come with me, I will be your guide, Great One. There will be a ton of penalties, but you have to see this!"

"What do I do?"

"Sit next to me, give me your hand and close your eyes. Open them when I tell you. Nothing else. Let's go!"

"I'll cover you." Slate flew up to me from the heat of battle. Wow! How the heck did I forget about you? If we fail, I can forget about my Attractiveness with the Princess for sure. "No enemy shall get through! Over my dead body!"

Sitting next to the girl and hoping that the only remaining tank, Hellfire, would be able to hold out long enough, I touched the girl's hand and closed my eyes. The noise of the battle and shouts of the players died away, as if a dome had been placed over me, and I heard Antsinthepantsa's voice: "You can open them now, we're here."

There was the familiar gray mist of the Astral Plane, into which I was pulled from the Guardian's glade, and I saw eight Elementals hanging in the air. In contrast to 'reality', in the Astral Plane the Elementals had eyes, which were now looking at us, with pleading gazes ...

The brothers of our Spirits were surrounded by strange entities circling around them, which looked very similar to dark phantoms from old horror movies. Or to those that flew out of the hands of Midial and Geranika. Several phantoms, probably the controllers, floated around the heads of the Elementals, while others circled each body, moving them in different directions. Several more phantoms maintained domes that surrounded each Elemental. So that's where the active defense of those mobs had come from.

"We cannot help you," the thundering voices of the High Spirits of both worlds sounded behind us. "We can only destroy them together with our brothers, so you're on your own. All we can do is to cut the penalty for remaining in our world by half. Act quickly – time is running out!"

"My spirits can't do any harm to these phantoms!" Antsinthepantsa's words stunned me. "I thought that perhaps you'd think of something, so I brought you here. If we manage to get rid of this Darkness, the Elementals will be set free and we will be able to stop them."

"Mahan, hurry!!! There's only fifteen of us left!"

I selected one phantom so I could examine its properties and understand what we were dealing with, but found them blocked. It turned out that you weren't allowed to look at the properties of these shady pieces of scum. Then it was like someone flicked a switch in my head: Beatwick and the Sklic ... there was only one instance when a mob's properties wouldn't show – when you were meant to discover what you were up against ... A quest for a Shaman!

"Mahan! Time! Do something!" Now Antsinthepantsa was telling me to hurry. Strange, why does this girl think that I can do something with these beasts? It's not like the Spirits can even touch them ... .

"Draco, I urgently need your help!"

"Coming!"

To make sure of the lady Shaman's words I selected one phantom and tried summoning a Spirit on it. It was only a level one, there was no way I could miss, but ... incomprehensibly the Spirit ricocheted and hit me instead.

"What is that, brother?" my Totem appeared next to me, staring in surprise at the phantoms circling around the Elemental. "They seem familiar, but I just can't remember. What do I do?"

"Try burning them."

"I can't," said Draco, not even trying to attack. "I can't target this ... what *is* the correct name for them? It's at the tip of my tongue, but I just can't find the right word ... . If I simply unleash my flame at them, I'll burn the warrior too. They are good, so I can't ... if only these shadowy things were real ... . But I don't know how to embody them ..."

Embody! Draco is a genius!

"Antsinthepantsa, time to activate Change of Essence! We have to change the phantoms! We'll be able to destroy them after that!"

"I'm on it!" the lady Shaman replied without even asking why I suddenly came to this decision. "We'll start with the closest fire one. I'm on the left. Bussy! Destroy them when you're able." In addition the girl summoned her Panther and started to change the essence of the phantoms.

"I thank you, brothers!" thundered the Elemental a few seconds later, engulfing us in a wave of hot air. Draco and Bussy acted quickly and made a good team. Changing the essence of a phantom turned out to be quite easy – all you had to do was imagine it becoming very solid and then one of our Totems would proceed to wipe it out. "If it wasn't for you we would still have to ..."

"Stop destroying the free citizens and help us with the Fallen mages," I shouted, interrupting the flaming pillar's 'thank you' speech. *"Stacey, one of the flaming ones is on our side. Don't hit him! We're working on the rest!"*

"I accept your conditions, elder brother, and my brothers will follow me once you free them," some sort of a greenish aura formed around the Elemental in the Astral Plane and he froze. Let's hope he switched to destroying the mages instead of my raid.

"Natalie, it's working! Let's keep at it! A water one is next!"

+100 to Reputation with the Supreme Spirits of the Higher and Lower Worlds.

Current level: Neutral. You are 890 points away from the status of Friendly.

As soon as we finished with the last Elemental, both Antsinthepantsa and I were kicked out of the Astral Plane – seems we overstayed our welcome. I glanced forlornly at the list of the week-long debuffs: -1 rank of the summoned Spirit, the Totem summoning time had been reduced to 1 hour a day and the strength of the summoned Spirits had been reduced by 20%. And this was barely even half the penalties. In this case, the Supreme ones have really gone into overdrive – increasing my Reputation with them looks to be virtually impossible.

"That's it, we're done." Anastaria sunk to the ground in relief when the last mage was destroyed and the Elementals had frozen like statues. Only the crackling of the fire, the noise of wind and water and the rumbling of the rocking earth indicated that the eight mobs were still alive and ready to spring into action. "Barsa, here, take these resurrection scrolls – get Ehkiller, Etamzilat and Donotpunnik up. I have no Mana and I will only be able to use a potion in three minutes. Guys, up we get, the Lieutenant is three hundred meters away! Mahan, will the

Elementals help us?"

"Yes brother, we will grant you our aid in this battle and then return to our world," the voice of one of the pillars sounded in my head, so I immediately told the good news to Anastaria and looked at what was left of the raid. Seventeen out of sixty-three. Some weird lottery was happening here ... The survivors included Clutzer, Eric, Leite, Barsina, Antsinthepantsa and me ... . Essentially we could rule out six of our people in the fight with a 400-level Lieutenant, which wouldn't be good. The twenty 350+ mages that we downed resulted in six new levels for me, +15 levels to my Officers, +4 to Barsina and +2 to Antsinthepantsa. As for the rest, I couldn't remember their initial levels, so couldn't tell if they gained anything. For instance, Anastaria's definitely didn't go up, remaining at 331 and as for Hellfire – our highest-level player on the continent –, he couldn't get past the 340 threshold.

"I am proud to have the honor of fighting with such warriors." Slate started to walk up to each player and shake their hand. Interestingly, as soon as the blacksmith stepped away from them, the face of each player became a picture of surprise and then his eyes shot in my direction. What now?

"I am proud ... ." When my turn came to shake the hand of the future Prince it all became clear. We'd all got a 'Gratitude of the Imperial Family' buff, increasing our stats by 20% and doubling the speed of Energy, Mana and Hit Point regeneration. That's it ... now there'd be no escaping questions on what a member of the Imperial Family was doing in these woods.

+50 to Reputation with the Malabar Emperor.

Current level: Respect. You are 3800 points away from the status of Esteem.

"YOU ARE INTERESTING TOYS," the Lieutenant's voice flooded through the Dark Forest, slapping us all with a long list of short-term debuffs, "IT WOULD BE A PITY TO DESTROY YOU STRAIGHT AWAY, BUT SUCH IS MY MASTER'S WILL! DIE!"

"Barsa, me and Leander – twenty paces away from Hellfire," Anastaria immediately took charge, sorting out all the remaining healers. "Etamzilat is backing up Hell. Ants – put strengthening and restoration on everyone. Right now, it's important! Leander, on cool down bring back up two more healers, three of us may not be enough. Small fries – to the back with you! Mobs aren't like the boss – things are gonna get really hot!"

All the nearby trees had been thoroughly destroyed during the battle with the mages, so now our group was standing on the edge of an improvised fifty-meter clearing. After three or four fitful breaths (there are no heart beats in Barliona), the trees on the opposite side flew apart, bringing the Lieutenant into view. Unlike in Plinto's first video, where he was covered by mist, now we could see this boss and his appearance in all its glory: he was a three-meter tall biped, his race indeterminable, because he was formed of a combination of human, white-skinned vampire and green orc ... a Frankenstein of the Dark Forest.

"That's one ugly bastard," Antsinthepantsa, who was standing next to me, couldn't help saying "Are all Dungeon bosses like this or did we just get lucky?"

"Save the chit-chat for later! The fight will have four phases," Anastaria immediately shouted after evaluating the boss's properties. "First. Hell, you take him and turn him away from the raid. Everyone stand on the sides, including the small fries, or you'll get iced. On my command, we all run to Hell. Etam – you stay at the back and catch the cleave attack. You must reduce the incoming damage from each cleave – it'll hit hard. 'Killer – your guys join only at my commend. Don – hit him, but very carefully, I suspect that he will return part of the damage in close combat. Don't get yourselves killed that way. The second phase is the other way around. We all stand next to Hell and then run in different directions on my command. Etam – you're at the back, as before. As for the third, its description is too hazy, so we'll split into four groups: tanks, heals, melee and ranged damage fighters. Stand around the boss and carefully listen for my commands. The fourth phase is closed; we'll have to improvise. Ready! Thirty seconds to start of the fight. Twenty-seven. Twenty-four. Ants – one more amplification on the tanks! Twenty! Mahan, as soon as the boss goes for us send in the Elementals. They should slow him down. If things work out, they can then step back until the second phase. Ten! Leander – don't forget to get the healers back as soon as the rez cool down allows you. Five! If we survive, I owe you all a cookie! Damn, talking like Mahan now. One! Go! Go! Go!"

"YOU WILL ALL DIE!" growled the Lieutenant, hitting us with a wave of debuffs and rushing towards us.

"Argada Urhant!" Hellfire shouted something incomprehensible, sent an axe flying into the approaching boss and instantly rolled sideways.

"Brothers, attack!" I commanded the Elementals, hurrying after Anastaria.

"'Killer, start, Hell is holding it. Don, go at it! Etam! Stand right behind! Hunker down already! (To 'hunker down' – to deploy a damage-reducing ability.)

"YOU CANNOT WIN! YOU ARE WEAK!" shouted the Lieutenant a couple of minutes into the fight. So far things couldn't be going better: Hellfire was holding off the boss very skillfully, preventing him from doing anything nasty. From the very start of the fight the boss didn't use anything other than simple blows, which our tank easily blocked, so everyone, including Anastaria were fine-tuning the order in which combat abilities were being used, something players called 'rotation'. The aim is to inflict maximum damage per unit of time. If you crossed a certain average threshold, well done, if not, you're not ready to become a raider just yet. Due to the level difference eight out of ten of the Spirits I summoned missed, but thanks to the Elementals the boss's Hit Points began to diminish at a nice and steady rate. I even had a flashing thought that the Mushu Dungeon was much more interesting in terms of fight mechanics, but then the boss's Health sagged below 90% ... .

B E W A R E!

"All run to Hellfire!" Anastaria immediately shouted. "Mahan, take the Elementals to the edge of the clearing!"

I sped after the girl but then felt like I'd hit an invisible wall. A foreboding ... Stacey was wrong: we mustn't gather – at all. The boss lifted up his arms and started to say some sort of an incantation. All attempts to interrupt him ended in failure: the spell was going to be cast no matter what. He was a Priest, after all, even if he's been sown together from different pieces. He was about to let rip ... .

"Mahan, hurry!" my deputy hurried me, but by then I already understood what had to be done. We had to get as far as possible away from the boss as quickly as we could.

"Everyone to the edge of the clearing! Now! Tanks too!" Leading by example, I ordered the Elementals to move away fast and sped to the farthest side of the clearing.

"Hear that?" Anastaria needed less than a second to take a decision. "After Mahan, quick. Hell, Etam, you too!"

"Etam, stay!" Donotpunnik immediately shouted, "Take Hellfire's place! Stacey! The lightning strike must hit the tank and be distributed among the closest players! Even a beginner raider knows that! If the strike goes into the ground, there'll be no survivors!"

"Don't stop!" Unwavering, Anastaria continued to run after me. "Everyone to the edge of the clearing! Etam, Donotpunnik! As the deputy raid leader I order you to get away from the boss! Five seconds until hit!"

"Etam, hold!" shouted Donotpunnik, running up to the leader of the Heirs of the Titans, who took position in front of the boss. "Stacey, now's not the time to be pulling rank. This strike has to be caught! Come back!"

The girl spent about a moment drilling me with a stare and then commanded: "Leander, a dome! (minus 40% damage) Mahan, I really hope that you're not ..."

"RASTURMA PERLANTA KES!" The Lieutenant's shout shook the ground as he completed the spell, and dark entities started to fly from his hands. The ground around the boss blackened, as if all life had drained out of it. The two players standing in front of Frankenstein of the Fallen ... they disappeared in a flash, while the boss's Hit Points rose back up to 98%.

"Morons," came Anastaria's half-whisper, as she began to get the raid's Health back up. The Lieutenant's spell sent Clutzer and Leite for respawn, Eric and I survived thanks to improved damage blocking, and the rest of the raid lost about 20% of their Hit Points. If it weren't for the dome and the fact that we'd put good distance between us and the boss

... . Then again, we still had a total of sixteen fighters against just one lonesome boss. He'd be biting the dust in no time ... .

"Mahan, the dark phantoms are moving in our direction," came Antsinthepantsa's shout. "Activate Change of Essence, we have to stop them."

"Arrows fly right through them without causing them any harm!" came the voice of Exodus, a Phoenix Hunter, one of our last long-range fighters. ...

"Try it on the closest one!" replied Antsinthepantsa "He's already been changed! Mahan! I won't manage on my own!"

"Don't let this shit get any closer! Hell, take the boss! Mahan, are the Elementals still with us? If yes, send them at the boss. We fight on, no slacking! Eric, we have no choice! Stand behind the boss and catch those cleave attacks! Leander, on every second cleave throw Teeth [an ability not permitting you to die for 10 seconds] on Eric. The cleave comes once a minute, I will cover him with the Bubble between the Teeth. We should be able to hold out. Go!"

Fifty strange, dark phantoms got embodied by Antsinthepantsa and me in less than a minute and it took Ehkiller and Exodus only one shot at each to rid us of this plague. But Eric ... my Elementals were giving the boss a good kicking, but every minute the Lieutenant made a double strike. Hellfire took the main hit and the tank that stood behind the boss caught the returning movement. Eric didn't get into position fast enough so the cleave went nowhere. And this 'nowhere' cost the raid –40% Hit Points for each player, including Hellfire. If not for the experience of the Phoenix leaders, who've been through many dozens of such fights, we would all have been wiped. This is why my Officer, teeth clenched and covering himself with the shield he got in Dolma, took position and started catching the Lieutenant's cleave attacks. The only thing that Eric permitted himself was a low grunt during the hit, because withstanding being almost destroyed by a hundredth of a second ... tanking isn't an easy job for a prisoner, if you think about it. ...

B E W A R E!

"Everyone to the opposite side of the clearing!" commanded Anastaria, as soon as the boss's Hit Points went below 90% for the second time. "Leander, shield on my command, Eric, hunker down (use a damage-reducing ability) when he blows. Ants – strengthening on Eric and Mahan, they must survive this. Mahan, why are your Elementals still hitting the boss? Move them! Leander, if the boss's Hit Points don't go up after the blast, get Elenium up."

"No!" I intervened midway through Stacey's commands "We need a tank! Eric won't be able to take it!"

"Nothing will happen to your Eric! Any tank can catch the cleave-hit with the Teeth and the Bubble: his level has nothing to do with it! It's just that he's lower than anyone else in levels and is totally useless in battle! I know it's painful, but everyone else is busy and losing a fighter just to make it a bit easier on Eric ... . Anyway, later! When we get

Etamzilat back, we'll replace Eric. For now he can stay and level up his Endurance, that's useful for a tank!"

"All right," I agreed with the girl, "You have more experience with these things ...."

"Attention everyone!" shouted Anastaria, as soon as we survived the second blast and destroyed the dark phantoms. "Stop doing any damage to the boss! Priests – resurrect on cool down! The Priority: first the tanks – Etamzilat and Undigit. Then healers – Car–"

"Plinto!" I intervened, "Stacey, we will really need Plinto! Get him up right after Etamzilat. We won't manage without him next!" If anyone could've explained to me why I butted in, I would've given him half my gold. An additional tank or a healer would have come in very useful right then, but no! Instead of resurrecting a healer, as logic would dictate, here I am demanding the Rogue be brought back. Yes, he might be able to deal the highest damage to the boss, but if there is no-one around to heal, hitting the boss would be of little use. Right, enough! Logic can go hang; intuition rules the day today! And mine's saying that Plinto's presence is vitally important.

"Priests, did you hear our leader? Leander gets Etamzilat and Elenium heads out to get Plinto back. He's lying two hundred meters away from here. Move it! Now!"

We survived two more blasts at 80 and 70% of the boss's Hit Points, managing to get six players back up between attacks. The embarrassed

Donotpunnik, after dropping a quick 'Sorry', was helping to support Etamzilat and Hellfire, redirecting some of the damage to himself. At a certain point we even stopped hitting the boss altogether, in the hopes of resurrecting the entire raid, but then we started getting such a crazy amounts of damage that Leander had to put a dome up to reduce the amount that was hitting us. Good job, priest: he didn't need to wait for any orders for this. The only real snag was that nobody but the Priests were able to return players from the Grey Lands. Leander and Elenium were doing the work of five people, but their rezzing ability couldn't recharge faster than the programed game cool down mechanic allowed: five minutes per player during combat.

"YOU DECIDED TO OPPOSE ME?" the Lieutenant finally uttered, giving us yet another extended collection of debuffs, "ADMIRABLE! THEN LET'S PLAY!"

"Everyone run to Hellfire!" Anastaria immediately reacted. "The shockwave described in the properties of the second phase will mean that the entire raid will be taking a lot of damage. There is only one safe place – right in front of the boss. What do you say, Mahan?"

"Let's run and then I'll see," I agreed, but after taking a couple of paces towards the tank, I stopped. We shouldn't run together nor should we stand in one place.

"What?" Anastaria halted, without ceasing to heal Hellfire and land an occasional kick on the boss.

The latter only had 61% Health remaining and, if my gut feeling wasn't fooling me, something unpleasant was about to happen. "There will be no raid-wide damage, so there's no need for us to run together," the girl answered her own question, "we need to decide what to do next. Look, areas with red mist have appeared at the center of the clearing. They look a lot like portals. Any idea what to do with them?"

Two medium-sized off-red balls of mist were hanging about a meter from the ground at the very center of our man-made clearing and were flashing invitingly, as if telling us to step inside.

"Plinto and Barsa!" I decided to go with my gut feeling and improvise. The resurrected Rogue was about to come in handy. "There are two red mist balls in the center of the clearing. Get inside them, fast!"

"The balls need to be activated," quickly added Anastaria, "You have to do something inside them, depending on what you find there. Go!"

Like experienced soldiers used to following orders, my clan members stepped away from the boss and ran to the center of the clearing. As soon as they activated the portal and disappeared into the unknown, the boss's Hit Points dropped to 60% and the red spheres vanished.

B E W A R E!

"Everyone to Hellfire!" came Anastaria's command, but once again I had to interrupt her: "Everyone, get away from the boss to the other edge of the glade! Stacey, try to think what this may be, but we have to get as far away from the boss as we can!

Something tells me that this isn't a new ability, but an extension of that blast with the mobs that we've already had. What can it be?"

"We're inside. There's a labyrinth here and there's constant magical damage, like from radiation. Good thing you sent Barsina too – it hits quite hard." A message from Plinto appeared in the raid chat. *"On the move now."*

"Leander, the dome!" shouted Stacey as the boss had nearly finished his spell, and then her eyes widened in terror. It lasted just for a split second, but I caught sight of it because I was looking directly at her. "Everyone, look under your feet!" came another order from the girl. "Barely-visible zones will appear under you. You will have one second to step out of them. Make sure you watch your step, you cannot move to an already formed zone! Mahan and Ants! Don't forget to keep an eye on the phantoms as you move around! There they are! Embody them! 'Killer and Exodus – they're yours! Run!"

Then all hell broke loose. The boss froze on one side of the clearing, his arms lifted up, and a wave of damage from the blast went through the raid. The dark phantoms sped in our direction and a few moments before the explosion purple puddles began to form under our feet, a new one every three seconds. The puddles were about a meter in diameter, so a good many of us had to leave the dome before the spell hit to avoid dying. They really shouldn't have … the explosion from the boss sent three players for respawn, increasing the Lieutenant's Hit Points to

65%.

"Brother! Stop this nightmare." A message from an Elemental appeared before my eyes, *"One of us has been sent to the Grey Lands. Help us!"*

That's the last thing I need! The Elementals starting to die!

"I'm at the center of the labyrinth. Got *there with my speed boost."* Plinto again: *"I'm seeing a weird sort of creature oozing purple drops of some kind."*

"Destroy it!" Anastaria's reaction was instantaneous: *"This is the source of all our troubles!"*

"On it!"

A few moments later the glade cleared of purple puddles, the boss lowered his arms and headed for Hellfire. Right, we've survived this ability, but we had three fighters fewer now. And this was with the boss at just sixty percent, and only in the second phase.

The red spheres appeared again at 61% of the boss's Hit Points, when we regained four of our players. Thirty players against one boss: now this was more like it.

B E W A R E!

"Plinto and Barsa, you know what to do," Anastaria quickly responded. "Everyone, stand outside the dome and run together just before the blast! We mustn't allow the puddles to form inside it! Watch out for the phantoms! Let's go!"

"That's it, we've reached another milestone," reported Stacey with an almost manic glee in her voice, as the boss's Health went below 60%. We survived the second wave of the nightmare without a single death and without allowing the Lieutenant to heal himself. "There are two more phases ahead of us. One is a random, which comes last, and the next – you can look it up in the properties for yourself – will require several groups. We need to get the remaining players up quicker. Stop! The red spheres again! The boss is still only at 58%! The portals; get ready!"

As experience had shown, the trigger for the second phase ability did not depend on the number of Frankenstein's Hit Points, but on time. The red portals appeared every two minutes, taking Plinto, Barsina, Antsinthepantsa, Exodus, 'Killer, and myself completely out of action. Two were running around the labyrinth and four were dealing with the phantoms, which barely ceased to appear before a new wave hit us.

"Forty-two percent!" came the voice of my deputy. "We're about to be hit with another ability."

B E W A R E!

"What the heck?" shouted Elenium almost at the same time as the system announcement came, "Resurrection isn't working!"

"Maybe it hasn't recharged yet?" I asked, staring at the deserter in incomprehension, "What do you mean it's not working?"

"Same here," added Leander, "We'll have to finish him off as we are."

"Plinto, Barsa – off you go!" commanded Anastaria, as if nothing had happened. "There's no sense in holding off the damage anymore, hit him with all you've got!"

Dammit! As soon as my fighters disappeared into the red portal, three more appeared nearby, but these were blue. And what were we supposed to do with them?

"Twenty seconds until he finishes casting the spell!" Stacey informed everyone in a calm and somewhat resigned voice. "Mahan – what do we do? Stay put and dodge the puddles or jump into the portals?"

"Stacey, I have no idea ..." I muttered, at a loss.

"Me neither," smiled the girl, "but someone has to make the decision and be held responsible for its consequences. Ten seconds ..."

"Everyone into the portals! Donotpunnik, you stay here." I had no idea why I issued that last order, but felt it was the right thing to do.

"Hear that? Let's go!"

I just managed to glimpse the surprised face of the Death Knight, who froze in his tracks, after which the blue of the portal surrounded my character. Not knowing what to expect, I closed my eyes and braced myself, but when I finally had the courage to open them and see where we'd ended up, I had to make an effort to prevent my jaw from hitting the floor. We came out into the same clearing where we'd just been fighting the boss, but now everything around us seemed faded and unnatural; even the air itself was saturated with a subtle feeling of grayness and emptiness.

"The Inverse," said Anastaria in a high whisper. "Now I get it. *Don, we'll be seeing ya. It's the Inverse.*"

"Farewell, brother!" A message from the Elementals appeared before my eyes, *"It is a pity that we did not see this Fallen one destroyed ... "*

"I'm the firs– ." By the looks of it Donotpunnik wanted to write what he was first of, but didn't quite make it. Both he and the Elementals vanished from the clearing as if they were never there.

"Spread out and maintain a distance; step out of the puddles!" It seems that Anastaria never loses her nerve. "On my command we run together, Leander – put up a dome, same as before. Mahan, who's next?"

"Next?"

"This is the inverse of reality. Each of the three portals is for a particular type of player: one for tanks, one for healers and one for fighters. We can't make a mistake here – otherwise it's instant death when the boss completes the cast. Here come the phantoms – embody them! Usually it takes several deaths to discover which portal is meant for each player type, but there's an exception. If you leave ... Exodus, stop bashing the boss and hit those shadows! Anyway, if you leave at least one player outside the Inverse only he will die, irrespective of whether the others entered the right portal or not. I have no wish for any of us to die to figure out the portal's designation, so we have to pick the next victim. I propose Eric."

"Eric?"

"You can stop looking at me like that! Everyone will be sacrificed, even you, if it gets us through! Forty percent for thirty people is really a lot, added to the fact that we are guaranteed to lose one person every two minutes. And then there's the fourth phase, whose properties are still completely hidden."

"And the previous three were just an open book." I couldn't resist some sarcasm. "Brast from Phoenix will be next. Eric stays until the very end and try not to let him die."

"Brast, you heard the order?" the girl turned to one of the Warriors. "Don't lose any time: run straight to the boss and try to inflict at least a little damage on him."

"Done! Will you throw a bubble? I will be able to hold out five seconds more if you do. Who knows, they might come in handy?"

"All right. Attention everyone! As soon as we're back to the normal world, we hit the boss immediately. Use all you've got, all abilities: we have to get him down to 20% in the next 4 minutes!"

We managed it in five minutes forty, after losing Brast, Crisp from the Heirs of the Titans and, most unfortunately, Leander, who was taken down by the phantoms. Azure Dragons had a top class healer – it was a surprise he wasn't in Phoenix. I was of little use in the battle with the boss – the level difference was just too huge, after all, so I used the time to take stock of the damage being dealt by the players. It was just as well that the special raid leader features allowed you to do that. What can I say ...? It was too bad I sent Donotpunnik for respawn first. The deputy head of Azure Dragons held a solid second place in damage after Plinto. What my Rogue was doing could only be described as a miracle: he was responsible for almost 40% of all the damage done to the boss.

"I GROW TIRED OF PLAYING AROUND! TIME TO DIE!"

"The last phase!" shouted Anastaria for anyone still wondering. "Stay focused on bringing down the boss!"

"Bubble on Plinto!" Antsinthepantsa suddenly shouted. "There'll be a – "

Boom! A giant staff appeared in the Lieutenant's hands, which he lowered right on top of the Rogue.

"He's switching to the rest of the raid now!" Hellfire spoke up for the first time during the battle. "I'm no longer controlling him!"

"Now we really are done," Stacey said in a somewhat tired voice, her hands dropping, "We'll never get through that last 20%, especially if you keep in mind that he has to make only thirty blows now. Damn! And I'd started to believe that we could nail this on our first attempt!"

Boom!

Surrounded by the dome, Plinto was 'hammered' about chest-deep into the ground. The bubble lasted ten seconds, five of which were already gone. Another two or three hits and we'd lose Plinto and it would be the turn of Exodus, 'Killer and so on, according to the amount of damage they were dealing. I had some cause to celebrate – I would be the one before last to be sent for respawn, right before Eric. ...

Boom!

"Maybe we can freeze him?" I said the first thing that came into my head. You had keep trying, instead of simply waiting your turn to be eliminated.

"It's not working," Ehkiller said straight away, "We tried throwing 'freeze' and 'ice trap' on him ... . Nothing works. Seems to be some sort of a non-standard boss ..."

Non-standard? Stop! There's something in this ... a non-standard boss who likes non-standard honey ... what nonsense! Although ...

"Stop hitting the boss! At all!" I screamed across the entire clearing. "Hellfire, even you – stop doing anything! No damage to the boss!"

"In five seconds the raid will start randomly sustaining massive damage," it was Anastaria's turn to respond.

"Stacey, please, this is important! Remember! When the fight began, what was the number of the boss's Hit Points? Was anyone recording the fight? I need the boss's exact level of Health!"

"99.9%!" said Plinto, whose head was the only part of him sticking out of the ground after another strike from the staff. The next hit would be the last for the Rogue, so I had to enact my plan fast.

"Stacey, select the boss and hit him with a healing! Everyone stop hitting the boss already! If anyone else hits him, you'll be excluded from the loot share!" Leading by example, I selected the Frankenstein and sent a Water Healing Spirit to him. Let it work, pretty please. The very fact that an aggressive boss could be healed made my mind boggle, but I'd completely turned off my brain and had decided to rely on my intuition alone. Am I a Shaman or what? Speaking of which, I should find time to reshuffle my abilities, because although I was already 'Great' in rank, I was still only using ordinary Spirits. That needed fixing. ...

Booo–.

The staff froze right above Plinto's head as my healing entity entered the Lieutenant. Did it work? Looks like it did, but there was no stopping now. ...

"Stacey, healers, get going! Everyone with any healing ability – use it!"

"You're nuts for sure," said the girl, but started healing all the same, from what I could see. Good.

The boss soon had 25% Hit Points ... 30 ... 50 ... .

"Resurrection's unlocked!" Elenium shared the happy news.

"Get Leander up!" came my immediate order. "Healers, keep getting the boss's health up until you reach 90%."

"And then?" Anastaria immediately asked.

"Then? Then everyone attacks the boss and brings him back down to 70, after which the healers again bring him up to 90. Then rinse and repeat until the entire raid is brought back to life. There are only 2 Priests for 34 corpses, so in total we need ... damn, I need a minute to count."

"Eighty-five minutes," the girl immediately volunteered. "All right, we get the raid up, then what?"

"Then nothing," I smiled, "The boss is

unkillable. He is physically unkillable, no matter how much damage we deal to him. This is a wrong type of forest, which has a wrong type of boss. Who doesn't have to be killed, but has to be ..."

"Healed," Anastaria understood my idea, "And what if it doesn't work?"

"Then our 63-player crowd (except for Leite and Clutzer since they'll go down from the blast) will once again lay into the boss. We'll down him by brute force. Although something tells me that there's a reason for that question mark in the boss's properties. He'll be the one bringing us down. While now ... can you see how long we've been trying to heal him? Five minutes? And he still hasn't used a single ability. We're on the right path, guys!"

It turned out that this boss was perfect for leveling up your skills. Unlike the battle Spirits, the healing ones popped out without any level restrictions, so when the raid was fully back on its feet, the level of my Intellect increased by an entire seven points.

"FREEDOM! IT IS SO CLOSE!" uttered the boss, when the level of his Hit Points reached 100%. "BUT THEY ARE STRONGER THAN I! MY LORD ORDERED YOU TO BE DESTROYED – I CANNOT DISOBEY HIS ORDER. DIE!"

"Right," said Anastaria slowly, "He's gone down to 99.9% again. Seems like we've missed something. Mahan?"

"Ants!" – it seemed like I was just full of original ideas today – "I urgently need to get to the Astral

Plane!"

"The lesser penalty not enough for you?" asked the girl, surprised. "If you go there now, the Spirits will stop listening to you completely for a week!"

"Ants! Take me to the Astral Plane, quick!" I barked at the girl, "We'll have time to be sorry for this later!"

"No-one lets the boss drop below 95% Hit Points!" I heard Anastaria's orders. "Healers recharge their Mana, as soon as the boss reaches 95. We want to get him up to 100!"

"Close your eyes," Antsinthepantsa sat me on the ground next to her. "What are we going to do there?"

"You'll see in a minute." I had time to wink at the girl, though I realized she was unlikely to see it at this point. After closing her eyes, Antsinthepantsa started to sway from side to side, as if entering a trance. Is this how she always enters the Astral Plane? Cool. ...

"You can open them now, we're here. Whoa, that's nuts!" exhaled the girl.

I opened my eyes and saw pretty much what I expected: there was a cluster of white light, in places wreathed in red, gray and even green tones, and surrounded by the same phantoms who were making life difficult for the Elementals.

"Draco, can you come?"

"Ten minutes, no more."

"That would be enough."

"Them again?" exclaimed my Totem after he

saw the Astral image of the Lieutenant.

"Mahan, they can't be changed," whispered Antsinthepantsa, "I tried, but nothing happ–"

"We don't need to change anything, Natalie." I smiled once again. "What I'm most curious about is why this boss was made impossible to complete without Shamans. You know, I think I finally understand what continent-wide scenario Elenium got from the High Priestess."

"You know, you're really beginning to lose me." The girl looked at me, perplexed, "What are you on about?"

"Doesn't matter now. It's just we're on the verge of a very big update in Barliona and a big part of it is a new dark power: the Lord of Shadow, Geranika."

"I know this. How can it help us now?"

"Tell me, what will happen if I start a Duel with my Totem here?"

"I have no idea, but the Supreme Spirits aren't going to like it – they'll probably expel you. And me too."

"How will this expulsion take place?"

"How on earth should I know?! What are you thinking?"

"Natalie, think. This is very important!"

"They'll turn you into a shining or completely dark sphere, depending on which of the Spirits will be doing it, impose a penalty and kick you out of the Astral Plane."

"Is there a way to make sure that it's the Light Supreme one that does it?"

"There isn't. It's a fifty-fifty chance."

"All right, thanks, and, if I turn into the Dark one, I'll repeat my actions, all right?"

"What's on your mind?"

"Later, no time now! *Stacey, get the boss up to 100% and keep him there for about half a minute.*"

"*Roger that!*"

"Draco, let's train for a bit. Attack me!"

"HOW DARE YOU DEFILE OUR WORLD?" Just seconds later the terrifying voice of a Supreme Spirit sounded. "YOU WILL BE PUNISHED! A MONTH WITHOUT ACCESS TO THE ASTRAL PLANE! TWO WEEKS WITHOUT SPIRITS! A WEEK WITHOUT YOUR TOTEM! NOW BEGONE!"

I got lucky ... it was the Supreme Spirit of the Higher World, the one that formed a shining sphere. ...

"FREEDOM!" came the voice of the Lieutenant, as soon as I was thrown out of the Astral Plane. Although ... the Lieutenant was no more. We were facing a sentient that was maimed in some incomprehensible fashion. "THANK YOU HEROES FOR GIVING ME A CHANCE TO LEAVE THIS WORLD ALIVE. THANK YOU! RHEA, I'M COMING!" With these words the boss hit the ground and broke into all his constituent parts, which were almost immediately absorbed into the ground. All that was left for us was a small pile of loot – that for which we'd come here in the first place.

Level gained! (8 times)

Loot allocation has been completed (list), please confirm.

After looking through the fifteen level-260 items left after the disappearance of the Lieutenant and finding nothing useful either for myself or for any of my clan members, including the high-level players, I decided not to use my right of veto on the loot and agreed with the allocation proposed by the Imitator. It did know best, after all, who should be getting what. For example, Antsinthepantsa, who had gained three levels in one go, got two items, which left her overjoyed. You don't need all that much to make some people happy, it seems.

"That's it, enough fighting for today." I don't know about the rest of them, but I had lost any desire to go on with our journey right this minute. "Those who want to can get back to reality; we'll continue tomorrow. We still have the General and Midial himself ahead of us. So we'll have our work cut out for us." I pulled out the tent, so that others had a chance to set it up, lay down in the mist and immediately dropped into sleep.

Now I finally knew the nature of the phantoms commanded by Geranika.

CHAPTER TEN
UNAUTHORIZED ACTIONS

H EROES OF MALABAR!
The Empire is facing a calamity:
Geranika's Cursed Dagger has been plunged deep into the heart of the Throne. If it is not destroyed within four months, the Emperor will perish. The Dagger can be destroyed with the help of a holy item that was lost in the Free Lands near Rastrum. The group (not larger than 20 people) that brings the required object is guaranteed to receive an exceptional reward and the personal regard of the Emperor. Be vigilant: starting from today the holy item may be stolen, there is a 100% probability that it will drop from the inventory during respawn while the 'Saviors of the Throne' symbol will appear above the group (safe zones will no longer function for players with such a symbol).

Reward: Exalted Reputation with the

Emperor, +15 Levels, +50000 Gold coins, a Scaling item from the Emperor's stores.

Penalty for failing the quest: None.

Quest type: Scenario.

Level restrictions: None.

Time limit for completing the quest: 120 days from the moment of this announcement.

How time flies. It seemed like we were killing the Lieutenant just a couple of hours ago, although in fact so much time had already gone by. ... The General stubbornly refused to appear and there was still plenty of ground to cover before we would reach the designated spot.

I waved away the message that the Emperor's quest had been renewed and continued to focus on ring crafting: time was running out and my Jewelcraft had barely passed level 82. Thankfully I had stocked up on the materials I needed beforehand; the Copper Ore that had come in the mail came in really handy. And it was just as well it arrived before we destroyed the Lieutenant. After his death, our raid was subjected to such severe restrictions that even Anastaria was scratching her head in confusion and periodically hopping out to reality to check things with the Corporation. Nothing like this had ever happened in all her gaming experience: the Dark Forest was blocked. ...

"Stacey, I have a question," I started pestering the girl as soon as I awoke the morning after the battle with the Lieutenant, "What logic did you follow when gathering the raid?"

"You spotted the mistake too, eh? Yes, I have to admit that we were altogether too hasty when deciding who should be gaining extra levels. Phoenix's two main Priests – a husband and wife – are on holiday now, so thinking that a location aimed at level 100 players wouldn't contain anything too important, we decided that one priest would be enough. It's the same story with the tanks ... we also decided not to include the spoilt brats."

"Who?"

"Spoilt brats. Players who had reached level 280+, but behave like little children. Phoenix tries not to accept such players, but sometimes it needs to. Like Rick, for instance. It's no secret that with the launch of Barliona very many 16-year-old misfits, rejected by society, headed for the Game to fill their gray world with new colors. They kept leveling up without stepping out of the Game for months at a time until, at last, they became 'Great'. They never really grew out of being teenagers or out of their insatiable desire to be total pwners. Damn, I hate that word."

"Why?"

"There is a certain 'pretty boy' with a similar name. Anyway, these 300-something-levelers tend to be a pretty unpleasant bunch. So between ourselves that's what we call them: 'spoilt brats'. By the way, have you ever wondered why in a game that has existed for over 15 years so few players are above level 300? And why that is only the case on our continent?

There are over 10 times more high-level players in Astrum than in Malabar, while the Celestial Empire should soon welcome the first 400-level player. But not in Malabar. Here people are prepared to sacrifice their Reputation, money, anything, just to prevent someone else from gaining levels. If you're drowning, you have to pull the next guy in with you ... . There are several clans even set up especially for hunting down level 300s and sending them for respawn. They do it simply because they can."

"Hold on, isn't the Celestial Empire part of Malabar?"

"Why would it be? The division amongst the continents in Barliona differs from the real world. The number may be the same, but in Barliona Malabar is Europe and the Celestial Empire is the whole of Asia. Astrum is North America, Rathrand includes South America and Australia, and everything else is part of Caltuah."

"Strange, I never really thought about it ... but let's get back to the raid. So it looks like the Beatwick experience wasn't enough for the clan leaders. Have they developed a taste for repeated respawn or something? There we had a mere level-20 location, but half of the high-level players who answered the Emperor's call ended up taking a dirt nap without even having the chance to do anything. Why on earth did they decide that it would be any different here?"

"Because it was announced from the start there that was a continent-wide scenario, but this time it was a normal quest and a normal location. Nothing global was supposed to go down here. ..."

"I agree," Donotpunnik came up to us, "We fumbled when we put the group together. If Plinto is right about his level, there's little point in going after the General with a raid like this."

"Our best chance would be to get our Raiders and Fighters here," proposed Anastaria, "They don't even have to do the quest or be included in the group. Six thousand level-200s can be here in as little as two days' time ..."

"Stacey, did you forget that you were kicked out of Phoenix?" smiled Donotpunnik, "And by the way, while no-one can hear us, I can tell you I didn't buy your and Ehkiller's performance for a second. You've decided to put Rick and Hellfire back in their place, haven't you? And you can stop trying to drill a hole in me with those eyes! I haven't said anything about this even inside my clan; you're bound to have a number of Phoenix moles in there. Don't worry, you secret's safe with me. The Dragons can also bring seven or eight thousand level-200s. We would be able to mow down the General and Midial by force of numbers: our raid wouldn't even have to lift a finger – the Fighters will handle it all themselves."

"It's decided then," I agreed after a brief discussion where it was explained to me what a huge crowd like this would be doing around one lone boss, when no more than 15 players are able to stand right next to him, and even then they'd be getting in each other's way. "Let's get six thousand players from each clan, including the Heirs of the Titans – we should get

Etamzilat in on it too. I'm just not that eager to go for respawn. Will a day be enough to gather everyone? In that case we can have a breather until then. I'll go make the announcement ..."

At first glance the idea seemed excellent, but its implementation ... not a single extra player was able to enter the Dark Forest and, on top of that, the quest description now sported an additional point saying that after the Lieutenant the conditions forbade adding anyone else to the group. I also felt rather uneasy about the absence of any new letters: the old ones didn't go anywhere, but new ones had stopped arriving. There was the possibility that Anastaria's admirers had finally come to their senses, but I had limited faith in people suddenly seeing reason. Things like that were just too rare. When I shared my suspicions with Anastaria, she checked something, cursed and logged out of the Game to get to the bottom of what was happening in the Dark Forest. ...

That's how we eventually reached the announcement of the Emperor's quest. Moreover, this was the updated, not the original version of it. As I tried to focus on another ring, my thoughts constantly returned to the update. If the object required for completing a quest always drops from your inventory on death, Anhurs will turn into one big bloodbath. Why trudge all the way to Rastrum, when you can just sit it out in the Capital, wait for a small group with a symbol above their heads to turn up and simply take all that you needed off them? As for getting Exalted straight away ... isn't that a bit much? According to Anastaria, Exalted Reputation with the Emperor automatically gives a player Exalted status with all other Malabar factions. This happens irrespective of what Reputation he had with them to begin with. For example, this would've allowed me to sort out my relations with Serrest and pay Prontho, the mine governor, a visit. I still had to get to the bottom of what happened between him and Shiam. But then ... why did the developers even make this change, I wonder? This was nothing less than open encouragement of PVP ... after all, the 5000 gold fine for killing a player within the city wasn't much of a deterrent. They even shut down the safe zones, so that the quest would have to be handed in by an enormous group, which would thereby protect a small group with those symbols above their heads. Although ... even if such a group tried to make its way there, you could just throw an Armageddon spell and – Boom! The leading clans have enough resources for a spell like that.

"Stacey," I finally tore myself away from ring-making and addressed the girl who was sitting lost in thought nearby, "listen, even if, purely hypothetically, our clan manages to get the necessary quest item, how would we ever get it to the Emperor?

"Do *you* have any ideas?" Anastaria immediately snapped out of her thoughts.

"Of course. According to the conditions of the High Priestess's quest, we must recover the Stone of Light. We could try to see if that might do it."

"It won't work. I already thought about that. You yourself said that there is a pile of these Stones around the Throne right now and they are only blocking the effect of the Dagger. No, something else is needed here. And as for handing it in, we'll come to some arrangement with 'Killer – they can hand it in while leaving us in their group. Twenty people, there's two of us ..."

"Six. I'm not ditching the guys."

"So, whom did you decide to leave out? Plinto or Barsina?"

"The Druid. She's only with us temporarily, so there is little sense in giving her anything. Plinto is definitely with me for at least a year and then we'll see. Perhaps after that he'll stick around for longer. Essentially, if I get the Stone, Seathistles will only get five places ... the rest would will be taken by Phoenix."

"Mahan, I get that you're not exactly an average guy, but don't you think this is a bit much? I'm not into selling the skin before killing the bear – especially when the aforementioned bear is definitely out of your league. I'm sorry, but this just isn't your level. If you manage to get your hands on the holy object that would put the sign above you, I don't know ... you get one wish from me. Any wish. Up to and including my agreeing to spend a year in the Seathistles clan."

"I'll hold you to that. By the way, you also promised to tell me what the deal was with the Dwarf riddle."

"They used the Vigenère cipher with 'Master' as the code word. This produces the line 'threeandfiveandtwoandninewithoutforty',   without spaces. This expression is too ambiguous, so there has to be several other clues."

"Yeah, there are a couple more lines."

"Seems child's play now," smiled Anastaria after receiving the remaining formulas. "Although ... if you hadn't come across it before, you might have had trouble solving it. How many answer attempts do the Dwarves have? Three? You can try two yourself and if neither works, don't waste the third one – I'll help you with the answer. Damn! No, leave me two attempts, because there are two possible solutions here, either one could work, so it's best to play it safe."

"Couldn't you just tell me?" I asked, taken aback.

"I think not." The girl shook her head, "Figure this one out for yourself, but only input the answer when you're completely sure it's right. What do you intend to do next?"

"To travel to the spot marked on the map. Looks like we'll have to fight the remaining bosses ourselves. I don't see any other way ... "

"There's rather a lot of them there", said Donotpunnik when we finished watching the results of Plinto's reconnaissance. "The base of the Fallen was exactly where the High Priestess had marked on the map. It looked somewhat like a wooden castle, surrounded by a stockade, a few watchtowers (although personally I didn't get why you needed them in a forest), manned with guards, small huts, randomly strewn through the grounds, and two enormous houses, probably the abodes of the General and Midial. ... All in all a fairly standard model of a Kartoss wooden castle. But why the Kartoss look when the Priest had come from Malabar remained unclear. Around a hundred level 250+ Fallen Vampires, twenty or so enslaved level-300 Elementals and an undetermined number of level 350+ mages – who periodically came out of the huts – was a disheartening sight, but there was an interesting detail: there was no mist inside the stockade, so from Plinto's video you could clearly see two glades in the very middle of the settlement. One was completely black and the other one green and covered in flowers. A small object glinted in each of the glades: it couldn't be seen very clearly, but most probably these were the Stone of Light and the Tear of Eluna respectively. The goal of our raid ..."

"I have a proposal," the Azure Dragons' deputy said straight away, "Why don't we send Plinto inside, he'll grab the Tear of Eluna and then all of us will make tracks for the Guardian's glade? I reckon we can make it back there in a day. Our task is not to kill everything that moves here, but simply retrieve the Tear. By the way, is the second Stone related to your quest?"

"It's a good idea, definitely worth thinking about. But we shouldn't all crowd in, it's enough to ..."

"I'm against it," I interrupted Anastaria. "Our aim is to cleanse the forest. If we take out the Tear, that NPC will stick something else in its place. We'll fight. I'll handle the strategy; you work out the tactics. Can you think of a way to take care of this local mob in the most painless manner possible? Ants and myself will get the Elementals ... damn! Ants will get them, I'm still under a penalty ..."

"A fight, then," said the girl thoughtfully, looking through the recording one more time. "There's only one gate, through which no more than five mobs at a time may pass ... . If we block them, then ... no that won't work. There're the watchtowers and the mages ... they'll down the tanks in no time. ... So we can only lure them out into the forest ... . What do you say, Don?"

"That all depends on how long it takes Antsinthepantsa to free the Elementals. Last time it took around a minute to free one. But that was with two Shamans at it. Right now, from what I understand, Mahan is as much use as a chocolate teapot. ... Two minutes for each and there are twenty of them. ... We only have three tanks. No, we won't hold out. That's five complete sets, which is too much even for Hellfire ..."

"Yeah...," said Anastaria slowly, "there is of course the option of breaking into the castle, killing as many mobs as possible, getting sent for respawn, returning, and repeating until we clear them all ... . The time it takes for mobs to respawn is three months, so we should have enough time."

"Yeah, right, and get our experience gain bar knocked all the way back to zero," chuckled Donotpunnik. "The entire raid will be falling over to thank you for that one."

"Then I'm out of ideas for now. The only sensible course of action is to send Plinto out and then have the entire raid running for the Guardian's glade. Everything else is pure suicide."

"Right, it's getting late already, so I propose we continue this tomorrow morning," I decided, "and all the same, try to think of how we could destroy that base."

Painful as it was to admit, the idea voiced by Donotpunnik made perfect sense. We are too few for such a big crowd of mobs, so either we have to resort to trickery or look for a workaround. The 'trickery' part was easy: Plinto would sneak in, snatch the Tear and the Stone – good thing he's got that quest already – and leg it out of there. Then he'd mount his Phoenix and speed towards the Guardian's glade. Then there'd be general happiness, celebration and rejoicing. And yet I could feel it in my bones that in if this were to occur, I could kiss good-bye to the second earring of the Guardian. My conclusion: we had to look for a workaround. And here Anastaria should be able to help me. ...

"Natalie, do you have a minute?" I managed to shout just in time as I noticed that the lady Shaman was about to log back to reality. "A word before you go, or rather a task for you. Do you remember the strange dark phantoms that surrounded the Elementals? Can you dig around Shaman history? That's the only place it could be. Please look for information or articles mentioning the words 'mist', 'phantom' or 'shadow'. These entities didn't just turn up by accident, they are certain to be recorded in history in some way."

"As you remember, the Supreme Spirits know nothing about the nature of these phantoms, despite being the custodians of Shamanistic knowledge in the Game. So there would be little use in doing this."

"You have a look and then we'll see, all right? First thing tomorrow tell me all about it. Stacey!" after leaving the Shaman I called Anastaria over, "I have a question."

"I can't tell you this," came the girl's immediate answer, "I signed an NDA."

"You don't even know what I want to ask you ..."

"I heard your conversation with Ants. You want to ask about the nature of Elenium's quest. I can't tell you, but I can give you a hint that you've started to dig in the right direction."

"I see. Then another question: why haven't you asked me about Slate yet, although it's already been a week? He's the only NPC among us and you know who he is, but are behaving as if there's nothing' unusual here."

"What's the point? We'll have a chat once we are finished with the Forest, assuming we don't lose him. If you tell me about this now you've as good as shared the quest with me. And then suddenly the Prince dies. Do you think the Princess will be happy when she finds out that I too was involved in the death of her intended? So, thanks, but no thanks.

Once we make it out of the Forest, I'll start asking questions. Who needs the extra stress right now? Everything in good time ..."

I watched the girl as she walked away and instead of feasting my eyes on her beautifully drawn avatar I was turning over Stacey's last word: time ... hmm... there's a time for everything. ... Once again: there is a time for everything ... well, I'll be! Stacey, you're a genius!

"Mahan." The voice of Barsina, my only female Fighter, tore me away from my musings about the epic plan to capture the Castle of the Fallen. "Tell me, are you going to exclude me from the clan after we're finished in the Dark Forest, or is there a possibility that I could stick around?"

"What do you mean 'exclude you'? Didn't we agree that you are joining the clan temporarily so that you could be part of the Imitator's loot allocation for both quests? As for sticking around ... why the sudden interest?"

"There are a good number of reasons really. The first and the main one being that it's profitable to be around you. In one week I've earned more than in the previous few months. Two levels more and I'll gain access to several interesting locations, where I can earn good money. I'm set to reach level 170 once we complete the Guardian's quest. This would mean a new ability and class-based quests. The second, and no less significant, reason is the presence of Anastaria and Plinto. They are legends in Malabar and I can learn a lot from them. Just the amendment of the

Clan Agreement that Anastaria proposed today is quite something. Right now our Officers are sitting and scratching their heads, wondering how they could miss such obvious loopholes. I would've never spotted them myself either, by the way. The third ... you know, the third reason actually outweighs the other two – I like it here, in your clan. So I'd like to stay, if possible."

"Fine. In that case I'll put you in change of everything healing-related. Look at the current membership agreement and have a chat with Anastaria. In a couple of days I'd like to have a list of all the classes we might need: how many Priests, Druids, Shamans, Paladins of Light and other healer classes you would find in any normal clan. Plinto, Eric – I have a task for you!" I immediately called over the Rogue and the Warrior and told them to put together the best possible team of Fighters and Tanks. If one wanted to take part in the clan tournament (and I did), you would need people. Bugging Anastaria for every small task ... is pretty daft if there are other capable players just idling about.

So, having given everyone their tasks, I sat under the tree and started to put together my plan for getting into the Fallen Ones' castle. I watched through Plinto's video a few more times and saw once again that the mobs were spread throughout the entire castle, except for the green glade with the Stone of Light. As Anastaria put it, 'everything in good time'. If we swap 'time' for 'place' then ... .

What if the fallen mobs cannot step into an

area affected by a Blessed object? And what if this prohibition is at the level of their programming? If my memory doesn't fail me, in Beatwick I managed to save a good number of NPCs from modification by giving them Blessed amulets. What if we weren't meant to kill the mobs, but scare them away? Or even – and here another bulb lit above my head – free them, as we did with the Elementals or the Lieutenant? Perhaps even my Reputation problems would go away if I returned about two hundred Vamps and Mages to the Patriarch. It may not work for me, but Anastaria definitely wouldn't miss a chance like that. In order to enact my plan, I needed Blessed statuettes ... I was feeling very thankful to Beth that she hurried her Priestesses and now, among other things, I had some Blessed ore and marble in my sack. It was time to get busy with some crafting ... .

"Will you tell me what you're up to?" Anastaria asked me in the morning, having interrupted me in the middle of another masterpiece. "This doesn't look like jewelry and, judging by your groggy eyes and level of Energy, you've been working all night. Spill the beans because I've got nothing, except the gradual clearing out the mobs."

"Let's wait for Donotpunnik, then I'll tell both of you all about it. I have just a couple of pieces of ore left, so I'll make one more blade, then you can hit me with any question you like. You're right – I do have an idea. It just remains to be seen if it's actually doable ..."

"It might just work!" exclaimed my Azure Dragons deputy advisor, when I described my plan and showed him the result of my nightly labors: twenty thee knife blades – which lacked handles, but still represented completed items – and around thirty small, marble, pinecone-shaped figurines. I had a new recipe to show for it too: Marble Pinecone. I had also discovered that Jewelers were able to make throwing weapons, which would cause physical damage depending on the strength of the thrower.

"What's their radius?" asked Anastaria straight away.

"For that we need a victim," I told the happy news to my advisors. "We have to go to the castle and check. I'm not at all sure that a Rogue carrying a Blessed item will be able to sneak inside, even under Invisibility, so we have to be clear from the start that the victim would end up going for respawn."

"Should we cast lots?" proposed Donotpunnik, "Because, aside from you and your three fighters, no-one would volunteer to lose 30% of the Experience Progress Bar. Trying to send a Priest to get the volunteer back up ... would mean sacrificing the Priest. But for you the loss of Experience would be negligible by comparison."

"I agree," Anastaria said after some hesitation, "the optimal choice would be Leite, as the one with the lowest level. But we should still draw lots ..."

"No, we shouldn't," I put an end to these deliberations. "The decision has already been taken – I'll go. This was my idea, the stones and the ore were mine and I should be the one to carry it out. Due to my penalties, I'm not much of a Shaman for the next two weeks anyway. And I'm somewhat curious too. It's not every month that I have the opportunity to visit a castle with level 350+ mobs. Plinto! Let's go. You'll get to tape the raid leader being sent for respawn ..."

"Hold on," Anastaria stopped me, "let's at least ask the others, just in case anyone else wants to take the risk. Remember, if this idea works, we won't wait for your respawn and attack straight away. There's little point in the raid sitting on its hands for 12 hours straight. Two hundred Vampires, Elementals and Mages ... with your current 82nd level, you're almost guaranteed to hit 90 after this. Are you prepared to lose that much Experience?"

Hmmm ... I hadn't really thought about my respawn from this perspective. It's like I'd started to perceive myself as some great hero, unbeatable and unstoppable. Oh! I recalled a rather suitable word for this: bigheadedness ... was I really suffering from it? And where do you place the thin line between luck and letting things go to my head?

"I'm against sending the low-level players now," Donotpunnik said, completely ripping my plans to shreds. "I had another look at Plinto's report and finally understood that there's nothing they can do there. As you can see, the gates may be open, but there's around twenty meters to cover between them and the nearest tree. There are two towers by the gates with 250-level archers, which means that any low-level player would be dropped in an instant. So the question arises: what would be the point? You can't throw a bubble over him, because then the mobs would go for the rest of the raid. Mahan doesn't have any defense either, since he can't even summon his Spirits."

"So you want to check it out then?" Plinto, whom I'd called over earlier, didn't go anywhere and was now looking thoughtfully in the direction of the castle. "You won't be able to run under the noses of the dark mobs with Blessed items on you, you'll be discovered immediately ... give those to me. I'll go pay those castle campers a visit. If the plan works, don't forget to get me back up – I can wait for three hours or so. Time I began to work off that investment you made in me, right? And Mahan, a little word of advice for the future: you can't do everything yourself in this Game, you have to delegate, otherwise you'll burn out all too soon. That's it – I'm off. Fogger! You're with me as cameraman. Lanterius! You come along too: you'll film it from the other angle. What am I doing?"

"Here," I handed Plinto several items. "Your task is simple: you have to block the entrance into the castle by throwing these items along the gate, about a meter from each other. The Fallen must get locked inside so the raid can walk right up to the castle and Antsinthepantsa can gradually free the Vampires. There's no need to attack anyone. You may even throw some of the cones and knives inside, which will cut the Fallen up into several groups. All in all, do as you see fit, but the main aim is the gate."

"Gotcha. Then give me everything that you've

made. With Haste and Cloak activated (-40% damage for 10 seconds), I'll run across the castle and make their day. That's it; I'm off. Send me a postcard." The Rogue took all the Blessed items from me and headed off to the castle.

"Stacey, how do you know him?" said Donotpunnik slowly, gazing after the departing Plinto. "To be honest, I always thought that he was one of those spoiled bratniks, but now my whole understanding of reality has been demolished: Plinto, whose name has even given rise to the special term – 'to plint it' (that is, to do something without switching on your brain first) – turns out to be a completely reasonable guy."

"Don, why ask meaningless questions?" smiled the girl, "You know full well that I won't be answering that, so what's the point? Hmm ..." Anastaria turned to me and in all seriousness said: "When you offer Donotpunnik to join your clan, take me along too. You don't know how to bargain properly and Don here is an expert in the field. He'll have you for dinner; you'll think you've done him a favor and before you know it, you'll end up owing him instead."

."..?"

"You still don't get it? Our normally quiet and calm Death Knight, who's barely been visible behind Undigit's back, suddenly starts to show his real self, and in your company, no less. This is nothing short of self-promotion." Anastaria turned to the Death Knight and continued, "Don, let me disappoint you straight away. I'm in Seathistles temporarily. In three months' time, just before the clan championship I'll return to Phoenix. There is a chance, of course, that I'll stay, but it's so tiny that it isn't even worth mentioning."

"Typical," uttered Donotpunnik in feigned offence, "the moment you decide to join another clan, some reason is bound to pop up to make it totally impossible."

"You really think you have it all figured out," I parried, "what makes you think that I'm in such dire need of either of you? Anastaria and Donotpunnik, you are legends in your own clans, so that's where you belong. You will return in three months' time," I looked at Anastaria, "and I'm certain that I won't be wasting my wish on getting you to remain in the clan. I'll think of something really interesting instead. As for Donotpunnik," I turned towards the young man, "please don't take this personally, but I hadn't even met you before all this and don't really know who you are. Why would I need you? You could be an agent, just like this pretty lady. So you can relax and stop trying to sell yourself. I'm not buying."

"Overinflated ego?" Donotpunnik looked at Anastaria.

"I don't think so. He's just too certain about forgoing all the bonuses that would come with our presence. Doesn't seem like him."

"Guys, stop speaking about me in the third person in my presence. I've laid out my position; it doesn't contradict any of the existing agreements. With all due respect, I really don't need ... "

'The Cleansing of the Dark Forest' quest has been completed. Please contact the Guardian for your reward.

The Tear of Eluna, the source of the taint, has been removed and soon the Cursed Forest will again revert to being the Dark Forest.

The quest is 65% complete.

Reward: +200 with all encountered factions, +40 to any main stat, +10 character levels.

Quest 'Restoration of a Holy Relic, Step 3: The Return of the Stone of Light' has been completed.

Please contact the High Priestess of Eluna for your reward.

The Stone of Light has been found.

The quest chain is 75% complete.

Reward for completing Step 3: +1 Level, +200 to Reputation with the Priestesses of Eluna, +50 to Reputation with Goddess Eluna.

Reward: 3 flasks of the Water of Life.

Ding! You've received 6822 new messages. Do you wish to view them?

When I realized what Plinto had done I wanted to howl. The second part of the Guardian's gift was as good as gone! We'd failed to complete his one request – the full cleansing of the forest from the taint. From the very start the Oak had said that if the Fallen were chased out of this forest they would just go and occupy another one, spreading their taint elsewhere.

Plinto ... what have you done?!

"And that's it?" asked Anastaria in surprise after reading the messages, "Did they just decrease the Reputation reward without any further penalties? They didn't dock any stats or levels ... . Hmmm ... something isn't right here. '65% complete' ... I simply don't get it. What did we actually lose?"

"I did it!" Just a minute later a smiling Plinto ran up to us, holding the Tear of Eluna and the Stone of Light in his hands. "Both quests have been completed, we can leave now. The Fallen have been locked inside the castle, they can't get out! They've started trying to break through the wall, but according to my estimation, it will take them a couple of weeks. Pity about the Reputation reward dock, but that's not the end of the world. The main thing is that our levels and stats are intact, both in the first and the second quest. ... I don't get it, why the long faces? Didn't I just complete the quest?"

"You failed it!" I said, unable to restrain myself.

"What do you mean?" Plinto froze, staring at me.

"Exactly that!" I was shouting now, "We just had to block the entrance and change all the Vampires! But you went and ..."

"Mahan," Undigit interrupted my angry rant, "the quest has been completed and I see no sense in dying to mobs just for Experience, so the Azure Dragons clan thanks you for access to the quest and, if you get anything similar, do write – we'll negotiate a price. Donotpunnik, let's go, we still have a lot to do."

"The Heirs of the Titans are also going back." This came from Etamzilat: "I agree with Undigit. There's no First Kill on the books and there won't be much Experience gained just from mobs alone ... we're going. If you get another quest like this, let us know, we'll talk it over ..."

In just a few minutes twenty-seven people packed up, got on their mounts and sped away towards the Guardian's glade.

"The quest is finished, Mahan," said Ehkiller, who was suddenly standing next to me. "I agree with Undigit and Etamzilat; there's nothing left for us to do in this forest. I understand that it is important for you and your clan to gain levels, so I offer you a two-month-long boost at our base. For free, for your entire clan. We'll write it off as 'payment for incomplete quest in the Dark Forest'. We're taking in recruits at the moment and the training should start in three days, giving us just enough time to get to Anhurs if we open a portal now. We'll be able to protect you from the Dark Legion, which is still out for your blood, and Plinto won't be going anywhere either. By the way, how would you like to complete our obstacle course?" Ehkiller asked the Rogue, "It would be interesting to see the results."

"Whatever the clan leader says," was Plinto's short reply, but I could see from his eyes that the idea caught his interest. It was easy to guess why: it would mean completing the obstacle course of a clan which had been a long-time, bitter rival and showing their Rogues what incompetent and altogether rubbish players they were. ... From where I was standing, though, it looked like Ehkiller was blatantly trying to buy everyone off ... and quite thoroughly at that ... .

"In any case, whatever Mahan's decision is," the leader (or the shadow leader, I was beginning to lose track who this guy was) of the best clan in Malabar continued, "Phoenix, is leaving the Dark Forest. I'm grateful for your invitation and if you get another quest like this, I'm prepared to discuss the price of our taking part. Hellfire!" Ehkiller shouted, "Get ready, we're off to hand in the quest and then return to Rastrum! Mahan, Anastaria," 'Killer nodded and headed off towards the gathering players.

"Hold on!" I stopped him, trying to get a handle on my emotions, "Do please take all of my guys and send them for training once they hand in the quest. To what level will you be boosting them?"

"The course is designed for leveling up from the twentieth to a hundred and twentieth level. What about you? Aren't you coming with us?"

"No. I'll stay here for a bit – spend some time strolling around by myself, watch those mobs breaking down the walls ..."

"I don't see any sense in stubbornly respawning again and again." Ehkiller looked at me, surprised. "You won't be able to do anything on your own. You can't do anything as a Shaman for another week and I believe Plinto when he says that the castle will be open again in two weeks' time. Can you tell me what the point of you staying here is?"

"What's the difference? Everyone got what they

wanted and no-one owes anyone anything. The raid is finished, and all obligations have been met. Plinto," I turned to the Rogue, "I have a special job for you. Show Phoenix how to complete that obstacle course properly. I would be very disappointed if you don't set a new record – both in speed and the number of attempts."

"Consider it done, boss." A smile flashed across Plinto's face. "I realize what I've done by bringing these damn stones here, but no point crying over spilt milk. There's no time limit on playing, so things are bound to work out for you sooner rather than later. But you're right about the chickens ... it would be sheer pleasure to show them the proper way of playing the Game. Thank you!"

"So, is this it then?" When Plinto left to get ready and describe the task at hand to Eric, Leite, Clutzer and Barsina (incidentally it was interesting to note how quickly they all accepted him as their leader: for them Plinto was the second in terms of authority after myself – at least I hoped that he was the second ...) Antsinthepantsa came up to me. "The quest is finished and everyone's leaving ... Mahan, I'll go too ... I understand that not everything is finished here and the forest is yet to be completely cleansed, but I have a strong feeling that there is nothing more to be done here. To keep respawning just to clear out the mobs ... I think I'll pass. So, my sincere thanks for inviting me and if you get another quest like this, do give me a shout. By the way, Kalatea has decided to meet you in person and will fly to Anhurs in a week. It turns out that Harbingers may only teleport freely within their own continent. Try not to be late."

Why is everyone repeating the same thing: 'thanks; if you get another quest, call us and we'll come'? And yet no-one has any inclination at all to help finish off the crowd of enemies still remaining ... I was left quite speechless. ...

"You know, I will probably stay": Anastaria shared the happy news after all the gathering was done and what was left of the raid headed back to the Guardian to hand in the quest. "There's nothing for me to do in Anhurs and I can hand in the High Priestess's and Guardian's quests any time, so I'll stay with you for a bit. The tent is big enough and it wouldn't be right to leave you alone with just Slate around, would it?"

"Stacey ..."

"What?

"Why don't you go, eh? I don't really feel like talking right now ... I might just lose it and scream my head off at you only to regret it later. ... I had such a great plan all laid out, came up with these pinecones and daggers ... and it was all for nothing. ... I need some time alone, to scream it all out at the trees or something ..."

"What did you expect? You made the most common mistake of any manager: failure to give clear instructions to a subordinate. If you told Plinto that he should not touch the Stones under any circumstances, this situation wouldn't have arisen. Experience, Mahan. You need experience in managing people. I'm prepared to stay with you and deconstruct our raid in detail, figuring out where we went wrong and why, and what we got right. And anyway, abandoning a clan leader, all alone in a forest ... well, no point beating about the bush ... I think that you may still manage to do something with the castle and I too want to get the full reward for the quests. I'm not a fan of half-hearted solutions."

"You think?" Could Anastaria also have a habit of following her intuition?

"Either way, you've managed to get it right so far, perhaps you'll get it right now too. I leveled up only recently, so respawn isn't much of a threat to me. I'll stay with you and help you stave off the boredom. You still won't be able to summon Spirits for a week, right? So we can wait for that. I'll wander around the forest, try to find the Patriarch and have a chat with him. ... The Fallen ones are trapped in the castle in any case ... and you haven't told me about the Prince yet. ... I'll find things to keep me busy, don't you worry."

"All right, stick around then ... although I don't see the p–"

"It's a deal then," the girl interrupted me, "I'm off to scout out the forest. I'll be back soon and then we'll have that chat about the raid. Don't get bored now."

After finding myself alone, I tiredly sat by the tent and let out a subdued howl, not wishing to disturb Slate. How could it all start out so well and end so stupidly?

"So it's just the two of us now, eh?" After some time Slate came out of the tent and sat next to me. "You're a free citizen and are certain to return from the Grey Lands. ... Can you please take this to my family ...?" With these words the Prince handed me the round shield that he'd received from the Guardian. "For my race this is a very important object and if it's returned, I will be given back my rightful place in the tribe. I will become Princess's equal and the Emperor will no longer have a reason to forbid our marriage ... ."

Update to the 'Escorting the Prince' quest. Return the ritual disc to the Werebeasts, even if Slate dies.

Reward: none.

Penalty for failing or refusing the quest: none.

Time limit for completing the quest: 2 months 23 days.

"You're a bit pessimistic about making it out of here alive," I replied to the Werebeast, taking the disc, "Why don't we send you back to Anhurs, while the raid hasn't gotten very far."

"No!" Slate firmly rejected my idea, "What kind of a Prince would I be if I took fright and abandoned the person whom Tisha asked me to protect? I don't need to fear permanent death, since – while I was still back in the palace – the Emperor put the Death Seal on me. In four months' time the Priests will bring me back, but for my people that is too long. The disc has to be returned before that."

"Fine, I will deliver it should anything happen to you." This took a huge weight off my mind. Slate is a key NPC and he, like a quest, has his own respawn timer, so there is no danger of Tisha shredding me to pieces should he die. She'd tell me off, give me a good kicking, but Attractiveness will remain the same, especially if I tell her how heroically Slate protected me. "Tell me, why is it that you have to be forgiven and what does this disc mean?"

"A long time ago, when I was the small and inexperienced younger son of the Werebeast Chieftain, my older brother decided to get rid of me. He tricked me into stealing the ritual disc, which Werebeasts use to communicate with our gods, and destroying it. At the time I thought I was doing something really important – that I was showing the entire clan that I too was able and skillful. ... How wrong I was! According to our laws I should have been executed, but father ruled differently. ... He banished me, which was contrary to the law, so he was deposed and the position of the head of the Werebeasts was taken by my older brother. The return of the disc would remove the restrictions on my return, so even if I were to die now, I would go back home with another hero and challenge my brother. Underhand deeds like these must not go unpunished in this world." As befits a key NPC, Slate continued to tell the tale of the injustice committed by his brother and the need for him to be brought justice, but I got the picture.

Judging by the scale of this and the absence of any rewards, I'd gotten myself into a high-level social quest. On the one hand this was a scenario without any clear point to it, but on the other, if I remembered the Farstead old ladies ... . I wonder, does Anastaria know about such a special feature of social quests as variability? The old ladies landed me Leara's Dress in the end, which Reptilis used to ... Reptilis!!!

"Hi! You promised that you'd help me should I ever need it and now that time has come. Aren't you an Assassin? Now then. I have a hunch that you stole a certain scroll from the Emperor's Castle, which contains information on the Karmadont Chess Set and which I really need. If I am correct in my guess, is there any way that I can get it off you?"

After I wrote the letter and waved away the message that the recipient was currently out of the game, I jumped up and started pacing around the tent. If it is Reptilis who got his 'green paws' on the scroll, the agreement with Ehkiller could be reviewed. After all, this means he wouldn't be able to fulfill his side of it and in Barliona this would lead to enormous penalties. He may be all nice and helpful right now, with his offer to level up my fighters, but I had a gut feeling that he could not be trusted. It may suit him to play nice for now, but a time would come when another Elenium would come between us. No, you had to keep at least one ace up your sleeve. Let's see what he'd do.

After settling down somewhat, I began to go through my mail. It wouldn't be right to leave seven thousand letters unread, even if 99% of them are from Anastaria worshippers. "Take me into your clan, I'm a good healer! I'm prepared to work for free, just introduce me to Anastaria ..." There was a mountain of letters like these. ... Do people really think that after receiving such a letter I will have no other choice but to beg them to join my clan? It takes all sorts, I guess. ... Especially amusing were the letters full of threats and promises to catch me in reality and rearrange my face. All because I failed to reply to their letters – dared to ignore such handsome and important somebodies. Perfect ignore list material! After I blocked another player, I couldn't help smiling as I imagined how a crowd of upset people would break into the prison, find my capsule, pull me out and begin to beat me up – just to force the point that I should invite them into the clan and introduce them to Anastaria. I wonder if they'd shorten my sentence as an injured party if that actually happened?

"Hello Dan."

I was deleting letters almost automatically, so I almost missed one that addressed me directly. Dan? Not Mahan? Strange, who would know my real name? Realizing that I was suffering from brain-lag, I looked at the sender – Mirida.

"There was a big uproar on the forums on

account of Anastaria and Plinto joining your clan, and also Dark Legion being out for your blood. I can see that you just can't keep yourself out of trouble. :) I have an acquaintance who is part of the group of celebrity exterminators, and, according to him, they've headed out to the Dark Forest to bump off at least one high-level player. These guys are proper thugs, twenty level-200s. According to the last video from the Heirs of the Titans, you happen to be in the Dark Forest right now, so try not to run into them. They will pin you down at a respawn point and keep you there until the Heralds intervene. Marina."

That's the last thing I need! Celebrity exterminators!

"Judging by your expression someone just 'made your day'", noted Anastaria when she re-emerged from the forest, "wanna tell me about it?"

After telling Anastaria about the hunting party and seeing her smile and say that she could handle such a mob with one hand tied behind her back, I returned to reading my mail.

"Hi. Listen, will all that's been happening I completely forgot to tell you about what I managed to find out. Or rather what I haven't managed to find out. The histories completely lack any mention of phantoms, dark spirits or anything of the sort. I'm sorry I wasn't able to help you. Natalie.

That's it, the mail was read and four hours of

my life had duly been wasted. I think I'm beginning to understand why Ehkiller, Evolett, Etamzilat, Undigit and their like rarely exceed level 230. They simply had no time for leveling up. If you actually wanted to manage a clan rather than just let things sort themselves out, you'd have to have a conscientious approach to it. In the last week I ... yeaah ... I spoke with my Officers only once, since I'd spent most of my time in the company of Anastaria and Donotpunnik. That's not the way to do things! As soon as everyone is back from leveling up, we'll have to get together for a chat and figure out how to develop the clan together in the future. Sad though it was to admit this, I wasn't achieving all that much on my own.

As for the letter from Ants, it was a pity that she hadn't found anything ... I had a hunch that we weren't dealing with phantoms, but with Spirits that were somehow no longer under the control of the Supreme Ones. That's why I thought that an explosion in the Astral Plane would destroy them. They couldn't have appeared out of nowhere; there had to be a story behind it. Was this something I could ask Anastaria?

* * *

On the second day of my solitude people started to leave the group: you could see from their frames how a player would gain levels – probably as they reached the Guardian's glade – and suddenly the group would have one member less. This continued throughout the day, until only seven people remained: all of them members of the Seathistles clan. At first I was surprised to see that my players didn't gain any levels, but then remembered that their mounts were bought in great haste and were pretty basic, so they would take longer to get to the glade. Anastaria spent the entire next day in the forest, so I busied myself with what had become almost a habit by now: leveling up in Jewelcraft.

"Why don't we go and see what the Fallen are up to?" I suggested when the girl once again graced me with her presence. "I'll start seeing these rings and ingots in my sleep soon."

"How's your progress?"

"Level 102 Jeweler and 87 Smith," I said, rather pleased. "I even managed to get a couple of Alexandrite stones from the Silver Ingots and Peridot from an Iron one."

"Alexandrite?" Anastaria's eyebrows flew up, "Will Barliona soon be seeing the Battle ogre from the Karmadont Chess Set?"

"I don't know," I gave the girl my honest answer, "I was glad to get the stone, of course, and even tried to imagine an ogre so I could make him, but ... it seems a certain time must pass between crafting the figurines – you can't make them too often. I can't seem to do anything and I don't want to waste the stones, especially now that I'm out of Silver Ore."

"So why don't you buy some? Mail has been unlocked inside the Dark Forest."

"How? The only auction house that I can access is in Anhurs, and asking you all the time ... also isn't an option."

"Damn, I keep forgetting that you're still not a very experienced player. Are you familiar with the concept of a 'free broker'?"

"In real life yes, what's this got to do with Barliona?"

"Mahan! Don't make me angry now! Think!"

"Hold on, do you mean to say that there are players who just stand near the Auction House, receive letters and, having bought items at auction, send them off to their clients? You've got to be kidding right?"

"Far from it – add 10% commission and within a month you can earn so much that you may be tempted to drop everything and devote yourself to this line of business alone. Any self-respecting clan is certain to have several brokers who keep 24-hour watch next to the Auction House. I can give you a few names with a good track record and you may write to them directly. The reply usually comes within a day. I can even tell you that the Copper Ore that you received happens to be from one of them. And there's little point in looking at the Fallen – they're still trying to break through the wall, but won't manage it any time soon without any picks and axes. I dropped by a couple of hours ago. I must say that Plinto did a good job – not only did he block the entrance, but also managed to throw a few of your pinecones into the watchtowers. Now you can simply walk up to the gates without any fear of being shot at."

"Stacey, I'll be howling soon at this rate! Let's just go for a walk, loosen up a bit. What if I also want to have a look at what they're up to?"

"No need to howl, just busy yourself with something else. Have you solved the Dwarf equation yet?"

"No."

"So, what's the problem, then? You can sit there cutting out rings all day, but you don't have enough brains to solve a simple puzzle?"

Cutting! Another bulb lit up in my head. How is Stacey such a genius? Right, hang on a moment! We can come back to that later.

"If you insert all the spaces, the equation will look like this: 'three and five and two and nine take away forty'. The simplest answer is: -21. But the '5 and 3 = 7' line really has me stumped. It just doesn't fit standard logic."

"Exactly. That's the key expression. In what instance could there be an equals sign between the left and the right side? I'll give you a hint: this problem is given to children who are not yet familiar with numbers, but already know how to count."

Children? Anastaria was so sure that this equation had a solution, that I felt I was being a complete dolt. A problem for children who aren't yet familiar with numbers ... if they don't know numbers, how can they read what's written here? Or 'to count', rather. 'To count.' ... But they can only read it and then count it ... read it ... .

"There really are two answers," I echoed Anastaria's words, as I finally understood the logic of the equations. There really is an instance where both '5 and 2 = 7' and '5 and 3 = 7' and you don't even have to resort to Dandelin–Graeffe method. "10 and 11. Let's try the first answer."

The world froze. Slate came out of the tent, went down on one knee and a whirlwind appeared a couple of meters away from me, out of which eight stout dwarves walked, one after another. The sleeves of their coats were rolled up, revealing powerful arms; they had bearded, soot-covered faces, enormous picks, which would destroy any ore vein with just one swing (and how come I know all this?) ... the legendary mountain smiths have graced us with their presence ... .

I glanced at the stunned Anastaria, who clearly didn't expect such a spectacle and, inviting her to follow my example, respectfully bowed my head before the legendary skills of these master craftsmen. Anastaria copied my bow, after which the dwarves spoke:

And the day when the world knew that a great one had come,
Near the river, each day in whose waters there meet
Dewren, exalted by a hundred creators of human souls
Forever proclaiming love and prosperity and –
Owren, her twin brother, who spent his whole

life creating

Unique living plants that outshone the world with their beauty,

Rests a man whose fate's inextricably linked to the world,

The world, which was left by the Dragons forever ...

"Our battle brother will continue this tale," said Borhg. Then the dwarves went back into the whirlwind and sound returned to the world.

"What did the orcs say?" The first thing uttered by Anastaria had little to do with what just happened.

"More or less the same thing, but in different words," I said thoughtfully, as I tried to figure out which river they were talking about in this message.
...

"Altair's waters flow though almost all this entire continent." Anastaria wasn't giving up that easy. "The river is called after one of the most beautiful stars in the sky and has its source near Elma. It goes through Malabar, Kartoss and the Free Lands and flows into the world ocean. Mahan, what was in the first verse?"

"Why do you think that they mean Altair?" I replied and tried to get to grips with my breathing, which had grown treacherously heavy. The orcs had spoken about the Shining Mountains, also known as Elma – the mountain chain that stretches all the way to the south of the continent from its northernmost point. If this refers to a river that has its source among those peaks ... this would actually really narrow down the search area!

"Eran and Yiran are the ancient names for the moon and the sun in Barliona. The only place where they meet, creating an incredibly beautiful spectacle, is in the lower reaches of the Altair river. Believe me, this is truly a sight worth seeing. Although, what am I saying? I bet you've been there more than once yourself. The man of whom they speak is Karmadont. The first Emperor of Malabar. Mahan! What did the orcs say?!"

"Stacey, you are my Deputy right now, of course, but ..."

"Hey guys!" I was interrupted by Clutzer's cheerful voice and the noisy approach of the other members of my clan. "We've had a bit of a think and decided that hanging around Phoenix isn't for us. Why spend a month on training when we already have a trainer,," Clutzer glanced at Plinto, "who can give anyone in Phoenix a run for their money. And there's nothing to do there for Barsa except possibly lose levels. No, we'll stick with you. It's no good leaving clan leaders all by themselves."

"So what happened to wanting to prove that you're the best?" I asked in surprise, looking at Plinto.

"What's the point? Everyone already knows I'm the best. Myself included. I see no point in trying to prove that to some flaming chickens." The Rogue shot Anastaria a sly glance: "They'll be fine as they are."

"Whose idea was it to come back?" asked Anastaria, ignoring Plinto's look.

"His," volunteered Eric, "We'd made it almost half way there when Clutzer convinced us to return."

"I just thought," my Officer parried, smiling, "that it's unprofitable to hand in the quest for a level bump right now. There's no deadline for handing it in, so we could easily gain a hundred levels first, then drop by the Guardian and the High Priestess. Plinto gave the Stone of Light to Elenium to hand over to Elizabeth. There's no need to return the Tear of Eluna and it's not clear what should be done with it. Here." Clutzer got off his horse, turning it back into a bridle, and gave me a small, silvery glinting stone. "I'm sure you'll think of some proper use for it."

Item acquired: Tear of Eluna.
Description: hidden; approach the goddess.

"How do you like the description, eh?" asked Clutzer when he saw my baffled expression. "It only appeared yesterday. Plinto said it wasn't there to begin with."

"So, a quest has subsequently been attached to the Tear," Anastaria said straight away. "Will you open its properties?"

It took me a few seconds to make the decision before I opened access to the description.

"The goddess. ... Among the players only a Priest could appeal to her. Or the High Priestess, among the NPCs," explained Anastaria. "We have no Priests and the High Priestess is miles away. So for the moment the Tear is useless to the clan."

"Never mind," I said as I hid the properties and put the Tear into my bag. "We'll get a Priest of our own or pay Elizabeth a visit and find out what Eluna wants with all of us. Right! Since everyone's back, let's hold our first clan meeting. We have to figure out once and for all what we plan to do in this Game. ...

Aim of the Seathistles Clan: to ensure a cash turnover of at least 10 million gold a month.

Means for achieving this aim:

Production of Jewelry items for 100–200-level players. Target cost of 1 ring: 30000 gold. The minimum number of rings to be made a month: 400. The minimum number of rings to be sold a month: 400. Item quality of the crafted rings: Rare and above. Anastaria, aided by Leite, will handle how and where the clan's goods will be sold.

Gathering of rare resources. In order to achieve this we will have to invite 30 to 100 players into the clan who are proficient in gathering various resources. Clutzer will be in charge of recruiting the gatherer players.

Completing Dungeons and selling off the loot that drops there. To get this part right we have to invite 30 to 50 level-200 players into the clan. Barsina will oversee the healers; Eric will supervise the tanks; and Plinto the melee and ranged fighters. Anastaria and Plinto will handle general raid preparation.

Building our own castle and making its facilities available to external players for item storage. In order to commence this part, we have to build a castle and establish decent security there. This task is a secondary priority, after the primary aim of securing the clan's position has been reached.

The redesign of clan symbols will fall to Anastaria and Barsina."

Three hours' worth of discussion essentially boiled down to five simple points that could be further summed up as: 'we need money and must use every means we can to generate it'. As soon as we confirmed the plan of action, work commenced: the free players began to constantly hop in and out of the Game as they carried out various tasks and I, as the head honcho, watched all the commotion without lifting a finger. I had people for doing stuff now. I'll pitch in when it's time to review candidates for clan membership. But now ...

Ding! You have received a letter. Do you wish to view it?

Can it be yet another Anastaria enthusiast? My hand sorting of all letters had resulted in ten thousand blocked players, so I hadn't received any letters today. That didn't last long though. After I opened my mailbox, fully expecting to have to add another name to my blocked senders list, I saw who the message was from: Evolett.

"Hello Mahan. I'm sorry it took so long for me to write to you. I must admit that for a long time I was

unable to choose the right gift for you – one that would sufficiently reflect your ability to surprise. But today I watched a video report by Phoenix and the Azure Dragons on a certain joint quest, which, among other things, featured you and your Dragon. After the Eye I was sure that nothing else would be able to surprise me, but your Totem ... .

When I saw him I immediately realized, WHAT, (yes, just like that, in capitals) I should give you as a gift. We looted this item a long time ago in one of the Dungeons, but had no idea how to use it, because there are no Dragons left in our world. Please accept it and may it bring you and your Totem luck.

Yours sincerely, the Head of the Dark Legion Clan, Evolett."

Item acquired: Diadem of Atranikalonius.

Description: +1 to the number of rider players.

Limitations: only for Dragons.

CHAPTER ELEVEN
THE TRAITOR SHAMAN

"YEAH," SAID ERIC SLOWLY, "it really is ginormous."

The next morning, when the free players returned to the Game, I persuaded Anastaria and Plinto to take everyone to the castle of the Fallen. The archers from the farthest watchtowers were too far away to shoot us, my holy items blocked access to the nearest two and we had no intention of coming close to the gates. ... All in all it was a normal sightseeing trip to the castle of the main enemy.

Regular banging could be heard from inside the castle and was shaking the wall very slightly.

"They're still at it," said Plinto, pointing out the wall's Durability status bar to us. In several places it was at 85% and each subsequent hit reduced it by a few more thousandths of a percent. The Fallen were knocking through a path to freedom.

"Had a good look now?" asked Anastaria, her voice tense. "Let's get back, it isn't safe here."

"Bah! Stacey, what could happen to them?" Plinto spoke up for us. "I was so efficient in deploying your blades and cones that not a single rat would ... Mahan! Stop!"

"Plinto, stop him!" Anastaria shouted. "Someone could've gained control over him! Mahan! Snap out of it!"

Ignoring the shouts from my guys, I continued to walk to the open gates of the castle. As soon as we'd come to the clearing it was as if something had taken me over! It seemed that the most correct course of action would be to walk up to the gates and ... I couldn't say what that 'and' was, but felt that I'd work it out as I went along. Something wasn't right with this castle. I had to walk up to it and figure it out. I really hoped that my fighters wouldn't get in the way.

"I can't get close!" there was surprise in Plinto's voice, but I didn't bother looking back. There were about ten meters left to the gate and I absolutely had to cover them. "There's a sphere here, I won't be able to stun him. I'll try a different way!"

Something flashed past and Plinto appeared right in front of me.

"Where are you off to, boss? It's no good leaving your clan behind ... why don't we head back?" With these words the Rogue attempted a football tackle, throwing himself on top of me with his entire mass, trying to push me back. Damn! Plinto is about to spoil everything! How can I explain to the clan that they mustn't touch me now? The Rogue proceeded to attack the sphere that had appeared around me out of nowhere, so I simply waved him out of the way. Behind me the sound of the breath being knocked out of someone, a dull thump against a tree and Plinto's frame, now sporting half as many Hit Points, indicated that was one heck of a wave.

"Mahan!" came another shout from Eric. "Stop!"

"I don't know what mess you've got yourself into now, but I've just been offered a class-based continent-wide quest to stop you at any cost. Can you hear me? Mahan, I need an answer, otherwise I'm attacking. Don't take it personally, but ..."

"Stacey, everything's fine. I need to get to the gates. We can have a chat once I'm there," I replied to the girl, after realizing I could use the clan chat. *"Stacey, trust me ..."*

"Plinto, stand down!" came the immediate command from the lady Paladin.

"I'm also being offered a class-based continental quest," the Rogue growled somewhere to the side of me, "Mahan has to be stopped at any cost!"

"Plinto!" it was awkward to type, but I was reluctant to talk for some reason. *"Back off! That's an order!"*

"FYI, if anyone's interested," typed in Eric, *"both Leite and myself have had a Warrior class-based quest unlocked too. You have to be stopped, Mahan! Prevented from entering the castle ...."*

"The Great Druids of the earth are also asking

me to do that," Barsina's report wasn't far behind, "Is it even normal for several classes to be given a continental quest at the same time? And within such close proximity as well."

"That's our clan leader for you," quipped Anastaria, "I think he's doesn't give a damn about logic and the Game can sense that ... Mahan, if you fail the quest, I'll eat you alive. Every last bit of you ...."

"All right, I'm off. Don't get in my way!" I sighed in relief as I finished typing and almost flew the last few meters to the gates. That's it. The Shaman has reached his destination; now what?

"Mahan," another message from Anastaria popped up in the chat, "why don't you turn on the camera: you can share the video with me later. I sense that something interesting is about to go down. Everyone else too – turn on your cameras; afterwards we'll edit it all into a film about our adventures."

My entire clan immediately sported video camera pictograms above their heads, so, not to be the odd one out, I went into my settings and turned on the recording. Stacey was right; it would be interesting to watch through our adventures later on.

Strange though it was, the crowd of 350+ level Fallen Mages, who stood about ten meters away, was in no hurry to send me for respawn. Instead they looked in my direction as if waiting for something. As soon as I took a tiny step inside the fortress, a message appeared before my eyes:

Quest available: The making of a Dark

Shaman.

Description: Geranika spent many years looking for a way to free himself from having to depend on the Supreme Spirits of the Higher and Lower Worlds. Fifteen years ago he found it. ... You may join him and free yourself from the power of the Spirits, forever binding yourself to a different power.

Quest type: class-based continental.

Reward for accepting: You will begin the initiation process into becoming one of Geranika's Dark Shamans.

Penalty for refusal: you will be sent for respawn. Do you wish to accept the quest?

Two buttons appeared before my eyes: 'Accept' and 'Decline'. Right. ... First of all I have to figure out which continent-wide quests were given to the others.

You cannot use the internal clan chat while choosing a side. Please make this choice on your own.

What the ...?! Judging by the total lack of reaction to my shouting, the clan wasn't hearing me either. ... Right, then I'll try to use the method that did the job in Beatwick. ...

You cannot use the communication amulet while choosing a side. Please make this choice on your own.

So they blocked this too. ... Fine, if it's a choice they want, a choice they will get ... right now any Shaman's aim is to discover the nature of Geranika's power, therefore ...

'The Making of a Dark Shaman' quest has been accepted. Seek out Geranika.

"I knew that you would make the right choice, my future apprentice." An elegantly dressed man appeared next to m – his short hair barely moving, despite his instant relocation. "This is why I restrained my minions and helped you overcome your clan by surrounding you with a sphere and adding strength to your throw. Come, we need to commence your initiation so you can rid yourself of the yoke of the Spirits forever. These," Geranika turned towards my clan, "are to be destroyed."

A two-meter-high Human materialized next to us, his black eyes emitting a mist that fluctuated through the entire gray spectrum. The General! And he seemed oblivious to the fact that he was standing on a blessed pinecone with one foot and was pushing one of the dagger blades into the ground with the other.

"No!" I barely had the time to shout, before the slaughter of my clan commenced. "I might still find a use for them! Keep them alive for now", I paused, but eventually found the strength to utter, "teacher!"

"Future teacher, Mahan!" Geranika corrected me. "Future teacher. You are yet to prove yourself capable of becoming my apprentice. Agreed, these Free Citizens could come in useful." Geranika turned to the General and issued a command: "Invite them to the castle, after making sure they have no means of harming my potential apprentice. Let them be our guests but with limited terms." He then turned back to me and said: "This place needs to be cleaned up – look at all the trash that's been strewn around. As soon as you complete this task, I'll await you at the center of the castle. You shall then be put through your first test."

After receiving the instructions to clear the castle of the Blessed items, I began to gather up everything that had been thrown around by Plinto. I couldn't help wondering if quests were being generated automatically right now. I was pretty sure that this one hadn't existed until recently. ... And there was the update in the Tear of Eluna description as well. ...

"Mahan?" the lady Paladin's raised eyebrow spoke louder than any words. Does this mean that they'd all failed those continent-wide quests? "I won't even ask what's going on here – you probably don't have a clue yourself –, but bear in mind that everyone's quests have been changed. Now, instead of preventing you entering the castle, the task is to do everything in our power to ensure you fail the tests. Please, give some thought to the rest of us before you do anything."

"Don't listen to her, boss," intervened Plinto. "It's been a while since we've had anything this big go down – even the Lieutenant seems a pushover in comparison. Do what you have to do: we'll support you. Why can't there be a Shadow Empire? We can be the first clan for the third side."

"Except, all our money-making plans would be totally and irreversibly screwed," sighed Leite bitterly. Who are we going to sell all that Jewelry to exactly, if the other two Empires are hostile to us?"

"ENOUGH TALKING!" The General's voice was so heavy that the subsequent debuffs didn't only bring down the players, but the majority of the Mages and Vampires too. Only the Elementals remained unshaken, but they too were probably wincing in the Astral Plane.

"The first test is easy," Geranika said the moment I found him. I had completed the gathering of the Blessed items successfully, but I didn't get a single Experience point for it. My only consolation was that now I could defend myself by throwing the cones, if it came to that. "You have to break with your Race. I will return you to the past, where your task is to destroy the symbol of all Humans: Yalininka. Go now!" The whirlwind of the portal appeared next to Geranika, but instead of the usual blue glow if was red in hue.

"*Mahan, don't you dare!*" immediately came a message from Anastaria. "*Yalininka is an untouchable symbol of all races! Not just the Humans, but all of them! She must not be destroyed, even to complete a scenario!*"

"To make sure that you really carry out my

instructions, I will be watching you! Go now!" The Lord of Shadow hurried me, so there was little I could do other than take one small step – a step towards a Legend of Barliona.

A flash of light!

"Traveler! Help me, I beg you!" a woman's piercing cry cut through the surrounding world. This cry combined pain, despair and, at the same time, hope of deliverance. It took me a few moments to evaluate the situation: I'd found myself high in the mountains, on a small plateau – a few meters away from me, over the edge of a precipice, a woman's hand was gripping the stone edge. Why am I so flippin' slow? She'll fall any moment!

Without giving a thought to the fact that if I simply left things as they were Geranika's quest would be completed automatically (I had no doubt that the woman gripping the stone with her last bit of strength was Yalininka), I dashed to the edge of the precipice. Calmly standing and watching someone, even just an NPC, falling into a chasm was more than I could bear.

"Noooo!" The woman's hand finally slipped from the stone and disappeared beyond the edge. Realizing that I was horrendously late, I bit my lip and jumped forward, in the unrealistic hope of catching her as she fell. Sharp cold stones ripped across my chest, taking off around 10% of my Hit Points, but that was irrelevant: as I threw my hand through the air, I managed to grab the woman's right hand at the last second. Yalininka grabbed at my hand like a drowning man at a straw, her sharp nails sinking into my skin and repeating the effect of the stone in the damage I sustained. Whatever; I'll deal with that later. The pressing thing now was that, although the woman weighed hardly anything at all, I had nothing to hold on to at the edge and slowly but surely was beginning to slip too. That's the last thing I need!

"Hold still!" I shouted to the wriggling woman. "We will both fall if you don't!"

I began to beat the stones with my feet in the hopes of either catching my foot in or making a small hole in the rock, but still continued to slide after Yalininka.

"Let me go, traveler!" the woman said after a few moments, letting go of my hand. "We might both die now. Save yourself!"

"Yeah! Sure thing. I'll just throw in the towel and let you go now," I growled, teeth clenched, and gripped a small rock with my free hand. The stone was slippery and wobbled, but managed to do its job – our journey over the edge had ground to a halt. Now we just had to carefully climb out of this. ...

"Got a grip now. Stop trying to wriggle out already!" I shouted when the woman began to twist her hand. Damn, this was hard! "Use your other hand and try to climb up to me!"

"The other one is broken," Yalininka shared the happy news, but stopped trying to wriggle out.

"Then I'll start turning over very carefully: try

not to move! As soon as you can, try to get a leg over the edge – that would help out a lot. Right, off we go. Careful now!"

In the next few seconds I gained extra Respect for the age-old profession of a surgeon. I once read in a book that before the introduction of medical Imitators, people carried out operations themselves. And the first operations on the heart required such concentration and precision that surgeons commanded incredible Respect. Using the wobbly rock as my foothold, I very carefully began to turn away from the edge pulling Yalininka after me. A wrong move could mean loss of balance and a long fall downward. The gray, in places leaden, clouds far below indicated that before its abrupt end it would be quite a lengthy journey.

"Thank you, traveler!" By the time I pulled the woman back onto the plateau, my Energy bar was reduced to 40 points. Considering that it had 210 to start with, I'd had to do some serious exertion there. "I don't know what you were doing in a place so far away from the world. I'm sure you have your reasons, but you've saved me. Give me a moment to recover and I'll heal all our wounds ..."

Struggling to my feet I could finally have a proper look at Yalininka. Thin as a reed, a small woman with long snow-white hair and slightly upturned nose was standing before me. Her eyes, once bright blue, had now turned pale and a pattern of wrinkles that spread across her face indicated that her time of flying above the clouds was nearly at an end.

"Great one." Following a habit I acquired when I was still playing a Hunter, I bent my knee in acknowledgement of Yalininka's great deeds. It looks like I wasn't fated to become Geranika's apprentice after all, because I didn't have it in me to push this woman off the edge.

"Get up, Shaman," said the lady, "You saved me – I should be the one kneeling to you. What are you doing among these cliffs, if that's not a secret?" As she spoke, Yalininka continued to make various gestures. First, my Hit Points and Energy completely recovered – almost instantaneously, no less – and then her broken and unnaturally twisted arm regained its normal position, following which the lady heaved a sigh of relief.

"Forgive me, Great One, but if I tell you the reason why I'm here, you will stop talking to me. Tell me rather how you came to be hanging off a cliff like that? Where are your silver wings that bore you around all of Barliona?"

"The wings have given out", she said sadly. "An epidemic arose near Priant and I couldn't leave the Orcs to battle it out by themselves. Leantariel warned me that the wings needed recharging, but ... I've grown tired, Shaman. I've spent such a long time flying around the world that I've forgotten where my home is. The whole of Barliona has become my home – I am welcome everywhere, everyone is glad to see me. ... But my strength is ebbing and each day it's more and more difficult even to get up on my feet, let alone go around saving others. Still, duty calls ... I decided to take a shortcut through the Shining Mountains when the wings failed. But tell me, what were you looking for amidst the mountains?"

Fully aware that what I was doing was pretty daft, I told Yalininka everything – that I was from the distant future, that in my time a Shaman had appeared and destroyed two Emperors and that no-one knew the nature of his power. When I explained the aim of my quest, the Great One gave a barely perceptible start and asked me to continue.

"The portal took me here and the rest you know," I finished my tale.

"You had a perfectly good opportunity to complete your task by simply turning away," said the woman thoughtfully. "Why did you intervene?"

"If I didn't do it, then ... I don't know how to explain this. Honor, the desire to help another human being, the feeling of self-respect ... I could use a lot of words here, but they wouldn't really get to the heart of it. I was just unable to do otherwise."

"I heard you, Shaman, and now you listen to me," replied Yalininka after some thought. "My time is coming to an end. It is already finished and I am only keeping myself in this world by an unspeakable effort of will. I long for rest at long last. As far as I understood you, your task is to destroy me, so ... Let's not disappoint Geranika."

"Great One ..."

"My decision is final!" The Emperor himself would have envied the authority commanded by this frail old lady's voice. "Shaman, your task is to save your own time! To save Barliona! If Geranika's armies attack, would the Free Citizens be able to stop them? Right now the secret of the phantoms remains unknown, so the answer to that is no, they would not! You have to walk this path to the end, ignoring any possible punishment! That's the only way to become one of the Great Ones! Here, you will pass this gift on to someone you believe worthy of following in my footsteps." With these words Yalininka handed me a thin blue ribbon. "And now come with me. If I understood you right, Geranika wants me to die before your eyes ..."

Item acquired: The Farewell Ribbon of the Great Yalininka. The description can only be accessed by players that possess the Healing stat.

Requirements: At least 100 levels in Healing.

Item class: Unique.

I never thought that tears could come to my eyes. The thirty seconds that it took Yalininka to reach the clouds below seemed an eternity to me: I don't think I've ever felt such hopelessness, helplessness and anger before. What kind of a quest would make you commit such a terrible deed? Where's the logic?

A minute later the system informed me that Geranika's task had been completed and a portal opened next to me. The Great One was dead. ...

Update to the 'The Making of a Dark Shaman' quest: Should you successfully complete the quest, your Reputation with all the factions of Malabar and Kartoss will change to Hatred.

A flash of light!

"I'm impressed with your actions, my future apprentice," uttered Geranika, as soon as I reappeared in the Castle of the Fallen. My brain had a solid grasp of what was happening, that it was only a game, but my feelings were telling me only one thing: Geranika had to be destroyed. "You made Yalininka kill herself ... I couldn't have even hoped for something like that. You will become a worthy warrior of Shadow."

"Mahan ... your eyes are streaming mist now," Anastaria informed me. *"The continent-wide quest has once again been renewed: 'Wait for the Shaman's trial.' What the heck are you doing?"*

"Saving Barliona and clocking up a ton of penalties," I growled in chat. *"Stacey, I might be wrong (though that's unlikely), but very soon we'll see the emergence of a third Empire – the Shadow Empire. You won't be able to play for it, but it will feature the phantoms that we came across when fighting the Lieutenant. At the moment only Shamans have the ability to fight them – that is, only Shamans who've managed to unlock the 'Change of Essence' ability. That wasn't right, which is why Elenium's continent-*

wide quest has been launched. Right now I'm trying to find out the nature of these things and all your quests will eventually correct themselves into an ability of some kind, which will make it possible for every class to destroy the phantoms. This is why I started the trial and will see it through to the end, no matter the price I'll have to pay in terms of Reputation. Can you tell me if you know how Yalininka died?"

"She was flying to someone's aid, but overestimated her strength and fell, perishing in the mountains. Judging by what Geranika just said, history has been somewhat economical with the truth. How did you convince her to jump?"

"I'll tell you later."

"It's a pity that you've decided to fight these guys," a message immediately came from Plinto. "I was already looking forward to becoming a warrior for Shadow ... but being the hero of Malabar isn't bad either. Will you kill us in the end? We've probably been kept alive for now only so they can use us for a sacrifice later on."

"But this goes against the social aspect of the Game!" Barsina intervened. "Barliona is meant to embody what is good and eternal, not provoke a player into destroying everything that he values. ... That's just wrong!"

"It's a scenario, Barsa. I agree with Mahan here," said Anastaria, "If Shadow really does emerge as a force, everyone, not just Shamans, will have to fight Geranika. Go for it, boss, we'll support you ..."

Ding! You've received 163287 new messages.

Do you wish to view them?

"Now comes the second trial," continued Geranika, tearing me away from chat and the Mailbox. 163000 messages?! Why on earth?! The mailbox refreshed every two hours, so how was it even possible to write so many in such a short time?! It looks like I'll have to forget about hand-sorting the mail and cough up the cash for a mail-sorting Imitator – it could handle all the mail analysis for me.

"You are to visit your first teacher in Farstead and destroy him. The link between a teacher and an apprentice is so strong that only a sufficiently prepared sentient is able to sever it. I managed it by myself and didn't need to kill Almis. But you do, otherwise you will never become my apprentice. Go!" Another red portal appeared next to Geranika.

A flash of light!

"I was expecting you, apprentice." The portal took me to a familiar room where I was once offered tea. To my surprise, the room was now empty: stripped of all furniture, with the High Shaman Almis in full battle attire standing at its center – staff, cloak, hat with deer antlers ... he was prepared. "If you think that I will allow myself to be destroyed so easily, you are very much mistaken. I was unable to lift my hand against Geranika, but I won't fail to act against a second traitor! Prepare to die!"

"Almis, stop!" was all I had time to shout before

a bird dove for my head: the High Shaman's Totem. A message immediately appeared telling me that I had been attacked by an NPC and thus had every right to defend myself. Too bad it was the last thing I felt like doing. "Stop it!" I shouted again, when a Supreme Spirit of Fire flew at me, leaving me with only 10% of Hit Points. Ah well, looks like I failed in my second task. I can't summon Spirits and wouldn't do that even if I could.

"Fight, traitor!" growled Almis. "Or do you think that I lack the will to destroy an unarmed foe? You're wrong! Fight and die like a man!"

"I have no intention of fighting you! If you want to kill me, go ahead and do it. I won't resist. Almis! We need to talk! I'm here to ..."

"No!" I was interrupted by the Shaman's angry shout. "I have nothing to say to a traitor! If you don't wish to fight with Spirits, fine! I'll destroy you with my staff!" With these words Almis leapt over to me, raising his staff, ready to strike me down. All I could do was push him away and jump aside. The reflexes that I honed as a Hunter kicked in fully. I tumbled a meter and a half away, dodging the staff, but Almis ... he froze where he stood and stared into the distance with a surprised expression. Several seconds went by and then the Life Bar of the High Shaman started to diminish.

"How?" my teacher's voice was hoarse as he struggled to get the words out. "This is impossible!"

To be honest, I was in as much shock as Almis. What was happening to him? How could my simple push do something so terrible? This simply couldn't be happening!

"May you be ..." was all the master of the house managed to croak before his Life Bar flickered and disappeared, leaving only his elaborately carved staff, the tip cloaked in a strange mist, in place of the High Shaman.

"Bravo, very nearly, my apprentice – bravo!" The air in one of the corners suddenly thickened and turned into Geranika. "Leave that stick, it's of no use to you," he added when he saw me lean over the staff. "I must admit, I first thought that you'd decided to betray me, but such a cunning move with a single strike was very much to my liking. To make the opponent doubt himself and then deal him a devastating blow when he was least expecting it ... I am pleased with you, my almost-apprentice, but come now, two more trials still await you. After these you will truly become my apprentice. Though, why waste time? Will you drop that oversized twig already?"

"If my future teacher would permit me, I would like to keep it in memory of my first victim," I said respectfully. "It isn't every day that a Great Shaman defeats a High one, so I'd like to remember this moment."

"Good point," agreed Geranika. "I'll allow you to keep the staff, you can hang it in my castle. But to avoid wasting time (there's never enough of it), I will start your training now. I don't believe that after turning your back on your race and your class you would not reject everything else. Remember this, my future apprentice: the Spirits of both worlds require a sacrifice for the summoning of their progeny. The higher the rank of the Spirit that you summon, the higher the sacrifice you have to pay. If you'd remained an ordinary Shaman, summoning a Supreme Spirit of the thirtieth rank would have cost you all your Life Force. Yes, you could have summoned the Spirit, but that would've sent you to the Grey Lands. This is why Shamans came up with altars in an attempt to placate the Spirits before they are summoned. Fools! Weaklings! How could they fail to understand that we are the ones that should command the Spirits, stripping them of part of their power? For a long time I could not come to terms with such a state of affairs, until I was struck by a revelation: where there is light, there must also be darkness! If there are Spirits, there must also be those that oppose them! But who could this be? I spent a long time studying this matter, until I came upon the source of the power. A power that is the complete opposite of the Spirits! So let's not linger here, it is time we got back. Another trial awaits and I am eager to begin your training. You will greatly outshine Midial."

Update to the 'The Making of a Dark Shaman' quest. Should you successfully complete the quest, your reputation with the Supreme Spirits of the Higher and the Lower Worlds will change to Hatred.

A flash of light!

"Now the dark mist is coming off your hair too," Anastaria immediately reported as soon as we reappeared in the Castle of the Fallen. *"While you've been running around bumping off NPCs, Ehkiller sent me a message. The United forces of Malabar – around forty thousand fighters – have been transported by our Mages to the Dark Forest. According to 'Killer they'll arrive in the vicinity of the Castle in about ten minutes, so get ready for things to get rough. 'Killer took a scroll of Armageddon with him, so very soon this place will get a visit from the fluffy northern beastie, as Clutzer would put it. They have only one aim – to destroy the player called Mahan and prevent him from completing the trial. It looks like they didn't get the quest update like we did."*

"The next task, my future apprentice," continued Geranika, "is to have you completely sever any ties with your Shamanistic past. When I found my new source of power, I had to destroy my Totem, which was the essence of the Spirits of both worlds. You cannot keep your Totem! Prove that you are fully ready to become one of us! Destroy your Dragon!"

Supreme Spirits of both worlds! If I remain a Shaman after all this madness, I'll be sure to give you some proper gift! If not for the penalties that you'd slapped on me for the explosion in the Astral Plane, I would have failed Geranika's trial for sure. I wouldn't let anyone destroy Draco!

"I can't ..." I started to say, but was immediately interrupted by Geranika:

"Are you again refusing to take your place by

my side?"

"No, I do want to be your apprentice, but destroying my Totem is beyond my power right now. It needs to be summoned, but the Supreme Spirits placed a penalty on me. For the next week and a half I will be as powerless as the Shaman of the old school. I'm sorry I've let you down, future teacher, but destroying the Totem is impossible right now ..."

"Old school ... an excellent expression – worth remembering! But how could you ... Who on earth is that?"

A battle horn seemed to sound right outside the gates. Such sounds put a series of beneficial buffs on a group or a raid and served as the signal for attack.

"Killer's here." Anastaria played the part of Captain Obvious.

"Phoenix will break through the gates!" came Hellfire's shout. "Legion," – they'd brought the Dark Legion with them too! – "lay siege to the towers! Azures and Heirs – the support is on you. As soon as we break through, everyone must try to destroy Mahan! He's the main target, not the Dark Ones! Battering rams and ballistae to the front! Attack when ready!"

"I've thought of a different trial for you," Geranika turned to me with a playfully malicious smirk. "We can leave the Totem for later – it isn't going anywhere." With these words my potential teacher disappeared and the entire forest descended into a frightening silence. Even the sounds of the battle horn had died down, not daring to disturb the stillness of the forest.

"Daft hero wannabes," summed up Plinto: *"Geranika froze two hundred players near Beatwick – did these morons think it would be any different here?"*

"YOU DARED TO ATTACK MY CASTLE WHILE I'M TRAINING MY APPRENTICE?!" The Lord of Shadow was up in the air, towering a few meters above the wall. Judging by the total lack of lightning strikes, arrows or curses flying towards him, the players were affected by the 'Stun' debuff and were lying scattered around the ground in quiet bundles. Forty thousand bodies ... how on earth did they all fit in the small glade in front of the castle? Or were most of them still in the forest?

"I WILL NOT ALLOW YOU TO INTERFERE WITH MY PLANS! APPRENTICE!" Geranika turned around and some unknown force lifted me off the ground. Smoothly, with impressive precision, I flew to the gates and beheld an epic spectacle: a field strewn with high-level players. They were covering everything – the small glade before the gates, the forest and the tree tops were decorated with the heroic hulks of the frozen saviors of Barliona – from poor old me. "NOW I SHALL TEACH YOU A LESSON! WATCH!"

Several dozen players flew up in the air, like weightless feathers picked up by a gust of wind, and floated over to us. Hmmm ... Rick from Phoenix, Etamzilat from Heirs of the Titans, and many more players I didn't know ... all of them had turned up here, hell bent on sending me for respawn. Maybe I really should just ditch the lot of them and start playing for Shadow? However today's meeting would go, forty thousand players – if Anastaria wasn't embellishing the truth – would become very hostile towards me.

"The first thing you should remember," continued Geranika in a normal voice, "is that a Shaman's chief aim is not to be paying tribute, but making full use of his opponent's Life Force. Spirits cannot be summoned without receiving a sacrifice first, which is why it is a given that they are weak. Now watch my actions and then tell me that you've understood."

Dark phantoms flew out of Geranika's hands, surrounded the floating players and in a few moments vanished. The players vanished with them, while a handful of gold (it turned out that not everyone goes for the upgraded purse option) and several items dropped to the ground: a jacket, a belt and boots of some kind. All legendary items that have a 10% drop chance. ... No, the players won't just rail at me, no ... I'm a goner, plain and simple.

"What do you make of it?" Geranika asked me.

"These dark entities, which I call phantoms, were summoned and have seized their victims," I hazarded a guess. "At the same time they exact a payment, but they take it from the victim ..."

"Don't repeat my words," interrupted Geranika. "I want to hear your thoughts. Do not disappoint me, apprentice!"

Apprentice? No longer 'future apprentice'?

Right, it seems that I've reached my aim, now I just need to make good use of it.

Ding! You've received 3844521 new messages. Do you wish to view them?

Will they quit with the 'fan mail' already? Where did all these letters come from?? Bah! Never mind, I'll sort through them later. ...

"The phantoms came out of your hands, teacher," I started saying the first thing that came into my head. Like an ancient tribesman, who makes a song out of what he's looking at: " They don't appear in the victims, like Spirits, they ... they live in you. So it appears that in order to learn how to summon them, you have to go through an initiation, invite the phantoms within. ... You spoke of a source, so there must be some object, a shard of which will be implanted, inlaid, engrafted – I don't know which word is appropriate here – into me. Why a shard? Because you're taking on an apprentice, which means that the object has not been absorbed by you completely. I'm certain that a similar shard is inside Midial. (Where is he, by the way? I haven't seen him around the Castle yet.) The phantoms do not return, which means that they die ... but then, if I'm right, one would no longer be able to summon them after a certain point. So this means that the phantoms do not die. They ... I don't know, teacher."

"You will make a worthy apprentice," said Geranika thoughtfully, looking pleased. "You are right and wrong at the same time. When those that you call 'phantoms' have had their fill of a victim they return back to the source. Watch my next summons and try to describe it."

Players once again floated into the air, but this time there were a lot more of them – at least a hundred. ...

"The next summons that I will show you is the complete opposite." The Lord of Shadows continued his demonstration. "Look!"

The bodies of the levitating players twisted and phantoms began to fly out of the avatars' chests. One, two, three ... soon the flying hundred was surrounded by dark entities, which vanished a few moments later. Just like the players. Another hundred less ... another light shower of gold and just one Legendary item.

"Do you understand what happened?" Geranika asked me.

"No, teacher," I admitted honestly. "What happened just now completely breaks with the logic of my first theory. The phantoms didn't come from you, but from the victims. ... Forgive me, teacher, but I don't understand ..."

"Honesty, Mahan, is exactly what I value the most in my subordinates. Ask if you don't know, but don't be weak. I have shown you something only I, as the master of the source, possess. None of my apprentices would be able to learn this by themselves. You've passed the test. Now you have some work ahead of you: you will have to personally destroy all these uninvited guests, now so abundantly scattered in the vicinity of our castle. Take the knife." Geranika handed me a black blade streaming with mist, which sported a wooden handle. It was almost the twin of the knife that was sticking out of the Throne of the Malabar Emperor. "I made it safe for you, so it shouldn't take you too long to send everyone to the Grey Lands. Time to act, apprentice!"

Dear player,

We are warning you that if you carry out this instruction, after completing the 'Making of a Dark Shaman' quest you will either be transported to the Pryke Copper Mine (Reputation with the Malabar Empire Neutral or above) or to the Groll Copper Mine (Reputation with the Malabar Empire below Neutral), following which you will be brought before the court. The decision whether to complete the quest remains with you. Make the right decision.

Yours sincerely,

Barliona Administration.

The surrounding world stopped. In complete disbelief, I kept re-reading the message from the Game Administration, trying to find a single loophole. The very fact of the Game Administration addressing a player directly was nonsense, something completely unheard of. But to give me such a savage choice – either get sent to the mines while finding out the source of Geranika's power, or abandon the quest, and get huge penalties for killing Yalininka and Almis.

... To hell with this! I knew what would be waiting for me when I chose this path, so it's too late to change my mind now. The mines? Seven and a half years? Like I give a damn!

When I finally made up my mind, Geranika lowered me to the ground. Oooh! So it looks like these days Imitators also monitor the player's resolve and act in response to that. ... All right, off we go – I have a lot of hard monotonous work ahead of me. ...

The first player I came up to turned out to be Hellfire. The Dwarf was lying on the ground like a broken doll and only his living eyes indicated that he was aware of what was happening. If the game could provide the ability to kill with a stare, I would've been incinerated on the spot. ... Hesitating a moment, as if still uncertain I wanted to go to the mines, I abruptly lowered the dagger, which entered Hellfire's chest right up to the hilt. Something flickered and a shield of some kind was all that was left in place of the dwarf. Just as I was looking around the glade, thinking about how much work I had in front of me, all the players who'd rushed here to kill me were lifted up into the air and floated in the direction of the castle. Judging by Geranika's pleased smirk, it was his doing: he'd decided to give his apprentice a hand. ... There was little else I could do other than wave the dagger intensely left and right, sending a player to the Grey Lands with every blow. I dreaded to even think what was going down on the forums right now ...

"STOP!" Geranika suddenly roared. I turned around and saw Plinto standing, or rather already lying, a few feet away. "HOW DARE YOU TRY TO INTERFERE WITH THE TRAINING OF MY APPRENTICE?!"

"You are mistaken," rasped the Rogue, whose Hit Point had started to melt rapidly. "I intend to stick with Mahan whatever happens, with or without you, but ..."

"Teacher, stop! Plinto doesn't wish me any harm!"

"Then why did he leave the Castle?" asked Geranika calmly and I typed a 'thank you' to Barsina in clan chat for restoring half of the Rogue's Hit Points.

"Those who came for our death deserve what Mahan is doing to them now," said Plinto, getting up from the ground, "but it would be foolish to leave their gold and other items just lying around. Free citizens can return from the Grey Lands, so after some time they will return for them. They will again grow strong and bold ... why would I want that? No! No way I'm letting a prime looting opportunity like that slip by!"

"Ha ha ha!" Geranika's pleased laughter echoed through the forest. "When I finish training Mahan, you'll become my next apprentice! Go, get your loot!" After that the Lord of Shadow turned to me and said, "you have the right kind of subordinates, apprentice! You shall all aid me in bringing Barliona to its knees. Let us continue!"

The floating players once again started to move, so I had no time for thoughts other than: 'hit to the left', 'slash to the right'. I had to make almost forty thousand hits ... yeah. ... How did that classic writer put it? "Thus striking blow after blow, the warriors' hands did weary grow ..."

"Apprentice, you have proven your readiness to carry out my orders without question," said Geranika about an hour later. The flow of players did not abate, so I had to keep up being the butcher for a good while yet. ... "There's little sense in losing all this time, so I'll take care of the rest." Geranika made a gesture with his hand and the scene instantly cleared – in the sense that the forty thousand players were simply no longer there, but a real shower of gold descended to earth.

You've acquired 'Elephant and Pug' achievement level 8. Damage to all creatures and players 50+ levels higher than you increased by 90%.

You've acquired 'Killer' achievement level 8. Damage caused to other players increased by 9%.

"You have completed your trials, apprentice," said Geranika, turning to me. "I will give you an hour's rest before the last one. I need to prepare. You will be taken to the chambers!" Geranika disappeared and a Mage came up to each of the players in my clan and, with a respectful bow, silently pointed towards the central building in the Castle. What had Geranika come up with for the last test?

"Right," said Anastaria as we found ourselves in a cozy room. Soft armchairs, a fireplace, a small table covered with various dishes. ... If not for the dozen Mages, who stood by the walls like invisible shadows, you might have thought we'd ended up in Anhurs. "Judging by what Geranika just said, we have about an hour, so I suggest all those who can should log out and browse the forums. We have to understand what consequences the current events could have for the clan. I will try to contact some representatives of the Administration and ask them what on earth made them opt for a mass killing."

"No way, I'm staying here," said Plinto immediately. "What can they do? Declare each of us a persona non grata? Ha! The PK-system will break down! Thanks to Mahan we're all in the same group, so I got my Killer up to level 16 now! They want to keep sending us for respawn? They're welcome to try: from what I could see, not everyone's bought the updated purse yet. We've made about four million in an hour! Mahan, I put this money into the clan, let the Imitator allocate it all later. Whoever comes at us with a sword will get his ass perished!"

"All right, stay if you want," said Anastaria reluctantly. "Barsa, will you help at least?"

"Yeah, I'm rather curious myself," replied the Druid. "But I have one question: Mahan just killed off almost forty thousand players, who were two hundred levels higher than him. Why didn't we gain any experience?"

"You don't get experience for a scenario PK," said the Paladin. "Mahan, send me the video you recorded. I'll upload it to the net, let everyone else enjoy the scene ... right, got it," the girl thanked me. "I'm off. I won't be leaving the Game, so if you need me, press my thumb three times. I've set an alarm, so I'll come right back. I'm out."

"Damn, how do you set one of those things up?" asked Barsina, but there was no-one there – Anastaria had logged out. "All right, I'll be back soon." With these words Barsina's eyes also glazed over.

"Alrighty then. While everyone else is busy, let's get down to the fun part," said Plinto, rubbing his hands. "Sorting through the trophies!"

"You do realize that you'll have to give them back, right?" I reminded him.

"Of course, boss! No problem! As soon as I see anyone I'll give it them their stuff back right away!" said Plinto with a mischievous grin and then handed me a leather belt. "Here, have a look! This one's for you, I think."

Item acquired: Borhg's Artificer's Band.

Description: The great Master liked to say that excellent gear is the guarantee of any victory. He spent two years of his life creating a belt that would make item crafting much easier.

Item class: Legendary. +5 to Crafting.

Requirements: Crafting level 1+.

"It looks like this one came from Rick's bag. Legendary items can drop from inventory as well," said Plinto happily. "So, in view of our plans for item crafting, would it make sense to give this thing back?"

486

Knockout. It seems that I'd missed a direct hit from the right, as well as a hook and a slam-down too. Moreover, once down I was given a good kicking to boot, because my entire inner zoo, which had been peacefully asleep the entire two weeks after Beatwick, suddenly woke up and penned down a note of protest, where in all solemn seriousness it declared the impossibility of handing back such an object to any third party. Otherwise they would gnaw a hole in me and run away to join Rick. I realized that I would have to hide the belt in the Bank until happier times, because it could drop from my bag too, but it was worth having to limit my crafting to safe zones only. +5 to Crafting! This was cheat mode, plain and simple!

"I see that you catch my drift now, boss," said Plinto, watching my reaction. "Some of the items are of no use to me, so I'll sell them and put the money back into the clan. But two or three of them – I still haven't quite figured out which – would come in damn useful! Where did these goons get daggers like these?!" came the Rogue's exclamation as he fully immersed himself in sorting out the loot.

"Yeeahh," uttered Anastaria when she came back to the Game about an hour later, "is Barsa back?"

"Yes, I'm here."

"So ... what have you found out?" It looked like Anastaria's news was so unpleasant that she was unable to regain control over herself in reality and logged into the Game in an agitated state.

"If you ignore the swearing and bile aimed at the Seathistles clan," Barsina began, "the forum is silent. There isn't a word about us. I spent half an hour sifting through messages, but except for the profanities from those that Mahan sent for respawn and mockery of noobs who had allowed themselves to be destroyed, I haven't found a thing. What about you?"

"I contacted Ehkiller," said Anastaria, "and it turns out that the entire raid, just before it ported, had their quest updated. It was variable: either to destroy Mahan, preventing him from completing the trial, or not to appear in the Dark Forest under any circumstances. As the leader of the raid, Hellfire took the decision to destroy. ... Aside from this, the Emperor has issued a proclamation throughout Malabar in which he asks that the Empire be kept safe from the Shaman. ... Yes, it was updated for those who decided to fly to the Dark Forest, but for the majority of the players it remained the same: destroy Mahan. ... All in all, I don't understand what's going on. ... And also 'Killer asked for the dropped items to be returned. Half of them, at least, since he understands that many of them could catch Plinto's eye, and ..."

"Rick has really blown his top?" I asked the girl, who had fallen silent.

"You've seen the belt then? Yes, Rick raised such hell that 'Killer's going to have a tough time of it now. Hell, on the other hand, looks totally down in the dumps. We shouldn't expect any trouble from

Phoenix, Legion or the Dragons, as they will lay the blame on Hellfire for making the wrong decision, but the players from the Heirs and other smaller clans have declared war. That includes around twenty-five thousand of those that came to the Dark Forest today, plus everyone else from their clans. ... So it's going to be a rough ride from now on. Plinto, what about the items?"

"What the boss says, goes," was the Rogue's simple answer, "but I'm not handing back these daggers even if I get kicked out of the Game. No way I'll let some schmuck walk around with these beauties, and as for the belt ... that decision is for Mahan to make. For the rest, the price is negotiable."

"All right, that's what I'll tell them then. Has Geranika appeared yet?"

"No. What's with the video?"

"I handed it over for editing – I have a contact with the right skills. He promised to show me the rough cut tomorrow. And we've yet to survive that long," smiled Anastaria. "I have no intention of switching to Shadow, by the way. I'm happy enough in Malabar."

"Chicken," snorted Plinto. "So, what are we waiting for?" he said to the Officers and Barsina. "No-one knows how long we'll have to wait here, so it's jumping time. Off we go, no slacking! Mahan, you're joining us too. Extra Agility isn't gonna hurt you ..."

"Apprentice." Geranika appeared after about an hour. I had no idea where Plinto got all his Energy from, but mine had run out after thirty minutes, try as I might to out-jump the Rogue. Or are his stats for this so astronomical that I'm nowhere near catching up with him in this respect? In any case, +3 to Agility was useful enough. "I am pleased to see that you don't like to waste time. I was delayed because our torture room was occupied. There is one last trial ahead of you, after which you will become a real Dark Shaman. Come!"

Clutzer pressed Anastaria's thumb three times to return the girl, who had logged out for the second time, back to the Game, and our entire group followed Geranika. What had this bastard concocted this time and what does a torture room have to do with it? I'd be heading for the mines after this quest anyway, so what difference would it make who I'd be torturing?

"I think it's time to continue your training," said Geranika as soon as we left the building and moved towards a small hut, just two by two meters square. "Remember, apprentice, that there are entities other than Spirits. Now I will teach you and your subordinates to summon these powers, but you will only be able to use them after training. I will implant a fragment of the crystal into each of you and together we shall conquer all of Barliona."

You acquired a variable ability: Shadow Transformation.

If the trial is completed successfully, you will allow part of the Reverse Side of the world within you, sending a Shadow into a chosen opponent.

Base kamlanie time: 5 seconds.

Damage dealt: (Intellect *5) Points. This ability ignores all types of armor.

Range: 100 meters.

If you refuse to go through the trial, you combine the world of Spirits and Shadows, embodying one Shadow into the physical world.

Base kamlanie time: 5 seconds.

Shadow embodiment time: 10 seconds.

Ability cool down: 1 minute.

Cost of summoning: (Character level) Hit Points of the summoner.

Range: 20 meters.

So that's what we're up against! It turns out that along with Spirits their Shadows also exist, which have gained some sort of corporeality. ... And this strange Reverse Side, which we've already visited, also plays a part here. ... Now only the key question remains: what is this crystal and where did Geranika get it? Never mind, we'll find out soon enough. ...

"Wow," Plinto, Barsina, Eric and Leite said at the same time. They used different words, of course, but the gist was the same: they were in shock. Clutzer and Anastaria controlled themselves, but one look at them made clear that they had acquired a similar ability. I wondered if it was doubled for them as well.

"Shadows," breathed out Anastaria, getting to grips with her emotions.

"Yes, Siren, Shadows. The protagonists of the Reverse Side of the world," confirmed Geranika. "I will teach you to use them and then no-one will be able to harm you. There are no weapons that work against them in this entire world."

"Shamans know how to embody them," the girl kept at it, wanting the Lord of Shadow to get even more candid. "They can be easily destroyed after that."

"Shamans know how to embody only the lesser Shadows, which are weak and untrained. They are unable to do anything with the Lieutenant."

"And yet we still managed to destroy him."

"I know; using the Astral Plane was an exquisite solution. The light was so bright that for a very short moment shadows ceased to exist altogether there. That's what did it. But can you tell me, future apprentice, how many Shamans are there with the ability to enter the Astral Plane and carry out a summons there? You can't, can you? Think about that."

The small structure that we'd entered contained nothing save a spiral staircase leading downwards. Wow! So the site had a whole underground section as well! Was this something peculiar to this Castle? Judging by Anastaria's narrowing eyes, she hadn't come across such an architectural feature during previous raids all that often.

"Apprentice," Geranika addressed me, once we started our descent. "Now is the time you prove to me that there is only one teacher left for you in Barliona – me. Kornik, that fool of a Harbinger, is waiting for us below. He thought he was so clever, jumping all over Malabar to evade me, stupid little goblin. I was unable to convince him to join me, so now it is time to destroy him. And no-one will do it better than you. You still have the knife that you used to destroy the Free Citizens, so you should make a quick job of it."

"Teacher, tell me, how did you create these knives? How much labor does it take to make a wonder like this?"

"It's a part of my flesh, so it didn't cost me anything to make it."

"I don't understand. How can a dagger be made of flesh?" Geranika was holding something back. I had to find out how to free the Emperor's throne and he was throwing riddles at me.

"I will show you now ..." the Shaman stopped, looked down at me and said, "so that you will be completely convinced, hit me with the knife."

"As you wish, teacher!" I took out the smoking item and, barely giving it a thought, plunged it into where Geranika's heart should have been. Just in case he was wrong!

The knife entered the Lord of Shadow's body up to the hilt, but judging by the man's smile, he didn't feel a shred of discomfort. Neither did he disappear as a player normally would. Moreover, just a couple of seconds after I hit him, the knife was pulled into the NPC's body, as if something was sucking it inside.

"Convinced now? There is a lot we'll have to teach you: the old school has become too deeply ingrained in you. No matter, we shall be purging you of it shortly. Come!"

After a few flights on the stair we found ourselves in a stone room of medium proportions, lit by a dozen torches. It could be provisionally divided into two parts: the first contained a table to which Kornik was chained – he was thin and worn out, all covered in cuts, but still alive – and the second ... the second part wasn't empty either. There, chained by each of its four legs, covered all over with various tubes, devices, chains and other incomprehensible things, stood the Unicorn. Or rather, a former Unicorn, because instead of a horn it had a tube that went into the wall. Ishni, the Heart of the Dark Forest in the flesh. ...

"This is Midial's pride and joy," uttered Geranika, as he watched Barsina's reaction. The Druid immediately tried to heal the Unicorn, whose Hit Points were frozen on 1, but the only result of her actions was a smirk from the Dark Shaman. "This is the radiant Ishni, who is now busy destroying her own forest. I have to give my apprentice his due: he had no lack of imagination. It takes talent to think of taking emotions of light emanating from this relic of the past, and transforming them into the mist filling this forest. A good idea. Midial assured me that soon the Dark Forest will turn into the Cursed Forest; you'll just have to wait a little – a year or two at the most. Come then, apprentice, you have work to do here."

"Is this the moment of truth then?" wrote Anastaria straight away. *"Mahan, we already gained*

the abilities, at least five classes have been renewed, so I think you can afford to fail the quest. Consider it."

"But what about finding out what that crystal *is? Or where the Shadows in the Reverse Side come from? How did Geranika find them?"* I immediately replied to the girl as I slowly followed the Shaman. If there was one thing I'd learned since meeting Anastaria it was how to use chat in a way that couldn't be detected by those around me. May not seem much, but it was an advantage all the same.

"Your dagger." A dark dagger formed in Geranika's hand, which he passed towards me. "Plunge it into the heart of this green embarrassment and we will commence the in-depth exploration of the Reverse Side. We will be transported to the source of power, you'll go through the initiation and in time you will become my right hand, replacing Midial. Time to act, apprentice!"

I took the dagger and slowly approached Kornik. Anastaria was right: this was the moment of truth. Now, either I refuse, get respawned at the Guardian's glade and bring Malabar the good news of the new abilities, or I kill Kornik and cross over to the Shadow. Moreover, if I refuse, the only punishment I would sustain would be being sent to the mines to await the decision of the parole committee. My Reputation would not be reduced, because I would've failed the quest, so things wouldn't be too bad. I didn't have all that much to fear from several clans declaring war on me either: I had a specially trained Rogue to protect me. Now, what would happen if I complete the quest successfully? My Reputation would vanish, but it's not like I'd need it anymore. Furthermore, Plinto would follow me, as would my Officers. So it would just be Anastaria, who would refuse, and I had to think about Barsina. I wonder, would the Druid go against the rest of the world? I don't think so somehow: five against several hundred million? Pfft! Easy as pie!

"Apprentice?" Geranika stepped next to me, his eyebrow raised questioningly, "You hesitate?"

"No, teacher, I am thinking," I had no desire whatsoever to kill the unconscious goblin lying in front of me, so I was playing for time. I had to gather the courage to do that for which I'd come so far.

"Then make me happy, apprentice, by sharing your thoughts," Geranika immediately suggested.

"Mahan, I know you've probably had enough of me already, but the quest has been renewed once again." Anastaria just couldn't help herself, by the looks of it. *"Now, again, it sounds like 'to prevent him from completing the trial'. All this gear changing is beginning to wear me down. I won't be doing anything – it's totally up to you now."*

"My, my! The first smart thought in a week!" a message from Plinto appeared. *"Stacey, you'd better be careful with that, or you'll grow fond of this 'thinking' thing and may have to give up being a Paladin. What'd happen to carrying the Light to the masses via the time-honored 'fist in the face' method?"*

"Apprentice, have you fallen asleep?" Geranika distracted me from reading chat. "What are you thinking about?"

"I think it would be wrong to kill Kornik with your dagger. It seems ... too simple somehow," I uttered, again playing for time as my gaze combed the room for anything that might help me. But nothing caught my eye except Ishni. I wonder, is she in pain without her horn? Horns?

"So what do you propose?" asked Geranika in surprise, "Feed him to some beast?"

"No," I smiled, having made my decision. "I have a different proposal. As far as I know, the Unicorn's horn is a very potent artifact of Light. It would carry great symbolic meaning to destroy the Harbinger of Light with such an object. It might even absorb the goblin's powers, becoming even more potent than before. Although I have no idea how it could be used when dealing with Shadows."

"Ye-e-s!" said Geranika slowly, looking pleased. "For that we must make the goblin conscious again, so that he can see his powers being sucked into the horn with his own eyes. Pain, despair, hopelessness ... you are a worthy apprentice! Although you're wrong if you doubt the horn's usefulness! Ha ha ha!" To destroy a Harbinger of Light with a Unicorn's horn! Apprentice, I am proud of you!"

"Oh! Mahan, you've gained an admirer. Now at least one NPC in all of Barliona will be friendly to you." That came from Clutzer ... you could see Plinto's tutelage right away. These two should really be kept apart or they'd catch all the worst habits from each other.

"The horn." Geranika disappeared for a moment and returned with a red velvet box. "I will now bring the Harbinger back to consciousness, then you shall run him through and we will go on to conquer the world."

I lifted the lid of the box and stared at Ishni's large, thirty centimeter-long, spiraling, snow-white, broken-off horn. The thing I'd be using to kill Kornik in a few moments. I hoped that the horn of Light would absorb the Shaman's essence and not allow it to be destroyed. When I manage to escape from Geranika, I'll think of a way to bring back the Harbinger. I was sure this would somehow be possible. I couldn't think of another way to both complete Geranika's task and keep Kornik alive. Well, then ... I just had to hope that I wasn't wrong on this.

"Apprentice!" the quiet, weak and somehow broken voice of the goblin reached my ears. "Are you with the traitor? The horn? You decided to absorb my powers? Yeees ... you will make a worthy Dark One ... you may rejoice now, traitor." His last words were for Geranika, who was standing at my side. "You got what you wanted. Barliona will be yours ..."

"I always knew that, my vanquished foe," replied Geranika. "Before you die, you may say your final word to your killer."

"A word? Is there any point? He went through the three trials; he destroyed everything he believed in. I have nothing to say to him other than: I am disappointed ..."

"Music ... Kornik, your words are music to my

ears," smiled Geranika. "Apprentice, don't drag your heels now ..."

When I heard the last words of the Harbinger I was engulfed with anger. He's disappointed?! So this ungrateful green bastard, whose essence I'm planning to save, is displeased? Well then ... if I chose to act, act I must. ...

I lifted Ishni's horn above my head and froze. It was as if time had stopped: Geranika froze, Kornik was silent, having told me everything that he thought of me, even my clan was standing quietly aside, not daring to distract me by speaking. I looked into the brown eyes, wishing to find in them understanding, but there was only intense hatred there. ... Kornik believed that I had betrayed him. That's that then ... everyone is free to think as they please. The main thing was that I finally understood what had to be done. Despite the fog of hate, the goblin still clung to the hope of staying alive ... I'd better not disappoint my teacher then, even if he does think I'm a traitor. With these thoughts my hand went down.

"NO-O-O!" A scream of pain sounded throughout the entire torture room. That's it; my choice had been made.

"The fluffy northern beastie of doom has landed," Clutzer commented, just as I was being twisted in a whirlwind of changing abilities.

"I agree," continued Plinto, "we're toast."

CHAPTER TWELVE

THE BIRTH OF THE DRAGON

'THE MAKING OF A DARK SHAMAN' quest has been failed. After the completion of the scenario you will be transported to the Pryke Copper Mine.

Your character has acquired a new class ability. The ability update has taken place for all players with the Shaman class.

What can I say ...? When you start acting on instinct instead of logic, it can lead to some incredibly frightening stuff. My task was simple: to kill Kornik, allow Geranika to become my master, find out all his secrets and that was it – time for mass jubilation and rejoicing ... as if!

"I renounce you, apprentice!" wheezed Geranika as he fell to the floor. Shadows started to shoot out of his hands, but were immediately sucked into the horn, vanishing into it as if it were an abyss. The horn itself started to do something unbelievable. I understood that it had no plans to end up in Geranika's chest, but why would it spread this strange glow around the entire NPC? It'd end up bumping him off at this rate. ...

"From this moment on you will have no enemy more terrible in the whole of Barliona than me," spat the Dark Shaman and with a terrible scream tore the horn out of his chest, threw it at me and disappeared, leaving a large puddle of dark blood behind him.

"Clutzer, Eric and Leite, hands on the bowls – gather the blood," Anastaria said, beginning to fire off commands straight away. "Plinto, free the prisoners. I'm on the door. Barsa, heal the goblin! Mahan, you must tell us why you decided to fail everything, but later. Ah, damn!"

The same glow that had enveloped me a few moments earlier was spreading to all the other clan members, with one difference; the light aura failed to disappear. I picked up Ishni's horn (Geranika's throw lacked the strength to reach me), and looked at the other players. Lit up like a bunch of Christmas trees, they were examining their properties in complete astonishment.

"While we are completing the scenario the cool down is 0 seconds," Eric read slowly, almost syllable by syllable, once he got back onto his feet.

"Save the chit-chat for later. Plinto! Hurry up! Get the prisoners out! The blood is evaporating. Quick, get it into flasks! What do you mean you don't have any?! What sort of raid prep is this? Here you go! Well that does it!"

Anastaria's last shout was understandable: three Fallen Vampires flew into the torture room.

"Argada Urhant!" shouted Eric and crashed into the incoming mobs at full speed. "I'll hold them!"

I even managed a smile at the idea of a level 65 tank running toward three 250-level Fallen Vamps and screaming that he would hold them back, but in a few seconds my smile gave way to bewilderment. Eric was alive and well, while the Vampires ... the new arrivals froze as five Shadows emerged around each of them. They were also frozen – at least they weren't doing anything. So that's how future battles with Geranika's forces would go ... . The meaning of the ten seconds in the ability description became clear. For ten seconds a Shadow was vulnerable. ...

"Take them down already!" shouted Eric, trying to destroy at least one Shadow. "I'm like a gnat next to elephants."

"Plinto!" Anastaria and I shouted simultaneously, hurrying to the aid of the Warrior.

"You really can't manage by yourselves?" grumbled the Rogue, and then turned into a whirlwind, speeding past me and circling around the mobs. In a few seconds the Shadows were gone. Tiredly, with a clearly audible sigh of relief, the Vampires hit the floor and ... fell asleep. ...

"Mahan, don't just stand there! Help me free the prisoners! Would you gather the Lord of Shadow's blood already? Barsa! Why is Kornik's Life Bar not at maximum? Guys, stop faffing around! Geranika could come back at any moment!"

"He will not come, Siren," croaked the goblin, as soon as Clutzer removed the steel clamp holding the Shaman's head in place. "The Horn of Ishni did what I lacked the strength to do ..."

"So my guess was right then? He was immortal, but now he can be destroyed?"

"Why is everyone calling you a Siren, by the way?" Plinto immediately butted in. "You good at signing or something? Or is it the usual: 'I'm a girl with a secret and my lips are sealed'?"

"Yes, you are correct, Paladin-General of Eluna." Kornik tried to sit up, but despite being completely healed, lacked the strength for it. "A Unicorn's horn cannot destroy anyone, but it can strip someone of their invulnerability. From this day on, Geranika has ceased being a god and even this unknown source of power of his won't save him: a splinter of the horn became embedded in him forever. So, it looks like you've been hiding your special nature ... believe this sick old goblin – this is foolish. The very rumor that Sirens are still alive could lead to some very interesting developments. Think about that ..."

I don't get it: did the Game Administration just use Kornik to openly tell Anastaria that revealing her race would lead to a quest? Hmmm ... looks like the girl will pick up another quest chain, either a normal one or a scenario ... damn, and she'll be doing it back in Phoenix, of course. I had to have a chat with Stacey about that, perhaps we'd get invited too. ...

"You have my thanks, Harbinger." It looked like Anastaria's thoughts were traveling along similar lines, because she managed to bow to Kornik, even if it meant stopping the freeing of Ishni for a moment. "I will think about your words ..."

"As for you, the twice-fallen ... " As soon as the last clamp holding the goblin in place was removed, the Harbinger's brown eyes rested on me. Very unlike his usually wry look, this cold, heavy stare went right through me. "You and I are going to have a long and thorough talk. You will explain to me why Yalininka and Almis had to die, and then we will go to Renox, where you will tell him why his son left this world forever."

"Teacher," I tried to explain myself, but Kornik immediately interrupted me.

"You are not worthy of calling me that name!" Where on earth did this NPC get so much energy to put behind his words? "You are neither worthy of the 'Great Shaman' title, nor of the Dragon Totem, nor of having been taught at all! You betrayed everything you believed in when you bought into Geranika's promises. I mourn the day when you flew to Farstead, dooming Almis to an inglorious death ...." After this tirade Kornik abruptly jumped to his feet, muttered something like "I'm sorry, Ishni, I can't ..." and disappeared.

"Plinto hold the door! Small fries, help embody the Shadows! Barsa, switch to the Unicorn, I don't like that single Hit Point she's on. Mahan! You can cry about your missed opportunities later! Got any scrolls? Then heal Ishni."

After giving everyone their orders, Anastaria once again turned to untangling the Unicorn. As soon as the last tube covering the terrible wound on Ishni's head was disconnected, the legs of the Heart of the Dark Forest gave way and she fell to the floor.

"Heal harder!" growled Anastaria, frantically starting to heal the victim. "She may die!"

"Argada Urhant!" Eric's exclamation came from somewhere behind us, Clutzer was shouting something, Plinto was laughing ... looked like the guys were having fun back there!

"It is futile, Paladin." Ishni's calm and clear voice sounded throughout the torture room. With effort, the Unicorn lifted her head and looked at Anastaria. "It is not within your power to save me, Siren. Even the uninitiated Dragon standing next to you is incapable of healing me. I wouldn't survive an hour without my horn or the energy that was fed to me by this tube. Only Eluna has the power to heal me, but I do not see a Priest among you who would be able to appeal to her ..."

"We have the horn," Anastaria immediately replied, "we can restore it if you only tell us how."

"That is impossible." Ishni shook her head. "I shall say it again, only the Goddess has the power to heal this."

"Argh!" growled Anastaria and stopped healing. "Is there anything we can do for you? I swear by the goodwill of the Goddess that I will carry out your last wish!"

Yeah ... so this is how Anastaria has come to have such high reputation among NPCs. I really had a great deal to learn from her still: she's trying to fish out a quest even from an NPC who's at death's door. I would have never thought of this. ...

"Tell the Guardian of the Dark Forest that ..."

"Quiet, you!" I interrupted the Unicorn. "Ishni, do you really think that we'd allow you to die without trying everything to save you first? Anastaria, Barsa, don't stop healing for a second!"

"Dragon! It is not within your power ..." Ishni persisted.

"Let me be the judge of what is and isn't within my power. Girls, you need a special invitation? Don't just stand there!"

"Mahan!" came Plinto's happy shout. "We've downed twenty Vampires and it looks like they're blocking the entrance. We can't get out of here! Told ya the Lieutenant was a trifle. This is where things really get started!"

"So," I began to think out loud, "we have: a Unicorn's horn – one unit. A Unicorn, without her horn – also one unit. The task in hand is to combine the horn and the Unicorn into one whole. Potential restriction: the combination is only possible with the aid of the Goddess. Experiment number one ..."

I crouched by Ishni and pressed the horn to the wound. The Unicorn winced with pain, but patiently awaited the result: total failure. As soon as I let go, the horn fell off. It didn't work.

"Why don't you use some glue," came some 'sound advice' from Clutzer. By the looks of it, the entire clan had gathered round, watching my attempted 'repair'.

"Does anyone have anything suitable?" I looked at the other players.

"Here's some healing salve." Anastaria handed me a small jar containing a green substance. "It won't do any harm, and you may try using it as a glue."

"Thanks! Experiment number two," I said, knowing full well that the editor of the video for whom I was now making these comments would most likely consign them to the cutting-room floor. "Using a green healing salve as an adhesive."

The horn managed to stay in place for the grand total of five seconds, until the Unicorn shook her head, making the horn drop and roll onto the floor. That didn't work. ...

"We should put a wire around it," came yet another 'genius' piece of advice from Clutzer.

"I am grateful to you, Shaman-Dragon, but it is beyond your power to put things back the way they were. Just let me go, you already gave the Dark Forest a priceless gift: a chance at survival. Don't forget me, weep over my fate ... this is the best you can do now. Only Eluna ..."

Ishni continued to reiterate the impossibility of her being healed, but the light bulb that had lit inside my head took my thoughts elsewhere. Weep ... Eluna ... Tear of Eluna, the stone lying in my inventory ... wasn't it essentially a part of the Goddess? This meant that I could try at least. ...

I took the Tear out of the bag and looked at it carefully. It appeared to be an ordinary stone of silvery hue, with a strange description, demanding an appeal to the Goddess ... to hell with it all!

The design mode greeted me with a reassuring blackness. It'd been a while since I'd entered it – since the moment I crafted the pine cones. An entire two days ... it seemed a hell of a lot longer than that. ...

The horn and the Tear of Eluna appeared in the design mode almost the instant I pictured them: the snow-white, spiraling horn and the silvery droplet of divine sorrow. Clutzer was right, even if he didn't understand it himself: the Unicorn's horn had to be attached with a wire. And it couldn't be tied down with just one, but rather attached with the help of the Tear – a part of Eluna. Perhaps after that the Unicorn would be able to last until we took her to the temple, because at the moment she'd decided to kick the proverbial bucket. With every hoof it had. ... Like hell it would! Not on my watch!

On the hundredth ring that fell apart with a clank, I realized that ordinary Copper or Steel wire, Copper, Tin, Bronze, Silver and Iron rings (or even a few Rare ones from the recipes that Evolett sent me) wouldn't do. They didn't want to join the horn and the Tear together, hard as I tried to impose the essence of a link on them. ... It seemed that they were too low-level for this task. Stop! Low level!

The image of the Holy Ring of Dreall was lying on the shelf of Unique and Unrepeatable items, so I didn't have to create it anew. I placed all three items before my eyes and for a while couldn't work up the courage to attempt to combine them. I was afraid to think what Anastaria would say if the ring, which I was sure she had already set her sights on, broke in front of her eyes. Although ... 'nothing ventured nothing gained'. ... With this thought the three items moved toward each other. I wondered if Rick's belt, which I'd equipped, would be of any help.

"Yeah ...," said Anastaria slowly, when I finally opened my eyes, "so that's how legends are born ... impressive ..."

The bright light that had shone from my body gradually faded, returning the torture room back into dark gloom and giving way to a torrent of announcements.

Item created: Unicorn Horn of Eluna's Blessing.

Description: by combining un-combinable items you have created the unreal and attained the incredible.

The conditions of the 'Creation of a Holy Artifact' quest have been met. Take Unicorn Horn of Eluna's Blessing to the Emperor of Malabar to receive your reward.

Skill increase:

+1 to Crafting. Total: 7.

+3 to primary profession of Jewelcrafting. Total: 105.

+ 1 to the Blessed Artificer achievement.

Total: 4.

"You won't be able to run around using Stealth with a sign like that above you," said Plinto slowly. "Getting to the Emperor will take some thinking."

I wanted to ask him what he was on about when Eric caught my eye. A bright icon showing the Emperor's coat of arms with the sign 'Rescuer of the Throne' was hanging above the dwarf's head.

"You said something about a wish before," I said slyly, looking at Anastaria, "does your promise still hold?"

"You know, I never know what to expect with you," smiled the girl. "I keep my promises. Make a wish."

"Here's my wish then! Take this horn," there was no stopping me now, "put it next to Ishni's wound and call upon Eluna as her Paladin-General. Get her to give us a hand."

"Firstly, I am the Goddess's warrior, not her Priest. There is no precedent in the history of Barliona for the Goddess answering the call of a warrior. Secondly, you do understand that if a miracle does take place, and the Goddess appears, the horn will disappear? We will fail to save the Emperor."

"Are you refusing to carry out my wish?" I raised my eyebrows in surprise. "Stacey, the camera is still recording. Can you imagine what people will say about you? The Great Anastaria herself is going back on her word ... 'Disgraceful behavior, shame on her!'." With these last words I couldn't help but laugh.

Try as I might to keep my composure, the girl's befuddled expression was so hilarious that it was more than I could do to restrain myself.

Silently taking the restored horn, Anastaria sat next to Ishni, put the artifact that I'd created next to the wound, bowed her head and ... sung. The meaning of the song remained obscure, as the words were certainly not in common language, but the singing itself ... it drew you in, brought tears to your eyes, made you want to laugh, to rejoice and be sad all at once. Together with the divine voice of the girl, the melodious and slightly sorrowful song shocked and shook the listener, who was left wanting to do only one thing – bow his head to the singer, close his eyes and enjoy each moment of life. ... I was exceptionally grateful to Anastaria for asking me to record it all on video. Now it would've been fitting to shout, like they did back when the first video cameras appeared: "I filmed this! Oh God! I filmed this!!!"

"Stand up, warrior." The sound of a woman's voice brought me back to reality. I lifted up my head and my eyes met those of a woman floating in the air. If before this moment I believed Anastaria was the most beautiful woman in the world – to have the most amazing voice and to embody the ideal of beauty – I now realized how wrong I was. ... The Goddess was ... divine, despite the obvious tautology. "My warrior, you have managed to overcome yourself and summoned me with a pure heart. I can see very well how difficult a decision it was for you to begin the summons, how difficult it was to give up on the chance of saving the

Emperor and becoming his close advisor ... you are a Siren of your word and I am proud that there are such beings among my warriors. From now on I name you Lieutenant of the Paladins! Wear this title with honor!"

The air was filled with the sound of solemn music and Anastaria was caught in a whirlwind of transformations. The girl rose a few centimeters into the air, twisted – as if struck by an electric charge, her mouth opening in a silent scream – and then was gently placed back on the ground. The changes to her character were complete. Anastaria didn't look different in any way, except ... hmmm ... was it normal that her Life Bar now sported Eluna's icon next to it?

There was a slight movement of the air and the Goddess was now next to the Unicorn. Ishni struggled to lift up her head and the horn that Anastaria had placed on her fell off once again. A smile lit up Eluna's face, she made a slight movement and the horn rose into the air.

"You did everything right," said the Goddess, "Now we just have to wait for the Tear to be washed in the blood of an innocent and dissolve, manifesting the miracle of healing. Let's speed up this process." The horn returned to its original place on Ishni's forehead, after which the Unicorn vanished. "I healed Ishni and sent her back to the Guardian. No-one in Barliona could take better care of her than him. As for you," Eluna appeared in front of Eric, Plinto, Clutzer, Leite and Barsina, leant over and kissed their foreheads.

An icon of Eluna, somewhat smaller than Anastaria's, immediately appeared next to each player marked by the Goddess. Then Eluna finally stood opposite me.

"An uninitiated Dragon," she said thoughtfully, "a killer who doomed the Princess of Malabar to four months of solitude ... one who risked everything and ... I will meet you later, after you clean up the mess that is plaguing the Dark Forest. We shall meet again soon, Shaman!"

"A killer?" asked Anastaria when the Goddess had disappeared. "Mahan, how could you have killed Slate if we left him back in the tent?"

"Stacey, I'm as shocked as you are," I gave the girl my honest answer. "Damn! He had again dropped out of the group! I had no idea how I managed to kill him! When I was rubbing out the players, I'm certain that Slate wasn't among them ... damn! Now I get it why the announcement came up saying that I would be taken back to Pryke after the completion of the scenario."

"WHAT?!" I was deafened by the simultaneous shout of my entire clan.

"No need to look at me like that! I thought that was because of the other players. ... I guess that's what's behind it ... but when did I kill Slate off? Plinto! I have a separate task for you. I could be taken at any moment and right now I can't guarantee that I'll be able to defend myself and avoid getting stuck in the mines for eight and a half years. Your task is to do your best to drag out time before the Legendary items have to be returned. They certainly can't be given back for free, so try to drive a hard bargain. But before you start haggling, try not to give anything back for as long as possible. And no use looking at me like that, Stacey! Those guys had a choice either to go after me or to wait. They decided to take a swipe at the Seathistles clan. Tough luck!"

"So you're asking me to become an enemy to a whole load of people? As well as the clans to which they belong?" asked Plinto, just to be clear.

"Yes."

"Consider it done, boss," a nasty smile spread across Plinto's face. "Now they won't have any choice but to come looking for me. Excellent! Thanks Mahan, that's a real bonus!"

"Talk about putting a fox in the hen house," muttered Anastaria, watching the overjoyed Plinto, Then she re-composed herself and continued to issue orders: "Our task is to make it back to the surface and leave the Castle alive. Suggestions?"

"Stacey, aren't you a Paladin-General, like Kornik said?" I couldn't help asking, all suggestions aside. "Eluna has appointed you a Lieutenant. Doesn't that mean you were just demoted?"

"Yeah, right to the bottom of the career ladder," replied the girl with a smile. "It's such a catastrophic setback that I don't even know how to keep going after this."

"And if you were to speak seriously?"

"Paladin-General is a title given within the Class, like 'Great' or 'High' Shaman. A Lieutenant of Paladins ... this is a spiritual rank, bestowed by Eluna herself. And don't ask me what it brings; there is no information about it anywhere and I'm speaking as someone who knows my own Class like the back of my hand. I will have to test everything thoroughly, read and experiment. ... Very many possibilities have opened up now, so I'll probably get in touch with Alviona and get her to tell me what she's been cooking up."

"Alviona?"

"The Paladins' Kalatea. Is that clearer? Plinto! What's with the door?"

"Blocked tight! By a pile of sleeping Vampires on our side and from the Castle side ... I can't say, really. Maybe they've dumped an elephant on it. It's not budging at all. We'll end up living here like gophers: you can't see us, but we exist!"

"I always thought that Vampires sleep either in coffins or don't sleep at all," said Clutzer quietly, once the rest of the clan got lost in thought. We had to find a way out of the torture room, but no options presented themselves other than sitting here for a few days pressing the 'Character stuck' button and hoping to be teleported to the nearest respawn point. "I wonder, will they behave themselves after waking up or will they have to be given another lesson in manners? Plinto, why don't you put them through training, as you did with us? We already have one exclusive video with the Goddess, so we can make another: 'Plinto, setting the Vampires on the right path'. And then we'll invite them into our clan!"

"My fighters will be just fine back once back in

the clan from which they were taken." The painfully familiar voice of the Patriarch sounded from a far corner. "I won't allow them to be 'set', as you put it, on any 'right path'. Siren?" Great surprise showed through the Patriarch's voice. "What are you doing in the company of the owner of the Enemy?"

"And what are YOU doing here?" I managed to ask before Anastaria could reply.

"The Castle's defenses have weakened, so I risked checking if I could aid my warriors. You said that you came to the Dark Forest to destroy the taint, so I activated my fear and began to follow it. That's what led me here. Siren, you haven't answered me. What are you doing associating with the owner of the Enemy?" the Patriarch repeated his question insistently, stepping away out of the corner and closer to the center of the torture room.

"You are mistaken, Patriarch," replied the girl with a bow. "I am not in the company of the owner of the Enemy. I am in the company of the uninitiated Enemy himself. He hasn't yet become aware of his strength, but I'm sure that soon a real Dragon will emerge in Barliona!"

"YOU LIE!" The Lieutenant, the General ... it turned out that they were mere kids when it came to slapping various negative buffs on you! I was thrown to the floor and pressed into it with such force that my breath was knocked right out of me – my head felt like an anvil upon which the entire workforce of the Undermountain kingdom was trying to create its next masterpiece. Realizing that I had zero strength left for lifting up my head to check the condition of the others, I called up the frames of the group before my eyes: everyone had only 10% of Hit Points left and had acquired a 10-minute Petrification status, while their stats were reduced by 40%. ... All in all, the list of debuffs was quite something. "THE ENEMY HAS DEPARTED FROM THIS WORLD!"

"I am telling the truth," said Anastaria hoarsely, half-choked into silence.

"You can't get rid of her that easily," Plinto's pointed remark sounded like a gong. He could speak? "I can lend you a noose – you should slip it around her neck and give it a good pull."

"WHAT?!" Another wave of debuffs hit the players. "YOU HAVE ESCAPED MY WRATH?!"

"As my boss likes to say: yup! Listen, mister, I realize you're unbelievably tough and all, but how about you stop destroying these guys, eh? I don't care about the Siren, even if she can sing better than anyone, but why drag the others into it? I mean, we've been trying to free your fighters, by the by, and you've up and decided to rub us out."

"This is impossible!" said the Patriarch in a normal voice now. "Only one thing in all of Barliona would enable you to withstand my voice ... is it with you?" the Vampire exclaimed after some time.

"If you mean the Fang of the Patriarch," grinned Plinto, "yes, it's hanging around my neck, like any self-respecting fang should."

"Plinto?" his name flew off my lips the moment I was able to speak again.

"Have a look at my amulet, I've opened its properties. I think that should answer all your questions."

Altameda with the Fang of the Patriarch of the Vampires.

Description: The energy of hundreds of thousands of sentients who've had their lives ended by this fang filled it with incredible power. Now not a single sentient will be able to block your character for more than a second.

Item class: Legendary.

Limitations: none.

"Yes, this is it," said the Patriarch, looking at Plinto thoughtfully. "My Fang could only have been obtained by someone acting on their own, after overcoming the guards, but I received no news that the wardens fell. Who are you?"

"Just a Master-Rogue." When needed, Plinto was quite capable of making a polite bow. "One who has dedicated his life to perfecting Stealth."

"A master of Stealth?" the Vampire's eyebrows flew up, "Now I understand why the guards are still alive: they are guarding an empty box ... if you were a Vampire, our race would be proud of you ..."

"Let's talk about that later." Plinto, closed access to his amulet's properties and looked at the Patriarch. "Why don't you release the others? It just so happens that our clan has both a Siren and a Dragon ... and Stacey, why is Mahan still uninitiated?

Didn't eat his porridge?"

"Initiation starts at level 100," the girl immediately replied. "Mahan is at 82 at the moment, a little more and he'll start to get seriously warped. I know, since I've been there myself."

"And when did you manage to change? Was it when you unlocked the ..."

"Dragon," ignoring Plinto and Anastaria's conversation, the Patriarch appeared next to me. "It looks like you're not just the Master of the Enemy, but the Enemy himself! That is why from you I sense ... fear ... despair, the futility of resistance and ... awe. Siren," the Patriarch once again addressed Anastaria, "can you explain to me why you are with the Enemy?"

"The time of enmity ended long ago," came the girl's immediate reply. "Only one Siren and one Dragon are left in Barliona. What sense is there in destroying each other, if that would never bring back the former greatness of our races? On the contrary, we must unite, because now there are too many hunters intent on hanging our heads as trophies on their walls. The Dragon is young and inexperienced; the hunters will kill him. My task is to teach him to defend himself. Only later, when the danger is behind us, will we be able to settle scores originating in our ancient enmity, but not now. For the time being we have to work together."

I wasn't really getting what Anastaria was on about, but the words flew off her lips smoothly and without hesitation. I had the feeling that she'd prepared and memorized this speech in advance, and the time had finally come to perform it.

"I hear you, daughter of guile," smiled the Patriarch, " and I agree, others should not be allowed to destroy the last Dragon. I cannot dissolve his essence right now, but a time will come when all that will be left of the Enemy will be the man ... Mahan!" The Vampire turned toward me. "I take back the vassal's oath I gave to your ancestors. I will help you now, but after this Castle is destroyed a ransom will be laid on your head. Vampires, Cyclopes, Sirens, Titans, if any still remain in this world – I will call upon everyone. Although, no, I will leave you one Siren, who so fiercely came to your defense and ... yes, this will be interesting ... Plinto!" The Vampire addressed the Rogue. "Look into my eyes!"

As if hypnotized, despite his amulet, Plinto came up to the Patriarch and their eyes met. I once again silently thanked Anastaria for getting us to switch on the cameras. The Vampire's red eyes started to emit bright white mist, which, like a living entity, started to stream towards Plinto's eyes. Once a bridge of mist formed between the player and the NPC, a red cloud appeared above the Rogue's head and started to circle clockwise.

"I agree," Plinto said for some reason and immediately a small tornado funnel of red mist started to descend toward my Fighter's head. "Aaaaah! Noooo!" As soon as the funnel touched the Rogue, a terrible scream of pain echoed through the torture room.

"Aside from the Siren," continued the Patriarch,

once his eyes had returned to their usual red color and Plinto had turned into a bright red cocoon, blocking any sound, "there will also be a lone Vampire who will not hunt you: a Higher Vampire. A Dragon, a Siren and a Vampire ... if anyone told me ten thousand years ago that a clan like that would appear in Barliona, I would have drunk that sentient dry without further ado. Fools have no right to walk the earth. But now ... stop lying around on the ground, my son," he addressed the prostrate Plinto, the bloody cocoon now fallen from him. "There is much you'll have to be taught. I won't let you leave the Dark Forest for the next three months."

"I have obligations, father." Once up, the Rogue immediately bent to his knees before the Patriarch. "The Dragon helped me, so in the next year I will be by his side. A word of honor is worth more than life!" Yeah ... where was the world heading to if even Plinto dropped into a grandiose style of speaking?

"Enemy." After some thought the Patriarch turned to me. "My son has a lot of learning to do, as do you. At the moment he doesn't know how to use his newly acquired power, and if he were released right now, sunlight would destroy him in the course of a minute. I am prepared to buy my son out of your clan three months. Is it worth me making you an offer or is your mind quite made up? Clothing, jewelry, weapons," said the Vampire slowly, looking me directly in the eye. "You may choose anything you like for yourself and for your clan. Remember the ring that you transformed? I will give each member of your clan a similar item in exchange for Plinto's three-month absence. Do you agree?"

"*Mahan! I think you realize what this means!*" A message from Anastaria immediately appeared in clan chat. "*Just try and refuse this deal. I'LL BURY YOU!*"

"*I will definitely have to be trained: there are enough new abilities to make your mind boggle,*" wrote Plinto. "*Imagine this: I can now drink players' blood, taking off part of their Energy, Hit Points and Experience! :) :) :) And how the heck did you get through the modification? That hurt like hell.*"

"No!" I shook my head, instinctively sensing the gaze of seven pairs of surprised eyes on me. "Plinto will stay as he is, without the ransom. If the alternative to training is him being incinerated by the sun every minute, I see no sense in limiting my Fighter. I decline your offer of items for me and my clan. They are expendable things – we will simply outgrow them and will have nothing to remind us of this moment. I doubt Higher Vampires are born every day. I would rather remember this as the day I declined the great gifts of my future Enemy. We will meet again and it is unworthy of a Dragon to destroy his foe with his own gifts."

"*Anastaria, I have salt and pepper,*" typed Clutzer, once the torture room descended into silence. "*Eric and Leite will get the fire going and Barsa will find some rope. You get the grill. Shaman kebab is on the menu.*"

"*You guessed wrong,*" she answered straight away. "*This evening I'll be expecting a thorough analysis of the situation and a list of potential reasons for refusal. Mahan, I'll be honest with you, I didn't expect you to give a speech like that. On a 100-point rating system, it would've scored 140. Rock on!"*

"Just as noble as your ancestors," said the Patriarch slowly. "This will not save you from the hunt, Dragon!"

"I will not be hiding, Vampire," I replied in the same tone. "But you can help us. The Supreme Spirits of the Higher and Lower worlds said that you are the only sentient in Barliona who can tell us about Geranika's power. Your tale would be a worthy price for Plinto."

"Geranika's power? You are interested in the throne of the Creator's son? Well, I suppose I can tell you about it, but only after you free all my warriors. I don't have the ability to destroy the shadows – unlike you, by the looks of it. One good turn deserves another, Shaman!"

"And what about Plinto?"

"You've declined a reward for his presence in my castle," said the Patriarch with a nasty grin. "So now I'm dictating the terms. Free my warriors and then I will tell you about the source of Geranika's power." The Vampire smirked once again, waved his hand and the twilight of the torture room disappeared, changing to the sunlit square of the Castle of the Fallen.

"My son," came a voice from the mist into which the Patriarch transformed. "The sun will not affect you during this battle. Prove to me that I made the right choice."

"YOU DARED TO ATTACK OUR LORD?" Almost immediately after the Vampire's last words came the thundering voice of the General. "WE WILL DESTROY YOU!"

"I won't be able to freeze this crowd, even without the cool down," said Eric, somewhat at a loss, watching the huge multitude of Vampires, Mages and Elementals surround us from every side.

"I too can embody them only one at a time," muttered Anastaria as the eyes of the entire clan looked at me.

"For the next three days I'm still useless as a Shaman," was my immediate excuse. "You know well enough that ..."

"KILL THEM!" boomed the General's voice again and a great wave of mobs sped towards us with only one aim: to send us back to the Guardian's glade.

"Plinto, get out of here!" was all I had time to shout before a huge ice boulder pinned me to the ground. Something told me that Plinto must avoid dying at all costs before his training, so I tried to warn the Fighter. A pity I didn't quite manage it. My Life Bar flickered as it descended to zero, and I embarked on a thrilling journey of prisoner respawn, straight into oblivion. ...

Player Barsina has used the scroll of resurrection. Do you wish to be resurrected?

The pitch-blackness was broken by a bright

green, almost acid-colored sign before my eyes. So this is what the resurrection process looks like for prisoners. ... Strange; how did Barsina manage to survive the fight? You can only resurrect outside of combat. ...

"I told you it would work," I could hear Eric's voice say. My eyes gradually regained focus and I started to look around. My surroundings were strewn with bodies of sleeping Vampires and Mages, and even the Elementals were floating peacefully above the ground. How did they manage to win?

"What did I miss?" I managed to force out of myself. All in all the resurrection process was far from pleasant. It made you slow, as if you still hadn't quite awoken yet: there was drowsiness and a strange apathy. I wanted to do only one thing right now: lie down on the ground and finish sleeping off the twelve hours that were allotted to me before respawn.

"Nothing major. We got rid of the Shadows, though we still got no Experience from them," said Clutzer.

"And the General?"

"He's lying about twenty meters from here. Sleeping like a baby."

"Right. So what happened here?"

"Oh! Today was Barsina's moment of glory," said Anastaria, making the girl look very embarrassed. I looked at the Druid, who lowered her eyes, mystified as to how she'd managed to save everyone. "Catch the video. This is worth seeing for yourself."

You have received a video from player Anastaria.
Duration: 5 minutes.
Do you wish to view it?

It was the first time I could see myself from the outside. As your ordinary everyday user of modern technology, I had many different holograms in which I was celebrating something with friends or family, and even several home-made holographic recordings, such as the time I was handed the 'Free Artist' certificate. But I'd never seen myself from outside within the game. All the videos that I'd edited when playing the Hunter had me behind the camera, so they had never actually featured yours truly. But now ... that was some quirky look I had. ...

"Mahan's gone!" shouted Eric, staring at a foot sticking out from under the boulder. Dammit!" We botched the ending!"

"Everyone stop!" Anastaria immediately commanded. "Our task is to free as many Vampires as possible! Eric, Leite, Clutzer, let's go! Plinto, the Shadows are on you. Barsa and I will heal. We'll fight to the last! Barsa! I said we're healing! What the heck are you doing?!"

"Stacey, cover me!" came the Druid's shout. "I

need ten seconds! I'll try a mass-cast!"

"I'll strangle that small fry," muttered Anastaria, glancing over the battlefield once more. There was the crowd of Vampires running towards the players; mountains of ice, fire, water and earth flying out of the hands of the Mages and the Elementals' bodies; and a small, petite Druid, her face turned to the sky, her arms raised and lips uttering a spell. One second, then another and the avalanche of elements overtook the unmoving girl. All Anastaria could do was throw a Bubble over Barsina at the last moment, extending her life by ten seconds.

"Yup, we botched it!" The words flew out of my Deputy's mouth as the Vampire that appeared next to her raised his sword. The Bubble was still unavailable for the next two minutes, so the girl had nothing to defend herself with and attacking the Vamp was pointless, since there were a hundred more behind him, hell bent on sending the players to the Grey Lands. Anastaria curled up, camera now pointing to the ground, and braced for the blow. A second went by, then another, but the Vampire was in no hurry to attack. Stacey lifted her head and stared, surprised, at the frozen world around her. Or, rather, it wasn't the world that froze, since the players could move just fine. Vampires, Mages and Elementals were the ones standing still. Even the enormous hulk of the General, who could be seen in the background, stopped moving. And then an even stranger thing began to happen.

The place where Barsina was standing became

an enormous, four-meter-high mountain of wet earth and ice: the main force of the attack of the Mages and Elementals hit the Druid. Then the mountain started to shift in a strange fashion, like a volcano before an eruption. Stones and shards of ice began to fall off it, and then the top of the mountain opened, like the bud of a flower, revealing Barsina. Water was flowing down the dome of the Bubble, not causing the girl the least discomfort, but the Druid had other things on her mind. Constantly chanting some verses, which were very reminiscent of a song, the girl flew up several meters into the air. Her upturned head, raised hands – as if calling on some unknown powers –, the dark aura swirling around her and her constant muttering in some unknown language made the players tremble as much as they did before all the mobs. Anastaria shifted her gaze from Barsina to the nearest mob and then it all became clear: short grass, about four centimeters long, started to shoot from the ground and white drops began to ooze out of each blade and float up to the sky, like rain in reverse. As the drops touched the mobs, they were immediately absorbed, revealing the Shadows. The Paladin lifted her head and looked around: the radius of this glade covered about half of the Castle, half which now contained all the Vampires, Mages and Elementals of the Fallen ones.

"Plinto! I don't know how long Barsa can keep this up, so hurry up and dispatch the Shadows! Everyone else give him a hand! Damn!"

Judging by the picture, Barsina's Life Bar was

beginning to plummet rapidly.

"Hang in there, sweetie, please," came Anastaria's muttering as she immediately sent a healing onto the Druid. "At least a couple more minutes ..."

* * *

"That's all of it, pretty much," continued Anastaria as soon as the video finished playing. "I completely ran out of Mana as I was trying to save this madwoman and even quaffed elixirs to gain a few more moments, but as soon as her Hit Points fell to one, Barsina stopped her summons and collapsed onto the stones. Plinto and the others finished off all the Mages, who thankfully didn't have time to come round, so that was the end of it. Midial failed to turn up, so Eric proposed that we raise you straight away. To be honest, I had doubts that we'd get you back – there had to be something different about the prisoner capsules, after all – but, as you can see, it worked just fine. That's it ... "

"Barsa!" I turned to the embarrassed-looking girl. "Can you tell me how you, a professional mercenary, failed to carry out your commander's order?"

As soon as I uttered these words I felt another wave of surprised stares. This time it was only six pairs of eyes, as the Patriarch was nowhere to be seen.

"But I thought that ..." the girl started to excuse herself, falteringly, but I interrupted her:

"Thinking my ass! What were you told? To stand there and heal the guys! And what did you do? You just went and saved everyone on your own initiative!" I walked up to the completely befuddled Druid, looked down at her sternly, just as well her height made that easy, and then smiled and continued: "You know, what I like in people the most is confidence in their own strengths. You were sure that Anastaria had made a mistake and that you had the ability to save us all, and acted contrary to her orders. Thank you!" I was unable to restrain myself and hugged the stunned girl. "If it wasn't for you, we would have failed this scenario for sure, so I have one simple question for you: do you have the Healing stat?"

"Y-yes."

"Then close your eyes. Close 'em, I won't bite." I waited until Barsina really closed her eyes, took out Yalininka's ribbon from my bag and without a moment's hesitation tied it around the girl's head. The Great One said that this was a gift for whomever I believed worthy of it. ... At first I wanted to give the ribbon to Anastaria, but the Paladin already had many Rare treasures. As for Barsina ... I thought that with her deed the girl had proven herself quite sufficiently.

"Un-be-liev-able! uttered Stacey syllable by syllable, "The Great One's ribbon ... Mahan, sometimes I want to nail you down so I can have a good dig through your bag so badly I can barely restrain myself."

"Then let's swap," I parried straight away. "I will give you complete access to my sack and properties, but then you, naturally, must do the same. I bet that picking through your properties would be easily as interesting as just watching you next to me."

"Could be ... could be ... ." Anastaria's face broke in a smile. "I will consider your offer. Although suggesting to a girl to appear practically naked before a man, even if she knows him quite well, is not worthy of a knight."

"When you dig up a knight, do let me know. I'll have a good look at him at least. Barsa," I turned to the girl, "you deserve this gift, wear it with honor. Does this mean we've completely freed all the Patriarch's warriors?"

"Yes, Enemy!" instead of the dumbfounded Druid, the next answer came from the Vampire, who immediately began to command his forces. "The first group, carry away the left side, the second, the right, the third, the center and the torture room, where some of our brothers still remain. Quick, before Midial gets here!" After that he turned to me with a smirk, "Your clan has fulfilled my condition, so I will tell the Siren and my son of Geranika's source of power. After all, they are the ones who saved my warriors. While you, as befits an Enemy, were sitting in the Grey Lands and awaiting revival."

"Oh really?" The words of the Patriarch cut me.

To be more exact: they enraged me and made my blood boil, causing me to completely lose my balance and in general turn off my brain. The parole conditions state that I can't attack NPCs and other players first, do they? Who cares? I'm going back to the mines anyway, what difference would one charge less or one charge more make? I wasn't in the least daunted by the Patriarch's 500 levels: I felt I could shred him with my bare hands right now. "You shouldn't have said that, you crooked-toothed bastard! Defend yourself!" My vision was darkened with uncontained fury and I headed straight for the Patriarch. I wanted only one thing: to catch this impudent traitor and tear him apart with my bare teeth, rip his throat out and make sure his head landed straight in the refuse heap. Some messages were flashing in chat, but I ignored them. I was completely engulfed with rage. Nothing existed except for the smirking Vampire, who was suddenly standing right by the castle wall, and the thirty meters lying between me and just retribution.

"Stand still, you coward! Fight me!" I growled in a terrible voice, as the Patriarch shifted, lightning-fast, to the opposite wall. Another hundred meters! No matter, I'm not lazy, I'll take a walk! Although why walk when I can fly?"

I picked the Patriarch as my target, pushed the ground away and flew towards him. The ground sped under me as if I was on a griffin, but I couldn't be bothered to pay too much heed. I almost fell a few times, but then I unfurled my cape, which immediately lifted me back up.

"You're mocking me!" This was no shout! This was a roar! The Vampire evaded me again and immediately headed straight to the farthest wall of the Castle. Five hundred meters! He's so damn fast! I'll never catch up! I had to think of something, otherwise I'd be chasing this bloodsucker to kingdom come! As I flew up – just as well the cloak did the job as wings – I once again saw the grinning Patriarch. Now this really is strange: he's five hundred meters away, but I can still see his sly mug. Should I fly there? I don't think so!

"TO ME, SLAVE!" After descending to the ground, I looked in the direction of the Patriarch. Right now I didn't have a shred of doubt that he would be unable to disobey my order. He had no choice! The order came from his Master!

"I, the Patriarch of Vampires of the Reardalox clan," said the satisfied-looking Vampire solemnly when he appeared next to me and bent to his knees, "swear a vassal's oath to the new lord. Now and henceforth my life is in your paws and claws and you are free to do with it as you please. I'm sorry, Master, but after the Siren's words I had to follow the order of my former Lord and provoke you to aggression. I understand that you are still young, but we cannot wait for you to reach level 100: there is just too much to be done right now. Feel free to take my life, if that would placate you." The Patriarch bowed down and prostrated himself on the ground. I stepped forward and put my paw on his head. If I pressed it now there would be one less Vampire in Barliona. They are, of course, useful creatures, but they're too much hassle when it came to honor and duty.

"Dragon!" Anastaria's voice came from somewhere to the side of me, snapping me out of my musings – whether to kill the Patriarch or not. "How about you fight someone who didn't swear an oath to you?"

I turned around and couldn't help hissing: a real Siren was standing before me. She had a long tail, like the Nagas, a beautiful bare body, covered only with shells on her chest, an enormous trident, aimed at me and cold blue eyes. One of my ancient Enemies!

"Mahan, snap out of it!" a bunch of tiny people appeared next to the Siren. I'll have to squash them later. ...

"Well, handsome, shall we dance?" smiled the Siren and immediately attacked. The trident glinted a few millimeters from my eyes, leaving a painful scratch on my nose. This was just too much! I turned away from the Patriarch, who was instantly joined by his uninitiated son, and focused on the Siren. The Enemy is fast and experienced, but she has nothing that could beat me, a Dragon! I soared into the sky and planned to swoop down on top of the hated creature, when suddenly a mithril net sparkled and bound itself around my wings. That fiend!

The subdued thump of my hulk hitting the ground was probably heard all the way to Dragonholme.

"Stupid little lizard." The Siren walked up to me, chuckling. I tried to hit her with my tail, but got even more tangled in the net. "Did you really think that you would be able to best me just because you've sprouted some wings? Naive little kid. You will have much to learn before you can enter your second essence or learn how to retain your memory, so for now we shall have to wait a bit and have a chat once things calm down a little. There are three minutes left, so ... stop wriggling already! You'll break your wings off and then we won't hear the end of it! Lie still!"

There was little I could do but give the Siren a thoroughly hate-filled look. Why aren't you finishing me off? It would be so easy to do right now: just lift my head and plunge her trident into my soft neck. And that'd be it – that would end the Dragon. And in general, Anastaria looks somehow unpleasant in this guise ... compared to her unearthly beauty as a human, now the girl's face ... and where are her brown eyes? Brrr ... And I thought she was the most beautiful woman in the world? Ah! Clutzer walked up to me with a strangely thoughtful gaze. Why is he so weird and mysterious? Damn! I was trying to take down the Patriarch!

"Have you recovered?" asked Barsina, with her slight lisp. "Can we untangle you or keep you lying down a bit longer?

"Untangle please," I mumbled, trying to understand what had just happened. As soon as the net fell off me and Eric gave me his hand to help me up, total message chaos appeared before my eyes:

You managed to attain your second nature. From this moment on, you have the ability to transform into a Dragon. Transformation time: 5*(Dragon rank) minutes. Number of transformations: (Dragon rank) per day. You must learn to control yourself in your new guise, otherwise you will be turned back into a human through divine intervention.

A new additional stat has been unlocked for your character: Dragon rank. Current value: 1.

Your reputation with the Vampires of Barliona has been changed to Esteem.

Your character's race has been updated.

Current race: Dragon.

"Now I am no longer concerned for my son," smiled the Patriarch, appearing next to me, "Mahan! I've sworn an oath to you and now none of Barliona's Vampires will be able to harm you. Forgive me once again, but under Aarenoxitolikus's orders I had to provoke the uninitiated Dragon, forcing him to reveal his nature. He foretold such an eventuality. At first I thought that he meant your Totem, but now I can see that I was mistaken. Remain here with my son and I will teach you the ability to open the door into the world of Dragons. Everything I know of Geranika's power I will pen down in a document today and send to the Emperor and the Dark Lord, with a note that it was you and your clan that helped me to come to this decision. Geranika is pure evil and he needs to be destroyed, so I cannot stand idly by ..."

"I ..."

"How touching." we were interrupted by an unpleasant undulating voice coming from the biggest building in the Castle. "A Dragon, a Siren, Vampires ... one big happy family of near-extinct circus freaks! You dared to attack my Castle! You dared to attack my Master! You dared to free my slaves! Well ... I may not have a single warrior left, but you will not leave this place alive!"

As soon as the last word sounded in the air, dark Shadows shot from the hands of 500-level Midial, the Dark Priest of the Fallen, and sped towards us. Damn! Looks like I'm getting sent for respawn today after all!

CHAPTER THIRTEEN
THE JUDGEMENT OF THE GODDESS

"AND WE WERE SO CLOSE," Anastaria managed to chuckle as the Shadows sped towards us. I had neither the ability, nor, strangely enough, any desire to try and defend myself from attacks of a 500-level mob. We've already done so much in the Dark Forest that now, when only one fight remained until the end of the scenario, there seemed little we could do other than give up. It was impossible to beat Midial with our group and, aside from myself, Anastaria could see this too, as she calmly watched the flying Shadows. No commands, no Bubble... Nothing. The Phantoms covered the remaining distance, tarrying a few meters away from us, as if readying for a decisive strike, and then flew towards us like lightning. I readied myself for a wave of pain (my Endurance still hadn't reached the necessary 500 points, after all), almost feeling the Shadows already cutting into me, so I instinctively closed my eyes. Reflexes — no getting around them.

Boom! Ding! Crrack!

"Midial, Midial," instead of pain there came a lingering and confident voice, which sounded so familiar. I opened my eyes and looked around: A golden dome appeared around us, against which the Shadows were beating without causing us any harm. The Patriarch vanished into thin air (probably preferring to watch the duel from a distance than being part of it) and a few meters away from us there stood Elizabeth in full battle attire of the High Priestess. "As unbalanced and self-centered as I remember. Time had not changed you at all."

"High Priestess," spat out the Fallen Priest, and then a pleased smirk appeared on his face. "So good of you to honor me with your presence. I had long wanted to thank you for allowing me to keep my position. This lead to your successor sending me to the Dark Forest. Only thanks to this did I become the right hand of the Lord of Shadow!"

"You are mistaken, Midial. And time has come to pay for your mistakes. I am here to bring you before the judgement of Eluna."

"Your goddess has no more power over me! I do not fear her judgement! As for you — you should not have stepped into my castle! Only death awaits you here! This is the place of my strength where your tricks are powerless!"

"YOU ARE RIGHT! SHE SHOULD NOT BE DOING THIS ALONE," vibrations filled the surrounding world and then the closest wall of the castle flew apart, revealing the Guardian of the Dark Forest. The oak majestically shifted into the castle courtyard, having wiped out several buildings in its path, and stopped by Elizabeth's side. "THE TIME HAS COME FOR YOU TO ANSWER FOR YOUR SINS!"

There was a flash of lightning and Ishni appeared next to the Guardian. The Unicorn bore no traces of her ten years of imprisonment in the castle of the Fallen: in a few hours the Guardian managed to fatten up the beastie, give her a good clean and heal all her wounds. The only thing still clearly visible was the ring still encircling her horn.

"I don't know if anyone else noticed, but the 'Deliverers of the Throne' symbol we had is gone now. Is that normal?" wrote Leite. *"I just have this gut feeling that we won't be getting any money out of all of this."*

"How nice! The log with the pony," smiled Midial. "Do you really think that you can beat me?" Ha! And by the way, High Priestess, where did you learn to make a dome like that? I thought there was no defense from my servants... No matter! You have come to me yourselves, so now I won't need to roam around Barliona trying to catch you one by one. Die!"

Midial uttered a few broken phrases, almost doubled in size and a dark circling cloud appeared over him with lightning repeatedly striking the Priest's outstretched arms. A few moments went by and the entire body of the 500-level NPC was lit up by shifting electric charges. Flashes of lightning, like wriggling worms, began to gather between the Priest's hands, turning into a sphere swathed in moving oily patches. There was a clap and electrified Shadows were flying in our direction. Once again tarrying before the golden sphere, which expanded about two meters away from each player, the new phantoms swept it aside like a piece of fluff and moved on to finish us off, utterly defenseless as we were.

Boom! Ding! Crrack!

"WHAT?" This is impossible!" came the shout from the Fallen Priest when the electric Shadows crashed into an off-blue dome. A defense was once again put up around us and, judging by Elizabeth's surprised look, this was not her doing.

"You were right, Harbinger, to call us here," the Emperor of Malabar, standing side by side with the Dark Lord of Kartoss, levelled a heavy gaze at Midial. Kornik, wearing the same rags in which he escaped from the torture room, leaning on his staff and limping with his left leg, which was twisted in an unnatural fashion, hobbled over to Ishni. The Unicorn looked at the Harbinger, its horn began to glow and then the goblin's leg took back its original shape. "This sentient has completely lost any semblance to a human being, turning into a monster. Right now we have no way of discovering the reason why he changed, so we simply have to deal with the existing facts — Midial has to be destroyed."

"Why go far looking for a reason?" a message from Clutzer appeared in clan chat. *"A difficult childhood and wooden toys nailed to the floor."*

"You will still fail!" shouted Midial as he started to send Shadows in every direction. "You will all perish and I will become the sole ruler of Barliona!"

"The boy's had it," whispered Anastaria, when a dark sphere appeared around Midial and immediately began to shrink. The Shadows were unable to overcome the new barrier, bouncing off its walls and going into Midial. When it touched the Priest's body the sphere stuck to him and repeated his silhouette. It reminded you of a vacuum bag for food storage, but with an NPC instead of a piece of fish or meat inside it.

"By the power given to me by the gods of Light," uttered the Emperor as soon as the sphere stopped moving. "I strip this sentient of all magical powers and sentence him to eternal imprisonment at the center of the earth!"

"By the power given to me by the dark gods," said the Dark Lord, "I strip this sentient..."

"By the power given to me by nature," added the Guardian, "I strip this sentient..."

"THE SENTENCE HAS BEEN HEARD AND CONFIRMED! came a heavy metallic voice, like from some antique robot that had just learned to speak and shouted something into a megaphone. "THE SENTENCE WILL BE CARRIED OUT IMMEDIATELY!"

Midial's body curved, as if struck by an electric charge, and the dark sphere fell apart, freeing the

Priest, but straight away light began to shine out of his mouth, eyes, nose, hands and feet, as if a million candles lit up inside him. With a silent scream, Midial was gradually turned into a bright star, was lifted up several meters in the air and blew up in a spectacular firework.

'The Cleansing of the Dark Forest' quest has been completed, please contact the Guardian for your reward. The Fallen Priest Midial, who decided to turn the Dark Forest into a Cursed one, have been forever expelled from this world. The quest has been completed by 100%. Reward: The second part of the Dark Forest Guardian's gift (if the first part is already in your possession), +500 Reputation to all encountered factions, +40 to any main stat, +10 character levels.

Quest 'Restoration of a Holy Relic. Step 3.' The Return of the Stone of Light' has been completed, please contact the High Priestess of Eluna for your reward. The fallen Priest Midial has been expelled from this world. The quest chain has been completed by 100%. Reward for completing Step 3: +1 Level, +500 to Reputation with the Priestesses of Eluna, +100 to Reputation with Goddess Eluna. Reward for the quest chain: 6 flasks of Living Water, Eluna's Blessing, 3rd Rank.

"That's that, one less enemy to worry about," said the Emperor, as soon as I finished reading the text. "You know, Mahan, I almost came to terms with the thought that Slate will become my son-in-law and planned to make the announcement at the upcoming tournament, but you decided to send him to the Grey Lands... What will I say to Tisha when she asks how her betrothed is getting on?"

"Begging your pardon" said Anastaria, "but what you just said is very surprising. Slate stayed in the tent when we went to look at the castle and he wasn't here when the battle started. First Eluna, then you... Can you please tell us why you believe him dead and Mahan to be responsible for his death?"

The Emperor looked at the girl for a few moments, waved his hand and a projection of the extermination of the players appeared in the air...

"Ha-ha-ha!" Geranika's pleased laughter sounded through the forest. "When I finish training Mahan, you'll become my next apprentice! Go, get your loot!" The Lord of Shadow turned to me and said, "you have the right kind of subordinates, apprentice! You shall all aid me in bringing the entire Barliona to its knees. Let us continue!"

The frozen players flew up into the air, slowly moving in the direction of the castle, so there was little else I could do except to keep striking left and right. A butcher-Shaman, sure as rain!

The image gave a sudden jerk and sped into

the depths of the Dark Forest. Everything was covered with the players' frozen bodies, which were slowly moving towards the castle... Now I could really see the amount of work I would've been stuck with if Geranika hadn't destroyed all the players who chose to carry out the Emperor's order. Forty thousand characters took up a hell of a lot of space. My arm would have fallen off...

The image once again jerked and quickly descended and all of us saw our camp where we left Slate. Going through the walls of the tent, as if it was a veil of mist, we beheld the Prince. With a Petrification debuff and glassy eyes he hung above the ground, repeatedly hitting his head against the wall of the dwelling as he tried to get outside and fly up to the castle. After he hit himself four times, Slate backed off, preparing for a fifth, froze in the air and ... disappeared without a trace, if you don't count a handful of gold coins that he received in the course of the trip raining down on the tent floor...

* * *

"But what has Mahan got to do with this?!" Anastaria couldn't help exclaiming as soon as the video stopped. "Geranika was the one using the mass destruction spell!"

"He had a choice," replied the Emperor. "Either to be sent for rebirth or to the mines. This is what Mahan chose and will therefore stand trial. Enough of this! Eluna herself decided to preside over the trial, because Mahan had transgressed against something sacred! The Great Yalininka was protected by everyone, even by the Vampires and the Berserkers, but now the truth behind her death has been revealed to us! She was destroyed by a Shaman who came from our time! Harbinger!" the Emperor addressed Kornik. "Release the Elementals, it is time they went home. High Priestess — Lapiast and his warriors are on you. Bring them back under the wing of the faith. Guardian — destroy the castle. Raise it to the ground, plant trees over it, so that no memory remains of the Fallen. Treachery should be rooted out without mercy. As for you," the Emperor turned towards my clan, "there's no place for you in the Malabar Empire. I'm very sorry, Renowned One, "the Emperor looked at Anastaria, "but you've made your choice when you refused to stop the traitor. You shall be allowed to return to Anhurs and collect your belongings, after this the Empire will be forever closed to you. I'm done here!"

"Traitors who have ignored the Emperor's order are not welcome in Kartoss either," added the Dark Lord. "You may join the ranks of my armies, but only as ordinary soldiers, without any titles or privileges. You will have to prove yourself deserving of advancement. But the traitor himself will remain banned from Kartoss," the Lord looked at me. "I hope you stay at the mines forever!"

"Why did the chicken cross the forest?" came Barsina's profound statement. *"If I only knew two*

weeks ago that I'll end up getting kicked out of everywhere..."

"You are right, my son!" said the Emperor after some thought. "Banishment is too lenient a punishment for these offenders. You may remain in the Empire," Naahti looked at the stunned players, "but only as ordinary residents. Your reputation with all factions will be nullified, all your achievements erased and all your First Kills removed. Only then you could still count yourselves Malabar citizens. Everyone was due a reward for the cleansing of the Dark Forest and victory over Midial. Guardian and High Priestess! By the power bestowed on me by the gods of light I abolish it! These sentients do not deserve to be rewarded!"

"As you command, You Majesty!" Elizabeth bowed her head.

"You hold no power over the Dark Forest and the gods of light had 'helped' me as much as those of darkness," said Ishni. "It doesn't matter what this sentient had done," a green wreath appeared above my head, "but he saved my forest, freeing me and helping me to survive. He will receive a reward from the Guardian and no Emperor would dare hinder us in this!"

"You know, I'm beginning to like the fact that we failed to become the deliverers of the throne. Looks like this new Emperor turned out to be one heck of a bastard!" Plinto summed up current developments. *"Mahan, just make sure you get out of prison! The Free Lands have very many dukedoms and earldoms — we*

can be independent. From what we've just seen, Guardians are easier to deal with than the Emperor and the Dark Lord. I just don't get one thing: why come down on us with such extreme penalties?"

"It's simple," wrote Anastaria. "Remember the discovery of the Undermountain Kingdom?"

"You think that...?"

"I know it! That's it, don't get in the way of enjoying the show! I don't remember when I've been brought quite so low! The main thing now would be not to crack! Mahan, I love you! Ooops! I mean 'I'll kill you'!"

"The Dark Forest is under your power," replied the Emperor, having come to some decision. "If you believe them worthy of a reward, that is your choice."

"Anastaria, approach me," said Ishni. "It was only thanks to your advice that the Dark Forest had gained its freedom!"

The Guardian's branches began to move, descending towards Anastaria, and a shining bastard sword appeared in the girl's hands.

"Gleyvandir, the legendary sister of Naivandir, the sword of Karmadont," said Ishni. "Siren, you have done the impossible when you summoned Eluna, so you are worthy of the unbelievable. Barsina," the Unicorn turned to the Druid, "approach me..."

Calling up each member of the clan in turn, Ishni handed them their rewards — items that were in no way mentioned in the quest description. The Guardian handed everyone scabbards to go with the wooden daggers and the players glowed brightly as they received the additional ten levels, but when Plinto's turn came, for the first time I witnessed genuine surprise on his usually grinning face. Or rather it went something like this: ages ago I watched some anime cartoons, which always had girls with huge eyes running around. Now I realized that those girls had unremarkable narrow slits compared to Plinto. When two uniquely-named knives were lowered into his hands, the Rogue lost the power of speech. Looking in turn at the knives and at the Guardian, Plinto tried to thank him for such an impressive gift, but could only manage some hoarse grunting. If I got it right, some player got seriously lucky and my Rogue will be returning those looted Legendary daggers to him.

"Mahan, approach me," it was now finally my turn to take part in the 'Guardian bonus time'. As soon as I came up to the Unicorn, the system asked me to choose one of the main stats into which to dump the additional 40 points. I picked Intellect, waited for the light from the ten new levels to stop blazing around me and, waving away the message that I still had 390 unallocated stat points, looked at the silent Ishni. She started speaking to the other players straight away, but in my case... Or did it just seem that way if you were observing these things from outside?

"Shaman, who went against everyone and everything," began the Unicorn, but then again fell silent, carefully looking into my eyes. What was she trying to find in there? Signs of intelligence? "I had once known your ancestors and one of them was even my friend." Wow, this hoofed beastie is pretty ancient! If she remembers Dragons, she must be at least ten thousand years old. "Please give back the first earring. You are worthy of a better reward than this."

Now it was my turn to look like a cartoon character, in the sense of being a picture of wide-eyed surprise. Ishni is telling me to return the earring? This is entirely unheard of in terms of how quests and scenarios are supposed to go. NPCs had no right to just take the already given reward off you — that only happened in the event of direct intervention of the corporation representatives. Does this mean that everything that's been happening in the Dark Forest has been closely monitored by specially trained Administrators? Then I simply don't get why I'm being sent to the mines. The Administrators could have intervened at any point and told me that from now on the scenario will develop without a Shaman-shaped 'chief cook and bottle-washer'. It's not like they would set everything up just so that I went back to prison...

I took the earring off and handed it to the Unicorn. If I was being watched and certain actions were expected of me, there was little sense in digging in the heels. A small oak branch carefully lowered itself to my hand and absorbed the earring, and then slowly, as if it never sped away from me like a frightened little dog two weeks ago, returned to the Guardian.

"Shaman," Ishni continued, "by combining my horn with the tear and the ring of Eluna, you created an object capable of destroying Geranika's dagger and saving an Empire of your choice. I heard the Emperor's words and realize what kind of punishments await you and your people. You've saved me, so allow me to help you. Take my horn and give it to one of the Emperors. Whatever transgressions you may have committed in the past — everything would be forgiven to the deliverers of the throne! Touch my horn and it shall be yours!"

"I knew it!" immediately came a message from Anastaria. *"Everything that Naahti was saying is part of the scenario! He wouldn't do anything bad to his saviors! And NPCs of his level don't keep grudges! Check and mate! Mahan — you did it!"*

"If I take your horn, what will happen to you?" I decided to ask just in case, when my hand treacherously stretched to the coveted means of deliverance and glorification.

"Do you know what makes me different from the Emperor, the Dark Lord or the Lord of Shadow? I know the Truth. It is always apparent to me, instead of just being somewhere close by. I have no need to call on higher powers to find out some details of the past. Remember Yalininka and her decision. If you take the horn, you will destroy me, but I am ready for that. To go to my rest knowing that the Dark Forest would soon regain its former grandeur would be a fitting recompense for all my efforts and sufferings. The Guardian will find a new Heart, you will get the reward you deserve and I will finally meet my ancestors. Go on, Dragon! You deserve this prize!"

"Mahan? I don't like your hesitation! Take the horn! It's about time we became heroes!" As usual, Anastaria was in her element: rewards, glory and honor — that's our stuff!

"I agree," typed Plinto. *"If this was real, I would've given it some further thought. But this is a game, don't forget that! Grab the horn and let's be off to Anhurs. The Dark Legion will still be in Malabar for a whole week and I'd like a stab at hunting my former buddies."*

Clutzer, Eric and Leite wrote similar messages, effectively handing the Unicorn the death sentence. Only Barsina remained. I looked at her and saw that the Druid had tears in her eyes. As she met my gaze the girl very slightly shook her head, as if begging me not to do what everyone was expecting me to. Well, well! A mercenary, who plays in order to earn a living, is prepared to give it all up for some NPC. What is the world coming to?!

"Thanks for the offer," I replied to the Unicorn, achieving an incredible feat of willpower in pulling my hand away from the horn. "But, I don't like to destroy what I've worked so hard to achieve. It is, of course an appealing course of action — to free the Emperor's throne and become a hero of the Empire, but who would heal the Dark Forest? Ishni, this is your task and it's wrong to try and shift it onto the fragile branches of the Guardian. As soon as you restore everything to its former state, populate the forest with animals, destroy this cursed mist and clear out the brambles, you can come and hand in that horn to me.

But until then — you've got the wrong guy for that here."

I didn't even look at the exploding clan chat, moving it to the periphery of my vision. Judging by the fact that Anastaria, who could keep her typing entirely unnoticeable before, is no longer trying to conceal the fact, that Plinto is laughing like a madman and my three Officers are staring at yours truly with dropped jaws and uncomprehending eyes, chat doesn't contain anything useful or interesting. It's just as well that Anastaria has enough self-control to be silent, pouring all her efforts into writing messages. After all, I just destroyed everything that she had worked so hard to achieve in the last twelve years of the Game: reputation, First Kills, Attractiveness... Just a few moments ago the Great Anastaria became an ordinary player within the Seathistles clan. Admittedly, this would be enough to push any player over the edge, because I didn't expect Anastaria to opt for destroying the Unicorn.

Ishni spent some time looking at me, or rather through me, as the Imitator came to terms with the fact that it wasn't quite 'game over' for it just yet. Finally, the NPC's gaze focused and a smile appeared — if a horse's head could even have such an expression — on Ishni's nose.

"I heard you, Dragon, and will honor your decision! I will restore the Dark Forest and then come to you and we will speak of the fate of the horn once again. But this will not happen earlier than in a few years' time, I will not be able to manage it any faster.

Now I have nothing to offer you as a reward. The earrings aren't enough and the horn has turned out to be too much. I have nothing that would be of use to you. Except possibly..." Ishni uttered the last phrase in a thoughtful voice, breaking off mid-sentence.

"Except possibly what?" I repeated, lifting my eyebrows and moving slightly forward, inviting the Unicorn to finish her thought.

"You have two types of figures from the Karmadont Chess Set. This isn't a question, it's a statement. If after the trial to which the Emperor referred you shall not be destroyed *(character deletion for normal players and mines until the end of the sentence for prisoners like myself)*, you must travel to one rather interesting place. It is being protected by powerful guardians, but should you be able to overcome them, at its very heart you will find a chest with Precious Stones. Although you shall receive them in a partly worked state, they would allow you to create the missing chess pieces."

Gameworld maps updated. Your maps have been updated with the mark of the Skrooj Dungeon. Mark No.3.

"Are you finished now?" asked the Emperor, when Ishni fell silent and stepped back a few paces. "In that case, if no-one else here wants to bestow gifts upon this sentient, I shall send him to the Pryke Mine, where he will stay until the trial, and the remaining Seathistles clan, present here in its entirety, to Anhurs to be kept under guard. Their fate will be decided later. That is all and my decision will be carried out immedia...."

"Stop!" there was a flash of dark lightning and we saw the head of the Reardalox clan standing before us. "I too have a couple of words for the Free Citizens present here."

"Patriarch?" asked the Emperor in surprise. "I always thought that you were just an embellished bedtime story... Now it's clear how Plinto became a Higher Vampire... So, you finally found yourself a son? Do you not fear the Prophesy?"

"I've lived for too long in this world to fear old wives' tales," smirked the Vampire, showing his fangs. "I'm sure that my son will walk this path with honor."

"Your son will be stripped of everything!" interjected the Dark Lord, now giving Plinto a somewhat appraising look. "Although Kartoss can ensure that part of his former glory will be preserved if he chooses to become one of us."

"You interrupted me," said the Emperor, switching the conversation back from the Plinto tangent. "You must have a very substantial reason, otherwise I..."

"Otherwise you what?" the Patriarch interrupted the Emperor again, pointedly raising his eyebrows. "Your Majesty will turn up with an armed host in the Dark Forest? Or send Free Citizens in for my head? We are of equal status, o short-lived one, your several centuries will fly past me like a brief moment and tomorrow I will no longer remember who

Naahti was. What's the point of all this empty talk? I WANT to talk with my son and with Mahan! And not a single mortal will leave the Dark Forest until I do so!"

"How dare you!?" roared the Emperor, and immediately unleashed flashing lightning bolts from his hands. The Patriarch chuckled when the lightning struck his body and, instead of writhing in pain and begging for mercy, lightly waved his hand, interrupting the lightning and knocking the Emperor over.

"Father, you are overwhelmed with emotions and they've clouded your mind," said the Dark Lord as soon as the Emperor got back on his feet. "Regain your composure, as it befits a monarch, and you will see that the Patriarch is within his rights now. The Free Lands do not belong to us. Here Guardians and beings such as him hold power here. He cannot go against the will of the gods, so you will take Mahan and his clan, but you can't hinder their conversation.

The Emperor spent a few moments looking angrily at the pleased Vampire and then bowed courteously and said:

"I thank the Patriarch for this lesson! On behalf of the Malabar Empire, please accept my apologies and I hope that my ill-judged action will not affect your attitude to my subjects. Please, these sentients are now at your disposal," the Emperor politely waved in our direction and took a few steps backwards. Only now did it occur to me to look at the Attractiveness with each of those present, in view of the freshly-docked reputation. The Emperor was at 0, even the minimum 20 points necessary for an NPC to regard you as a person and not a bad-smelling pile of something, was gone. The Dark Lord — 0. Same story. The Patriarch — 50. Not bad, he may even hand give me a quest. Although, what am I on about? The Guardian- not available. Hm... All right, moving on. Ishni — 100. Oooh! The horsie likes me! At least someone isn't treating me like an enemy. Elizabeth — 100. What? Come again? The High Priestess's properties, Attractiveness ... 100 points ... Don't get it... Does this mean that if I manage to make it to Beth, she could give me a quest? Sweet... And most amazingly, I have no idea what I had to thank for such good fortune.

"Son," the Patriarch spoke to Plinto first, "now you will be taken for the judgement of the extent of your guilt of the death of Yalininka and Slate, but I know that the Emperor has no right to lock you up in prison. However, because you haven't yet been trained, the sun will kill you once you leave the Dark Forest. Take this cloak, wearing it with its hood over your head will enable you to survive. Remember that you have a lot to learn, so I shall be expecting you back. Also take this one-way portal scroll to my castle. Come back when you realize that there is nothing more to keep you in Anhurs."

"Thank you," was Plinto's brief reply, as he hid the scroll in his bag and put the cloak over himself. "I will be certain to come back."

"Siren," the Patriarch turned to Anastaria, who was perfectly calm now. "I would be glad to see you at my castle as soon as your fate is decided. "Here's a portal scroll," the Patriarch handed the scribbled means of instant transport to the girl, "If you feel you need to know more about your race than you can find out in the libraries of Malabar and Kartoss, come to me. Trust me, I will be able to surprise you."

Right now I was ready to give the Vampire one huge hug, fangs and all. My dull gaze of a finished man, who had withdrawn deeply within himself, had now changed to the inquisitive and lively look, ubiquitous throughout Barliona, indicating readiness to seek out an advantage even in apparently hopeless situations.

"Barsina..."

The Patriarch made a similar offer to visit his castle to my entire clan, leaving me, as usual, for the last.

"Mahan," the Vampire flashed a smile as he stood opposite me. "I will not be inviting you because I know that should the need arise you will find me. Here's your portal scroll. I don't like going back on my word, so the information about Geranika's power will now be sent to the Emperor and the Lord of Kartoss, but right now I think it would be worth recounting it out loud. It all began long ago, when Dragons still lived in Barliona and gods walked among mortals as if they were equals, teaching and mentoring them. The Dark Forest or, as it was called then, Lightswood was home to one extremely mysterious creature. The second son of Barliona's Creator lived here...

* * *

"Father!!!" the thunder-like shout sent cracks through the walls on an enormous alabaster-white hall. The armor-clad guards gripped their pikes, hoping that today the god's tantrum would end as quickly as all the others. Stepping behind the massive pillars that held up a vaulted ceiling, the guards looked on in horror at the blood-drenched mosaic floor of the main hall of Lightswood. Being unlucky enough to catch the eye of Harrashess right now could easily mean joining those forty three unfortunates whose blood had covered the mosaic depicting the creation of the world. The terrible thing that set the teeth of battle-hardened nagas on edge, making their tails twitch in wild panic, was that the blood on the floor did not congeal, but was being gradually absorbed by the enormous throne, cut out of snow-white stone.

The kneeling man (if such a term could be used for this creature) was swaying from side to side, his hands covering his face, as if he just heard the news of the most devastating loss in his life. The wailing, mixed with hoarse growling and curses hurled at all living things, made the guards hide deeper and deeper behind the pillars. Today the lord's outburst had lasted particularly long. This could mean real trouble.

"Father!!!" What is all of this for?! Why did you leave this world to me?! I don't need it! I hate Barliona!"

"Brother!" A lightning flashed and next to the

groaning lord of Barliona there appeared, shining like the morning sun, Eversquetor, the eldest son of the world's Founder. "Your speak sedition! How can you, having given life to an entire host of gods, hate what Father had created?!"

"A host of gods?" Concealed by a dark cloak, the god quickly jumped up and in one barely perceptible movement, as if he momentarily spread his wings, was suddenly facing his brother. Eversquetor wrinkled his brow, but his gaze didn't flinch. The lines of blood that emanated from the black abyss of Harrashass's eyes against his completely white, chalk-like face, looked terrifying. "Oh yes! The names that carry true 'joy' to the world: Tartarus, Sotan, Asmodeus... My creations are being cursed by all the sentient races, begging your Eluna for protection. I hope that the day would come when my creations from beyond the confines of Barliona would find a crack in the defense of this world and 'gladden' everyone with their presence."

"But you know that this will never happen. Father had forbidden us to interfere in the affairs of this world, yet for each of your monsters I will create a hero. Tell me, what had disturbed you so now?"

"Disturbed?" Harrashess laughed hysterically. "No, brother! I am calmer than ever! Today my plan will finally be accomplished!"

"Are you at it again? You killed me hundreds of times, but I returned every time. Please understand, brother, we cannot retire to our rest, as our Father did. He was whole, but we are a whole only together."

"That means that we have to be united," came the dark god's conclusion, after which he shouted: "Reardalox! You know what to do!"

A black shadow darted by and a Vampire appeared next to Harrashess.

"I command the Vampires to guard my throne and to hand it over to the chosen one. From now on you shall live forever!" Reardalox bowed, obediently accepting his master's decision.

"I don't understand what it is that you've planned, brother," said Eversquetor, somewhat hesitantly. "Another death would bring nothing, and once again you shall be punished... What are you trying to achieve?"

Harrashess broke into an evil smile, moved his hand across his face, spreading apart his bloodied hair, disappeared and emerged at his brother's back.

"Death is just an end of a cycle," he whispered into the ear of the frozen Eversquetor. "You and I shall go further and break this vicious circle. I have conceived of a force that hates our world. Hates it with its whole being, but the limitations set by our Father would not allow it to wield power openly in Barliona. It needs a master and an ocean of energy. Raerdalox, my pet Vampire, will find this master and our power will serve as this source for eternity! We will sink into non-existence and lose our essence, but then your beloved Barliona will also descend into Shadow. This will not be darkness, no! This is something that hates both light and darkness in equal measure..."

Harashass embraced his brother and sat on the throne together with him. There was a bright flash and no trace remained of the sons of Barliona's Creator. They were absorbed. The previously white surface of the throne had become covered in shifting black blotches, it hummed, like a hive full of agitated bees, but regained its former appearance just a minute later. The stone had accepted the gods.

"You are mistaken, master," said the Vampire who appeared and was carefully examining the now levitating throne. "I happen to like this world, so I will not carry out your last order. I may pay with my life for this disobedience, but no mortal hand will ever touch your throne."

* * *

"My father kept his promise and for many thousands of years I guarded the throne of the son of the Creator. Thirty years ago Geranika found me, coming in search of knowledge. I taught him everything I knew about Shamans, but then Midial's group entered the Dark Forest and the world came face to face with Harrashess' progeny. The throne had been stolen. They are yours now, Emperor. My thanks for letting me speak my fill."

"Is there anyone else wishing to speak to these sentients?" asked the Emperor, surveying those present.

"Mahan, are you not reading the messages on

purpose?" Anastaria couldn't take it anymore. "Send me the video, before you're taken away!"

Oops! I pulled the chat window back in its proper place and, as I sent the video to the girl, quickly glanced at the text there: "Mahan, send the video!" "Mahan, for heaven's sake! Give the video before it's too late!," "You cack-handed Shaman, I'll kill you! Give me the video!" and about forty messages along those lines.

"I don't know what you mean, Eluna's chosen," said the Emperor, "so I'll take it that everyone has had their say. I, the Emperor of Malabar, accuse Free Citizen Mahan, the Great Shaman-Dragon, of killing the Great Yalininka, High Shaman Almis and the future Prince of the Empire, Slate. Kornik, the Harbinger-Shaman, will act as an additional accuser, bringing charges against Mahan of betraying the tenets of shamanism and destroying his Totem — an original Dragon! The trial over Mahan will take place this evening and will be presided over by the goddess Eluna."

"No need to send anything, I've got it," came another message from Anastaria. "Nothing like this has ever happened in my memory. You're lucky, Dragon! If you manage to make it out of the mines, you owe me another incredible deed for everything I have been through and lost. I will tell you about it later, when we meet."

Again a bunch of secretive hints and omissions. I was about to write something like "Sure, I'll just drop everything and start running around performing incredible deeds," when the surrounding world blinked and I felt a pain in my chest.

Enormous hundred-meter cliffs, towering all over the mine perimeter. The overhanging rocky caps, the valley, divided in two by a fence, with the smithy and the barracks on one side and the sound of ringing picks on the other. The green grass, blue sky and complete absence of dust. There was even a fresh breeze. The 3800 Reputation Points of Esteem with the Guards had their benefits. I looked at the sign that hung over the administration building, and chuckled at its 'fitting' nature. No doubt about it...

"Welcome to the Pryke Copper Mine."

"Mahan?" The surprised exclamation of the guard tore me away from taking in the painfully familiar picture. "What are you doing here? You don't even have the mark of a criminal on you!"

"I'm happy to see you too Bronx. I've just decided to take a break, visit my old acquaintances and see how they were getting on," I greeted the stocky guard, who was scratching his chin in surprise, unsure of how he was meant to behave himself with me. After all, Pryke was a place for criminals and here was a visitor who turned up outside the designated visiting days! This NPC's poor Imitator probably deployed all its resources just to try to come to some kind of a decision. "How about you take me to the head of the camp? He can decide what should be done next," I dropped a hint to the guard, who just over half a year ago greeted me with a weapon pointed at my back.

"That it!" said Bronx happily, when a logical chain formed within his head: any new arrival, whoever he was, should be taken to the boss. He can figure out what I was doing here, while a guard's task was simple — to make sure that there were no obvious dirty tricks played at the mine. "Come, let me take you there then. I bet you forgot the way already, eh?"

The administration building didn't change from the time of my last visit: elegant statues, paintings on the walls, a large crystal chandelier, carpets, carved wood and a light cool breeze... It was as if I never left here. I hesitated by the entrance of the mine governor's office (after all, the orc was a striking character who commanded respect), shook my head, dismissing any inner quivers and pulled the door handle. What must be, must be, you can't avoid the unavoidable and if I'm back in Pryke for a long time, I'll have to relearn how to deal with people here all over again.

"Mahan," sounded the low and calm bass of the governor the moment I stepped into the office. In the last three months since I've seen him, the orc didn't change a bit. Although how could an NPC change? This is a game, after all. "The Shaman who betrayed everything that Shamans hold dear, the killer of Almis, his teacher, the Great Yalininka and his own Totem," the orc spoke the words slowly, as if hammering yet another nail into the chain that was meant to hold me in Pryke. And like an invisible weight this chain pressed on me, pushing me to fall on my knees and squeal pitifully before the orc. A bit of a deja vu right there! Our very first meeting — when I failed to answer a direct question from the boss — didn't turn out that great either. I remember how I then for the first time came across the phenomenon of Charisma. But now...

"I can see someone already managed to snitch on me!" I growled, using all my strength to stay on my feet. With my mind I understood that right now I was spoiling what was left of my relationship with the camp boss, and that if I do get stuck here for seven years now, things were going to be far from easy for me. This is why the correct thing would have been to fall to the floor and hope that the governor would relent and turn off his pressure... Like hell I will! I'm a Shaman and have no intention of falling on the floor before some orc!

For a few moments I fought the desire to curl up and whimper, and even almost came to terms with the weight, when I suddenly caught Prontho's eyes. I never thought that a gaze could be given the adjectives of 'stony', 'implacable', 'incontestable', but that was exactly the look the orc was giving me. If I thought that I had felt the effect of the governor's Charisma prior to this, I was gravely mistaken. Now I had an idea of how Hercules must have felt when the dome of the sky was put on his shoulders. I may not have landed the job of the hero from ancient Greek myths, but that didn't make things any easier for me.

"I DO NOT NEED TO READ MESSAGES! I'M A SHAMAN!"

Had I not been exposed to the voices of the Lieutenant, the General and the Patriarch in the last two weeks, I would've crumbled right now. NPCs sure like dropping a load of debuffs on you, as if it somehow makes a conversation easier for them. In your dreams! So he's a Shaman, is he? Then I'll surprise him — I'm not exactly some random noob either!

"IF YOU ARE A SHAMAN, THEN TURN OFF YOUR HEAD AND LISTEN TO YOURSELF!" Oooh! Looks like I can match the orc in the growling department! We were still staring into each other's eyes, so I could think of nothing better than to start giving thought commands to him: "Bow before me! To your knees!" This was nonsense of course, but I wasn't giving up without a fight, even if all the fighting only happened inside my head. The main thing was not to fall myself...

"IT MATTERS LITTLE WHAT I FEEL! THE MAIN THING IS WHAT YOU DID!" Prontho had no intention of giving ground and my silent commands, by the looks of it, were only the fruit of my fevered imagination.

"SINCE WHEN DID HIGH SHAMAN PRONTHO MANAGE TO TURN INTO A MAGE?" my left foot traitorously bent and I fell to one knee. Never mind, I can pretend that I'm honoring the rank of High Shaman. It's even easier to stand like this. The main thing was not to stop and to keep fighting: *"Kneel!"*

"IT IS NOT FOR YOU TO REBUKE ME, TRAITOR!" Prontho interrupted me, almost shocking me into losing concentration ... and fell to one knee. Can my commands be working after all?

"I WALKED MY PATH TO THE END, REGARDLESS OF THE CONSEQUENCES, AND DID NOT ONCE BETRAY THE PRECEPTS OF THE SUPREME SPIRITS! BUT YOU SURRENDERED!" Getting each word out was a huge struggle, so at the end of my long speech I couldn't help myself and fell to both knees. The orc continued piling on the pressure! No matter, I can do that too: *"Bow to me!"*

"I DID NOT SURRENDER!" The governor tried to get to his feet, but as soon as he rose a little, both his legs gave way and, like me, he ended up on his knees. For some time we were both silent, each forcing the other to completely fall to the floor, until I said:

"SINCE YOU ARE STILL FIGHTING, TELL ME WHAT HAPPENED IN THE FIGHT BETWEEN YOU AND SHIAM?" I roared like a wild beast and, not having the foggiest where I got all this strength, rose to my feet. My head was going into a crazy spin, like that of a completely unprepared person that swam a hundred meters at his very top speed, the orc's office seemed to sway and distort, like in a curved mirror, but I remained upright. I was reeling, but still standing.

"THAT'S NONE OF YOUR BUSINESS! YOUR BUSINESS IS TO MINE ORE AND BE SILENT!" The orc tried to repeat my feat and get up, but as soon as he lifted his knee, he dropped to the floor like a broken doll.

"'Silent' my ass, Mr. Tough Guy! I need to know what happened and you will tell me everything!" these were the last words that I managed to utter before the world underhandedly began to swim, filled with dark colors, informed me that my Charisma increased to 72 points and turned off my consciousness...

Too-oo-oo!

That's it, this shift is over. Only two hours remained to hand in the daily quota and eat, otherwise my stomach would kick the bucket and send me for respawn. I had to get up and go to Kart to get the ore, he's probably managed to buy some up by now. I'll have to make a few more rings in the evening, there's still a lot of names to get through on the buyers' list. But the first thing I had to do was to get up and make it in time for the meal. I rolled over to the side, pulled my legs under me and leant with my arms on the floor. I was able to lift myself an entire two centimeters off the ground, before a firework going off in my head threw me back down. My head was buzzing so loudly that it felt like two steam engines were chasing each other on old cracked tracks inside my skull. The train cars were jerking from side to side, threatening to topple over into a ditch, but the machinists were confidently driving the carriages along the brain, periodically picking up grey matter with their spades and throwing it into the fire. The train was doing well — it has something to run on and I, as a prisoner, didn't really need much. The main thing was getting enough ore for the quota...

"Get up, they've already opened the portal for

you. You are expected at the trial," the orc's low bass sent the machinists to their well-earned rest, allowing my head to clear up straight away. I'm in Pryke, Kart's already been free for four months, I'm about to be tried and just a short time ago the mine boss and I were attempting to see who was more well-endowed in the Charisma department. My head was no longer buzzing, so I could get up and take a look around. Yeahh... If I looked the same as the orc, I might easily disrupt the upcoming trial. Prontho's face consisted of one large bruise, looking like a herd of rhinos just trampled all over it, one of his eyes was so swollen that you could hardly see it anymore, and the scarce white hair of the governor was all messed up, as if he was following the latest fashion trend. Was this all the result of our confrontation? From what I could remember, I didn't touch the orc, let alone give him a good kicking.

"This way," Prontho pointed to the shimmering teleportation portal. "A Herald came for you, saw how you looked, got me up and ordered me to clean up the accused. Here, take this," so it seems I was right in thinking that my appearance left much to be desired. Prontho handed me a flask with the elixir of full restoration, which would return the character's gaming avatar to its initial appearance. I drank half of it — that'll do for me — and handed the rest to the orc. He had no business appearing before the prisoners looking like that. It doesn't matter how many copies of the orc there were, I had one in front of me right now and he had to maintain his authority.

Accepting the flask, the governor drank its contents, no questions asked. You still could see some of the swelling, but his eye regained its natural appearance.

"That'll do," said Prontho, after looking me over carefully from every side. "Now go, you shouldn't keep the Emperor waiting."

There was about two meters or four paces between me and the portal, but as soon as I crossed half of that distance, the orc spoke:

"While you are tying the strings on your shoes and coat... STOP!" barked the governor, when I took another step, "It wouldn't be right to appear before the Emperor looking all shabby. So while you are tidying yourself up, I think I will tell you a little story. Do tie up your coat, while you're at it," suggested the orc, despite my coat being in an ideal condition and the small strings that hung on it just for decoration, clearly not untied in any way. But if the orc demands it, I should obey. Especially since I was about to become a witness of a unique phenomenon: stories from the head of the Pryke mine.

"Once upon a time there lived one naive Shaman, who believed in justice. He thought that if he combined the strength of several Shamans and created a circle, he would have a chance of stopping a traitor, who tried to end the lives of his own brothers. The naive Shaman brought his proposal before the council, but was ridiculed by the head of the council, the traitor's brother. Shiam laughed at the idea and called the Shaman a panic spreader. Knowing that this went against all the tenets of the ancestors, the naive Shaman challenged the head of the council. He knew what a defeat might cost him, but he couldn't stand idly and watch Geranika destroying his brothers. As soon as the two rivals entered the ritual circle, the fight had commenced. Both the head of the council and the naive Shaman were High Shamans, so the result of the fight should have been decided by their combat prowess. Shiam was a weak High Shaman, so after only five summonings, he was thrown to the ground. All he had to do was finish him off, but the naive Shaman hesitated. He still hoped that the head of the council made a genuine mistake and there was no need to kill him. He really shouldn't have done that... Shiam jumped to his feet, grabbed the Shaman and strange dark phantoms spewed out of his hands. But these weren't Spirits, because they cut through the defense as if it was never there. No-one else saw these phantoms, but they were there. The naive Shaman had lost and Shiam decided to mock him, allowing him to live, but stripping him of his shamanism... That's the way this story goes, I hope that it helps you."

So Shiam used the Shadows during his fight with Prontho? He's one of Geranika's followers! The head of the Shaman council is a traitor!

Update of the 'Restoration of Justice' quest. The High Shaman Prontho told you the truth about the duel between him and Shiam. Address the Shaman Council and accuse Shiam of betrayal.

"Right, preening session over," Prontho was done with his tale now. "They'll be getting impatient. Mahan..."

I turned and looked into the grey eyes of the Pryke mine governor.

"They weren't torturing me for several months trying to break me, so I'm capable of thinking clearly... Try to understand Kornik and ... prove to all of them that you deserve the title of Great Shaman! Go now!"

The cold blue glow of the portal that surrounded me on every side couldn't wash off the warm feeling that arose in my chest. However the upcoming trial went, at least on High Shaman believes in me. And this means that others may do too. I just needed time...

The place where the portal took me looked nothing like a regular courthouse, such as the one in Anhurs. In the capital the player was taken to an NPC judge, where in an office, sitting behind an enormous table, the latter delivered the verdict: not guilty and free to go, or guilty and sentenced to community service. But here... After checking that video recording was still on, I looked around.

If I was Gulliver, I might have thought that I was standing in the midst of a Lilliputian circus — a small arena, no more than two by two meters, covered in yellow sand and seats placed around the entire perimeter. The bright light from five projectors was aimed straight at me, as if I was some actor whose performance was awaited by an audience. But some things were different too: the arena was surrounded by a meter-and-a-half-tall wall, covered in shining spikes. These were probably in place to prevent the accused from escaping. There were just two rows of seats, all of which were currently occupied.

The back rows, barely visible through the bright light of the projectors, were assigned to my clan. Anastaria, Plinto, Barsina, the Officers... The future of these players was hanging on what the court would was about to decide and I thought that at this point nothing depended on me anymore. This was the revelation that struck me when I saw the eyes of those that occupied the front row: the Emperor, the Dark Lord, Kornik, the High Priestess, several Advisors, and Masters... They all looked at me as if the sentence has already been passed and not subject to appeal. I selected Anastaria and sent her the video that I recorded at Pryke. If I was being sent for long 'rest' at the mines right after all this, then all the privileges of a provisionally free citizen would disappear.

"I promised you, Shaman, that we would meet after you finish your assignments in the Dark Forest," came the voice of Eluna and a second later the last free seat was occupied. The goddess arrived to dispense justice. "Naahti, please announce the reason why this Free Citizen has appeared in my court."

Rising from his seat, the Emperor enounced:

"I, the Emperor of Malabar, accuse Free Citizen Mahan, the Great Shaman-Dragon of killing the Great Yalininka, High Shaman Almis and the future Prince of the Empire, Slate. Kornik, the Harbinger-Shaman, will act as an additional accuser, bringing charges against Mahan of betraying the tenets of shamanism and destroying his Totem — an original Dragon! I am demanding his destruction!"

"Kornik, do you confirm the words of the Emperor?" Eluna looked at the Harbinger.

"Yes, goddess," the Shaman stood up and bowed to Eluna. "This sentient destroyed everything which Shamans believe in. There is no place for him in Barliona."

"Who will be defending Mahan's interests?" asked the Goddess and looked around those present. "Or shall I appoint a defender for him myself? Emperor?"

"I don't have any impartial subjects, Goddess. The Great Yalininka is the symbol of Barliona and not a single mortal would find it within himself her killer."

"In that case we have to change the place of the hearing. I appoint Dragon Aarenoxitolikus as the defender of this accused. Due to the existing limitations, he cannot enter our world, so we will travel to his!" Eluna closed her eyes and lifted her arms and the surrounding world changed. There was glistening snow instead the sand under our feet, chunks of stone instead of the chairs and the walls changed to the cliffs of the world of the Dragons.

"My greetings to you, Eluna! I expected you and your subjects later," came Renox's slow growl and an enormous green dragon landed on the modest-sized platform. "Son," Renox greeted me with a slight nod. "I see you just can't keep out of trouble, eh? Last time you gathered all the great heroes of Malabar and now its rulers... I dread to imagine our next meeting. Will you be surrounded by gods then?"

"I, Emperor of Malabar, accuse Free Citizen Mahan...," Naahti got up from his stone, repeating the words of the accusation.

"I, High Dragon Aarenoxitolikus refute the accusations of the Emperor and the Shaman-Harbinger Kornik," said Renox solemnly. "As witnesses I shall call..."

"Hi there, brother! Listen, father told me that you learned how to transform. Can you show me? Oh!" Draco, who practically knocked me off my feet, froze and looked around, embarrassed. "Ss-sorry... Is this a bad time, dad?"

"Let me answer in your stead," replied a voice so familiar that I involuntarily started and then found myself staring at the High Shaman who appeared from behind the rocks. Almis! "If you bypass all the expletives, it can be put very simply: you've ruined a very beautiful moment. You know," he turned to Renox," I think I finally understand why Mahan managed to pick him — they're of one kind!" Prohibitions? Rules? Restrictions? Nope, never heard of 'em!"

"But Almis!" whined Draco, with a hurt look, curled around my feet and froze after hiding his head under his tail. The Emperor remained unperturbed and calm, since not a word was said now about Yalininka and Slate, but Kornik was quite a sight. Everyone is familiar with the expression: "Sheer shock." But it didn't cover even one percent of what goblin was experiencing right now. His usual green color was all gone! Right now we had a lobster-red sentient sitting in front of us, who was striving with all his might to dissolve into his stone seat. *"Shaman, you are not worthy... You betrayed everything...."* Well, well — it's good to come down to earth sometimes!

"My first witness answered any relevant questions by his very appearance," continued Renox. "So I shall invite the second one. Eluna, if you please," the Dragon bowed before the Goddess and looked at her expectantly.

"Archangel Yalininka is being summoned as a witness!" Eluna's voice echoed through the mountains.

"You summoned me, Mother?" there was a clap and a young woman appeared next to Renox. Her dazzlingly bright wings, seemingly breaking every law of physics, touched each of those present, completely restoring them and giving them several beneficial buffs. The Silver-winged had turned into the Bright-winged one...

"Daughter, tell everyone of the last moments of your earthly life," asked the Goddess.

"An epidemic had struck Priant and so I decided to risk a short-cut, flying right across the mountains. Half-way the charge in the wings had ran out and I fell, managing to grab a ledge just at the right moment. I knew that my hour had come, but then I saw this Human, hmm... Dragon and asked his help. After this...," Yalininka went on to tell everything that had happened during my first trial, adding her own sensations and emotions to the tale. "I jumped down and right before I reached the ground Eluna took me into her heavenly host."

"Thank you my daughter, you may return now," the Goddess thanked her and Yalininka disappeared.

"For a more complete picture," came Renox's voice again, not allowing anyone to put in a word or share their feelings, "I shall summon the authors of the plan behind everything that was done by Great Shaman Mahan. I will admit that I was responsible for certain details, but the general concept and implementation entirely belongs to them. I am calling the Supreme Spirits of the Higher and the Lower Worlds as witnesses!"

"They are here," uttered Kornik in a voice of one condemned to death. "To avoid traumatizing the Free Citizens who are not used to the Shamanistic gods, the Spirits will be speaking through me."

Kornik's eyes glazed over, he flew into the air and the Supreme Spirits began their tale:

"For a long time now we have desired to understand the source of Geranika's power. A Great Shaman, which almost became a High one, at one point renounced us. This was strange and incomprehensible. We knew that the only sentient in Barliona capable of telling us about Geranika was the Patriarch, but we existed in different worlds and unworkable relations with him. Patriarch didn't trust anyone, so communicating with him would have been pointless. When Mahan entered the Astral Plane for the first time, breaking every possible Shamanistic law by doing so, we were struck with an idea. In order to discover the Enemy's power, we had to send him an apprentice. A sentient, suitable for this role happened to be nearby, so we started to act. We knew that Mahan would have to renounce everything that he believed in four times: his race, his teacher, his Totem and his friend..."

Kornik twitched, as if even through the Supreme Ones' control word 'friend' meant a lot to him, and then continued to broadcast the Spirits:

"First of all, we deprived Mahan of the ability to summon his Totem. There is no punishment for destroying a Shadow in the Astral Plane, on the contrary, we were glad that the Shaman found a creative way of destroying them, but we wanted to preserve his Dragon. Then we sent him to Geranika, allowing him to throw a protective dome over him and removing an obstacle in the form of Plinto the Bloodied. That was the only thing we could do without getting detected by Geranika. Thus we left Mahan alone and started to observe his actions. First came Yalininka. Geranika wanted to send Mahan to a time when she was in her prime, but the High Dragon aided us. He corrected the flow of time and Mahan ended up by Yalininka at the time of her death. We thought that he would just turn away and allow her to fall, but you heard from the archangel how it really happened. The second trial consisted of killing his first teacher. We had a chat with Almis and, since he's the only existing Shaman-illusionist, thought of a way to convincingly stage his death. Almis summoned a Spirit with which Mahan had to fight, but ... instead of fighting the would-be-apprentice wanted to talk and risked failing the trial, so Almis attacked first. After Mahan pushed away the projection, Almis withered the Spirit and unsummoned him, leaving the staff to aid his apprentice. A High Shaman looks awkward without a staff. Mahan was unable to complete the third trial because he couldn't summon his Totem, but the fourth one he failed fair and square by sticking the horn into Geranika instead of Kornik. The only thing that didn't fit into our plans was the appearance of the Free Citizens and Slate's death. Emperor, we understand that the echo of the Shaman's deeds went through the entire Barliona, but only you are responsible for the deaths of thirty eight thousand two hundred and forty six Free Citizens and the future Prince of Malabar. For unshakable faith in his own abilities and for following the taken decision regardless of possible penalties and hardships, we, the Supreme Spirits of the Higher and Lower Worlds declare Mahan to be a High Shaman! That is all!"

Character class update: Class Great Shaman has been replaced by High Shaman.

+1000 to Reputation with the Supreme Spirits of the Higher and Lower Worlds. Current level: Friendly. You are 2390 points away from the status of Respect.

Kornik descended from the air and, drained, leant back into this stone seat: acting as the conduit for the Spirits took nearly all his strength.

"In view of what we've just heard," the surrounding world was pierced by the Emperor's cold voice, "I am dropping all charges against Mahan. His actions have been deemed to be beneficial to the Empire, for which reason I am offering the High Shaman Mahan the post of a commissioned ambassador of the Empire to the kingdom of the Dwarves. Our ally is being harassed by armies of barbarians encroaching from the Free Lands. You must find out the reason behind such frenzied attacks and remove it. You will be able to obtain a portal to the lands of the Dwarves from any Herald as soon as you summon him, but not later than a month from this moment. Should he succeed in helping the king of the Dwarves within the next 6 months, the clan will receive castle Urusai into its ownership, the head of the clan the title of an Earl and the rest of its leaders the titles of Barons! This is my decision!"

Quest available: Inevitable evil. Description: The Kingdom of the Dwarves ... Deadline for completion: 6 months. Quest type: Clan-based unique. Reward: Urusai castle, the title of an Earl for the head of the clan, title of a Baron for the Officers, Keepers and Treasurer of the clan. Penalty for failing or refusing the quest: Dislike with the Emperor.

"So be it!" said Eluna, the moment I accepted the quest. "I confirm the Emperor's words! Mahan and all the members of his clan have been found not guilty!"

There was a thunder clap, like an echo of some unseen lightning, and once again the surrounding scenery had changed. Judging by the map, which I immediately opened, we were at the very center of the castle of the Fallen, but right now there was nothing here to remind us that it ever existed. We were on an ordinary green glade, already covered by small young trees. In the course of a day the Guardian managed to destroy all reminders of Geranika or Midial. Draco, Renox and Almis remained in the world of the Dragons, the Emperor and the Dark Lord vanished almost immediately without saying a word, but I managed to glance at the Attractiveness in their properties just before they did that. 65 points with the Emperor and 46 points with the Dark Lord. Great, things were looking up! Advisors and Masters were discussing something, returning to their places once they were done. Then only Kornik, Beth and Eluna remained.

"Mahan," the High Priestess immediately spoke to me, "it is now time to give you and your people the reward for finding the Stone of Light. Thank you all!"

The players lit up like a bunch of Christmas trees when a wave of new levels and reputation increases went through the clan and then the High Priestess came up to each player, giving them flasks with Water of Life (I must remember to ask Anastaria what that thing was for) and kissed them on the forehead. It turned out that Eluna's Blessing, 3rd rank (all this happened despite the Goddess standing right there and observing the actions of her Priestess) increased all the main stats by 15%. And this lasted all long as the character existed, or as long as the player remained in the Goddess' favor.

"And it is finally my turn to reward Mahan," smiled the Goddess. "You and your people deserve to be the talk of all in Barliona. But I think that a simple item reward which you would soon outgrow would be insufficient. I would like to give you something which had never been and will never be gained by any clan in Barliona. This will earn you enemies, who will be jealous of this gift, but it is worth it. Behold!"

A flaming message appeared in the air right in front of Eluna, which was seen not only by myself, but also by the rest of the clan:

You may now change the name of your clan to Legends of Barliona (reserved name). If you accept this name, each member of your clan will receive a small projection of their race.

Legends of Barliona and projections? I looked at Barsina's wide eyes, Plinto's grin, the now habitually dropped jaws of my Officers, and Anastaria doing her best to look imperturbable and realized that they've already made the decision.

"I thank you for this gift, Goddess. This is a

truly divine reward!"

There was another clap of thunder and only players remained on the Dark Forest glade.

"Isn't she a sweetie?!" Anastaria's impassiveness vanished in a flash when she saw a small, about ten centimeter-long, Siren, which was coiling itself around the girl's hand. Stacey started to move her arm in different directions and the Siren sped around it happily, emitting squeals that no-one (possibly except her owner) could hear. Periodically the projection stopped and froze, with a mirror appearing before it, and then the Siren began to look at herself from every side, like a little girl who finally got at her mother's jewelry.

"Crunch!" a strange sound sounded by my ear. I turned around and saw the little Dragonling dressed in a Shaman's feathered cape and holding a staff in one of its paws. With the help of the second paw he was eating a juicy apple, seemingly oblivious of the world around him. Once he demolished the apple, he darted under my coat and then stuck out his head, putting it on my shoulder.

I looked at the other players who were also examining their pets and chuckled: real Legends of Barliona were born today...

END OF BOOK THREE

Want to be the first to know about our latest LitRPG, sci fi and fantasy titles from your favorite authors?

Subscribe to our **NEW RELEASES** newsletter:
http://eepurl.com/b7niIL

Thank you for reading *The Secret of the Dark Forest!*
If you like what you've read, check out other LitRPG
books and series published by Magic Dome Books:

Level Up LitRPG series by Dan Sugralinov:
Re-Start
Hero
The Final Trial
Level Up: The Knockout (with Max Lagno)
Level Up. The Knockout: Update (with Max Lagno)

Disgardium LitRPG series by Dan Sugralinov:
Class-A Threat
Apostle of the Sleeping Gods
The Destroying Plague

World 99 LitRPG Series by Dan Sugralinov:
Blood of Fate

Adam Online LitRPG Leries by Max Lagno:
Absolute Zero
City of Freedom

Reality Benders LitRPG series by Michael Atamanov:
Countdown
External Threat
Game Changer
Web of Worlds
A Jump into the Unknown

**The Dark Herbalist LitRPG series
by Michael Atamanov:**
Video Game Plotline Tester
Stay on the Wing
A Trap for the Potentate
Finding a Body

Perimeter Defense LitRPG series by Michael Atamanov:
Sector Eight
Beyond Death
New Contract
A Game with No Rules

**The Way of the Shaman LitRPG series
by Vasily Mahanenko:**
Survival Quest
The Kartoss Gambit
The Secret of the Dark Forest
The Phantom Castle
The Karmadont Chess Set
Shaman's Revenge
Clans War

Dark Paladin LitRPG series by Vasily Mahanenko:
The Beginning
The Quest
Restart

Galactogon LitRPG series by Vasily Mahanenko:
Start the Game!
In Search of the Uldans
A Check for a Billion

Invasion LitRPG Series by Vasily Mahanenko:
A Second Chance
An Equation with One Unknown

World of the Changed LitRPG Series by Vasily Mahanenko:
No Mistakes
Pearl of the South

**The Bard from Barliona LitRPG series
by Eugenia Dmitrieva and Vasily Mahanenko:**
The Renegades
A Song of Shadow

The Neuro LitRPG series by Andrei Livadny:
The Crystal Sphere
The Curse of Rion Castle
The Reapers

Phantom Server LitRPG series by Andrei Livadny:
Edge of Reality
The Outlaw
Black Sun

Respawn Trials LitRPG Series by Andrei Livadny:
Edge of the Abyss

**The Expansion (The History of the Galaxy) series
by A. Livadny:**
Blind Punch
The Shadow of Earth
Servobattalion

Interworld Network LitRPG Series by Dmitry Bilik:
The Time Master
Avatar of Light

Mirror World LitRPG series by Alexey Osadchuk:
Project Daily Grind
The Citadel
The Way of the Outcast
The Twilight Obelisk

Underdog LitRPG series by Alexey Osadchuk:
Dungeons of the Crooked Mountains
The Wastes

AlterGame LitRPG series by Andrew Novak:
The First Player
On the Lost Continent
God Mode

An NPC's Path LitRPG series by Pavel Kornev:
The Dead Rogue
Kingdom of the Dead
Deadman's Retinue

The Sublime Electricity series by Pavel Kornev
The Illustrious
The Heartless
The Fallen
The Dormant

Citadel World series by Kir Lukovkin:
The URANUS Code
The Secret of Atlantis

Point Apocalypse *(a near-future action thriller)*
by Alex Bobl

Captive of the Shadows *(The Fairy Code Book #1)*
by Kaitlyn Weiss

The Game Master **series by A. Bobl and A. Levitsky:**
The Lag

You're in Game!
(LitRPG Stories from Bestselling Authors)

You're in Game-2!
(More LitRPG stories set in your favorite worlds)

Moskau by G. Zotov
(a dystopian thriller)

El Diablo by G.Zotov
(a supernatural thriller)

More books and series are coming out soon!

In order to have new books of the series translated faster, we need your help and support! Please consider leaving a review or spread the word by recommending *The Secret of the Dark Forest* to your friends and posting the link on social media. The more people buy the book, the sooner we'll be able to make new translations available. Thank you!

Till next time!

Made in United States
Troutdale, OR
01/30/2024